FIASCO OF ADVENTURES

FIASCO OF ADVENTURES

VICTOR JAMES

Sana Abuleil, Christian Neumann

The Megacosm

This book is dedicated to my mother, Sandra. Hope she enjoys reading this in heaven. And yes Mom, I will write that one thing one day. I promise.

Special thanks to Christian for his great cover art, and to my editor Sana for reeling me back in.

Fiasco of Adventures

By Victor James

TRUE MEGA

New Haven, Summer

Even over the coursing wind, the silver engine on the white Chevelle ahead ripped out a chainsaw-like roar that reverberated off the brownstone houses. Fiasco winced, and his head sunk into his shoulders from the noise. Streams of ashen smoke plumed from the rust-stained twin exhausts and rushed over his blue force shield in a blinding haze. Iron-tasting spittle filled his mouth, and the odor of the monoxide-filled gas burned Fiasco's nostrils — a noxious fume that twisted his stomach further into knots.

You will fail, the voice whispered, and Fiasco nodded.

Warm summer winds whistled over his exposed jaw and ears, clearing out the murk. The crown of his head down to the tip of his nose were concealed behind a deep sea- blue leather mask. The straps used to tie the mask together behind his head snapped like small whips as they caught the current. Flying parallel to the street, the concrete below him became a solid, gray mass, licked with yellow lines, rhythmically beating into his mind as they came at him in faster intervals with every breath.

"Don't look down again," he thought.

Behind a pair of white goggles that he had rescued from a second-hand store, Fiasco shut his eyes from the sight. Those yellow strips on the road were why Fiasco usually kept to the skies and avoided the streets. Whenever he tried to do so in the past, the cadence of the street lanes would churn the bile in his weak stomach.

He swallowed hard—attempting to ignore the nausea—and peaked through thin eyelids.

"Get yourself together, loser," he muttered into the current, breathing out to push down the retch.

On either side of the street Fiasco sped down, tall, black, metal lampposts blinked on like orange fireflies as dusk descended on New Haven. Cars, northern red oak trees, and shocked faces on his peripheral vision blended with the pale light, turning into colorful streams curving back behind him. But even with the prismatic show, all Fiasco could think of was the yellow street lines that were inches from his face. Again, nausea gripped his stomach like a fist.

On his hands were glimmering gauntlets made of blue, intricately patterned lights that curved to a point-like scythe halfway up his forearms. He brought his left glove to his mouth as he held back the sickness.

Failure is all you know, the voice said, and Fiasco concurred with a slight nod as he sailed through trails of exhaust.

The whistling wind turned to a scream when Fiasco corrected his course to get back behind the Chevelle he pursued and struggled to keep pace with. The engine thundered with each shift of a gear. The streetlights glinted like orange shooting stars off the muscle car's chrome bumper. Small dips in the road tested the fleeing car's suspensions that squeaked and groaned from the stress.

Each beat of light that rolled over the rear window illuminated the shadows moving within. Fiasco counted four silhouettes in total. Two sat in the back, their faces vibrating to a blur from the power of the muscle car. Their teeth were tinted orange from the street-lights as they pointed back at him, fogging up the rear window with their laughter.

"Keep laughing, thieves," Fiasco whispered into his glove. His voice was lost in the wind swirling over his aura shield that glowed about his body.

Beyond the two in the backseat, the black shadow on the passenger side leaned in towards the driver, arms and hands swept about furiously as it spoke, fanning the light from the front window. Fiasco had to swallow back more bile. As they spoke, the Chevelle jumped over a speed bump that propelled it further ahead rather than slowing it down, the engine growling as the automobile soared. Faint sparks glinted from the undercarriage as the car landed and kissed the pavement. Inside, the driver's shadow overlapped with the passengers. Streams of orange light bled between them when the two shadows separated and bumped darkened fists.

The Chevelle downshifted again, let out another roar, and became a white streaking bullet before Fiasco's eyes as the distance between him and his quarry tripled in six seconds.

"Damn muscle cars," Fiasco thought as he passed through the gaseous cloud the Chevelle left in its wake.

You know you will fail, the voice reminded him again.

"Yeah, I know, I know," Fiasco said, bathing in the negative emotion the voice's words created. The negativity sparked his emotions, which in turn fueled his power. He let the energy from the ridicule wash over him, pouring from within.

In the middle of his chest was a white circle trimmed in gray with a blue letter *F* that Fiasco had hand-stitched in the center. The symbol stood out against his dark-cyan colored suit and pulsed, sparking blue spouts of light. A wave of warm energy rippled outward from it, rolling like water, flowing down to his feet, propelling him forward. Wind rushed over his body. The brilliant streams of color on either side of the road faded to black as Fiasco's speed increased, and his view narrowed in concentration.

"Tune out the world. Don't think about the road and those yellow lines. Focus on the car," Fiasco repeated. The white blur of a car widened and grew as he closed the gap, and the long chrome bumper was all that he could see.

Fiasco fought the turbulence as the chase reached what he estimated was over ninety miles per hour, and his mind geared toward the citizens. There was no love lost between him and the people of New Haven, but he realized that the extreme speed of the chase was dangerous for the pedestrians still on the street. The New Haven Police department had done their best to clear the pursuit route, but their cruisers were lost in the hunt blocks ago in a tangled pileup of police cruisers. None had arrived to take their place. It was up to the Mega-hero to capture the thieves and return the stolen property all on his own.

"You don't need them, Fiasco," he said to himself. "You can do this alone."

Unlikely. The voice mocked. *Failure is certain.*

Pushing through the headwinds, Fiasco reached out with his gloved right hand. Focusing on the image he had in his mind, the light fueled by his internal power twisted and morphed into a thin, blue line that snaked out from the palm.

You know this will not work, the voice said. *You are a loser, and your ideas never work.* Fiasco nodded in acceptance.

The symbol pulsed on his chest, gaining power from the surge of negative emotion, and the curling light from his hand thickened from the swell as it gained on the fleeing Chevelle.

"Just catch it," Fiasco thought, as if trying to coax the manifestation to obey him with his words. "Just hook the bumper."

The end of the light morphed from his thoughts, twisting and bulging, transforming into the only hooking device Fiasco could think of in the heat of the chase. The end curved at the head, and sharp azure teeth jutted outward. His view narrowed further when he concentrated on the small point where the manifested blue crowbar scraped against the bumper once with a spark, then twice near the narrow space where the trunk sat atop the fender.

It will not work.

"Just a bit closer. Come on, you can do this," Fiasco encouraged himself as he nearly missed, nicking the bumper further away than the previous attempt.

Just think about what you are trying to do, the voice said with derision. *It cannot work.*

Warm sweat pooled beneath Fiasco's mask, leather sticking to his skin like wet swimwear. Whispering beneath his breath, he said, "Shut up. I'm almost there."

Pushing out his hand as if it held a solid tool, the teeth of the crowbar scraped over the bumper, inching slowly towards the gap until the Chevelle's suspension rasped as it ran over a deep pothole. The bumper dipped down out of Fiasco's eyesight, pushing his hand and the shimmering crowbar upward in reaction. A curse nearly escaped his lips until the car hit the other side of the pothole a second later, sending the rear end careening skyward. Through blind luck that Fiasco convinced himself was skill, the teeth of his manifestation left deep trenches into the metal as it slid at an angle along the bumper. It skimmed along the surface until it managed to catch between the gap, hooking down onto the bumper with a grating crunch.

Secured, Fiasco's arm jerked forward from the strength of the engine.

"I got it!" He shouted with more astonishment than he wanted to display to anyone who might have been listening. Luck had never been on his side. If it had been, then he would have taken a different codename—not that he truly had a choice in that matter.

Hooking his target sent a stunning burst of happiness down Fiasco's spine. In reaction to the injection of joy, the power emanating around the *F* symbol on his chest flickered, then dimmed to a pallid luster, weakening the strength of his tether. Cursing himself for the lack of concentration, Fiasco drew upon the well of power reserve he kept inside for such moments and twisted the blue tendril in his hand like a rope, preparing to pull the line in.

Ahead, the engine of the Chevelle let out a low growl, as if it were angry about having to tow an unwanted passenger. Yet, Fiasco's grip held true, blue sparking off his aura when he scraped against the course road. Reeling the line in, the distance closed further still until, appearing below him, twin streaks of black curved crescent moons on the asphalt. The string of light from Fiasco's gauntlet connected to the crowbar mimicked the arch as the Chevelle made a hard right turn, tires howling in clouds of black smoke and burned rubber. Fiasco had only begun to react to the sudden turn when the sound of rending metal shrieked back to him, and the bumper ripped free from the muscle car with a sudden jerk.

The colors of New Haven returned to stark view, and the nausea seized Fiasco's body once more. The crowbar manifestation from his hand melted away as the bumper tumbled down the street toward him, bouncing at odd angles. It shrilled through the wind, missing his head by inches as it sailed over. The shattering of a windshield behind made Fiasco's shoulders flinch, knowing the damage would further burden his reputation. Glancing to his right, he saw the Chevelle squeal down third street, red brake lights gleaming through a dark gray mist. The muscle car turned away from the New Haven hero who continued streaking forward, caught in his own momentum.

Lost in nausea and choking haze, bright stars and concrete switched like a kaleidoscope as Fiasco bounced and tumbled forward. Pebbles of pavement broke away and pummeled against his shield, resonating like hail against glass. Skipping off the street, a burst of blue aura attempted to correct the tumble, but only sent his flailing body airborne. Fiasco's stomach-turning journey ended when the left side of his head and shoulder crashed into the side of a three-story townhouse with a metallic thud. An audible grunt burst passed Fiasco's teeth, pouring out along with the air in his lungs as he fell backwards onto the sidewalk in a shroud of red concrete dust and debris.

I told you it would fail.

Flat on his back, Fiasco's head slowly nodded up and down, despite the pain that gripped his neck. Dust motes danced in pale orange streetlights as particles fell like snow about him.

"Ta-da," Fiasco groaned.

Debris crunched in his now bare right hand and dug into his palm as he lifted himself up at the waist. The sight of the cloud from the disintegrated brick of the townhome made him instinctively cough and check for wounds. There was still pain, but his force shield had absorbed most of the impact. He could taste tepid metal on his lips from where his tooth had punctured the inside of his cheek, but examining the rest of his body, he was little worse for wear after striking a stone wall at that speed. But he knew that it was not real stone that crumbled to dust in his hand.

The fine, red powder slipped like sand through Fiasco's fingers as he stood upright. Through his adventure as a Mega, a cottage industry of home protection had sprung up in New Haven that was specific to his exploits. The Savoy Corporation, the lone mega-corporation in the emerging city, had begun offering reinforced siding for businesses and housing.

Thick, flexible metal was installed in specific locations and bolted along walls where analysis suggested Fiasco was more likely to strike while patrolling. It was covered by faux siding, made from the same sponge-like material used as movie props, placed over the metal to resemble original brick. Last Fiasco had read, New Haven Finance Weekly mentioned that the service had doubled in profit each year of his activity and would soon be offered in cities where other Megas were active. Fiasco Proofing® is what they coined it.

He reached out and touched the sharp edges of the scar left behind on the wall. The Fiasco Proofing was not absolute, however, evident by the way the homeowner burst from the townhome into the night. He was dressed in a gray robe cinched at the waist; his face twisted in rage. The man ran down the skinny stairs, knees pumping through the slit in the front of the robe.

"What the hell is going on? Damn!" the older man yelled with a theatrical thrust of his arms as Fiasco held back a snicker. The man peered between Fiasco and the cavity in the fake brick, his rage growing with each glance. Even under that soft streetlight, the hero was sure he could see the caramel skin of the angry stranger turn a shade of red. "You have to be kidding me!"

"Please stay calm, citizen. The damage is minimal," Fiasco said, but his words did little to soothe the man's ire. He hardly believed them himself but felt the need to reassure him as a true Mega-hero would. However, given that the stranger looked like he was closer to taking a swing at him than offering a hug, Fiasco realized that his words had the opposite effect.

"Minimal!?" the man screamed, his voice a high-pitched whine. "Have you seen the inside of my house? It looks like it has been hit by an earthquake you fuckin' moron!"

The internal energy that fed off the man's hostility pulsed as Fiasco pictured crooked picture frames, cracked lamps, overturned tables and vases, and some colorful liquid spilled on a white couch caused by his impact. Heat crawled up his neck as more neighbors emerged from houses connected to the man, undoubtedly drawn by the sound of the chaos and the shouting. They too were in a state of undress which made Fiasco aware of the hour growing late. It was night in New Haven, and he was running out of time for another engagement that he couldn't miss, which left little time for whining citizens.

"So, what are you going to do about my house, man!" the stranger screamed. At his side, his hand curled into a fist.

The older man stood nearly four inches taller than Fiasco, and his body doubled his thin frame. The features on his face reflected the neighborhood's rage. Yet, even with the obvious physical advantage, the man kept a safe distance between them. Fiasco noticed that the murmuring crowd would only get so close as well, forming a semi-circle with nearly five feet of berth between he and them. He had seen it before and knew that the people feared him.

Your people hate you, the voice mocked. Fiasco nodded.

Through the commotion, he nearly forgot about the fleeing thieves. Finally remembering that he was out on a job, the power pulsed from the symbol on his chest and flowed over his body, bathing the onlookers' faces in a soft, blue light. With the activation of his power, the glowing gauntlets returned to his hands as he rose into the sky to clear the crowd. As he hovered above the ground, he tongued the gash inside his mouth. Blood trickled asymmetrically from his mouth, and he wiped it away with the back of his hand. The blood rasped, then burned away on his glove as he peered down Third Street where he last saw the car turn.

The pungent stink of burnt rubber still permeated the air. The driver was skilled but had struggled to maintain control over the Chevelle. Fiasco made note of the zigzagging tire stains, and the long, fresh sliding gash on the side of a gray Altima that had been rammed onto the curb. But the driver had regained control. Down the street, the Chevelle registered as nothing more than two red, burning dots in the distance as its brake lights shimmered at least four or five blocks away, shrinking every second that he lingered.

Fiasco considered pursuit when the voice reminded him of the one choice it always suggested.

You should give up, or next time, you will hurt someone.

With a nod, Fiasco acknowledged the voice's wisdom. It was a blessing that the angry man had Fiasco Proofing to begin with. Had that been a normal dwelling, his aura shield would have caused him to plunge through the side of the home like a cannonball. The momentum could have even carried him through more than one house. He looked down at the people below him, men, and women with small children hugging their hips, shivering despite the warmth. Fear was apparent on all their faces even through the shadows his light created. Fiasco thought of the harm that could have fallen upon the most innocent citizens.

Realizing that it was best to add another loss to his long list of failures, the defeated hero's chin lowered as he started his descent back to the street. Back to the angry man and his neighbors, who still sought answers. Glancing one last time up to Third Street, Fiasco's breath caught in his chest when he saw a small black and gray object drop like a streaking comet from the night sky. It landed on the hood of the Chevelle with a boom that drew gasps and audible whoops of surprise from the people below. Fiasco shared in their shock, as he held out his hands to stop his descent.

Floating, the entire spectacle came to Fiasco all at once. Metal crunched and twisted on the front of the Chevelle as the hood imploded inward. Cars on either side of the street trembled on rubber tires, caught in the concussion wave from the impact, their alarms bleeping in an offbeat cacophony. The two red eyes of the taillights jumped in unison—twice as high than when it struck the pothole earlier. The vintage undercarriage scraped against the concrete in a shower of sparks when it returned to the earth. The roof flattened upon impact, sending glass exploding outward like gleaming missiles. Jarred from the collision, the left rear tire broke free from the chassis, wobbling as it rolled out of sight in the shadow between two parked cars whose yellow hazard lights blinked off and on.

Then, as fast as the crash began, it was over. The calm of the night returned to the neighborhood. Crickets were heard singing their songs in the bushes outside the homes, a relaxing ballad in stark contrast to the flashing hazard lights and intermittent car alarms that alternated beeps down the street. What was left of the Chevelle sat half draped in shadow, the other half beneath the wan orange lamplight that flickered on the left, damaged from the debris of the crash. Thin wisps of white steam rose from the mangled hood, curling into the night. The metal exterior was no longer gleaming from the great care of a loving owner but was instead an entwined mess of sharp jagged edges whose paint appeared dark and depressed.

"The hell was that?" Fiasco wondered.

Hanging in the air, the exposed jaw beneath his mask was clenched tight as eyes from below crawled along his skin, each one suddenly seeing him as the authority figure. New Haven was a quaint town nestled in the middle east of Oregon. It did not have the cache or catchy nickname of Portland, nor the posh, bourgeoisie reputation like its neighbor state to the south that overflowed with Megas. It was a headline on local news whenever a mainstream Mega would even cross the border and fly over their town.

Once, they had a big named Mega, Scarlet Valor, someone even he admired as a child, until he left the state, chasing Hollywood to be a celebrity hero. Counting himself, Fiasco knew there was only one other Mega that called New Haven home. After seeing the breadth of the destruction of the automobile, it had to be him who ended the Chevelle's run.

He is better than you, the voice said. Fiasco's jaw clenched tighter.

"Well," a woman in the crowd asked him dryly. She had lit a cigarette to calm her nerves, holding it close to her mouth between two fingers. "Aren't you going to take a look?"

"Of course I am," Fiasco replied, embarrassed that she felt the need to ask.

Leaning forward, he raced down the street, leaving a gust in his wake. Within seconds, Fiasco had made up two blocks. After reaching block three, shards of metal debris strewn along the street below began to glimmer a light blue, leading him to the wreckage. As he approached the site, he watched a bulky figure cloaked in a shadow pull the caved-in door on the driver's side off the hinges with his bare hands and toss it carelessly away. It clanged against the ground as it wobbled, until it settled to a stop.

One limp body was pulled from the wreckage and tossed over the figure's left shoulder like a sack of flour. The shadow leaned over again, holding the limp man in place with a thick arm, then pulled out another body that Fiasco surmised was the passenger, tossing him over the opposite shoulder. Fully laden with unconscious criminals, the figure walked away without acknowledging the megahero's presence, disappearing into the darkness on the other side of the shattered vehicle.

A blue trail followed his wake as Fiasco reared up. He curved his body until he was vertical to the street, and then gently floated down behind what was left of the Chevelle. An acrid mix of gas and oil tweaked Fiasco's nose as he walked into the buzzing streetlight. He passed the protruding rusted metal hinges that held the erstwhile bumper and walked towards the exposed driver's side, studying the shadows and darkened alcoves swathing the houses but finding no one hidden within.

As he walked, Fiasco investigated the crash. The hood of the car was caved in, black racing stripes resembling twisted lightning. He gingerly placed a hand on the roof, careful to avoid sharp metal splinters, even though his gauntlet would keep him from harm. He leaned into the mangled opening on the driver's side, showering the cabin within a light blue.

The driver had indeed been taken out by the figure, but he was wrong about the passenger. The driver's seat had been pushed forward off its railing so that the person in the rear who had laughed at him earlier could be safely extracted from the wreckage. The other passenger in the back was slumped to the right. A thin trail of blood trickled down the upholstery where his head rested. Studying his chest, blood-stained fabric failed to move and there was no indication that the young man was still breathing. Fiasco leaned in closer, reaching out to grab hold and pull the injured criminal towards the driver's side.

"Trying to steal my catch?" a voice whispered in his ear.

The light about Fiasco burst outward with an azure brilliance. Flinching upward, he hardly felt the bump as he knocked his head on the broken roof and jumped back out of the car with one quick motion. Looking upwards, he saw Talon's face, in the reflection of blue light, towering over him with a churlish grin.

"Ow!" Fiasco said, rubbing the back of his head, feigning injury. "Dang it, Talon, I told you about sneaking up on me like that!"

Talon chuckled, and Fiasco stood astonished. He had made sure to check the shadows when he approached, ensuring the Mega wasn't there lurking to jump out. Yet, Talon was still able to sneak up on him without a sound. Considering his size, his stealth was a feat of nature.

Fiasco drank in Talon's costume, still rubbing his head. Where his was that of a classic Mega, complete with a white lightning bolt belt, boots that matched his suit, and deep blue carbon fiber guards sewn on his suit from his shoulder down his arm, Talon's outfit epitomized simplicity.

His black hair, faded on the sides, tapered up to black spikes that waved upward. A light gray mask contrasted against his golden-brown skin and sat on the bridge of his nose yet held tight to his face. Thin screens covered his eyes, making them appear a solid white. Fiasco always wanted to ask what material Talon had used to create the mask, since it was malleable, able to move and change according to his expressions; however, his shame at having run of the mill goggles never allowed him to broach the subject. A leather knife belt lolled around Talon's hips. Twin curved dagger's filled loops on the side, their edges marked in red, and it was armed with a twelve-inch bowie knife on the opposite side.

The only gaudiness of his outfit was the silver buckle latching the knife belt, engraved with two knives to form the letter T. Across his broad chest, against a black t-shirt, was a smoke gray silhouette of a snake eating eagle perched on a branch, biting into the wood. The bird-of-prey's head was canted to the right, gray-blue eyes looking down at a prey off in the distance. Its wings were poised, arching up, ready to take flight with feathers resembling knives spread like fingers.

You are jealous, the voice said, *because he is better than you.* Fiasco sighed.

Talon's smirk broke into a toothy grin with his perfectly straight teeth that radiated white. "You're sloppy as ever," he said. His voice was deep, yet simultaneously immature. He moved around the collapsed hood, silent, like a stalking panther and made his way towards the passenger side that sat in the shadows. "I followed your chase since you made it out of downtown, when that crash you created hemmed up the cops."

Embarrassment brought heat to the Mega-hero's cheeks. Arriving to the chase late, the police were spooked when Fiasco flew between two cruisers and joined the pursuit. His aura was bright— perhaps too bright—and blinded the officers. He barely evaded when the interceptor on his left swerved violently and pitted a fellow cop. The following crash left a glut of damaged police cars on Goode Street, and him alone in the chase with the fleeing thieves. Just remembering caused a wave of humiliation, and enough negative emotion to add to his power reserve. The effect was only compounded now that he knew Talon was there to bear witness.

"You were there this entire time?" Fiasco felt obliged to ask, yet he wasn't truly surprised. He could fly, but his chase for the Chevelle was street level. Talon's mastery was that of a roof rat. The scaffolding, metal stairs and rooftops were his domain, as he seemed able to crisscross the city in minutes using those means. It wouldn't be hard for the Mega to keep up with the pursuit given his unnatural speed.

"Yeah. I was there," Talon replied with more than the proper amount of sarcasm. Fiasco searched, but there wasn't even a hint of sweat on his brow from the effort. "I saw that you had at least a dozen chances to end this before..." Talon's white eyes looked up as if searching for the words. Then, he continued, "Well, fiasco, for lack of a better word, before it came to this."

"I don't need you watching over me," Fiasco declared as he followed Talon to the passenger side of the Chevelle. "If you were paying attention, then you would know I tried. It's not my fault that they turned too fast, and I couldn't keep up."

Talon's mask furrowed at the brow, and his mouth twisted up like a question mark. "Tried? You mean that crowbar thing?" He guffawed and put one meaty hand over the knife-like glass that was left over from the side window. Glass crunched in his palm, and without a hint of pain, Talon bent over to look inside.

"Look, you've been at this—" Talon began, then paused to look over at Fiasco with the whites of his eyes wide and pleading. "Can I get a light?"

Fiasco sauntered to the car and leaned over.

He thinks you are dumb, the voice mocked, and his power waved until his aura swelled several shades brighter, turning Talon's face a cerulean hue and illuminating the inside of the car.

"Thanks," Talon said, then put his head back inside the cab. It turned right then left, surveying the damage. His voice echoed off the crumpled interior as he continued, "You've been at this, what, three or four years now?"

It was five, but Fiasco did not feel it was prudent to correct him, since he awaited the greater point.

"Four years, many of them with me, and all you could think of was a crowbar?" Talon leaned back out; his arms outstretched. "That's bush league, Crooked F."

The nickname that Talon used made Fiasco bristle, slicing through what was left of his pride. His costume had to be hand-made with his clumsy hands, which could have been likened to a meth addict trying to perform heart surgery. It had taken days of sneaking away in a closet at his parents' house, head tilted, with just a flashlight tucked under his neck for light. Using navy blue sewing thread, he was excited while stitching the stylish letter *F* into the white circle on his suit but misjudged the lining by millimeters due to his angled vision. It was enough of a mistake that the symbol tilted slightly to the left whenever he stood up straight.

At first, no one noticed. It wasn't until local news outlets—who seemed to have hated him since day one—picked up on the glaring mistake. 'Crooked F' trended as a joke at his expense, but 'Fiasco', another name the press created, became his official moniker. No one ever asked what he originally meant by the letter. Talon still enjoyed using the original nickname and wouldn't let it go.

"Surely you can do better than that by now," Talon taunted.

Putting his hands back on the Chevelle's door, Talon's arms flinched, pulling the door off with twin crunches at the hinges. Glass tinkled along the asphalt. The passenger nearly spilled out onto the ground before Talon caught the unconscious man with one arm and slung him over his left shoulder. With his right foot, a swift kick sent the passenger seat over the center armrest and through the driver's side, sending both seats skidding along the street. With the opening now wide, Talon pulled the last passenger Fiasco nearly rescued out of the backseat by the top scruff of his shirt.

"Hey, easy there, Talon," Fiasco said. "That one seems really hurt."

A black eyebrow jutted up above the mask on Talon's face. "You were about to pull him clear through the other side just a second ago," he stared accusingly. "But relax, they're fine."

Fiasco's head tilted to the side. "How do you know?"

"I listened," Talon replied, and nodded to his left. "This one just has a few cracked ribs. I can hear them grinding as he breathes," he said, then shook the other man whose limbs flailed like a doll. "And this other one just has a concussion. Probably. I don't know. Can't really listen for a head wound, can I? I'm not a Praetermind."

"You listened? I didn't know you could do that," Fiasco bleated. He tried to tongue the cut inside his cheek, but it had nearly healed, feeling like a sore, thin stitch.

He is better than you, the voice taunted, and Fiasco's aura flushed.

"I'm sure I told you before. You just don't pay attention half the time," Talon chuckled as he walked over to a manicured lawn and laid the two criminals next to the other two, he had rescued earlier. "They're breathing at the very least and quit trying to change the subject. You always do that, you know? You need to listen."

Fiasco sucked his teeth. He hated talking about himself. As far back as he could remember, failure was his constant companion. It manifested in the voice when his powers activated at seventeen and turned into the evil jiminy cricket that was quick to remind him of his inadequacy.

Megas normally gained their power at puberty, the voice whispered. *You were a late bloomer.*

"You know what you did wrong don't you?" Talon asked.

"Yes," Fiasco replied, but it was more a question than an answer.

"Well? Tell me."

Fiasco's shoulders sank, and he looked at the ground. "I'm a born loser, I guess. A Fiasco. I mean, it's in the name," he replied, trying to sound sarcastic, but channeling the voice's negativity. "Is that what you want to hear?"

Talon's mask bent sharply at the bridge of his nose. "What's the matter with you, Crooked F?" His mask shadowed along the edges to display his disapproval. "Why do you always talk like that? It's like speaking to an emotionally stunted child sometimes." He crouched like a baseball catcher near the head of one of the robbers, studying his wounds while he let out a breath. "If you undervalue yourself, rest assured the world will not raise your price."

"What the hell does that even mean?" Fiasco said with a laugh. "Who said that, Talon? Don't even try and claim it as your own."

Talon turned on his ankles to face him. "I don't know. Some dead guy, but at least I remembered it." The two laughed together and Talon's face softened. "Look, I don't want to hear that crap out of you anymore. It's self-defeating. Now seriously, what did you do wrong?"

"I don't know, Talon," Fiasco replied and crossed his arms over his chest. "Seriously."

Still crouched, Talon measured Fiasco's face, then slowly stood to full height. Fiasco squirmed, feeling like he was being questioned and scolded by his father.

He will never love you.

"You weren't prepared," Talon finally said, "You saw only the here and now, and wasn't prepared for what came next."

"What's wrong with the here and now, anyway?" Fiasco asked. "That happens to be where we live."

"A true Mega must always be prepared for what comes next. He has to be steps ahead or risk being left behind." He turned and gestured back to where Fiasco had crashed into the brick wall. "Case in point."

Fiasco's chin dipped into his chest. "Very funny. So what, you want me to be like Scarlet Valor or something?"

Talon's face hardened again. His mask framed his eyes and brows, giving it a menacing visage. "Forget that guy. He's corporate. A Fraud. He doesn't care about this city, even though they love him."

The sudden show of anger from Talon nearly made Fiasco feel what he sensed was apprehension, until he heard police sirens echo in the distance. NHPD had finally broken through the snarl and almost caught up to the pursuit. Red and blue lights blinked behind Talon where a crowd had formed and watched as the two Megas looked at each other in silence.

"I can see you, Fiasco," Talon finally said, his tone more somber than before. His face relaxed again as he walked toward him, his voice lowering as he approached. "You have to step it up. People are talking, and words travel fast these days. Now the wrong people are talking, and the wrong people may be listening."

Despite being cocooned in his warm light, Fiasco shivered. He knew Talon hinted at the Megahuman Defense Command. The M.D.C. They were the boogeymen of the MegaStream forums. A government trained law enforcement agency comprised of Megas who specialized in policing Megahuman affairs. They normally only dealt with nation-threatening events. Last Fiasco checked, his notoriety polled less than the girl Mega in Wyoming who could speak to dogs. Yet, their presence was still a dark shadow of fear that loomed over anyone who chose to put on a mask.

"Well, it's not like I'm some Mal," Fiasco countered, using the sobriquet for Malignants, Megas who use their power for crime. Perhaps there was a modicum of luck in Fiasco's life since he had yet come up against such a vicious foe, and it was his intention to continue that streak going if he could. Mal's were not known to leave Mega's breathing after encounters.

"We're a mid-level town in Oregon for God's sake," Fiasco continued. "No one cares what you do Talon, and even less me."

The silence between the two Megas was oppressive. The white screens over Talon's eyes shielded any attempt by Fiasco to gauge what he was thinking at all. Talon's eyes hadn't wavered from his stare until the big man sighed and shrugged incredulously with both shoulders, breaking the tension.

"Well, you never know what could happen. Times change while you're not paying attention." Talon said, then nodded to something behind Fiasco's shoulder. Fiasco turned and saw that several local news agencies had set up a small village of vans and cameras half a block down the street. Reporters were scampering about, getting their camera crews together, while hurriedly trying to beat the other network. New Havenites drawn by the noise and news coverage began to pool around the news camp.

A hand slapped down on his left shoulder and Fiasco flinched. Talon stood tall on his right. The perfect smile had returned to his face, as if their contentious conversation had never occurred. He walked him with a muscled arm firm around his shoulders towards the media. Noticing the two Megas approaching, the reporters met them halfway in bursts of white camera flashes and microphones, questions firing in rapid succession.

"Fiasco, did you kill them?"

"How does it feel to fail again?"

"Does it bother you that your approval rating is at eighteen percent in the latest New Haven poll?"

Their questions were a sonata of voices speaking over one another. Talon put both hands on Fiasco's shoulders and stood over him as he would a child.

"Now, now. Leave Fiasco alone. None of this is his doing," Talon asserted. The two Megas exchanged a glance before Talon stepped in front. "Because it was me who actually brought these thieves to justice."

With that proclamation, the flashes from the media's cameras burst like a firecracker display of white. Talon's smile widened, spreading his arms to drink in the adulation as he walked forward into the attention. His large shadow draped over Fiasco so much so that it was difficult to even tell that he was behind him, except for his pale blue glow that seemed to lend Talon his own shimmering aura.

You only make him look better, the voice said. Fiasco nodded. The energy around his symbol throbbed from the inferiority he felt, and his power surged until he slowly lifted into the air.

Talon looked up. "You're leaving already?" he asked, the white eyes on his mask growing wide.

"Yeah, I think you have this part covered," Fiasco replied dryly. "I have to go let some strangers into my house."

"Oh yeah, the party. For that professional Mega league team, right?" Talon replied, putting the latter part of his sentence in air quotations. Talon's perfect toothy grin appeared on his face, as if he was in on a joke that Fiasco was not privy to.

To Fiasco, the Mega league was simple, but brilliant in nature. At its core, the league was just common football, but played by Megas. The field was twice as large in width and length than a national football team's stadium to accommodate the players powers. Megas were almost common if the term was stretched to include the lower ranks. The Mega league was reserved for Deltas and Charlies— specifically for strong men and Speedstras, Megas who could run faster than Mach One. Sometime, Microclimate practitioners—Megas who could manipulate the weather like rain, wind, or snow—were able to join, adding new facets to the game. Beta's were too strong, and there were no Alpha level Megas, as far as Fiasco knew.

There were twelve teams in the league. New Haven was one of two recent additions, thanks to the Savoy Corporation, representing the pacific northwest. The other addition was in Salt Lake City, representing the Rockies. For an emerging town, New Haven was abuzz with anticipation, and Fiasco had been talked into celebrating the acquisition, even though he normally shied from human contact.

"Well, good luck with the party. And with that girl," Talon said.

"We're just friends Talon," Fiasco replied.

"Right." Talon mocked with a purr. "Just do me a favor and have a little confidence in yourself," he said. Then, pointing up to Fiasco, he added, "Oh, and take a shower too. You smell like a filthy ass farting sulfur in that suit."

"Jerk," Fiasco mumbled, barely audibly, as he rose into the sky.

Talon's white eyes narrowed. "I heard that," he responded.

Looking down, Fiasco gave Talon his own smirking leer. "I know," he said, then offered a soft salute up to his brow with two fingers.

"Wait," Talon shouted. "Before you go, I didn't find any money or merchandise in the car. What exactly did those guys steal anyway, so I can return it? Make it look good for the cameras. You know how it goes."

Fiasco tilted his head. "The Chevelle was the merchandise, Talon. It was an original with all the parts that they stole from Tomas Savoy himself."

Surrounded by citizens and media, the svelte Mega turned and cursed beneath his breath. Fiasco suppressed a laugh, then looked up into the sky.

"Fiasco!" he shouted, half singing his name in an off-key note that echoed off the neighborhood. Then, he took off like a blue bottle rocket upward into the clouds. The breeze in his wake swept up the grime and debris, swirling it among Talon, the media, and the citizens equally, leaving a thin coat of dust on everything—and everyone—in the vicinity.

Cool air greeted him, as Fiasco soared over the city. He headed north over the whaling cop cars driving south toward the Chevelle wreckage below. On his right, past highway one-twenty-six, with its lines of white and red headlights, he saw the expanse of land where the new Mega league stadium was going to be built. Parked trucks and large foreman trailers were lit up by the bright halogen lights being erected at intervals around the site.

Looking left, he saw downtown, where the teeth-like silhouette of office buildings rose against the night sky. As he thought back to a time when he couldn't fly, Fiasco noted that the old skyline he remembered as a child of trees and mountains would eventually be dwarfed by the corporate Savoy tower that had begun construction blocks away, creating a new center in New Haven. Orientating from those landmarks, and the gray quarter moon in the sky, Fiasco veered to the left, turning toward Longreach district, where he lived.

As he flew, Fiasco pondered the encounter he just had with the citizens and press, realizing that coating them in dirt would not endear him to the people of New Haven. Nonetheless, he was already resigned to being the town pariah. The local hooligan. No amount of glad-handing or baby holding would change public opinion. There was never really a need to live for or please someone else. Yet, Talon's words still lingered.

Removing himself from the here and now, training his mind to think steps ahead, and the overall concept of being a true Mega did not register. He was just Fiasco—no more, no less. There were no rule books for the game he played. Talon's advice came in handy from time to time, but he could only play the game as it came to him. Why play chess when he was better at checkers? For Fiasco, it was best to know his limits and embrace mediocrity.

You will always be a failure. Fiasco nodded in affirmation, assured that more failure awaited him later that night. Failure that went by the name of Julianna.

Julianna

Lukewarm water trickled down Kevin Jones' face, turning maroon from the brick dust that crusted his skin, when he heard the first rap on his door. Although he had rushed home from the Chevelle wreckage, there was only enough time for a quick bird bath. This entailed standing in the middle of his bathroom on the cheap, cold tiles that chilled his feet, while washing down the important areas with a soapy washcloth. Water dripped from his chin while he leaned over the sink basin, pausing as he waited to make sure he heard something.

The door rapped again with three knocks. Kevin leaned into the hallway. Soiled water trailed down to his bare chest as he looked at the clock painted blue and gold and shaped like a stylized football helmet on his living room wall, emblazoned with New Haven's Mega league team logo. The bath had given him a good forty-five minutes to prepare his apartment for the party that was supposed to start at nine. Whoever was at the door was frustratingly early.

The knocks came again with more impatience.

"Hold on!" Kevin shouted, then looked at himself in the mirror. His hair was a wet, sloppy mess, with dirt-laden sweat still falling from his face, mingling with the sink water.

"C'mon. Give me something so I can dry off, you prick," he muttered to the mirror, but the voice that readily spoke up when it came to derision did not respond. It worked on its own schedule, not on command. It only seemed to activate when he was at his lowest —to kick him when he was already down. Or when he dared for optimism. With no other choice, Kevin winced as he slid faded jeans over his damp leg. Hopping as he slid the other leg through, he wondered if it was Julianna waiting on the other side of the door.

At his day job at Blanchet Consumer Receivables—BCR for short— he had heard about Julianna even before seeing her. She was the fourth-floor beauty with creamy, smooth skin, and hourglass-shaped hips that worked in the records department upstairs. She had all the male bill collectors talking, and the few females in his department jealous. Warren, his best and only real friend who he shared a squat desk with, had seen her before he did. He often said that the key to Julianna's extreme beauty was that you could place a thin board right in the middle of her nose, and each side of her face would be identical to the other. She had that golden ratio—perfect symmetry.

Another three raps hit his door, soft, but more rapid in speed.

"I'm coming!" Kevin yelled. Warren wouldn't have knocked; in fact, he probably would have just walked in as if he owned the place. Dry socks rolled over damp feet, stumbling in his haste as he imagined Julianna standing outside, frustrated, and ready to leave.

Calm down, the voice said, almost like a true friend, then continued, *you will never look good to a woman like her.*

"There it is," Kevin said as his chest warmed.

He let the power cascade over his body. A few swipes with hands warmed by his power did enough to smooth out the deep wrinkles in his jeans. A swish of cool mint mouthwash stung his throat that he then spat out into the sink with foaming white bubbles. Looking in the mirror, he ran a brush over his messy hair until it appeared decent. Satisfied that he was at least presentable, Kevin spritzed on cologne that had sat unused for months on his counter, then hurriedly slipped on a t-shirt as he walked towards the front door.

At the door, he noticed the character on his shirt and fanned the bottom out with his hands. "I wonder if she'll know who this is," he thought.

You are too much of a nerd for someone wonderful like her. Kevin agreed.

With a deep breath, he counted to one, then opened the door. The scent hit him first— pomegranate with a hint of citrus and lavender— but it wasn't the peony flower smell he was expecting. The woman standing in front of his door had large green eyes and wavy black hair that fell to her shoulders. She wore a short gray shirt that stopped at her navel, above jeans that looked painted on. She stood several inches taller than him in black leather heels. She was pretty, but she wasn't Julianna.

"Hi?" Kevin said. He did not know her by name but thought he may have seen her around the office a few times.

The woman rolled her eyes when she caught sight of his shirt.

"Is Warren here?" she said flat, and with an attitude he didn't much care for.

"Uhm, no. He doesn't actually live here," Kevin leaned back and glanced inside at the clock on his wall again. "You're a little early, but you're welcome to come in and wait for him. I have some food—" He didn't even finish before the girl huffed, turned, and stormed away.

Even the tight apple bottom that sauntered down his concrete landing to the outdoor stairwell could not quell the flicker of anger he felt inside. "Yeah, nice to meet you, too!" Kevin shouted, his voice dripping with disdain. "Asshole," he whispered as he slammed the door.

Women do not like you, the voice reminded him, as it was apt to do.

Leaning against the door, a warm blast of air rushed through Kevin's nose as he tapped a tune with his fingers on his chest where his symbol would have been in costume and nodded in agreement. Not even one guest in, and he could already predict that the night would be a typical Fiasco evening. Yet, with all the negative things that could be said of Kevin Jones, breaking his word was not among them.

He surveyed the mess that was his apartment and sighed, "Might as well get this over with."

Using the power he collected from the rude girl's visit, Kevin sent out glowing blue lines from his hands, using the tendrils, to clean his apartment from top to bottom. Afterward, a glowing hand dimmed the ceiling light fixture overhead in the living room, while he turned on two free-standing floor lamps, spindly like spider legs, which stood in the far corners of the room, both adding to the soft beige light.

The party began with a trickle of guests arriving, followed by an awkward tension of no one wanting to mingle, as if they were all strangers that did not actually work together. The discomfort lasted until more guests arrived to crowd the interior of his apartment. Kevin lost count at twenty, but their proximity at least forced people to chatter. He first noticed a problem with the latest batch of arrivals. Most were strangers that must have invited themselves by word of mouth. Party tourists.

As more tourists continued to occupy his apartment, Kevin decided to wait in the foyer and act as the party doorman. With every knock or doorbell ring, he greeted the new arrivals and let them in.

"Come on in, you guys," he said as a welcome. "Make yourselves at home. There are refreshments in the back."

But most guests never acknowledged his presence as the host, at most passing him a coat or jacket to put in the closet behind him as they made their way like a herd toward the free beer and food. The apartment Kevin was able to afford on his meager salary was cheap, with thin floors and walls, but spacious in footage for its price tag.

In the den to his left, a few guests had congregated in the small niche enjoying themselves huddled around his PC playing a dungeon role-playing game. The real action was in the living room, where a musty heat had built up from the bodies even though the patio door that led to the balcony was open to let in the night air.

The large entertainment center— a weighty donation from his parents that they just wanted out of their house— dominated the wall that closed off the kitchen. The music was low from his stereo, but the bass still thumped from the speakers' proximity to the wall. The volume was muted on the television, but the clear image on the screen played the coverage of his botched car chase with the Chevelle in a continuous loop, acting as a constant reminder of his latest failure.

"Hey," Kevin said over the music. "You guys don't want to watch something else? You know, maybe music videos, or some reality show? Or whatever you people like?" But no one answered.

A couch sat on the opposite wall, just passed a glass coffee table. Several of the fairer sex sat along the length of the couch's arm watching the television. Red-haired Jenni West, one of the rare females on his bill collector team, appeared to be the ringleader, dominating the middle. She had skin of porcelain to contrast with the fire red hair cascading down her back and black shirt. Her pale legs crossed under a gray and black skirt. Three more girls formed a half-circle around her, holding their red plastic cups with both hands as they giggled and swooned whenever Talon's chiseled brown face appeared on the television.

Tired of seeing Talon's perfect smile, Kevin walked through the den, ducking under a silver and glass chandelier that hung far too low, to get a view of the rest of the party.

A glut of his guests had crowded into the small kitchen nearly shoulder to shoulder, and he could imagine the smell their mass of bodies had conjured. Dirty liquid streaked his bland linoleum floor, stained with black, dirty shoe prints of various sizes and treads. The kitchen was a thoroughfare and opened into a ten-by-ten-foot dining room where his tendrils had set up the folding table to hold the pizza, chips, and finger foods that had to be littering the floor by now.

"It's like I can literally see my security deposit dwindling," Kevin muttered.

Looking at the helmet clock, only forty minutes had passed since guests had started to materialize, and Warren had yet to arrive. Neither had Julianna.

"Whatever," Kevin thought, resigning to the fact that her agreement to attend was just lip service. "Who needs her here, anyway? Probably would have caused a riot based on this lot."

Face reality, she does not like you. Not even as a friend.

He was nearly ready to send everyone one home, until a gush of wind rushed up his back from the foyer area. He turned when the crowd let out a cheer of recognition. At the foyer, the door was swung open to welcome a familiar person standing in the entrance, arms spread out like Jesus, bathing in the cheers just like Talon would do.

"Okay, everyone, calm down, I'm here," Warren said as he picked up a case of beer with his right hand, and slid his phone back into his pocket with his left. The din and tone of the party increased several notches just with his friend's arrival.

Weaving his way through the crowd, a glasses-wearing, shaggy-haired, coding nerd from the IT department named Ethan Johns made his way to the landing. Ethan was tall, but unkempt, with a spare tire around the midsection that stretched his tucked in shirt. He was always hovering around Warren, like a pilot fish beneath a shark. He was a project of Warren's, like the plot of a ninety's teen movie, but his friend had his work cut out for him to turn the frog into a prince.

Grinning, Ethan took the case of beer from Warren with both hands without being asked, as a small crowd formed to greet Kevin's friend. A smart grin etched Warren's face that extenuated his left dimple on his caramel skin as he shook hands and fist bumped the male party goers. The women who came up to greet him put their heads into his chest and wrapped their arms around his waist to pull him in for hugs. Jenni was the last in the line of women, and her embrace lingered longer than the other girls, leaving behind strands of red hair on his shirt when they parted. Warren held her by the hips, nodding and smiling as they talked, before he finally noticed Kevin watching, and greeted him with a grin and a hand wave.

Warren strolled towards him, his confident glide making him seem much taller than the other people around him. His hair was dark, short, and wavy with a dim sheen that was tapered on his forehead down to manicured sideburns that stopped sharply at the earlobe. The well-shaped hair only made his dark eyes shine brighter.

Kevin had never seen Warren dressed in anything less than business casual. He walked into the party wearing a white button-down shirt that was tailored to his toned, lengthy frame. The sleeves were unbuttoned and pushed up his forearms, revealing a dark tattoo of Golgotha, with the three crosses spaced on a hill on his right arm. Dark slacks complimented the shirt and were enhanced by black wing-tipped dress shoes.

"At least he left the sports coat," Kevin thought, suddenly feeling severely under dressed in his t-shirt that wrinkled at the collar.

The two friends met just at the edge of the foyer.

"Hey!" Warren exclaimed, shaking Kevin's hand with his right, while simultaneously pulling him in to wrap his left arm around his neck. Pulled in close, Kevin could smell his cologne, a secret mixture of Warren's own design.

The music thumped in the living room but was less so near the foyer where they stood, sounding more like low bass coming from a car. Sweat already glistened on Warren's brow as he pulled away and looked around.

"Well, this is more people than I expected. Glad word got out," he said, still grinning.

Kevin glanced about. "So, this is your fault?"

"Yeah. Why? Is that bad?" Warren laughed as he leaned back to open the foyer closet door and produced a dark gray sports coat that Kevin didn't even realize was there.

Kevin knew what sporting the coat meant for the night. The coat was like a hunter covering himself in an animal pelt. A target had been acquired— one that had been identified even before his arrival— and Warren needed his best hunting gear. Kevin had no idea who he had in mind but knew it could have been any of the women who came to embrace him earlier. The way he and Jenni stared at each other looked promising as well. Or he could have been after that rude girl who still had not returned. Either way, given the state of his dress, Warren could have his pick of them all.

"Well, yeah, it's a problem, Warren. I mean, look at how many people are here," Kevin swept his arm behind him. "Plus, most of them didn't bring their own beer like I asked, and I bet they've eaten all the food by now, too." He felt his stomach growl as he spoke, recalling that he had not eaten since before the chase with the Chevelle.

"That bad, huh?" he replied.

With vigorous nods, Kevin pointed accusingly with his hands at the numerous guests that invaded his apartment.

Warren bit the side of his lip. "I can admit, this is more than I expected," he said, scanning the crowd. "Still, it's not like I forced you to host."

"No, but you guilted me enough," Kevin replied. "You have the stereo, Kevin. You have the room because you have no furniture, Kevin. You're off that day, Kevin. You are right in the middle for everyone, so it's the perfect location, Kevin. Do it for the Mega team, you said."

"False!" Warren pointed his own accusing finger in front of his smile. "All I did was explain the reasons why it would be good for a guy like you to be known for hosting a good party around the office."

"A guy like me, huh?"

Warren's eyebrows curved downward at the top of his nose. "You know I didn't mean it like that," he said with a sigh. "What I'm saying, is that you need to open up a bit. You can't just hang with me for the rest of your life, like some life mate."

Kevin stiffened. "Now what does that mean?" he said. His eyes darted to Ethan behind Warren, who looked away once he noticed that he was caught eavesdropping on their conversation.

Warren glanced to the left as he searched for the words. "What I mean is that you need to put yourself out there man! Get some tail for once," he finally said with a soft punch to the shoulder.

It felt as if everyone at the party had heard Warren's statement, and all eyes were fixed on their embarrassed host. "Gee, thanks, Warren," Kevin said in a high whisper. "Say that louder because I don't think they heard you on the balcony. You're really being a pal tonight."

"Man, I keep screwing this up," Warren said, putting a hand briefly on Kevin's shoulder as he laughed. "What I'm saying is that, really, this party is for you. I mean, look how many women are here. You know how hard it is to get a turnout of females like this? Usually, these house parties end up being a hundred dudes showing off and fighting over the four or five women who happened to show up."

Kevin crossed his arms over his chest. "They came here for you, Warren."

"So?" he laughed. "Man up a bit! Be proactive. This is your house, so act like the king of the castle. You need to get your carrot wet to get that stick out of your ass and lighten up a bit."

Kevin cocked an eyebrow at his friend's colorful euphemism for sex. Warren had noticed that gene to conquer the opposite sex seemed to be mute inside him, and sleeping around was out of the question, since he was raised with different standards gleaned from the church. Being single was a comfortable bubble that he could retreat into, away from the chaos of being Fiasco. There was no conceivable reason to invite someone else in to potentially ruin the tranquility.

Before he could respond to the lewd advice, a sharp breeze raised the hair on his arms, and Kevin noticed that someone had left the door open behind Warren. "See, this is what I'm saying, Warren," he protested, pointing with his hand as he moved to close the door. "Leaving my door open. Running up my electric bill. I should have followed my instincts with this party."

"Wait, hold up Kevin," Warren said, pushing out his hand, but it was too late.

Kevin pushed the knob, but the door came to a stop with a sound of clinking glass. On the other side, he heard a mouse-like 'ouch' squeak through the opening. Looking down, there was a slender knee, and below that, a brown leather high heel shoe that belonged to a woman. He was smacked in the face by a sweet, spicy flower scent that wasn't overpowering, but triggered a pleasant remembrance as he opened the door again. Heat rushed to Kevin's face as Julianna shouldered her way in, carrying a brown paper grocery bag cradled with both arms that crinkled like newspaper as she slid inside.

"Hi," Julianna said. Even though she appeared a bit disheveled from climbing the set of stairs of his apartment, it was still as if a royal had graced his humble shack.

All the available light seemed to glint off the light brown flecks in Julianna's almond-shaped eyes, making them shine like stars. A smile spread on her pink lips that glimmered with a light sheen of gloss. Kevin glanced over at Warren who stood behind him with one eyebrow raised and puckered lips that triggered both dimples on his lean face. Flustered, and finding himself with a lack of words, Kevin took a step back and let the door open fully. Julianna walked in and bumped the door shut with her hip as Kevin's eyes followed her shapely curves.

"Hi, Julianna!" Ethan beamed. He waved a chubby palm, causing the case of beer to slip from his grasp. The way his face turned a beet red said that he probably had a crush on her. Looking around, Kevin thought that at least half the men at his party showed up hoping she would appear, sharing in Ethan's affection.

"Hi, Ethan! So glad you could make it," Julianna huffed, winded from the flights while burdened with the heavy looking bag in her thin arms. Ethan's face brightened with euphoria just being noticed by her.

That was why Ethan, and others like him, held such admiration for her. Julianna looked at Ethan and treated him the same she would anyone else, despite his low office popularity status. One of her gifts was making everyone feel equal, even the less attractive men, despite knowing that she was the queen that wore the tiara in most of their minds.

Moving next her, Warren said, "Sorry, but this is why I was late. Someone," he nodded over to Julianna, "wanted to follow me here. And she just had to stop by the liquor store, too."

"Don't blame me for having manners. Who comes to a party empty handed?" Julianna panted as she shimmied the bag back up to her forearms, the movement dropping a lock of hair before her left eye. Her beautiful eyes looked up at Warren, who was several inches taller. "And you're welcome for that beer, by the way. Cheapskate."

Warren patted his pockets and pretended to check his coat jacket then spread a pretty grin to distract from his lack of having money to cover the beer.

"Oooh. Yeah," he whined in a soft, gentleman way with a snap of his finger for emphasis. Julianna rolled her eyes, making Kevin's mouth twitch in a brief smile. "Remind me to get you back later, okay?" Warren continued, licking his bottom lip.

Warren and Julianna exchanged glances—his with the best, sad puppy dog he could parody, and hers a beautiful faux rage. The standoff only lasted an instance before the two laughed together. Julianna bumped him with her shoulder, with a sly smirk. Watching the two share an inside joke stoked the power inside Kevin.

All at once, he understood who Warren had targeted at the party.

You never stood a chance, the voice whispered, and melancholy washed over Kevin, knowing the voice was correct once again. The revelation of their relationship almost felt embarrassing, and images of her and him together, embracing, laughing between pecks of lips played in his mind as his best friend got the girl once again.

"Hey, where did you go, Kev?' He heard Warren ask.

Then all at once, the images subsided, and Kevin looked between Warren and Julianna. The two stared at him together, their faces strained as if they could see the pictures he had just imagined. The low thumping bass behind them that matched Kevin's beating heart seemed to only add to the awkward tension.

"Thanks for the beer. And the liquor," Kevin stumbled as he spoke to Julianna, trying not to catch her eyes. "Forgive me. Here, let me get that for you," he continued as he took the bag of liquor from her arms.

"Thank you," Julianna exhaled before playfully poking Warren in his ribs for not offering first.

They are adorable together.

The bag was packed so tight with content that he heard a tear in the paper when he grabbed it, jostling the bottles inside. Looking inside, the bag was filled with mixing agents, juices, sodas, and various hard liquors, like flavored vodkas, whiskey's, rums, and tequila. It was an eclectic mixture of drinks made to get people drunk fast while saving a dime.

"Here, take this," Kevin said to Ethan as he balanced the bag atop the case of beer he held. Ethan groaned from the extra weight, but Kevin paid it little mind, seeing it as payment for eavesdropping earlier.

Free from the bag's burden, Julianna took off the small jean coat she wore, and folded it over her arm. Surveying the party, she pulled her purse strap that had fallen back over her shoulder. Then, those light-brown eyes set on him.

"Cute shirt," she said. "Thank you for inviting me, Kevin."

Julianna must have noticed his apprehension. As she moved a lock of hair from the front of her eye and pulled it back over her left ear, her eyes narrowed to slits. She let the rest of her dark, straight hair frame her face and unfolded down to skinny shoulders that sparkled with a soft sheen. A sky-blue sundress set on her shoulders with thin spaghetti straps. It flowed like water over her generous breasts and curvy, tempting hips, buttoned down the middle with small buttons. The dress was accentuated with brown leather heels about an inch in height that latched just above her ankle, raising her up to his eye level.

Noticing that he hadn't yet replied, Kevin finally said, "Oh no problem, Julianna. Glad you were able to find the place."

"You should thank me then!" Warren said. He moved between the two and guided the trio from the foyer to just outside the kitchen. Ethan lagged behind, pushing up his glasses as he struggled to keep the bottles inside the paper bag balanced on his case of beer.

Warren flicked his finger towards the kitchen. "Put that liquor in the dining room, Ethan, and could you do me a favor?"

"Sure, Warren, shoot," Ethan replied, his voice barely audible over the music that Kevin had noticed was louder.

"Can you make me a drink real quick? I would really appreciate it," Warren shouted to be heard.

Ethan smiled and nodded vigorously, nearly shaking off his glasses again. Before he left, he glanced at the black-haired beauty and the red brightened on his puffy cheeks when she grinned at him. Then quickly, Ethan followed Warren's orders, lumbering into the kitchen with the case of beer and bag of liquor.

Warren then pointed with a limp hand to no one in particular in the dining room and shouted, "Hey! Someone clear off that table in there! Time to get wet!"

The crowd wooed and raised their cups, knowing that getting wet for Warren meant a binge session of the drinking game, Waterfall. The game made Warren a legend around the office. At every party, he would organize and host the parlor game, ensuring everyone would get drunk equally and generally have a good time. Yet, even with the frequency he hosted the game, no one seemed to tire of it. Two minutes in and Warren already owned the party that he barely felt noticed in.

You only make others look better, the voice reminded.

Kevin stood before the opening of the kitchen. Julianna gave him a quick glance before squeezing Warren by the forearm. "I'm going to go talk to Jenni," she said.

"Oh, okay," Warren replied. Before she could go, he reached out and grabbed her by the hand, bringing it up to his chest as he looked at her deeply. "Hey, try to be back to make the first round, okay?"

Julianna nodded, snorting a laugh, then walked away, Warren's hand lingering at the tip of her fingers before he finally let go.

Rubbing the center of his chest with callused knuckles, Kevin realized that he had held his breath while Warren and Julianna touched, bracing for a passionate hug or kiss before she left. As close as they were, he wouldn't put it past his friend to shove his latest prize right in his face. But then, part of him wondered why he even cared. He and Julianna were just friends after all.

"Let Warren have his party," he thought, "and the girl for that matter." He could just walk out to his favorite bar, eat a BBQ chicken pizza, and not come back until everyone was gone. There was little doubt anyone would even notice, and there was no reason to hang around to see Warren and Julianna act like a couple after the liquor had lowered their inhibitions either.

Losers are skillful in the art of self-pity. Kevin accepted the rebuke.

Together, Warren and Kevin watched Julianna disappear, hips swaying and hair, still with a glowing sheen even in the darkened room, bouncing against her back as she walked. The crowd in the living room seemed to part for her, with the men admiring as she passed, and the women scrutinizing her from hair to toenail polish. Near the arm of the couch, she and Jenni squealed as if they had not seen each other in years.

As irritated as Kevin was with the thought of the two being together, since Warren would only grow more insufferable, he realized that if he were a real friend, he would find a way to be happy for him. That is what a true Mega would do.

Interesting. The voice said, then mocked, *you are setting yourself up for failure and heartbreak.*

"Ooh wee," Warren moaned as he put his arm tight around Kevin's neck and bit his knuckle. "I know what you're thinking bro," Warren continued, "but you're wrong. She absolutely does stand a chance with a guy like me."

Then he laughed in Kevin's ear—the kind of self-satisfied laugh that suggested he was just kidding about being an overconfident prick. Kevin could almost feel the attraction his friend had to

Julianna. Sensing that Julianna too probably held the same feelings as Warren, Kevin squirmed from beneath his friend's arm and pulled away.

"Hey!" Warren snickered. He had his hands out wide and held a joker-like grin. "Look, I was just joking, so don't give me that condescending look you sometimes get. Anyway, I thought you'd be happy that I brought her here, but you're not acting grateful. I just legitimized your party."

Slender arms crossed over Kevin's chest. "I guess. I mean, I am glad you brought her here. Julianna's a friend, but I know what you're doing, Ren," Warren only let Kevin call him that nickname. "The jacket, the drinks? Don't pretend you brought her here for me."

"I don't even know what you're talking about," said Warren, sucking his bottom lip. His eyes had focused back like a panther on Julianna and Jenni, discrediting his statement.

When it came to women, Kevin followed the unwritten man code, but Warren grew up in a different part of New Haven that did not follow the same rules. Competition was his code, especially when it came to the opposite sex, and he wanted them all—or more accurately, he wanted them all to want him. To his best friend it was let the best man win. Warren only ensured Julianna's presence at the party so everyone could witness his triumph.

He is better than you in every way.

While they were talking, Ethan arrived, grinning as he handed Warren a drink in a plastic cup.

"I got your drink, Warren," he squeaked.

Warren sipped the drink, and his face soured as if he had swallowed a lemon.

"What the hell is this?" he stammered and coughed.

Ethan's face turned strawberry red.

"Tequila sunrise?" he replied sheepishly, looking between Kevin and his mentor.

Warren nearly spit the drink back up, but forced himself to swallow hard, orange spittle still on his lips.

"You wasted that liquor on this bullshit?" he asked, then shoved the cup in Kevin's chest, nearly spilling the contents onto his superhero t-shirt. His face was still twisted when he turned to Kevin and said, "Look, I need to get in there and make sure the game is set up properly, and that no more liquor gets wasted, apparently. I'll be back, and we'll finish this talk then."

Warren gave him a swift and strong one-armed hug, and before Kevin could reply, he left with Ethan. Curious, he looked down at the orange liquid that still swirled below the rim and took a swallow of Warren's drink. Citrus flicked the taste buds in the back of his throat. It was far too sweet, even with ice, and tasted almost like orange-flavored syrup. Yet, the tequila still burned like fire going down his throat.

Forcing down the drink and feeling awkward that he was standing out in the open all alone, Kevin shouldered his way through the crowd in the kitchen to the dining room. Whoever had listened to Warren's orders to set up the game had done a decent enough job. The food had been cleared, and plastic red cups filled with liquor shots and beer bottles still glistening with condensation dominated the center of the table. Stacks of cards circled atop the table. Warren was lining up some players, alternating between boy and girl, around the edge. He once told Kevin that this arrangement allowed for more interactions, and potential hookups once the booze kicked in.

Kevin had never played waterfall before, since he never attended office parties, but Warren had explained it to him so many times that he probably could be considered an expert. A player would grab a card from the circle and have to follow the rule associated with that number or face card. Warren would give the instructions of each card to the players before they were too drunk to remember.

All the rules ended with variations on binge drinking, either alone or with someone else. Waterfall happened when someone chose an ace card, meaning the entire table was forced to drink one cup after another, only able to cease when the person before them did so. It went around the table like a waterfall.

Moving to the arched opening leading to the living room to give players more space, Kevin scooped ice from the chest at his feet to water down the tequila sunrise, then took another sip. It was still too thick and far too sweet. He could use the power to melt the cubes to water it down quicker, but then he would be left with a warm cup of watered-down liquor.

"You going to stand here all alone or are you going to play?" a soft voice said into his ear.

For some reason that still eluded his understanding, Julianna had persisted in their friendship, despite the cold shoulder Kevin gave her initially. Months after joining the company, she had worn him down with just pure sweetness and engagement. They even had quick conversations whenever she came into the office, a feat shared only with Jenni.

She pities you.

"Maybe later," Kevin replied, regaining his composure as the fire burned his throat. The walls of the den did well to smother the bass of the music, so he was able to keep a smart distance. "Going to let the guests get started first." He continued.

Julianna replied, "What a gracious host you are."

"Stop staring at her like a perv," Kevin thought while he chewed the side of his lip and buried his free hand in his pocket.

"I'm actually surprised you showed up," he said to her. "Thought you were always in the books. I was pretty sure you would flake on me."

"Flake?" she giggled. "How old are you?"

The heat returned to Kevin's cheeks, but Julianna did well to let it go.

"No, not tonight," Julianna continued. "I mean, my dad is a foreman so," then she nodded over her shoulder at the Mega league clock on the wall.

Kevin followed her eyes to the ornament then pointed. "Oh, so you mean your dad got the contract to work on that new stadium?"

Julianna nodded. "Yup."

"Wow, given the size of that thing, it must be a massive contract," Kevin replied.

"Sure is," she agreed. He could see the joy and pride in her eyes swell from her father's accomplishment. "He said it was a Godsend. We weren't doing too well before then, since he refused to work for the Savoy's, and wouldn't build their tower. But he says he can retire based off this contract alone." Her smile widened. "So, once I heard about you celebrating New Haven getting the Mega league team, well, I felt it was a good time to put down the books and relax for once."

Kevin smiled inwardly because he knew what she admitted was only partially true. It never crossed his mind at the time to ask her to come to his hovel, but he noticed that she lingered near Jenni's desk, picking at the dust on the ancient monitors, after he told her about the gathering. Getting a nod from Warren, he could hardly get the invitation out of his mouth before Julianna blurted out an emphatic yes. Given her reaction, it made sense why she came to the party with Warren, since logic dictated that it had to be his handsome best friend that made her so excited to attend.

"Well, that's awesome about your dad. Hey, congratulations." Kevin said and lifted his cup. "Here's to Mr. Jove, then." Julianna hailed from Catalonian lineage, and it took him several corrections to pronounce her last name properly with 'jova' instead of 'jove'.

A thin grin spread across Julianna's face as she wiggled the fingers on her empty hands. It took Kevin a moment to realize what she was trying to impart.

"Oh, that's right! You need a drink." Kevin exclaimed. He peered inside his cup, but the saccharine stench wafting from inside made his stomach jump. Looking back at the kitchen, he was about to get Julianna a drink of her own until Warren walked up, handing her a cup that smelled like mint as it passed.

Warren's nose wrinkled up when he noticed Kevin taking a sip of the sunrise.

"You're drinking that piss?" he asked.

Kevin glanced over his cup from Warren to Julianna and swallowed a mouthful of the syrupy content.

"Well, yeah. Not going to waste the liquor," he replied with a smack of his lips. "We're not all rich like you, Ren." Kevin tapped his pockets with his free hand, then snapped. "Oh yeah, that's right."

Julianna giggled with a back hand to her lips. Warren's eyebrows bounced up from the slight, and he tapped Kevin lightly on the chest with the bottom of his fist.

"We have more liquor, dude." Then, he clapped his hands loud enough to make Julianna flinch and nearly spill the contents of her cup. She giggled into her hand again when she saw that Kevin had noticed. "On that note, are you two ready to play? I left spots at the table open for both of you."

Julianna's eyes flicked over at Kevin before she replied, "Uhm. I think I'm going to pass this round."

Warren mouthed the word *what* to her, eyes pleading, and Kevin stifled a laugh. From the expression on his friend's face, it was as if Julianna had spoken in some foreign language that he could not quite comprehend, and it was obvious that he was not used to being told no.

"Come on," Warren exhaled. He held Julianna's hand in his and bent his knees to look her in the eyes, licking his shapely lips. "Just one round to get your feet wet. We have to catch up to these people anyway. It's not every day you get to celebrate hitting a lick."

Julianna's head went back as she laughed. Jenni came from the balcony almost hopping up to Julianna, her natural red hair rebounding against her black shirt. With the high heels, Julianna was taller, so Jenni smiled up at her friend and tugged on her elbow. Her fair cheeks were already flushed from drinks, yet her skin still held a pale glow.

"Come on, Juli. Don't make me play this game by myself," Jenni said, pouting with her eyes. Julianna was being double-teamed and Kevin could already see her spirit to not play dissolving.

"Go ahead," Kevin encouraged her. She had taken enough pity on him by coming to the party and even checking up on him, so it was time for her to have the fun she was searching for. He was comfortable enough alone.

"You sure?" Julianna asked, as if her participation was up for debate. He appreciated the gesture of having a say, even if it was just that.

"Yeah, yeah. Go. I'll probably join you later," he replied with a wave of his hand.

Julianna's body relaxed. Warren winked in his direction and Kevin squinted in return. Julianna never looked back at him before she took her spot at the table next to Warren, who smiled triumphantly.

Losers always defer to their betters.

He forced down the last of the sunrise, which was more tequila than any other mix at the bottom, but its fire was quenched by the power that held steady inside. One reason Kevin declined to play Waterfall was the fact that it took an exorbitant amount of binge drinking to overpower the energy within. Drunkenness could be achieved, but only with great effort and expenditure of capital.

The power treated the alcohol like an attack to his system, a wound that needed to be burned away and then healed like the cut in his cheek. If he stood out at all instead of being easily ignored when he went out for the occasional drink, someone would notice him nursing one drink all night, or drinking so much that he was still impossibly sober.

Through a pair of shoulders, he could see Julianna straight ahead. She was to the left of Warren, and her face shined beneath the light from the wobbly ceiling fan. Warren leaned close into her ear, probably explaining the rules of each card that he had already told the others. Kevin waited to see her make a face, but Julianna only smiled, seemingly comfortable with his proximity to her neck.

Reaching down, he pulled two bottles of beer from a chest just inside the dining room that he stuffed into his pockets. The cool felt good against his legs as he kneaded his way through a mass of people standing in front of the balcony door.

"Excuse me," Kevin said, and elbowed his way through the musty people.

As he walked through the open balcony door, a whoop rang out from the dining room as the game had begun in earnest. Smoke hung outside as he passed a group of men and women smoking cigarettes, huddled together in the left corner. He found an empty spot on the opposite side of the balcony, away from the stench. Another whoop, and he could hear Warren's voice barking his rules to shape the experience.

Fetching a beer from his pocket, Kevin twisted the top and took a short pull. The cold of the iron railing was a relief to his still sore back as he propped his elbows up and watched his guests get on without him. The clamor indoors grew louder as booze-infused voices talked over one another. The music had been turned up several notches in response. Dancing had begun in the den, spreading quickly to the living room as others took up the beat, the floor creaking from the writhing bodies.

"Here's to you and Warren's party Kevin," he said as he raised his beer and drank again, swallowing several times to force down the cool liquid.

A soft breeze swept across Kevin's neck as he picked at the label on the bottle etching his Fiasco symbol in with his thumbnail, thinking over the Chevelle chase, and what he could have done differently had he thought ahead. Time passed as he went over various scenarios when a muted cheer reverberated through the dancing crowd coming from the dining room. Shadows of two raised arms bopped on the walls. The game must have ended with someone crowned the winner. Warren liked to play the first round with a shortened deck just to get everyone used to the rules but, lost in thought, he hadn't realized so much time had passed. Kevin took another swig of beer when Julianna poked her head through the balcony door.

"There you are!" she said. Her face was tinted red, and her neck glistened with perspiration. A vexing lock of hair fell over her eye as she walked towards him on slightly unsteady legs, then leaned her forearms on the balcony beside him. Quickly, he pulped the label with a swipe of his thumb.

A pine-scented breeze swirled on the balcony from the nearby trees.

"Oh my God, it feels so good out here," she said, waving her hand over her neck and face to aid the gentle wind. "That was intense."

Kevin turned around and leaned over on his forearms, as well.

"I tried to warn you," he teased.

"No, you didn't!" she exclaimed and pushed his arm. "He plays that game every time?"

"Every time." Kevin nodded his head, and with a mischievous grin, waved the spare bottle of beer he fished out of his pocket in front of her face.

"Oh God no," Julianna covered her mouth and laughed. "I'm probably going to throw up already. I might have had a bit too much since I was the last in the waterfall."

Kevin let out a sympathetic laugh. "Warren's plan working to perfection," he thought. "The last one always has to drink the most."

"Here, hold this one," he said as he gave his open bottle to Julianna. "Don't drink it though. I'm going to get you some water."

"Thanks," she replied with an eye-catching grin Kevin was sure only Warren had witnessed before. It was almost enough to make him not want to leave. But she needed the comfort of water more than he needed to pretend her smile meant anything more than just a smile.

Music pounded his ear drums and the bass thumped against his skin as Kevin made his way back to the kitchen, this time forcing his way through the crowd with his arms. Part of him wanted to call on the power to bulldoze them all away with his blue light. There was a rush to get to the cooler where he had seen bottles of water and make his way back to the balcony. An internal clock ticked away as he ran into Warren just inside the dining room, going in the opposite direction.

"Hey!" Warren said with excitement. The music made it hard to hear him.

"Hey," Kevin sighed back. His friend's eyes were wide with a hint of pink, and he could tell he had reached the early stage of drunkenness.

"Man, you missed a good game!" Warren said. "People about to get jacked up in here. Hope you found a way to lock that bedroom door, if you know what I mean," Warren leaned in and tapped him with his elbow, still with that leering grin. Kevin noticed that he held a cup of pungent liquor in one hand, and a bottle of water in the other.

"So, have you seen Julianna? She didn't look too good after

the game. I thought I would bring her some water," Warren half shouted, turning his head to look around.

Even though Warren was several inches taller, Kevin moved in front of him to add the top of his head into his field of vision. Looking around as well, he saw in the distance that his den was fairly packed with people. With the dim light and bobbing heads dancing in the shadows, it was hard to make out the various faces in the small alcove.

"I think I saw her over there," Kevin said, leaning in to be heard, and pointed in the direction of the den.

"Cool." Warren's head kicked up in a nod, flashed him a grin, and threw up the peace sign with two of the fingers that held his drink.

"I'll take that, though," Kevin said and snatched the water bottle from Warren's hand, walking away before he could protest.

On his way back towards the balcony, he wondered why he was even trying to match Warren's competitiveness. He knew, once Julianna and Warren started dating, the affiliation between them would be altered forever. He had seen it before with other women who had dated Warren. Most had only pretended to associate with him just as a bridge to get to Warren. He would no longer be Julianna's friend; he would slowly morph into being her boyfriend's friend. Being one step removed would dilute whatever relationship he and Julianna had cultivated and something inside him wanted her to be his friend alone for a few more hours.

You were born to lose, the voice recalled.

A chill had kicked up on the balcony, signaling the end of summer. The skin on Kevin's hands and cheeks felt damp as he moved to the corner where he left Julianna, and the air smelled pregnant with rain.

"Hey! I thought you weren't going to drink that?" Kevin said.

In the corner of the balcony, Julianna was hunched over. Her long, dark hair covered her face and hands as she stealthily took a drink from the beer he had left in her possession. Hearing Kevin's voice, her head turned and looked at him like a puppy caught stealing food in the kitchen. Then, she burst out laughing, wiping spilled beer from her mouth with the back of her hand. Shaking his head, Kevin twisted the water bottle open and took his beer back in an exchange of drinks.

"Here, lightweight. You're going to be passed out by midnight at this pace," he said, but part of him was impressed. School was almost all Julianna ever talked about, and it seemed to consume all her time, so it was good to see her having fun. A mission had presented itself, and he knew he had to ensure she could enjoy the time off for as long as possible. It would be his last act and gift to her while they were still truly friends.

"You're a lifesaver," she replied.

The dew from the bottle smeared against her skin as she rubbed it over her forehead, then swallowed a quarter of the contents. She turned to look out into his parking lot. It was a Friday, so most of the cars were gone from the spaces. Mist played in the streetlights. In the distance, past the opposite row of apartments, moonlight hung over the trees and gave them a pale, hazy blue glow. Kevin joined her looking at the scene, their elbows nearly touching on the rail.

"It's actually pretty nice out here," she said.

"Well, it's dark. You can't see the needles and trash right now."

"It's not that bad," Julianna giggled and bumped him with her shoulder. "But you're doing good out here, Kevin. You have your own place, while I still live with my parents."

"Yeah, well, you're still in school, so it makes sense. My dad said it was either school or leave," Kevin replied. "So, I left."

"Well, you should be proud. Not a lot of people our age could cover a place without having any roommates."

"This place is a shithole in the ass crack part of town, built by obvious drunks, so it's affordable," Kevin snickered. "Plus, I need my privacy."

He almost wanted to her tell her why he was living among people who looked the other direction. But the voice sneered, *Fiasco is a joke. You better not dare.*

"Quit talking like that. I like it out here. It feels peaceful," Julianna declared.

Julianna was right in the fact that his neighborhood was indeed somewhat well-maintained given its more insidious nature. As New Haven's prosperity grew, Longreach had been renovated to include cheap, affordable housing, but the city was foolish enough to let poor people like himself move in. Now Longreach was like a beauty queen infected with cancer on the inside. Crime had become so prevalent, that most of his Fiasco business came from patrolling just a few square miles away. But at least the scenery was pleasant when you were being mugged.

Standing upright, Kevin gave her back the beer she had stolen a drink from earlier, while he took the spare. "To your dad's contract." The two finally toasted with a clink of their bottles.

A breeze swirled the mist in the streetlights and floated the flowery scent of Julianna's hair. They stood in silence, and some-how, he wasn't uncomfortable like he normally would be. The gentle wind kicked up again, ruffling the bottom of her sun dress, forcing out a shiver. Crossing her arms over her chest to rub bare shoulders, Julianna moved closer until their shoulders touched. Noticing the warmth against his arm, Kevin looked over at her bright, brown eyes. The lock of hair that had been bugging her all night had fallen out of place again, fluttering in the breeze, and slowly his hand went to fix it.

Do not dare touch her, the voice chastised.

Kevin paused, feeling as if he had been yelled at by his father.

The tan light shined in Julianna's eyes that never wavered, as if waiting for him to make that move before she saw that he wasn't and tucked the errant hair back over her ear. Her pink lips puckered into a smirk before she turned and looked back at the forest.

"Why are you so warm?" she asked.

"I don't know. Must be the beer?" Kevin replied.

"A few beers make you that warm?' she replied with a chuckle, grinding her arm into his. "And you call me the lightweight."

Ensuring Julianna wasn't looking as she kept her eyes forward, Kevin closed his eyes and concentrated on the warmth of her skin touching his. The comfort of her touch sent a chill of happiness down his spine, enough to quell the well of power he kept inside, lowering his body temperature. Just in case it returned against his will, he leaned away from Julianna, breaking contact to ensure that there was space between them again.

You cannot drown me, the voice said in a low growl. *You are just another loser without me.*

"You're such an asshole," Kevin muttered.

"Who is?" Julianna asked.

Before he could answer, a pair of elbows pushed them further apart. "Hey, guys," Warren beamed. "It took me a minute to find you." It was his turn to squint at Kevin for the wild goose chase. Then he turned to Julianna, who had parted to let him in, and flashed that winning smile. "We're getting another round of Waterfall going. You ready to play?"

"Not me," she said, putting her hand up with a grin. "I think I need to coast from here on out."

"I'll play," Kevin said to Warren's back.

Julianna leaned her head out over the balcony to see him, jaw slacken. Warren turned around with nearly the same expression. His eyes narrowed as he studied Kevin's face, trying to ascertain why he suddenly was game to play. Then, he nodded slowly.

"Okay," Warren said, rubbing his hands and licking his lips with anticipation. "Okay, game on. Let's go."

Julianna walked in first, and Warren followed, head tilted down and hot on her heels. As he passed, a woman in the smoking group shared her cigarette when he leaned his head over. She held it out in a flirty manner between two fingers, and Warren took several pulls to get enough nicotine in his system before he followed Julianna inside. White odorous smelling smoke curled and trailed behind him. As Kevin followed, he noticed that the woman who had shared her cigarette had her eyes fixated on Warren, as if waiting for a thank you that would not come. The disappointment he saw within her pained expression fueled his own emotions and power, which made it easier to carry out what he had planned.

The game table seemed to be the only thing still somewhat clean in the apartment. Waterfall was already laid out, with the card deck separated into piles and arranged strategically in a circle around the food. The shot cups had been replaced while Warren was gone, and spare red and green plastic cups full of beer were placed where there was room, in case more beer was needed by some sudden rule change.

Warren leaned in and looked at the participants around the table who were only men at the time.

"The game moves counter clock-wise, and remember that wooden leg boys," he said as he chose the first card and held it to his chest. "Ladies, make your choice."

The women wooed as they filed in between the men. Kevin took Julianna's previous spot next to Warren, forcing him one spot down. He made sure not to stand anywhere near Jenni West. The first advice Warren ever told him about the game was to never stand next to a true red head in a drinking game. To his left, Arial, a pint-sized, chubby brunette with pouty lips and dark-rimmed glasses, squeezed in-between them quiet as a mouse. Jenni was on Warren's left again, her face gleaming as she brought four bottles of beer trapped between her fingers. Warren laughed when he leaned over, and she whispered something into his ear while pushing the bottles onto the table. Julianna stood behind Arial, still able to watch the game over her head.

Warren raised a hand, and the drone in the dining room died down until only the thump of music was heard as they waited for the reveal of his card. He flipped his wrist. Random voices in the room murmured, "Seven of diamonds." It was almost phrased as a question, as the alcohol had clouded the rules in their minds. It wasn't until Kevin raised both arms to the sky that a wave of realization spread around the table, and hands shot up with shouts and giggles. There was one, however, who raised his hand last.

"Got 'em! Drink, Marcus!" Kevin yelled, pointing to the man at the opposite end of the table.

"You're an asshole, Kevin!" Marcus said. With a resigned grin, he pulled his thick dreads behind his back, and took a long pull from his beer bottle, then slammed it down on the table to cheers.

Arial chose next and pulled a five of spades that she showed to the rest of the players.

"Never have I ever," she said, needing no reminder about the rules. She glanced over her shoulder at Julianna and pushed her glasses up her nose. "Kissed a girl."

Julianna brought her beer bottle before her as if it would ward off the flirtatious minx. Her eyes were wide, and she looked over at Kevin, who gave her a shrug, his mouth tight, and eyes red as he stifled a laugh.

The game went silent for what felt like minutes, until Jenni raised her glass and said, "Well, shit. Here's to ya boys!" then took a long drink of her beer.

The participants in the game glanced at each other.

"Hell yeah!" a male voice in the crowd rang out. The men in

the room let out a cheer in response, as if their soon-to-be Mega team had scored a touchdown. They too had to drink since the rule stipulated that anyone who did the opposite of the declaration had to drink, which made the fact that the pretty girl with the fiery red hair was drinking along with them more enticing.

"Holy shit," Warren mouthed to Kevin, then took a long, hard pull, smiling down at Jenni from his beer.

The laughter increased when others noticed that poor, red-faced Ethan did not take a drink. Marcus reached over the table, nearly spilling a basket of pretzels and mussed his brown hair.

"Awe, poor baby," purred Yuna. She was a thin, cute Asian with short black hair who worked in some department Kevin had trouble remembering. She moved around the table. The noise in the dining room swelled when she grabbed Ethan's shirt into her tiny fist and pulled him down. Being short, Yuna still had to stand on her toes to reach his head, giving him a full kiss on the lips. Kevin could see the whites of Ethan's eyes, but he did not pull away. Instead, he used his long arms to lift Yuna up into him by the small of her back.

"There we go!" Warren said, jabbing his finger at his protégé. The game had escalated just as he designed, and it was only the first round.

After several seconds, Ethan let Yuna down and the two parted with a rousing clamor. Yuna wiped his bottom lip with her thumb and smiled before walking back to her spot at the table. His face apple red, the mentee reveled in his first female kiss, bathing in praise from the men and women alike. They pushed and pulled him back and forth, mussing his hair and further wrinkling his clothes. Now Ethan could take his drink.

Taking advantage of the sudden distraction, Kevin stretched out his index and middle fingers on the edge of the table. Thin, blue tendrils moved out from his fingertips, nearly invisible against the dark tablecloth. Before anyone could notice, he let the lines of energy lift the edge of the cards in the pile closest to him ever so slightly, one by one, until he found the card that he wanted. The tendril pulled out the edge of the card from the pile, just enough for him to reach over the table and appear to pull it from the top of the pile.

Kevin held the card to his chest.

"I got my card," he said, loud enough so that the noise of Ethan's celebration died down. He lifted the card to show the others.

"Eight picks mate! Eight picks mate!" Jenni said, bouncing and clutching the cloth of Warren's sports coat, almost singing the words.

"For my mate, I choose," Kevin looked over and watched Warren's face wane. "Warren."

Choosing a mate meant that whenever Kevin had to drink, so did Warren. Not only did he have to drink along, but he would be forced to continue drinking during that round until Kevin was done. This was his plan when he decided to join the game that round. Whenever it was his turn to drink, his power would burn the alcohol down, and when it was time for Waterfall, he would take full advantage of the spare beer bottles around him.

It made sense to play the game that way to get Warren drunk and out of his way. He was not ready to concede his time with Julianna. At least for that night. He was not ready to lose her when she and Warren would become a couple and planned to use his power to keep that round going long enough to leave Warren flat on his face.

Kevin cocked his head towards his one true friend, raised his bottle, and then the two shared a drink. The clatter of the guests rose like a crescendo as he took long, deep swallows. Beer dribbled from Warren's chin onto his crisp, white button-up shirt, his pink eyes watering as he tried to keep pace and save face. With his head dipped backward, Kevin tongued out the last drop of beer, admired the empty bottle, then sat it down gently on the table. Leaning in on both hands, his eyes bore through Warren, who breathed deeply and wiped the dribble from his mouth before putting down his own bottle.

"Okay, then," Kevin coolly said, "Let's continue the game."

*****

Friday night slipped into Saturday morning. It was just Kevin, Julianna, Jenni, and Warren, teetering on wobbling legs, forbidding the night to end. Ethan, the ever-present dutiful ward, attempted to stay, but awkwardly noticed that he was the fifth wheel, and was the last to leave.

Walking from the kitchen back to the living room where the rest were, Kevin said, "Let's watch a movie," holding a cardboard box while chewing on a mouthful of cold pizza that tasted like heaven. His words slurred more than he expected, even with the power, prompting another bite.

"Yeah! Good idea!" Warren said loudly from the booze, his face brightening as an idea seeped into his drunken head. "Let's show them that one," he stammered.

Pointing a sagging slice his way, Kevin swallowed hard and said, "We're not watching *Hallrats* again, dude. If they never saw Cashiers, it wouldn't be as funny."

A lazy smile spread across Warren's lips. "No, man. Not the Skewverse. That one with the guy and the exploding head."

Julianna's nose wrinkled below the brow. "Exploding head? Is it gross?" She was standing near the couch holding a bottle missing half its content, taking small sips to nurse her intoxication.

"Who cares, let's watch!" Jenni said. It was unsurprising that she agreed with him; she and Warren had become simpatico during the night, each appreciating the other's ability to match their drinking prowess.

Kevin raised his pizza over his head in agreement even when a piece of sausage broke loose and rolled beneath his coffee table. "Sure, put it on," he said and flopped on the couch, setting the pizza box atop his lap. Warm air seeped from the worn cushion as it accommodated his weight.

"Found it!" Warren exclaimed, holding up the DVD box for all to see.

"Hey," Julianna said with a slap on Kevin's knee. "You didn't answer me." Her eyes were sincere when she leaned down and whispered, "Is this going to be gross?"

The shrug and smile Kevin replied with seemed to do little to calm her fears.

"What the hell," Warren said, "What kind of movie player is this? This disk won't even fit!" He was kneeling in front of the television, fumbling.

"Oh, for Christ sakes," Jenni sighed. "You're a hot, drunken mess. Here, let me do it." She snatched the disk and slid it onto the waiting tray, pushing it closed.

"Thanks," Warren slurred, breathing through his mouth as Jenni picked him up by the hand and led him around the coffee table.

Julianna took the cushion next to Kevin, laid her purse on the ground, and taking her shoes off to curl her legs beneath her dress, smoothing it down with her hand.

"Is this okay?" she asked, pointing to her legs.

Kevin chewed the garlic buttered crust and swallowed as much as he could. "Have you seen this couch?" he replied through a mouth half full.

She leaned in close enough for him to catch her scent and whispered, "What movie is this again? For real, is it nasty?"

Kevin reached over and grabbed the remote from the coffee table and sat it on top of the pizza box. "It's just the best drunk movie of all time. Riki-Oh. And no, it's not gross. Not really. Cheesier more than anything, but wait," he looked over at her. "You're not squeamish, are you?"

Julianna put her elbow on the back cushion, resting her head on her palm. She peered down at the beer bottle and swished around the meager remnants inside.

"Well, not right now." Her breath smelled like amber when she let out a small hiccup.

"There you go," Kevin said and toasted her bottle with what remained of his pizza slice.

Jenni curled up in the beige recliner on the other side of the couch that croaked as it slowly rocked. Warren sighed as he slid onto the cushion next to Julianna. Kevin offered him the pizza box, but he declined with a hand wave, then he sat it down on the edge of the coffee table. Looking down, he noticed that Warren had sat awkwardly with one leg beneath him so his other knee could touch Julianna's foot.

Kevin chuckled internally because he knew persistent touch was Warren's final stage when making a move. Hand on the back; shoulders touching while leaning on the bar; even a hand on a knee if things were going well—anything that allowed him and his catch to interact. By the end of the movie, he expected that Julianna would probably be asleep in his arms. It was human nature to want to be held and comforted, something that he could hardly empathize with at all. His preference was to not be touched if he could avoid it.

All four were enticed as the movie played, laughing at the silly but graphic practical effects of the kung-fu movie set in a dystopian, vicious prison. Watching the movie together for what felt like the hundredth time, Kevin and Warren played off each other, cracking vulgar jokes back and forth that made the two women laugh even more. The frivolity only lasted an hour before fatigue took hold.

Warren was the first to fall. His head tilted awkwardly to the right while his legs splayed out wide in front of him. To his left, Jenni was curled in a fetal position on the recliner, her head resting on the armchair, and Warren's sports coat pulled over her shoulders for warmth.

Even given her rookie party status, Julianna had outlasted them both. Kevin watched her face contort when she held back several yawns, but by sheer force of will, she seemed to be forcing herself to stay awake. Then came the scene that had driven her ambition. Nails dipped hard into his shoulder, and beer nearly spilled out of her nose when the random extra in the movie had his head crushed by one of the antagonist's massive hands in a vicious spray of fake blood and gore.

"Oh my God, that did not just happen!" she laughed. The beer in her bloodstream made the scene funnier and her eyes watered as she shook Kevin by the scruff of his shirt. "Rewind it back! I need to see that again!"

"Yeah, play that shit again," Warren murmured, giving the equivalent of a death rattle before he sank further into the couch.

"I told you," Kevin laughed and let her hands guide his shoulder as he reached for the remote. "Watch; it only gets better the second time."

He could feel the warmth of the grin on Julianna's face as the two watched the movie together. The alcohol and sweat did little to dampen her beauty, and instead gave her skin a healthy glow. Every time she spoke or laughed, she fumbled with the piece of hair that kept tickling her eye. Frustrated with her constant head flipping, Kevin swept the lock from her face and wrapped it around her ear. Julianna stood still, looking at him with a knavish grin as he pulled a few strands of hair over it and tucked it under a tuft to hopefully keep it from falling out again.

When he was done, Julianna patted that side of her head. "Well, you're good at that," she said, her eyes twinkling from the television light. "Thanks."

"I have a sister," Kevin said, forcing himself to look away from those soft brown eyes. "But my pleasure."

Julianna stifled another yawn. It was clear that the long, strenuous night had taken a toll, but she at least had her fun. When Warren and Julianna finally got together, Kevin wondered if perhaps he had earned her friendship as a separate entity.

"One can hope, right?" Kevin thought, but the voice was quick to give its opinion.

You will lose her eventually, the voice said. Kevin began to nod when a floral scent wafted to his nose.

No longer able to hold back the exhaustion, Julianna yawned as she flattened herself a bit on the couch and put her head on his shoulder. A cold sweat chilled Kevin's brow and he could see the tip of her nose looking down. An anxious swig of his beer cooled his throat, as he slowly lifted his arm over the back of the couch.

Careful, the voice warned. *She is going to be angry with you when she awakens.*

"Quiet," Kevin said while holding his breath.

Julianna fell into the nook of his arm with a low moan and settled on his chest. Nervously, he let his arm fall over the goosebumps on her bare arm.

"Holy hell," Kevin thought.

Her soft, rhythmic breathing lifted his arm with every breath. He breathed in the aroma from her hair that was just below his chin and enjoyed her body warming against his. It felt surreal having the stunning woman in his arm, as if he were dreaming, but he knew he didn't drink that much.

With the click of a button, he switched to regular TV, frantically turned down the volume so the sudden noise wouldn't startle Julianna awake. Looking down, she was still asleep. Watching a rerun, Kevin sat there on the couch, the last one standing, his left side stiff as a statue. Although he tried to concentrate on the screen, he couldn't help but sneak glances at Julianna's face, the perfect eyebrows, cute tiny nose, and succulent lips. Eyes closed, lost in a dream.

"What the hell am I doing?" he thought.

She will not want your arm there when she wakes up.

"Should I take it away?" he wondered.

Yes.

"But it's not like I made her lay on me."

You were never very smart.

"This can only end bad, right?"

Agreed. The voice said, but, looking down at her peaceful face, try as he might, Kevin could not bring himself to take his arm away.

The power inside trickled through his skin and down to his arm. It heated the skin that touched hers to keep Julianna warm. She groaned again, sliding her legs in closer, and he kept his arm around her for the rest of the morning.

Hours later, the sun rose over the mountains. Its rays streamed through the vinyl blinds like shiny gold fingers that landed on Julianna's face. The light worked like an alarm clock, and she began to stir on Kevin's chest. Eyes dried and strained, Kevin had not slept a minute, and quickly his arm went back to the top of the couch. He held his breath as she lifted herself up. Julianna looked around the room, gathering her bearings, then looked at him with pink eyes.

She covered her mouth with the back of her hand when she said, "What time is it?" Her voice was dry as a desert.

Kevin studied her face, waiting to get yelled at for crossing the line, then looked up at the clock above them. "About six thirty," he replied.

"Shoot!" Julianna scrambled off the couch. Her feet unfurled beneath her dress and hit the floor. Quickly, she sat up and gathered her purse and shoes. "Shoot! Shoot! Shoot!" She was pulling up the straps of her heels. "I have a paper I was going to edit and submit, and then be at work at nine." She looked up at him. Her hair had fallen over her eyes as she leaned down. "I need to get going. Sorry. I wanted to help you clean up."

"They really did wreck the gaff, as Jenni would say," Kevin looked around at the mess his guests had left that was more apparent in the sunlight. "Uhm, it's okay. This is going to take hours. Besides, it's time Warren earned his keep for this place since he's here all the time." He looked back at her. "Will you let me walk you out?"

She smiled through her loose, dark strands, her lips still with a polish of gloss. "Yeah, I don't mind."

The two tip-toed over Warren's outstretched legs. A thin line of drool spilled from the corner of his partly opened mouth, and his fingers were intertwined with Jenni's outstretched hand.

"Typical Ren." Kevin thought with a snicker.

Julianna retrieved her coat from the closet, Kevin his shoes, and he slowly opened the apartment door so not to wake his slumbering guests. A chilly morning air touched their faces. It had rained overnight, which lowered the temperature several degrees. A morning mist hovered over the grass as the sun warmed the water into glistening dew.

"Okay, that woke me up," Julianna said with a throat clear. Shivering, she put the thin jean coat on, but still hugged and rubbed her shoulders. "You're not cold in just that t-shirt?"

Kevin looked down and examined himself. "I don't know. I run hot, remember?"

"That's right," she replied and moved in closer to take advantage of his warmth. Sweaty hands rubbed his legs inside his pants pockets. Somehow Julianna had forgiven his earlier folly of holding her throughout the night, or at least had the decency of not bringing it up. Moving a suitable distance away, he did not want to push his luck further.

Side by side, they slowly descended the staircases that led to the first floor, then walked towards Julianna's car.

"It was fun tonight," he said to break the silence.

"Yeah, I had a good time." She continued her self-hug with one arm, but still held the back of her hand to her mouth as she spoke. "Again, thanks for inviting me. I know I keep saying that, but I honestly don't get invited to things often."

"You?" Kevin replied. "That's surprising. Seems like everyone knows you at work. It takes you an hour just to walk through my floor."

She laughed. "Yeah, but that doesn't mean people want to hang out often. Besides, I have so many responsibilities outside of work. So, I think that's a turn off."

"Well again, glad you could make it." He replied. "You messed up, though, by telling me you like it out here, because now I'm going to be inviting you over more often."

Julianna put her head back and laughed again. "Don't worry, I'm down. I need to finish that movie, anyway." She looked at him with those eyes that had begun to clear. "Just no more Waterfall."

The corner of Kevin's mouth turned up and he replied, "Deal."

They reached a beige Toyota Corolla. Stopping behind the trunk, Kevin wondered if she could see his heart beating through his shirt. Was a hug appropriate, seeing as they were now true friends, or was that too much since Warren claimed first dibs? Would not doing anything at all be an affront to her that would end their friendship? And how hard could those thin arms slap his face if he were to try something else entirely? Julianna shivered in her coat and dress, twisting her foot in the ground, and glancing about as he stood like a doofus, contemplating his options.

Do not even entertain the idea.

"Well, bye," Kevin croaked. He took his hands out of his pockets to give her a hug that was quick as a Mega Speedstra running down the block and back.

"Bye," Julianna replied softly. Her full lips parted, and her hand slid down to his forearm as they moved apart.

You have never had a great idea, the voice said, almost beseeching him. *Fiasco is not just your name; it is your life.* It continued, unrelenting. *This is the reality. You are the Fiasco. Do not add making a fool of yourself to the list.* Kevin nodded.

For a moment, they did not move until Julianna's hand let go of his arm, and she turned to get into her car. Kevin turned away, chewing his lip as he put his hands back into his pockets and started back to his apartment. He thought about how the voice was never wrong, fed him power and kept him out of any trouble that he couldn't handle. When it first manifested with his powers, he fought against it, disagreeing. As a typical teen, he believed he knew best. Each time had turned into a disaster, where his power would pitch and start when he needed it most from the conflicting emotions his defiance wrought. His failures as Fiasco began with that denial, and so obedience has been the clear way to go ever since. He found that it was best to nod and agree and drink from its miserable wisdom.

"Ah, to hell with this," Kevin said.

He turned on his heel and marched to Julianna. Shiny black hair fell down her back, as she rummaged through her purse for her keys. Kevin gently grabbed her by the elbow. Julianna turned with a surprised whoop as he pulled her in close and leaned in to kiss her. Julianna tried to say something just before their lips met, but quickly gave up and responded in kind, moaning as she wrapped her arms around his neck, cradling the back of his head.

With his eyes closed, Kevin's emotions cascaded inside with a tidal wave. She was not the first girl he had ever kissed, but that moment felt vastly divergent from the others. His finger tightened, pulling her in until her breast spread against his chest. The circulation of the morning air cooled his skin, but the softness of her body against his sent warmth from his navel to sternum. Her curved hips filled his hands, covering every inch with bone and flesh until he moved them to the small of her back, fingers interlocked at the nape, just below the cuff of her jacket. She moaned again, holding him tighter. Even the voice was silent, Julianna's passion quenching its misery, and the world seemed to fade, while the two melted into one another.

Before risking losing himself forever, the warmth subsided, and Kevin pulled away. Julianna leaned back in his arms, head down but still smiling. She licked her bottom lip, putting a hand on his chest where his crooked F symbol would have been.

"I'm sorry," Kevin huffed, heat from embarrassment flushing his cheeks. "Were you going to say something?

"Just," she started. Red spread against her cheeks as well, and she rolled her eyes away, smiling. "I was going to say something about my breath."

"Your breath?" Kevin said, surprised. "Well, that's better than what I thought you were going to say."

"And that was?"

Kevin's eyebrow kicked up when he said, "I thought you were going to tell me you weren't drunk anymore!"

The two laughed together.

"Wow," she said, and rubbed a warm palm on his cheek. "I've been waiting for you to do that all night. For weeks now, even. I was beginning to think you didn't like me."

"You've got to be kidding me," Kevin replied.

She looked away. "You'd be surprised," she said.

Her face softened as some memory came to the forefront. His hands pulled her in closer, hoping his warmth would burn the hurt away.

"Well, it seems impossible to me that someone wouldn't like you," he said. She breathed out as he placed a soft peck on her forehead. "You're wonderful, and I'm just an idiot. I guess I just needed the right motivation."

Her right eyebrow raised, and her beautiful smile returned. "So, what was your motivation?"

Kevin thought about the question. It could have been Warren's relentless competitiveness that ignited his testosterone. Or the voice's demeaning negativity. Or, it may just have been Julianna's stunning beauty, and how well they got along all night. Perhaps it was her persistence to break down his walls. It could have been all those reasons, or none at all.

Kevin grinned at her. "It doesn't matter now," he said softly, then kissed her again.

He had no idea how much time had elapsed, but Julianna groaned and reluctantly pulled away, "I really have to get to work." She softly tapped her hand on his chest.

"I know," Kevin said and put his forehead on hers. "Guess I'm going to have to call you now, huh?"

Julianna shut her eyes and giggled. "You better."

They pecked once, twice, then a third time before she forced herself to separate.

"Okay, okay. I really need to go before I do something bad," she laughed, then looked at him with an affection he could feel.

"Bye," she said.

"Bye." He held Julianna's hand until she got into her car. She waved him back with a laugh as he blocked her from closing the door. Once he finally moved to the curb, looking back, Julianna shook her head then kissed her palm, blowing him a kiss.

"So, this is how Peter Parker must have felt meeting MJ," Kevin thought, and waved as he watched her pull away.

He thought his power had flared inside, twitching like a fish gasping for air from the sudden rush of happiness, but it was only the sun peeking through the clouds that warmed his body. Kevin touched his chest and concentrated; he could hardly feel the power there at all. Just a small drip of energy shuttering like a pilot light waiting to be ignited. He thought about Warren up in his apartment, and grinned. He had to tell him that he kissed Julianna. *The* Julianna.

"I'll make him call me Tiger," he said with a smirk. But he knew that, even reluctantly, his friend would be happy for him, and it would not be an act. To Warren, and his adherence to the survival of the fittest code, Kevin had followed the rules of the game. The best man won. For a moment, Kevin expected a rebuke for even thinking that he was the best man, but the voice was unusually silent, most likely, stunned by the sudden turn of events.

"Nothing to say, prick?" Kevin thought as he made his way to his apartment. There was no response.

He hurried up the steps, pumping his knees, as he finally began to feel the cold.

"No snarky comment? No put down to fuel yourself? After all this time, you're quiet?" He stopped in front of his door. "I'm almost disappointed." He waited.

"Maybe this is a new chapter," he looked around, speaking to the voice as if it were all around him. "Maybe I don't need you anymore."

His fingers touched his chest, but the tips remained cold. An ear-to-ear smile spread on his face as he opened the door and began to walk past the threshold. Then, his body froze. A coldness swept from his heart down to his legs, sapping his arrogant smile.

Please.

It sounded like a dying voice carried on the wind. Kevin's mouth tasted dry as cotton. Shivering, the air around him stiffened as a sudden rush of sadness fell upon his shoulders like a snow mound. His knees felt like water and buckled so much that he had to hold himself up by clinging to the edge of the door with both hands.

He did not know the voice even knew that word.

Please, the voice whispered again, *do not screw this up,* then it added, *Tiger.*

The Introduction

New Haven, Fall

"Come on! Open up!" Kevin shouted with his fist pounding the door.

The cinched-up tie itched like a noose around his neck. The gray suit jacket Julianna had forced him to wear felt too tight, even on his barely-there biceps, and pressed like an anvil against his average chest from the tapered cut. Futile as it was, he snapped and pulled down the fabric on his arms to stretch meager gains of room along his back so he could breathe, but it did little to alleviate the constraint. The skin on his thighs itched from the thin fabric that did nothing to hold back the wind, and his toes ached from the cheap, black dress shoes he bought the day before. Being thoroughly uncomfortable from head to toe, he wondered how he had even let his mother talk him into coming over for dinner.

He pinched the fabric against his groin. "Whose idea was it to make men's suits so skinny?" Kevin said. "Whoever it was, I want to kick his ass. I can't breathe in this thing."

'Sure." Julianna's lips pursed and her eyes rolled. "Like you could beat up anyone Kevin."

"Oh yeah?" Kevin flexed the arm hers was wrapped around. "Feel that lady."

She gave the bicep a squeeze, as if testing the softness of a tissue roll. "Wow, I stand corrected." she quipped, then pulled him down and planted a peck on his cheek, just light enough not to mess up her lipstick. "My hero," she whispered in his ear before she pulled away.

Grumbling, Kevin picked and pulled at his suit.

"Stop fidgeting; you're going to wrinkle it," she replied. "Besides, you look handsome."

She leaned in and pressed the small, white circular doorbell. The chime echoed inside the house with a ding and slow dong.

"I hope you kept the receipt Jay, because I'm taking this back right when we're done here."

A smirk made Julianna's face even prettier under the light from the porch lamp. "Don't lie to me. You never take anything back. We just donated a whole bag of clothes of yours that still had tags on them."

Kevin frowned then stood up straight. "But this time, I mean it. I'll walk out of here naked just to keep this suit pristine if I have to."

The light made Julianna's red lipstick glisten as she laughed. There was a hint of smoky eye shadow that highlighted her light brown eyes and perfectly curled eyelashes. Diamond-shaped earrings sparkled as she moved. A tight French braid swept over her forehead and melted into her hair. She wore a thin, black, wool trench coat that was loosely cinched at the waist and stopped at the top of her leg. He tried to convince her to wear something heavier since it looked too small for the cold, but Julianna refused, protesting that it was the only coat she owned that wouldn't crease her dress underneath.

As they waited for the door to open, Kevin felt the swirling winter air that had descended on New Haven; it chilled him to the bone. Shivers ran through his body, and he blew into his hands again while pumping his knees. If he were that cold, then Julianna must have felt glacial standing on the porch, exposed to the elements with nothing but a thin coat to keep her warm. Yet, she didn't show her discomfort. She held his arm tight to her body, her back remaining regally straight.

Hearing no sounds coming from inside the house, Kevin pounded the red door with his fist hard enough to make the metal door knocker clang with each blow.

"C'mon mom, it's freezing out here!" he shouted with the final swing.

"Sssh!" Julianna admonished and pulled his arm down. "It's not even that cold." Her brow furrowed. "Is everything okay? You seem to be colder than usual these days."

"I'm fine. Seriously, I was only kidding," he smiled at Julianna to put her at ease, which was much better than telling her the truth.

Instinctively, the fingers on Kevin's free right hand moved over the fabric of his dress shirt, and between the taunt buttons. Now when his fingers touched his chest, there was nothing there. The space where his symbol normally would be was devoid of energy and warmth.

The truth was, in the few months that they had dated since the party, Kevin and Julianna's time together had been wonderful. He had never let anyone get close to him before her. Not even Warren. But Julianna was like an ace fighter pilot that could maneuver past his metaphorical defenses. Since they both worked for BCR, they were together almost every waking moment— and he still never tired of her presence. They usually spoke on the phone while he drove to work, and they always ate together at Kevin's desk, no matter how much the guys in collections ribbed him for it. Julianna had nearly as many clothes at his place as Warren, and even kept a toothbrush on his bathroom counter for sleepovers. She had stabbed deep into his being in those months, and it was enough to keep the power at bay.

The power waned because of the good, positive feelings Julianna helped manifest that silenced the voice and dimmed the well of energy it normally cultivated. As a reaction, his body was colder without the power, after spending years used to the heat it created. He was transforming from a Mega and acclimating into a normal human being that was encountering the elements again for the first time in years. Just regular, normal Kevin Jones who got cold from gusts of wind.

The experience of normalizing should have been jarring, but often, Julianna was there to fill the warmth that the power left behind. He could no longer play the failed Mega, but it was worth abdicating that broken crown if it meant he could be with her more often.

"Stop!" Julianna whined as Kevin's fist inched up towards the door. But before he could pound it again, the door opened in a rush of warm relief from within.

"Hi!" Caitlyn panted. Sweat dampened her face as she fumbled with a round, purple earring on her left ear.

"Sorry, I had to pull something out of the oven, then finish getting dressed."

"It's okay, Mrs. Jones," Julianna said. She smiled and reached out her hand.

Kevin's mother took it in both of hers and led her inside. "Oh honey, you're freezing! I'm so sorry. Come in. Come in already and make yourself at home."

"I'm fine too mom," Kevin muttered as he followed the two inside. It was crowded in the small foyer, but he was happy to be out of the cold.

"Quiet, Kevin," his mom rebuked, then turned back to Julianna. "Here, let me take your coat."

The foyer was slick with melted snow that made Kevin slip when he closed the door behind them. Julianna, on the other hand, navigated it with grace. She pulled the trench coat off by the shoulder and revealed the black Etsuko style dress. The tight sleeves stopped at mid-forearm and covered her chest and shoulders in decorative, dark lace. It ended above the knee and was cinched around her curving hips with a thin, black belt and silver buckle. The black flats made her have to look up at him for once, which Kevin appreciated.

"My, that's a beautiful dress," Caitlyn said as she hung the coat on the wooden coat rack on the wall. "And I love those earrings."

Julianna touched the glimmering diamond earring in her right lobe.

"Oh, thanks. They were my grandmother's." She looked down at the dress and spread out the bottom with pinched fingers. "And yeah, this dress is useless where we work, but I fell for the marketing that said you could move from the boardroom to the bar in this." She looked up at Caitlyn and grinned. "But I've had it in the closet for months, and still don't know where the boardroom is at work, so I thought, what the heck?"

Caitlyn's high-pitched chortle brought Kevin back from admiring Julianna's beauty. His mother stood on black high heels but was still several inches shorter than Julianna. Her skin was smooth and hid her nearly fifty years. Her salt and pepper hair fell below her shoulders, and she wore an elegant dark purple dress with a portrait collar and loose skirt that bounced against the back of her legs as she led Julianna upstairs.

Still in the foyer, Kevin searched around before crouching at the edge of the separate stairway that led down to the dark basement.

"Where's the dog?" he shouted up to this mother as she and Julianna climbed the stairs to the living room.

Jordin, the bushy black and brown half German Shepard and husky dog that was his best friend throughout high school, should have already scrambled up from the basement after hearing his voice. He would have to keep her off him since she seemed to shed almost year-round, but it had been months since he had seen her last, and he looked forward to introducing her to Julianna.

"We put her in the garage," Caitlyn yelled back.

"What?" he stood up and put his arms out wide. "But it's freezing in there!"

Thumping steps moved quickly along the carpet from upstairs and stopped at the edge of the staircase. Caitlyn looked down at him, her face flushed as if she was about to burst.

"We have a heater in there. Besides, you know how she gets around females for some reason," his mother yelled in a whisper, both hands on her hips.

A grumble rose from Kevin's throat, but he knew his mother was not wrong. When he occasionally would have a girl over, just the sight of her would send a normally gentle Jordin into an angered frenzy. Her hair would stand in a line down her back like bristles, and her front paws would stiffen, spread out wide as she followed the girl's movements with piercing, brown eyes.

Still standing at the edge of the stairs, Caitlyn beckoned him rapidly with her hands.

"Now stop all that yelling and get up here. She's waiting. Now." That last word landed like an anvil, and Kevin sagged beneath its weight. His mother wasn't asking.

"Yes mom," he said softly, and promptly jogged up the steps.

Kevin's mood lifted when a savory, pepper and garlic aroma met him in the living room. The overhead chandelier light was on, but the gas fireplace to the left cast the room in an orange ambient glow that played like ocean waves on the walls. The eggshell-colored couch on his left was empty, but he noticed the occasion was special enough for his mother to have brought out the tan throw, embroidered with intricate maroon flowers.

Julianna sat on the matching loveseat against the wall on his right, giggling as she played with his kid sister, Angie, who had climbed on her knees to play with her braid. His mom had dressed her in a simple pink dress and matching shoes and braided her hair into two pigtails that fell behind her back.

"Hi Kevin," she said as her tiny finger played with Julianna's intricate hair style, until he tickled her sides.

She wriggled under his fingers with an irresistible giggle that drew Julianna in. "Leave her alone, Squirt. You're going to crease her dress."

"It's okay," Julianna said with a look and pulled her back on her lap. "She's lovely."

Kevin shrugged, then followed an unmistakable crackling sound of beef being cooked in the kitchen. The table that stood just outside the kitchen was large, rustic, and made of solid wood that shined from a layer of lacquer. It could seat six people, even though there were only four in his family, ringed with tall wooden chairs that matched the hand-brushed finish. It was far heavier than it looked and sat on a large black iron stand that nearly broke his back when he had helped his dad haul it up the stair's years ago.

In the kitchen, an orange pan with creamy, white liquid sat on the black stove top, coming to a simmer from the gas fire beneath. A large saucepan was next to it with thin wisps of gray smoke winding from the top. His mother hunched over the stove in a plain white apron hastily thrown around her neck.

"Oh man, you're making beef stroganoff!" Kevin said and made his way inside.

"Well, I know it's your favorite, and it's not like I get to see you all the time," Caitlyn replied, then pinched his cheek. She leaned over and pulled the oven open, using a rag on her shoulder to inch out the center wire rack. A sweet, rich, fragrance made Kevin's stomach sing as she pushed a toothpick into the center of the two brown cakes that were baked next to each other.

"Almost done," Caitlyn said and gently closed the door again. She stood up just in time to catch Kevin stealing a small sizzling chunk of peppered steak from the pan, tossing the steaming piece into his mouth.

"Kevin!" she shouted beneath her breath so Julianna couldn't hear in the living room. "Did you even wash your hands?"

His cheeks puffed as he blew out warm air and chewed the molten hot, but savory meat. His tongue burned as he spoke. "Wash my hands? It's like a thousand degrees in that pan mom."

Her shoves were gentle but firm against his shoulder. "Get out Kevin! You're getting in my way."

"I thought you wanted me to help?"

"No, just leave it to me."

"I'll help Mrs. Jones." Julianna stood at the edge of the kitchen. Her arm swung back and forth from Angie at her side, who looked up at her with a snaggle-toothed grin.

Caitlyn's mouth drooped into a frown. "Oh no, honey, you're our guest. Guests don't cook, especially in that dress."

Julianna hung her purse on the back of a chair at the table and pushed her hair over her shoulders with both hands. "It's okay. Ask Kevin, I love to cook." She looked him in the eye as she passed Angie off, who bear-hugged both his legs like a little koala clutching a tree. "Besides, he talks about this dish all the time, so I want to learn how to make it, if you don't mind?"

His arms crossed over his chest— as much as they could in his snug jacket— before he gave up and leaned an arm on Angie's head. "I can cook, you know."

"Since when?" the two women said in unison, then laughed together. It always amazed him how the other sex could come together in such a tight bind of sisterhood when they cared about the same thing but seemed to hate each other otherwise.

"Women," Kevin muttered to Angie. "Don't ever become one of those, okay?"

Her nose wrinkled up and eyes shut tight as she grinned, the missing front tooth making her look even more adorable. "Become what?" she asked. Kevin only smiled and gave her a peck on the forehead.

"Take your sister out of here," Caitlyn said with a smack on his rear. "And tell your father the food is almost done."

Kevin breathed out and tried to walk, but Angie held onto his left leg tighter.

"You're going to wrinkle my pants, too, squirt," he said to her, but she only giggled, and her grip went tighter in response. Seeing that the little girl wasn't going to relent, he was forced to duck walk, exaggerating his long strides as he lifted Angie off the ground with each step, that elicited whooping laughter. At the edge of the staircase, he peeled Angie off, lifted her up, and held her under the legs as she wrapped them around his tight jacket, ensuring that it would match his wrinkled slacks.

Knowing what was to come, Angie held her ears as he leaned over the stairs and yelled, "Dad! The food is almost ready!" Jordin's subdued whining barks echoed from the garage and wafted up the stairs in response to his call, but there was no reply from his dad.

Caitlyn poked her head out of the kitchen. "Kevin! I told you to stop that," she stuttered, and he knew she was correcting a curse word in her head before she continued to speak.

"What? He can hear me," he looked at Angie. "He heard me, right?" Angie knew she shouldn't smile, but couldn't help it, and the two nodded together.

"What am I going to do with you two?" Caitlyn sighed. "Just stop yelling, and go down and get him, please. I have to show Julianna how to put this all together."

"Want to do me a favor, my beautiful little tulip of loveliness?" Kevin said to his little sister. "Can you go get dad?"

"What do I get if I go?" Angie asked in a mouse-like tone that belied her extortion attempt.

"How about I sneak you an extra piece of cake?"

The smile on his sister's face grew brighter and she said, "Okay. Deal."

He shook her little hand, then she climbed down off him and ran down the stairs in small plastic clicks from her shoes. Jordin whined and barked again from her presence in the basement, but he heard the clicks turn right towards his father's study.

"Dad! Dinner's ready!" She shouted, the noise melting further down the hallway as she went.

A quick inspection found that his suit was a wrinkled mess and stained from some grease on her tiny fingers, making it impossible to return later. All the movement made it at least feel less like a straitjacket. Swipes of his hands smoothed the front as best he could.

Julianna and his mother chatted like old friends as they moved around the kitchen, putting all the food together. On the table, the plates, spoons, forks, and butter knives were already set out for the five seats atop white cloth napkins. Sculpted wine glasses that tapered near the top were next to each setting, filled with a burgundy liquid, except for Angie's seat, where a plastic cup sweated condensation from the pink lemonade inside. Near the center of the table, a fresh oval-shaped loaf of white bread his mother perfected in the Dutch oven cooled on a wood cutting board, its top layer hardening to a thin, brown crust. Next to it was a large, round, wooden bowl. A matching wooden tong was half hidden by the tossed mixed vegetables and cheese inside that glistened with beige Caesar dressing.

When he looked up, Julianna traipsed slowly towards the table. She held another smaller bowl with both hands out before her like a person performing a sacred ritual that swished clear liquid with each step.

"Don't drop it," Kevin joked with a slight flinch, but Julianna kept her eyes on the vinegar in the bowl.

"Shut up, Kevin," she said, not reacting to the movement until she carefully sat the bowl down next to the salad, smiling after not having spilled a drop. The smell of the tangy vinegar that smothered the limp cucumbers and thin cut onions rose from the bowl. His stomach grumbled; the anticipation of the delicious meal almost more than he could bear.

"You went all out, mom," Kevin said, taking in the aroma with sniffs, then looked at his mother who was still in the kitchen. "Cucumber salad, too?"

Caitlyn winked at him as she walked to each plate with the black pan, scooping out steaming sauce covered egg noodles in generous portions.

Julianna rubbed his arm and whispered in his ear. "I have no idea how she made that cucumber salad. It was already in the fridge when we got here."

"Don't worry, it's not hard. I'll show you," he replied, warmly rubbing her hand for even wanting to know.

Kevin walked Julianna to the long side of the table close to the window and pulled out the chair for her, eliciting a slight nod of satisfaction and a smile from his mother.

"Well, who do we have here?" a pleasant voice asked beyond the table. Still holding the chair, Kevin looked up, and saw his dad walking towards them with a stunted gait as Angie giggled and clung to his leg.

"Howard, this is Julianna," Caitlyn said, her face beaming as if she had introduced the queen of England.

"Hi, Mr. Jones," Julianna said sheepishly, straightening her dress to stand and reach out her hand.

Howard leaned over the table and shook her hand with a warm smile. "It's a pleasure to meet you, Julianna."

As he leaned over, Kevin could smell his signature Old Spice scent. Howard stood over six feet tall, a trait he would have appreciated more than the bad stomach he inherited. His gray hair thinned near his temples, but there was still enough to give him a smart, textured crop. Wrinkles creased his forehead and the corner of his eyes behind thick dark glasses but were just enough to give his face a dignified air. A five o'clock shadow, that was more white than black, framed his wide, pinkish lips. The top of his father's khaki pants was more wrinkled than Kevin's from Angie's ride, but he hid it well beneath a light brown vintage sports coat that still had the dark brown patches stitched on the elbows, like something from an eighty's sitcom.

His father produced a silk cloth from his breast pocket and proceeded to clean his glasses.

"Kevin," he said with almost an imperceptible nod.

"Dad." Kevin replied, just as cold.

"You look skinnier since last time I saw you," Howard looked up, squinting as he made circular motions with the hand that held the glasses. "Here, around the chest area."

"Dear Lord, Howard," Caitlyn breathed out.

He looked at her with a puzzled expression. "What?" he replied, perfectly drawing out the word. His father had perfected saying it in such a genuine tone that it was difficult to tell if he actually knew what he said was a mistake. Julianna looked between the two of them, not daring to move. The situation made Kevin's neck start to sweat.

"Everyone sit before the food gets cold," Caitlyn said, clapping to cut the awkward silence.

She peeled Angie from Howard's leg by the arm and led her away. Free from the encumbrance, Howard walked to the far end to take his spot at the head of the table. Julianna edged over the chair Kevin had pulled out closest to his dad, and he slid it beneath her as she sat. He took the chair next to her and smoothed out his jacket on his lap. His mother sat at the other end from Howard, while Angie climbed up onto the tall chair to her left across from the couple, having the entire opposite side to herself.

Howard leaned in over the plate of food and took in a deep breath of the garlic, pepper, and cream sauce. "This smells wonderful, honey." He looked up at Caitlyn with his glasses full of steam from the warm plate.

"Daddy, your glasses," Angie sniggered in a low tone because her hands covered her mouth. Howard's eyes went cross-eyed as he looked down, making his sister laugh even harder before he took off the offending pair to clean again.

"Can we eat now? It's getting cold," Kevin said. His stomach grumbled like a cement mixer, so loud that he had to squirm in his seat. A smile sprinted on Julianna's face because she had grown used to hearing the strange noises his stomach often made, making the joke that it was talking to her whenever her head lay there.

Howard put on his glasses. "Julianna," he said, ignoring his son's pleas. "Do you mind if we say a prayer before we eat?"

She shook her head. "No sir, we do the same thing at my house."

Before they even started dating, it only took Kevin days of talking to Julianna to find out that they had religion in common. They both had a similar upbringing that included church, bible study, vacation bible school and, of course, the pensive rebellion of it all when they reached their teens. It was only recently that they had both taken steps to get back into organized religion together, finding a non-denominational church that satisfied them both. Caitlyn already knew that information, so it was more than likely his father knew as well, and it was just one of the small tests Howard liked to give people.

Howard nodded his approval at Julianna. "Very good. Everyone, please hold hands and bow your heads."

Julianna slipped her hand in Kevin's; it was warm and damp with anxious perspiration. He rubbed his thumb over the top of hers to ease the apprehension. Julianna smiled and her fingers tightened in reaction before she closed her eyes.

"Heavenly Father," Howard said. "Thank you for this bountiful food. Bless my wife for her hard work, and I ask that you watch over our guest, Julianna, as we welcome her into our home. Amen."

"Amen," the table said in unison. Kevin gave Julianna's hand a squeeze and she turned at him and smiled again.

His dad mixed the noodles and sauce with his fork, twisting it several times before putting a portion into his mouth.

"Mhm," he exclaimed while chewing. "See, Kevin. Still hot." Then winked behind his glasses.

Kevin's eyes narrowed at his father as he stabbed cucumbers from the bowl and piled them on his plate. The vinegar ran off the vegetable pile and mixed with the cream sauce. Then, after a few twists to the noodles, his palate exploded with buttery cream sauce and a hint of garlic that mingled with the peppery steak he ensured was in the bite. His father was correct that the food was still warm, and each satisfying bite made it worth the wait.

The bread loaf crunched and splintered as Caitlyn cut off a slice on the blunt end with a silver bread knife.

"You want some bread, sweetie?"

"Sure," Kevin said and lifted his plate.

"Yes, ma'am, that would be great. Thank you." Julianna replied, smirking, and looking at him with the side of her eyes.

Caitlyn shook her head at her spoiled son and tossed the round stump end of bread onto his plate, then cut a fresh slice from the loaf and passed it to Julianna's plate. Across from him, Angie was unwilling to wait for the adults. Her face was the picture of concentration as she used both small hands on the wooden tongs and struggled to pull out an over-sized portion of salad, sending bits of tomato and lettuce spilling over the side. The worry lines on his mother's brows creased, and she stole the tongs from her daughter to finish pulling out the salad for her plate.

Julianna's eyes closed as she chewed. A low moan escaped her lips. "Oh my," she said, then swallowed. She pointed at the stroganoff several times with her fork. "Kevin, you were not lying. This is amazing, Mrs. Jones."

"Told you," he said between chews.

Nails dug into his pant leg. "I just said you did," Julianna said sweetly, but her eyes flashed a more vulgar tone. His girlfriend had very little peeves, as almost nothing seemed to get under her skin but, 'I told you so's' were on the short list.

That compliment seemed to be the signal Caitlyn needed to eat, as she finally forked out her own morsel of stroganoff. "Thank you, hon," she said as she took a delicate bite of the noodles.

"So, Julianna," Howard said. "Tell us about yourself?" The bread crunched with each pull of the knife as he cut off a slice.

"Yes," Caitlyn said. "It seems like you two have been dating for so long you would think we would know more about you by now."

"It's only been a few months," Kevin swallowed hard. "And I know what you're trying to say, mom."

She touched her chest in dramatic fashion.

"What?" she said, in the same perplexed tone his father gave earlier. "It's been five months already, Kevin," Caitlyn continued. "I am just saying, you don't date often, so a mother should meet the woman that got her son off the couch when she couldn't."

"Well, with comments like that mother, I can't believe I never brought her over before now," he replied.

Julianna pressed her hand to her mouth and snickered behind it.
Caitlyn had hinted at the dinner several times before they agreed
on a date, almost insulted that they went to visit Julianna's family
first. Kevin had met her family weeks prior, but that felt like a
different experience. While her kin were normal human beings, his
family seemed to be deprecating manifestations the voice had sent
to speak when it couldn't. Even Angie, as her child innocence was
able to blurt out the hurtful truth at any moment.

But there was something else that had stayed his hand and kept
Julianna away from his family. Although visiting Julianna's family
went well, something happened during the introduction which had
stuck to Kevin like an annoying splinter beneath his skin ever since.
In the Jones' backyard, he found himself alone with her father,
Josep, next to the barbecue that still smoldered with heat from the
applewood inside. Julianna was inside with her mother, chatting
and cleaning up. Josep's skin was a shade darker than Julianna's and
hardened to leather from his time out in the sun. Josep was only a
few inches taller than Kevin but was broad and muscular from years
of manual labor.

When he and her father talked while sharing beers, Kevin expected the usual, 'What are your intentions with my daughter?' type
of question. A lifetime of television and coming of age movies had
prepared him for that moment. Yet, he was struck with something
much more profound when her father asked instead, "Where do you
see yourself in five years?"

It was such an uncomplicated yet poignant question that cut
deep as Kevin stumbled to answer it. Before dating her, he would
have answered something about wanting to be employed and not
homeless, outlining the depth of his ambition. But now that he was
gifted with Julianna, he knew he had to be more to suit her. With
Julianna in his life, there were so many variables to consider that

were not previously there, and he asked Josep for time to ponder the question.

Her father gave a weak smile but didn't press further. Mr. Jove never mentioned it again that night, but Kevin could sense that he had given the wrong answer—or at least not the answer Josep wanted to hear, which still eluded his understanding. He never told Julianna about the conversation, but it had created a hairline fracture of doubt about their relationship, as Kevin pondered whether he was worthy of her. Trying to avoid a similar situation with his own family, he had postponed the introduction which seemed futile given the results so far.

"So, I heard that you were going to college. Is that right?" Howard said, and Kevin sighed. It was only a matter of time before the community college professor brought up education— or Kevin's lack thereof that seemed to stick like a needle in the history teacher's eye.

"Yes, sir," Julianna said. "Just two semesters left. Finger's crossed."

"Oh!" Caitlyn whooped. "So, that's what, six more months left there about? I bet you're excited."

A hand covered Julianna's mouth as she nodded and chewed quickly.

"More like nervous," she said after swallowing. She glanced in Kevin's direction. "I feel like I have a countdown now and can't figure out what I want to do next."

His mother reached over Kevin's plate and rubbed Julianna's hand, looking her in the eyes.

"Well, that's the fun part, hon. Getting out into the world and figuring yourself out." She leaned back in her chair and waved her hands across the table for emphasis. "Ask Howard. It took me months after I graduated to figure out what I wanted to do. So, I think you'll be fine."

"Much better than someone over there," his father chimed in with a mirthful tone, and pointed to Kevin with his butter knife. "His sister will graduate before he does."

Silverware clanged against a plate. "Howard, my God, really?" Caitlyn gasped.

"What?" His father's smile broadened.

"You're embarrassing him!"

"Cat, he knows I'm joking," Howard leaned forward and peered over his glasses, mouth frowning. "Kevin, you know I'm kidding, right?"

The corner of Kevin's mouth tightened up and he gave his father a tilted nod. Beneath the table, Julianna's fingers intertwined with his and she pulled his hand into her warm lap.

"He'll graduate one day," she said, her voice confident and without a hint of frivolity as she peered into Kevin's eyes. "Kevin's smart, funny, and talented. He's just pacing himself." Any anger he felt from Howard's words was lost in her eyes.

"Pacing himself?" Howard straightened with a chuckle and pushed his glasses up his nose. There was a pause for emphasis before Howard dug his utensils back into the noodles. It would take a hummingbird to see the nearly imperceptible nodding of his head as he twisted the noodles on his fork. "Kevin, I have no idea how you pulled this off, but you need to keep this one. She actually believes in you."

Caitlyn's utensils clanged against her plate again. Holding the edges of the table, she glared at Howard in exasperation, but Kevin ignored the exchange he had already seen a million times between his parents.

He mouthed a thank you to Julianna and put his hand over hers. No one had ever stood up for him before. The fact that she had intimidated his father on the first day of meeting him didn't go unnoticed or unappreciated. He didn't think it was possible, but Julianna had just reached a new plateau of eminence in his mind.

"Well, I plan to," he finally said to his father, but his eyes never left hers, sharing in their unity.

"Good," Howard said, head down, still chewing. "You two should get married."

That declaration forced Kevin's gaze from Julianna's face.

"Oh, come on now, dad." Howard just stared at him, slowly chewing, as if he hadn't said anything at all. "Now you're just being obscene."

"You're using that word wrong." Howard countered quickly.

"You should, Kevin," Angie interjected between smacks, forgoing the fork to put individual noodles into her mouth from her plate. "I like her. Then she could braid my hair like hers and play like she promised to."

Howard shrugged, his face a picture of smugness. He pointed at his little sister as if a priest had blessed his preposterous suggestion. Julianna looked down, her brown skin turning pink as she played with the napkin on her lap. Even as she peered down, Kevin could see a wan smile spread on her face, bemused by the situation.

Kevin glared at his sister, and said through gritted teeth, "You be silent, woman!"

Angie blinked, but the blank expression on her face never wavered as she replied softly, "I thought you didn't want me to be one of those?"

Kevin pointed a finger at her and suppressed a smile, "I knew you heard me earlier!" Then, he turned to his mother and pleaded for rational assistance, "Mom, a little help please?"

Caitlyn chewed on her fork. "Well, it's not exactly a crazy idea to start thinking about, Kevin."

"Really? You too, mom?" he said in exasperation. "This isn't the eighteen-hundreds anymore."

"Oh, don't be so dramatic, honey," she said. "Your father and I were married by your age. And well, there is nothing wrong with planning ahead."

Betrayed on all sides, Kevin knew that he had to defend himself or lose the narrative for the rest of the night. It could be Howard's declaration that would give Julianna the sliver of doubt he couldn't afford—just when he was finally getting used to having her around.

"That's because, mother," he said to Caitlyn, "people had to pair up during the Cenozoic period for warmth and survival. Nowadays, we can take our time."

Julianna buried her face in his arm, and her shoulders bobbed up and down. Her laughing breath was warm in his fabric. He smiled, knowing that she was now firmly back on team Kevin and Julianna.

His mother's face hardened. "That's not funny, Kevin," she said, patting down the gray part of her hair.

"What's the cenzo period?" Angie said as she bit off a piece of bread.

Kevin turned to his father and pointed at Angie with his hand. "And you're a history teacher?"

The quip seemed to annoy his father, who looked at him with narrowed eyes, and slowly tongued morsels of food out of his back teeth. The joke had one important fan. Julianna squeezed his hand tighter, and her head fell further down his arm so that he had to stifle a laugh of his own.

They had only been together a short amount of time, and they were still young. There had been jokes about marriage between the two with the amount of closet space he was losing and how quickly Julianna cluttered the bathroom vanity. But the two had not discussed it in detail, or with jokes aside. He was still a boy, who couldn't even answer a simple question from her father. Marriage seemed like an absurd notion at that moment in their relationship.

Composed again, Julianna straightened up; her cheeks were a

cherry red as she carefully dabbed the tears from her eyes with her napkin and blew out a long breath.

"Wow okay, I wasn't expecting all of this," she said.

After a long drink of wine, Kevin said, "Well, I tried to warn you. I told you these two were mentally deranged."

"Careful now Kevin Jones," Caitlyn said in a slow, deep tone. Her face trembled as she admonished him with her eyes, until she burst into laughter. "Okay, Howard, it looks like we've embarrassed him enough." She smiled over her glass at Julianna as she took a sip of wine.

Kevin looked between his mother and father who seemed to have plotted the entire humiliating scenario together. "Yeah, no kidding, mom. You two done already?"

Awe, my poor baby," Julianna said, still laughing as she rubbed his cheek with the palm of her hand. Her eyes softened. "But, Julianna Jones, it has a nice ring to it. Doesn't it?"

Now it was Howard's turn to bellow with a laughter that echoed in the dining room, breaking his strait-laced character. Caitlyn laughed as well, winking at Julianna as she sipped more wine. His sister laughed in soft giggles, as well, although the confusion on her face said she did not quite seem to know what was so funny.

Kevin couldn't help but join in. It was an astute joke told masterfully by his girlfriend, and he had to give her credit. It shredded any remaining tension, and practically ingrained her status as one of the family by joining in on the ribbing. For him, it was worth the heat, since it was all in mirth, but that feeling lasted only until he looked in Julianna's eyes again.

To his parents, what she said appeared to be a joke, but Kevin knew Julianna far better. There was something behind her soft, brown eyes that glistened as she looked from Caitlyn and Howard. They hid a truth that hit him harder than any bullet against his aura shield. Her countenance, along with that smile and the soft touch of her fingers beneath the table, were all pieces of a puzzle that, when pulled together, implied that perhaps Julianna had seriously thought about marriage before. The thought lasted only an instant that Kevin shook it off, fearing he was reading into something that wasn't truly there.

Yet, the speculation made a sharp pain tinge Kevin's stomach as if a fiery pebble had been dropped down his throat.

"You okay, son?" Kevin looked up at Howard, whose dark brown eyes were sharp behind his glasses.

"Yeah dad, I'm fine," he replied in a low tone, and slipped his hand out of Julianna's. His fork turned over the noodles that didn't seem as appetizing as before, with the cream sauce turning brown from the air. He thought about the question Mr. Jove had asked, and the answer seemed even more elusive.

"Julianna, what are you majoring in, if you don't mind me asking?" Howard asked as he swiped a piece of bread through the cream sauce and tossed it into his mouth.

Julianna gave Kevin a queer look as she sensed his trepidation, then turned to Howard, steepling her now empty hands in front of her.

"Uhm, I'm a graphics design major," her voice trembled, but the composure returned. "You know, pamphlets, images, symbols, logos, wedding invitations. Things like that."

"You create them yourself?" Caitlyn asked.

"Mhm," Julianna gave an embarrassed, repressed smile. "Right now, I use a Mac that's almost on its last leg. I'm trying to guilt my dad into getting me a new one as a graduation present."

Caitlyn cleared her pallet with more wine. "That's very interesting. Is there a huge market for that here in New Haven? Graphic design, I mean."

"Well, yes and no. With the way the city is growing, I'm feeling out interest in local companies. Savoy Industries is hiring."

"Savoy Industries?" Howard said. "Funny you should mention them because I met Tomas Savoy recently."

His mother leaned forward on the table. "Really, Howard? You never told me this," she said. Kevin noticed that her face seemed to contort with what he thought was mild annoyance.

Ever oblivious, Howard nodded and swallowed. "Yes. It was at a NHCC luncheon about an important exhibit we're trying to obtain at the local museum. We had a good talk, he and I. We've been exchanging emails sporadically ever since. I could speak to him for you, Julianna, if you'd like. See if they have any openings at his company?"

Julianna exhaled. "Oh no, Mr. Jones. Thanks, but I don't know. I know it would be great working for such a large company, but I did some research, and I am not really feeling their...ethics? If that makes sense."

"Good girl. A woman with integrity," Caitlyn said with a nod of pride. "So, if not with Savoy, do you have other places you are looking at?"

"Well, there are other strong local companies, but it's nothing like what you would see in Eugene or, uhm, Portland." Her eyes glanced over at Kevin, knowing his negative feelings towards that city. "Or L.A.!" The smile returned to Julianna's face as she spoke. "L.A. is a mecca for graphic designers with all the industries there."

"L.A.?" Kevin asked. The night had been full of new revelations.

It was the first he had heard that Godawful Californian city as a possible destination for her. The Jones family had taken a vacation to L.A. when he was younger, and it wasn't great, to say the least. The taxi driver, who reeked of urine and motor oil, had taken them to the wrong hotel, then driven off with his father's money without giving back his change, a hefty twelve-dollar tip. Angie was a baby at the time and whaled incessantly throughout the trip. They later found out she was infected with croup that had spread throughout the over-priced hotel. His mother's foot was cut by a piece of glass on the beach that later became infected, as well, and he was shocked by the filthy, skid rows that seemed to dot every other street downtown.

It was a step above Portland, for sure, but only by a few degrees, as far as he was concerned. After the family left early, he was relieved to get back to his small, but clean town of New Haven, and promised himself he would never step foot in that hellhole city ever again.

"Well yeah, L.A.," Julianna answered. "There are so many companies and start-ups there that I can intern with to get my foot in the door."

The pain in Kevin's bowels spread to his diaphragm and pulsed like scalding water through his veins, making him wince. Looking around the table, his father was the only one who seemed to notice, but looked away, wiping his mouth with a napkin to cover his staring. He contemplated why Julianna had kept L.A. as a destination secret from him. It was enough to make him wonder if she wanted him to accompany her at all. Maybe she was planning on ending their relationship when she graduated to get a fresh start?

New Haven was perfect for Kevin's nature, and he didn't feel bad saying it, but that was when he was only concerned with his own life. Now that he was in a relationship, he had to think about what Julianna wanted, as well. They were quickly becoming one instead of two. Or so he thought until that instance. Julianna was a well of creativity and ideas that seemed to overflow one after the other. Perhaps she needed a much bigger canvas than New Haven could provide?

As if she could read her son's thoughts, Caitlyn asked, "So, you would move then, Julianna?"

Kevin breathed out. "What's with all the questions, mom? And you too, dad," his hand went to his girlfriend's thigh beneath the table. "She has to keep all the options open." Their eyes found each other again, and it was Julianna's turn to mouth a thank you.

Caitlyn, feeling the rebuke from the united couple, leaned away and picked up her glass of wine to take a drink. "I just don't want anything to happen to you two, is all," she replied in a somber tone that Kevin noticed.

Julianna leaned over and placed a peck on his cheek. He allowed her hand to slip back into his beneath the table as she rested her chin on his shoulder.

"Don't worry, Mrs. Jones. I don't plan on anything happening to us." Her jaw tickled Kevin's shoulder bone as she spoke, and he smiled inwardly. The pain that had moved to his sternum seemed to ebb from her proclamation, believing that she meant every word.

Bored by all the grown-up talk, Angie held her head up by her palm as she lazily stabbed at the nearly empty plate before her. "Can we have cake now?" she whined.

Normalcy descended on the table, and the rest of the dinner went on without another road bump, even though Kevin found it hard to concentrate with the whirlwind that clouded his thoughts. Julianna charmed his parents with her honesty, excitement, and laughter, while Angie fawned over her as if she were the big sister she always wanted. Even Howard contributed to the mirth with his unintentional bouts of humor and humiliating stories about his students and moments from Kevin's childhood. Kevin did his best to keep the conversations topical and light.

When the dinner had concluded, Caitlyn retreated to the kitchen to put the icing on the cake, with Angie hot on her heels, vinyl shoes patting the carpet, knowing better than to hold onto her mother's leg to catch a ride. Seeing that Julianna was able to survive his father if his mother was around, Kevin excused himself from the table.

Julianna clutched his arm. "Are you okay? Is It your stomach again?"

With a shrug, Kevin replied, "Sometimes you must pay what you owe, Jay. And the porcelain god demands his sacrifice."

"Gross, Kevin," she replied with a twisted mouth.

With a laugh, he laid a peck on her cheek. "I'll be right back."

He offered his father a nod as Howard twitched his eyebrows up. Kevin walked past the loveseat and down a long hallway but stopped just outside the bathroom door. He noticed that his former bedroom door was ajar further down the hall.

It was awkward growing up and having his room directly across from his parents' master bedroom. Music had to be low or listened to with headphones on, and any racy movies were watched in the darkness on mute, with the remote nearby in case his mother barged in without knocking. When he could convince a girl to sneak over in high school, If he could get her past Jordin, he also had to battle his mother's uncanny instincts that seemed to know when another female was present. Still, there were many good memories he had in that room, where he spent most of his time alone.

Curiosity tugged at him, and he wondered what his parents had done to his room since their unceremonious parting. The door creaked as he pushed it in, just as it had done for years. Muscle memory made him click the switch on the left, and the room was flooded in a brown light, almost dingy in color since one of the bulbs in the ceiling fixture had burned out, and the other covered in dust. The air was stale and cold but had a welcoming aroma.

The sliding door closest to his right was still empty. His queen-sized bed was still there, prominent in the middle of the room, with its broken faux wood headboard that Jordin had chewed at the edges. A large wooden chest was next to it, between the bed and double windows that Kevin knew was filled with old comic books, magazines, and childhood toys. It weighed nearly as much as their dining table and took up so much space that he was forced to leave the chest behind when he finally moved out.

He walked in further. Turning to his left, his eyes widened when he saw that his mom had kept his prize possessions adorned along the wall. As a child, he discovered superheroes in comics, an obsession that exploded when real life Megas were canonized within its pages. As a lark, he convinced Caitlyn to let him plaster his biggest wall with bagged and boarded comics. He had arranged them in a checkerboard pattern, stapling the sleeve so he could flip up the plastic flap to change out the issues based on his weekly rankings. They were still on the wall, their bags still gleaming and the issues inside as pristine as he had left them.

The door creaked again, and Caitlyn walked into his room alone.

"Where is Julianna?" he asked.

Rubbing her arms against the cold, Caitlyn replied, "she's with your father."

"You left them alone?" His father was hard enough to deal with when other family members were around. Thinking about how much worse his father could be in one-on-one situations, Kevin moved to intervene, but his mother caught him by the arm as he passed.

"She's fine," Caitlyn breathed and pulled him in. "They're getting along like peas in a pod. Listen."

Their voices were muted through the wall, but he could hear Howard speaking in the quick, higher-pitched tone that he always got whenever he grew excited about the topic. He couldn't imagine what it might have been about. Perhaps aliens. His father was as practical and reasoned as one would imagine a professor to be, but his guilty pleasure was watching hours of alien shows and speculating about other civilizations.

Looking back at his mother, Kevin asked, "What are they talking about?"

"Music," Caitlyn replied with a chuckle.

"Music? What music?" he turned to face her. "I don't remember the last time I saw or heard dad listening to anything. Even in the car, he only listens to books."

"You don't know him as well as you think, Kevin." The stare his mother gave him was almost sympathetic. Then, she pulled his arm over her shoulder and turned toward his wall of comics. "And you need to give Julianna more credit. Right now, she's in that beautiful dress with your father, going through his record collection on the floor. He can't believe how much she knows about the classics."

Lost in thought, Kevin muttered "I guess I should give her more credit. But I have time."

His mother's hair smelled like peppered beef and sweet cake, reminding him how much work she had put in that evening. Kevin wrapped his other arm around her thin neck.

She reached up and held his forearms. "This jacket is really tight," she said, examining the fabric between her fingers. "But stylish. I'm surprised you're wearing something modern."

"Julianna likes it," Kevin sighed and chuckled. "I know, I've become whipped. I'm as bad as you dressing dad now."

"Oh, stop that," Caitlyn said. Kevin could feel her smile. She closed her eyes and swayed in his arms. "Julianna is amazing, Kevin. I am so happy for you."

Kevin smiled along with her. "Yeah, she really is."

"Even Angie loves her."

"Who doesn't she love at first sight? I worry about that girl and stranger danger," Kevin said. Caitlyn huffed, but he gave her a squeeze to ensure that he was joking. "Think Jordin will love her too?"

Caitlyn turned to look up at him. "I wouldn't risk it," she laughed. "She's scared more than one of your exes away. Like that terrible Marny you dated."

"Marny," he breathed out her name. "In my defense, she was

really, really tall. Great legs, longer than my body, with great jeans. Hips like a coke bottle."

"She was an amazon, Kevin," Caitlyn said dryly. "She nearly crushed me when we first met. And she was rude."

"Yeah, she was pretty bad, but she never wanted to come back after meeting Jordin. That girl really has a way of sniffing out the bad ones," Kevin replied. "But it all worked out. I'm really lucky to have Julianna."

"You're extremely lucky."

"Hey," Kevin moved his head away to the side so he could see her face. "I just said really lucky. I can pick my own adjectives."

"You mean adverbs." Caitlyn's mouth pursed like a fish, and she smacked his forearm with her hand. "You really need to go back to school, Kevin."

"Ow!" Kevin exclaimed. "And you need to stop hanging around dad!" He pulled her in for a hug, and the two shared a laugh.

With his arms still wrapped around her neck, they admired the comics. He remembered a time when he had almost taken them down, tired of being made fun of at school for his hobby and getting beaten up again and again. But Caitlyn talked him out of it, imploring him to be himself. As far back as he could remember, and before Julianna blessed his life, Caitlyn was his best friend, and the only one that could force a relationship between he and Howard. She was the glue that kept the Jones' family together, and he wouldn't have even ventured over that night if it wasn't for her persistence.

He glanced from comic to comic, wondering just how much money he put into his hobby. "I can't believe you kept all these up."

Caitlyn smiled and rubbed his arms. "Well, you left so suddenly, and it was such a bad time. I wanted to make sure you knew you were welcome to come back."

He squeezed Caitlyn tight, imagining the passive-aggressive

things she had to put up with from his father just by keeping them up. His mother would scold him when he was wrong, but he always felt she had his back. That was why he was surprised she played along with the whole marriage conversation at the dinner table. A woman who would put up with his father just to keep up some comic books on the wall would not have put him in such an awkward situation. There had to be something more.

"So, what was with that wink you gave Julianna at the table when you trapped me with that marriage talk," he asked.

He felt Caitlyn tense in his arms. "You saw that?"

"How could I miss it? You two were practically talking in some subliminal, girl language across the table." He waited for her to answer. "So. Are you going to tell me?"

"It's nothing," she said, and rested her chin gently on his arm. He knew his mother only shut down when she was hiding something. It was interesting to him that Julianna did something similar whenever she tried to keep a secret.

"Tell me," Kevin whined, softly shaking her for emphasis. Caitlyn could never resist his whine. Angie was picking up on the tactic as well.

As he planned, Caitlyn relented but he wished that she had held her tongue in the end.

"It's nothing. We just talked when we were cooking, and things came up," she paused. "You two came up. Your future together."

Kevin's eyebrow arched up and he wondered how deep their conversation could have been in such a short period of time. "And?" He asked.

His mother hesitated before declaring with a dismissive wave of her hand. "Well, I told her that if you don't commit and ask to marry her soon, she would need to move on. That's all."

"What!" Kevin exclaimed. His arms weakened and loosened

around her shoulders as he pulled away. "How could you do that to me mom?"

She had said it with such nonchalant confidence, that at first, Kevin thought it was yet another joke put on by his mother. Caitlyn clutched his forearms and held them in place with surprisingly strong hands. She never turned around to meet his eyes, but instead moved her head to look at each comic on the wall, as if she were studying art at a museum.

"I love you, baby, but you are so non-committal. And you never really plan ahead," her head bowed, but she held firm onto his limp forearms. "I never said anything, but Julianna reached out to me before tonight."

"Really?" Kevin replied. He remembered that once she had asked for her parents' number, and he gave it to her, never thinking she would call without telling him.

"Yes. We've been talking on and off for weeks now," Caitlyn continued. "Nothing really specific since we were saving it for tonight. But she has plans Kevin, and a wonderful future, and you, well, if you can't just grow up and reach your own potential, then you shouldn't hold her back."

Air caught in Kevin's throat, making his tie feel even more constricting. He thought his parents' banter with him that night was to break the tension, but instead, they were the prelude to a Brutus level of betrayal. It was sabotage. His wonderful mother had conspired to light the fuse that would eventually lead to their demise.

"Don't be upset, Kevin," her hands squeezed his arms, voice cracking from emotion that cut off her breath. "House and wealth are an inheritance from fathers, but a prudent wife is from the Lord. That's in the bible. She's a blessing, Kevin, and I truly did it because I love you."

"Unbelievable," was all Kevin could reply.

Yet there was a nagging question that turned over in his thoughts: Was his mother wrong? He thought of all that had transpired. Julianna's amazing personality had cowed his intractable family into loving her in just one night. She was even able to create a bond with Howard, which was something he could not accomplish in two decades plus of time together. Obviously, her mother loved her, as well, if she was able to throw her own son beneath the bus on her behalf. It was clear to anyone paying attention that Julianna was special. A precious flower that would grow beyond New Haven.

'Where will you be in five years?' The question Julianna's father asked echoed like a cruel joke. He thought of it as an equation. Math was his least favorite subject, but even he knew that there were multiple variables affecting the total, and most variables were positive between he and Julianna.

One positive variable was the hope that Julianna had introduced into his life. So effective was its potency that it stifled the voice, and even improved his bill-collecting efforts at work. Just her presence made him look forward to waking up and going to work. The months with her were his most financially successful ever at BCR.

The equation was modified again when he added the fact that Julianna's own family seemed to enjoy his company. That bucked the norm when it came to the first impressions he usually made. More than once, relationships had ended after the first time he looked parents in the eyes, as they could sense his lack of commitment. Kevin enjoyed Julianna's family in equal measure, despite her father's question. Josep was easier to talk to than his own father, and far more down to earth. It did not feel like a chore to be around them.

Yet, Julianna's life was the part of the equations put in parentheses that was supposed to be factored first. Graduation was just around the corner for her, and based off her grades and contacts, companies and jobs would soon be lining up to recruit her. There was little doubt in Kevin's mind that Julianna could survive wherever she landed given her work ethic, brilliance, and charm, whether in the north, or even L.A. She could accomplish this with or without him. But, if he had read her body language correctly at the dinner table, Julianna did not want to go it alone.

Doing the math, at that point in their relationship, it seemed as though things were going well for their union. There was an overall positive total if he were to stop at just those variables. But there was one more twist to the equation that would change the aggregate.

Absent were his own positive contributions to the problem. Julianna had followed her dreams, working hard to graduate in her field of choice. For some of that journey, Kevin was by her side, playing the devoted boyfriend that wanted to do his best to lift her up when needed, and stay out of the way when necessary. Yet, what had he truly accomplished in that time that was not attributed to her?

In his youth, he dreamed of owning a store that catered to comics, but that dream died when he was bored senseless while taking business classes in college, which eventually resulted in the friction with his father. There was a second dream, but that too was crushed when he failed at being a Mega of any notoriety. He was more embarrassed than proud to admit to being Fiasco, and he counted it as a blessing that Julianna's presence had ended that portion of his life, but even the absence of the power had been accomplished because of her. So, he wondered just what Julianna's benefits were for being with him.

Thinking of nothing positive he added to balance out his contributions, Kevin divided the sum of the positives and negatives by their future prospects. Where Julianna's trajectory would lead to the stars and beyond, yet, by his mother's own admission, his future likely led to stagnation. In the end, he could hardly begrudge his mother's ultimatum. How far could Julianna truly rise when she was standing in quicksand?

There was only one result when he equaled out the expressions.

In five years, you will be without her, the voice whispered. Kevin swallowed hard, his throat dry and aching, and felt his head nod in agreement.

"Are you okay, Kevin?" Caitlyn asked. She turned around in his arms and looked up into his face. Sweat misted her brow, and her dark, slate eyes were full of apprehension. The worry lines about her forehead were deep and furrowed as she studied his face. With the back of her hand, she traced his head and cheek, then moved her hand down to the center of his chest.

"It's suddenly so warm in here now, and your heart," she continued. "You're burning up."

The Jordin Test

Kevin sat on the edge of his bed, thumbing the eye holes of his leather Fiasco mask. "Damn that dog," he thought. The stale cowhide stench of the mask that had sat unused for months made him fight a sneeze. "The least you could have done was buy me some time."

After they left his parents' house, Julianna cooed in the passenger seat, "I love your family." She laughed and brushed away black and brown hair that clung to her dress like cactus needles. "Even that crazy dog." Nothing could remove the smile that seemed permanently branded on her face after she had passed the Jordin test.

After his mother's revelation, Kevin had brought the furry Shepard husky upstairs and held her firmly by the collar to meet Julianna. The hair on Jordin's spine bristled when she caught wind of his girlfriend. It grew worse when she finally saw Julianna standing in the living room. Looking between him and his new girlfriend with eyes more yellow than brown, it was as if Jordin instantly put them together. She bared her sharp teeth like a wounded wolf, and with a deep growl, he felt her collar vibrate. Her legs tensed and spread wide, and her back arched as if she would pounce if he let her go.

Caitlyn nearly made him take her back to the garage downstairs, until Julianna took one tepid step forward, then another, with her hand out limp so Jordin could take her scent. Jordin sniffed, short hairs on her nose tickling along Julianna's knuckles, then looked up at him. Kevin smiled to simmer her down and ruffled the burly white fur beneath her neck, eliciting a whine and long, warm, tongue-licks beneath his chin. That interaction was all it took before Jordin was in Julianna's lap, ears pinned back and tail thumping against the carpet. Just like that, she had cowed his family's harshest critic.

On the drive to her house, Julianna looked out the passenger window that fogged from her breath and winter air, still smiling. "I really do love them," she said softly. "I honestly wouldn't mind being a part of your family."

There it was. His answer to the most important variable in the equation was out in the open. There was something in her tone, subdued and a bit somber, signaling that his parents' gambit had worked. His mother started a fire with her ultimatum, while his father poured gasoline on it during his impromptu marriage talk. A countdown had begun, and it would terminate six months from that moment when Julianna graduated.

The rest of the drive was quiet compared to their more raucous evening. It ended with a soft kiss, and a whispered bye from Julianna, who seemed to have sensed his looming depression. As Kevin pulled into his apartment parking lot, he had made the decision that the only way he could prove he was not the crab in the barrel that would pull Julianna down to his depth, was to excel at the one thing that made him unique. He had planned to succeed where he previously failed and make Fiasco someone respectable. He vowed to be someone Julianna would be proud to be with and could not leave.

Back in his room, the warmth rose as the negative emotions of insecurity and insignificance swirled within, and he loosened the tie at the top. Sliding down the side of the bed, Kevin knelt on the floor, elbows on his mattress. Ruffling the mask in his hands, he brought it to the top of his head, and his eyes closed. He mouthed a prayer, trying without success to dampen the voice that said, *you will fail.*

Non-Proportional

The spring rains came down like heavy tear drops. They pelted the shimmering blue aura that surrounded Fiasco and the manifested blue gauntlets on his hands that curved up his forearms as he soared south through the New Haven sky. The rain sizzled and evaporated away upon contact with the shield in small, white puffs of steam. It was nearly dusk, but the rolling gray cloud that stretched into the horizon and dropped a downpour upon his head already shadowed the city in a dull overcast.

The Savoy Corporation tower that was in mid construction loomed on his left like a monolith growing taller by the day. To the southwest, he saw the tall cranes and the orange dots of excavators masked in heavy mist. There were bulldozers and other construction equipment parked within the hole where the Mega League stadium was being built. Julianna's father had taken him on a tour, and he was amazed by the size of the cavity and what humans could accomplish without the aid of Mega powers. He repressed a smile from the memory. There was work to be done.

Beneath him, the city shimmered in coral streetlights. New Haven looked strange, larger than he remembered. The square rooftops of the office buildings strewn with rainbow-colored patio furniture blurred and ran together. In the months since his return, Fiasco had learned to keep his eyes ahead to the trees or open skies, so he would not trigger his stomach pangs. No longer heading into every incident on the verge of heaving was a benefit to his endeavors, yet he was still able to admire the view in short intervals.

The rekindled adventure as a Mega-hero began small, and with various levels of success. Often, Fiasco would patrol near his home, rousing violent drunks who stumbled about and fought after last call, or bust the drivers who swerved on the nearly empty roads. But the airwaves were suspiciously quiet about his return, as if the town had left him in the past, so he had to step up his activities to gain any notice.

Recently, he had graduated to facing armed robbery again, with the usual Fiasco results. The media took notice again when Fiasco had surprised a tweaked-up robber who saw the Mega and replied by opening fire, emptying his magazine in a fit of anger and fear. The bullets bounced off his aura like white streaks of lightning. One clipped the poor young clerk who was cowering beneath the counter through the arm, severing his triceps off the bone.

It was as if Fiasco had never left at all, and his notoriety returned with gusto, even though the clerk would have lost his arm had he not stemmed the flow of blood and cauterized the wound with his power. Headlines like 'Local Menace Returns', and 'Fiasco for the Fail', peppered the newspapers and website headlines alike. While his failures mounted, so did the backlash, with Mega forums online going pages deep in vitriol from Mega groupies and parents worried about what kind of role model he represented.

When they first began teaming up again, Talon had called in some favors— with whom he would never say— and pulled enough strings to give him access back to the MegaStream, his authentication to the server having expired during his hiatus. The MegaStream was an online encrypted site for only true, verified Megas and would age off the desktop if not used. It also acted like a pseudo

Mega-human dispatch since it streamed the latest crimes relevant to a geographical area in real time.

He had heard that it was moderated by Megas who could read minds. Apparently, that was how they knew where crimes were occurring, but that information was never verified. The stream could be tough to navigate. Events as low as pets stuck in trees, to a Mal-Mega attacking a tech company seemed to be entered haphazardly line by line. Even the vernacular was different for each entry, as if hundreds of different people were entering data into the stream all at once. But the MegaStream was imperative to the life of a Mega-hero. It was unrealistic to go searching for crime with no leads, hoping to catch crimes in the act.

It was in the MegaStream that Fiasco found the lifeline that had forced him to venture out in the awful weather. In the socializing section, Talon had reached out for aid. The opportunity of redemption had presented itself when the saturated one-twenty-six highway had caused a vicious pileup along the Modoc Bridge. It only took minutes for the crash to appear in the stream as a developing emergency, and only seconds after that came Talon's message. It read, 'Get your ass out here now -T', in red flashing letters.

Kevin and Julianna had dinner plans at Mama Rena's to sample New Haven's best tacos, but he couldn't pass up the possibility of raising his Fiasco profile. The memory of the disappointment on her face made his aura thicken.

Slosh and rain licked the blue light in low hisses as he veered to the west. In the distance, a snow-capped mountain range peeked through the clouds surrounded by a gray mist. Juniper trees jutted from the landscape; their spiky green limbs heavy with rainwater. On the ground, snow retreated from the downfall, revealing pockets of brown grass and sagebrush beneath him as he moved from the bright city lights of New Haven to the high desert plains.

"You can do this," Fiasco thought, but the voice made sure he knew otherwise.

You are going to fail.

From Fiasco's altitude, he could see that the highway was lit up for at least a mile. All the cars heading out of New Haven were at a stand-still, bumper to bumper. Horns blared, and a congestion of angry drivers stood out in the rain, casting blame at each other. This slowed the progress of ambulances and fire trucks who attempted to ease through the gridlock to reach the scene. He buzzed over the blockage, a blue blurring streak that wanted to be seen by the crowd and headed towards the bridge.

The description he read about the accident on the MegaStream did not properly describe the chaos he found once he arrived. Dark smoke mixed in with the heavy rain. Just before the bridge's entrance was the zigzag of passenger cars that tried to stop last minute on the slicked road, but instead, smashed the car in front of them one after another like dominoes.

All four lanes were clogged at various angles, like a post-apocalyptic scene. Bloodied survivors soaked from the rain tended to others off to the side of the road, using what was available to set splints and tie off seeping wounds. One car had plowed through the trunk of another as it drove up the roof, soared over several others, and landed on its side atop another vehicle. Given its position, balanced precariously at a slant on a caved in roof, Fiasco decided that car was most deserving of his attention.

Curving up until he was horizontal, and floating down, Fiasco landed gently on the car's backseat door. The car moaned with every careful footstep toward the front. Rain pattered on his leather mask as he powered down his aura, knelt, and peered through the driver's window that was strangely crumpled inward. He kept the gauntlets powered on high, and they cast the inside of the cab in stark blue light. The steering wheel was dotted with dark black stains, and the windshield spider-webbed with cracked glass, but there was no one inside.

"You're late as usual," a man shouted behind him.

Fiasco turned toward the stranger who spoke to him. He was kneeling on the ground. The shirt sleeve on his right arm was torn off, the skin beneath heavily bruised. He held a woman's head in his lap with his crumpled shirt to her forehead. Her eyes fluttered from the falling rain as she stared at him. Blood matted her forehead and streaked her blonde hair red. A crowd of fellow survivors had gathered in a crescent shell around them.

"Talon already got us out," the man continued, licking the rain from his lips. "Like a real Mega would." The crowd stirred and joined in his disdain.

"Of course he did," Fiasco sighed, then stood to full height.

He will always be better than you.

Fiasco looked at the bridge. Further down the highway, an orange light blinked on the back of an overturned sixteen-wheeler that obscured what was beyond.

"Be careful citizens. Aid is on the way," he replied.

Drinking in the bump of energy the voice had given him from the crowds' rebuke, the aura returned in a snap, and Fiasco took off like an azure rocket, overturning the car that tumbled off the roof in a scream of grinding metal.

"Fiasco!" he shouted, and his name echoed off the wreckage as he continued towards the Modoc Bridge. Reaching the truck, he slowly circled around the red cab pockmarked with damage from the crash. He searched, ensuring the driver had been evacuated by his friend, before landing on the side of the upturned trailer. Water pooled over the company logo painted on the side, and Fiasco knew it belonged to the company building the stadium that Mr. Jove was contracted to. Walking to the edge, and standing in front of a larger rubber tire, he could see the rest of the damage on the other side.

Reflecting the blue-collar nature of the New Haven citizens, the Modoc Bridge was old and simple in design. It was buffered on each side by four-foot-high silver metal guardrails, attached to concrete blocks that were now cracked and marked with gashes and holes. As he gained an unobstructed view of the crash site, Fiasco realized that the true extent of the crash was worse than he was led to believe.

Through the clamor of driving rain, screams of pain echoed through the darkness. Metal and glass were strewn along the road. Coupes, mini-vans, trucks, and sedans, in various states of wreckage, littered the Modoc Bridge into the horizon that was masked by a haze of precipitation and smoke. Even while the rain continued, a blazing fire raged in the middle of it all, fueled by gas that leaked from severed tanks.

It was apparent from the dark rubber skids burned in the road that the truck he stood upon was headed east into New Haven. It had overturned when it tried to evade a silver oil truck that had lost control on the slippery road going in the opposite direction. The oil truck had skidded to a halt when it burst through the guardrail on his right, ripping the iron outward like tinfoil. A thick, black sludge leaked from the oil trailer along a small tear that was opened by the jagged rail, and pooled on the ground, threatening to add its fuel to the blaze. The truck groaned as the cab teetered several feet off the bridge. It reeled side to side and appeared as if a strong gust of wind could send the entire truck careening down to the river raging below.

"Crooked F! Get the lead out!" Talon yelled, which echoed through the bridge, and off the canyon below.

"Yeah, sure Talon," Fiasco stammered, struggling to comprehend the disaster before him, rain dripping over his goggles. "Get the lead out. Sure, whatever you say."

Taken aback by the severity of the crash, Fiasco did not notice Talon amid the chaos. He wore the same number eight shaped mask as before. The rain had slicked his jet-black hair down and ran down his exposed chest that held a bone necklace interspersed with curved knives hanging low. A black leather vest, etched with the bird-of-prey symbol on the back, caught the ambient light from the heavy rain that pasted it to his skin. His blue jeans were soaked through—resembling a dark black. Black boots splashed in the puddles as he moved among the dangerous wreckage. No motion was wasted as Talon kicked in windshields and wrenched car doors off their hinges like tissues, pulling out survivors even as the fire grew behind him, threatening to overtake them all.

Rescued Havenites walked along the far side of the bridge like zombies, some with arm, leg, and head injuries that were more severe than what Fiasco had seen outside the bridge. Their faces were blank, rain dripping off slacked jaws, staring ahead as if stunned silent from the totality of the crash. For the first time, Fiasco did not envy Talon's superior hearing. He could still hear the screams bouncing off the metal and asphalt, but the rain, smoke, and darkness made it impossible to pinpoint what direction they originated from. He realized it wasn't possible for everyone to have survived the accident, not with the amount of damage he witnessed. The thought of someone dying in the wreckage froze Fiasco's blood and soured his weak stomach.

"The fire," Fiasco thought, sensing the greatest threat facing the surviving victims. "Got to get control of that fire before anyone else gets hurt. If that oil hits it, this will be an even bigger disaster."

The gas fire dominated most of the center of the bridge, growing as it consumed the leaking fuel, and trapping injured New Haven citizens on one side, away from ambulances and aid coming from the city. Mind made up, he zoomed forward off the trailer. Floating horizontal above the burning conflagration, he repeated, "Fuel, ignition source, oxygen." It was the mantra he learned as a cub scout on the components of a fire. It was one of the few things he picked up before he grew tired of being forced to interact with the other children and quit just before making bear.

The hungry flames reached up like fingers at the blue aura on Fiasco's boots. Power flowed through his gauntlets, until it poured out from his hands. With a mental command, it curved downward beneath him like a bell. The bell expanded, slithering out until it covered much of the firestorm in a makeshift azure dome. Fiasco lowered his hands and the dome descended, landing on the asphalt with a thud. Hands twisted right and the dome turned along with them, grating a thick groove as it dug into the pavement to ensure the fire was properly deprived of the food it needed to grow.

Sweat misted the brow beneath Fiasco's mask, and dripped stinging drops down into his goggles. He could already feel the heat from the blaze begin to subside in the canopy.

"I've got the fire!' Fiasco shouted.

Yards from where he floated, Talon's rescue efforts had slowed to a crawl, as he had to gently navigate loosing a minivan that was crushed like an accordion between two sedans. Fiasco couldn't see anyone inside the shattered window, but the careful attention Talon was giving that vehicle meant that someone must have been trapped in the wreckage.

Talon never turned to look at him as he pushed against the car in front of the minivan. A hose inside the hood broke free from the engine, wriggling like a snake, and splashed a steaming liquid across his face, but Talon did not so much as wince. As if impervious to pain, his hand pushed against the crumpled trunk of the other vehicle. Pushing outward, the metal screamed as he decoupled the two vehicles with a stiff grunt.

"You waiting for a prize?" Talon grunted as he pushed. The strain of his effort made the back of his arms ripple. "Don't just float there like some pansy, get the other people out. I'm busy here!"

Fiasco searched around, looking down at his gleaming hands, wondering how he was supposed to help more. The fire still was not quenched beneath the dome, and his power was currently indisposed trying to snuff it out.

"What am I supposed to use, my dick? I'm trying to quench the fire!" Fiasco shot back. The dome around the fire flickered from his bout of anger. He knew it was not the time for levity, but the patronizing tone of Talon's voice got under his skin.

Talon glared over his shoulder from the remark. Rain dripped down from his stiff, square jaw that was clenched tight. "You have two hands," Talon said through his teeth. "People are dying, so yes, use your dick if you have to."

Fiasco could feel the resentment even though they were several feet apart. He stared at his hands. Eyes fixed, he put one hand atop the other, transferring the strand attached to his right in the left gauntlet. Moving his right hand out slowly, he watched to ensure that the dome did not waver in strength. The power glimmered about the left glove like a blue star as he freed his right hand, and he pumped it full of spare energy, so much that he could not see the fingers beneath the brightness. Although Talon's acrimony was not appreciated, he did have a point. The extent of the fire had caused so much trepidation within Fiasco, that it never occurred to him it would take only one hand to tame it.

Because, below the surface, you are stupid, the voice said. *And a coward.*

Fiasco nodded in agreement.

Behind his goggles, he closed his eyes and began to concentrate. He fixated on the malice and disappointment in Talon's tone, and the fact that the voice had nailed its assessment of his abilities yet again. The energy burned just under the skin of his chest from the negativity, then flooded into his arm, down to his free hand.

Blue tendrils curled outward from the tips of his fingers. Weaving the lines through the wreckage, Fiasco's face was tight with deep concentration. Using the lines, he probed for trapped survivors. Beyond the point where Talon had finally freed the crushed minivan, the strands felt along a vehicle that had slammed into the metal guardrail. White smoke steamed from the caved-in engine, and the tires were ribbons of shredded rubber on gnarled rims. There was a child in the backseat, his shouts muted as his tiny fist beat against the cracked glass.

The stench of oil, gas, and smoke flushed through his aura as Fiasco floated closer to the wreck, dragging a thick line from his left hand that held the dome tight over the fire. The tendrils on his right hand melted together just outside of the window that refused to give.

"Get down!" Fiasco shouted.

He wasn't sure the kid could hear him over the distance and rain, but he seemed to have put things together, and his little head ducked down into the back seat. Fiasco's fingers pressed together into a pyramid. The blue energy curled into a muscled cobalt fist with the middle knuckle protruding outward as it tightened. Fiasco flicked his wrist and the blue knuckle lightly tapped on the glass that splintered outward from where it struck. He flicked his wrist again, and the glass tumbled inward, falling under its own weight. Fiasco cupped his hand upward, and the energy fist responded, cupping the bottom of the empty windowsill through the broken glass.

Sweat mingled with the rain and streamed down into Fiasco's suit as he pulled back with his arm, straining enough not to rocket the remaining glass fragments at the boy inside. Glass tumbled down and slid into the cab regardless, and Fiasco cursed beneath his breath. With another tug, the door finally gave and peeled back like the edge of a book cover. Rain dropped on the fabric of the now exposed back seat. Nothing moved in the car.

Then, as Fiasco held his breath, he saw a small head with stringy brown hair peak out. His glowing fist almost disappeared completely from the sudden elation of the sight. Looking about as if lost, the boy climbed carefully over the glass, passed the ruined door, dirty and with blood on his knobby knees. Fiasco wondered why he turned back inside until he saw the child guide his frightened sister towards him. Her yellow dress was stained with dirt, and her brother held her beneath the armpits so she could make the small jump down to muddy ground.

"Well done, kid," Fiasco thought.

After checking the dome, Fiasco repeated the effort on the passenger door, peeling it back off the latch until he could reach inside. His hand flattened and overturned, and the powered fist mirrored his movement. It shrank and cooled with his mental command as he pushed his shoulder and slid the hand gently inside the cab. Through the power, he felt around and touched a body slumped towards the door on the driver's side. The body wasn't flushed completely against the door but seemed to hang like a marionette on its stand. The tendril-like fingers played through what felt like long hair. He reached further inside and discovered another face slumped against the steering wheel horn that failed to beep. In his mind, he imagined a woman— likely the kids' mother— pressed against the father who was slouched on the driver's side, both unconscious from the crash.

Slowly, he closed his fingers. His forehead itched as it furrowed in determination, moist with sweat and chafing against his leather mask. The aura had kept him relatively dry below, but the deluge of rain obscured his field of vision.

"Use the energy," he thought. "It's a part of you."

He felt around with the glowing hand, and gently slipped blue fingers around the father's torso. Sensing through the light, his breaths were shallow, but at least he was still breathing. The thumb on the glimmering hand stretched and curved beneath the woman's arm and over her chest. Fiasco lifted the two and floated back inches above the wet pavement as he slowly pulled back his arm. Lightning strikes of pain shot through his shoulder from the combined weight. Beneath his forearm, the curve of the gauntlet dripped down to the ground, acting like a crutch that kept the manifested hand steady. Slowly, he pulled the couple out, ensuring that his hand projection did not scrape against the skin piercing metal remnants of the door he had torn off.

Rain hissed as the fist reached open air. Once the pair were safely outside the door, he opened his palm to lay them flat along the cold, wet asphalt. The woman rested atop her husband, splayed out like two sleeping dolls, as rain assailed their bruised faces.

"Mom!" The boy yelled as Fiasco recalled the hand back toward him. The husband stirred first, then the mother followed, startled awake by the shower. The boy held his little sister by the hand. Small splashes parted the accumulated rain as the children ran to their parents.

"That's one down," Fiasco thought as he separated his fingers and the hand reverted into lines of separate lights. Moving further into the wreckage, the tendrils took the initiative and searched for more survivors.

Take your pedestrian victory and flee. The longer you stay, the more likely you will fail.

Climbing into the sky, Fiasco elevated, stretching the blue strand attached to his left hand to keep the dome intact, gaining a greater overview of the scene. The fire felt all but quenched beneath his dome, so he was able to transfer power from that hand into the other, sending out more tendrils that snaked out of his fists to double his rescue efforts. Talon handled the most critical accidents, while Fiasco cloned his efforts several more times, dealing with the things Talon couldn't attend to. The survivors mostly tended to each other as he probed over fender benders and light scrapes further at the end of the crash. After what felt like hours, he and Talon's work seemed complete, and Fiasco allowed himself to finally relax while floating back to the earth.

A puddle of rainwater rippled away beneath Fiasco's feet as he touched down on the pavement. With his aura fully restored, rain steamed upon touch. Looking left to right, Fiasco scanned for something he could have missed in the wreckage, until a screeching noise pounded against his eardrums.

"What the hell was that?" Fiasco said aloud. The ear-splitting shriek was loud enough to pierce his aura shield, raising the hair on the back of his neck as he searched about for the origin of the noise.

The small lapse of concentration was just long enough for the dome around the fire to disappear in a blink. The strands of lights he had out among the wreckage followed suit, breaking apart like ash before fading away. Heat escaped from beneath the bell and rushed over his body like a wave. Ashen colored smoke followed the heat and hung low like a pungent mist that stung his nose.

When the cloud had thinned enough for him to see the dark outline of wrecked automobiles through the haze, he searched around to find where that unnerving sound had originated. A fortunate gust curled more smoke into the heavens, further clearing the bridge, and it didn't take long to find the perpetrator of the sound.

"There you are," Fiasco thought.

In his efforts to quickly rescue survivors and shut Talon up, Fiasco had forgotten about the oil truck that had broken through the guardrail. Fresh rubber on the wet street said that either a tire had moved, or the weight of the cab that tottered over the edge had lurched the truck forward. The noise he heard came from the oil barrel whose gash on the side had ripped open even further when the truck slid forward. Black oil streamed like a faucet onto the road. The pounding rain, or pure blind luck, was all that kept a single spark from igniting, taking the bridge, injured survivors, and himself along with it.

Move, you loser, the voice said. Fiasco responded. With both hands outstretched before him, he shot a concentrated beam of blue energy at the guardrail.

"Watch the heat," he reminded himself, sending out a mental command to cool the temperature of his power, fearing it may ignite the fuel. The glowing hand he used to rescue just moments ago reformed at the end of his beam. He parted his arms, and the manifestation separated in two.

"Two hands are better than one," he quipped to calm his nerves. "Going to need them both to pull this off."

The tendril on his left hand plunged inside the hole on the side of the tanker. Inky black spilled onto the ground. With it, Fiasco probed through the sticky black substance, moving slowly until he found the jagged end of the guardrail. A blue light of energy pulsed from the symbol on his chest. It rippled down through his power line so he could blunt the sharp edges. With his other energized hand, he gripped the bent and broken iron guardrail outside of the truck.

Fiasco crouched down, bending at his knees. Then, at the shoulder, he pulled back the tendril inside the tanker. Straining, he almost wanted to drop his aura to let the rain cool his body that seemed to be perspiring from every pore. Rain had made the outside guardrail slippery even to the manifestation, so he released more power, and the glowing fingers clenched down with a crunch for a tighter grip. Buried deep into the earth, the rail shook in its moorings, but held firm.

"Do it," Fiasco said to no one. "Do it yourself, before Talon does it for you."

The left arm that pulled at the rail inside the tanker ached from the effort, but the iron proved far more stubborn than the car doors and refused to budge. It was not until the voice reminded him that Talon was better that Fiasco manifested enough energy to feed into his creation. The metal groaned, then screamed as the rail was bent away from the oil truck. Once the oil drenched guardrail was safely outside of the barrel, Fiasco waved his hand in front of his face from right to left. The movement forced his created hand to bend the rail over on itself until it resembled a twisted candy cane of metal, ensuring that nothing could accidentally strike the match that would ignite the oil.

However, before he could even think of celebrating its extraction, the error of his move became apparent and struck like a bolt of lightning. While the rail had presented a danger of igniting the oil, he realized that its strong moorings were the only thing that kept the truck from sliding off the bridge.

"Ah, hell," Fiasco muttered, his aura shield brightened as his anxiety deepened.

With its wheels sitting on the edge of the bridge, the red cab made one long and slow revolution and that was all it took. Unfettered from its anchor, the truck jostled and lurched forward along the pavement. The mechanism that attached the tanker to the cab lifted like a precarious pyramid. Metal scraped together like rusty knives before the weight and momentum pulled the entire truck forward, bringing it a step closer to plummeting into the river below. Even with the heavy downpour, Fiasco doubted the river was high or deep enough to swallow the entire payload. If it fell, there would be an impact with the sharp, unforgiving stones beneath the water. He could not foresee the consequences, but based on the movies he'd seen, Fiasco predicted an explosion was sure to follow.

"I can fix this," Fiasco breathed.

You will fail.

The rainwater separated before Fiasco as he rocketed inches

above the pavement. Sliding to a halt behind the tanker, and arms outstretched, he shot out gleaming rays of light from each hand. They passed through the air like whips on either side of the tanker, sliding through and over tires and gears on one side, and slithering over the round barrel on the other before they merged at the front of the cab. Heart beating in his ears, he took panicked breaths, before he closed his eyes to think about his past failures to try and conjure additional power. His memory instantly went back to a brawl he had in middle school. He thought back to when children he knew formed a circle to watch a much larger bully extract his payment of blood, raining thunderous blows. The embarrassment he felt from the memory poured more energy into the well.

When you fail, Julianna will be so disappointed in you.

Rain thumped against his goggles, and his shoulders sagged from the thought.

"I know she will," he mumbled.

The crooked *F* on his chest pulsed and flared in a firework of cyan and gray light. The tendrils thickened, crawling, and spreading over the breath of the truck as Fiasco morphed the energy into a shimmering web. The strain of holding the netting felt like it would pull his shoulders out of their sockets, as the truck inched forward in a screech, pulling him along the ground. His memory raced, trying to think of another terrible thought he could mine from the past. Then, a voice from the cab reverberated off the bridge foundation below and sent a sobering chill down Fiasco's spine.

The tanker hung over the bridge like a deflated balloon. The cab of the tanker swayed left and right, rain seeping through the cracks and crevices. A hand frantically waved out of the shattered window, a gold watch glinting off the light of his power.

"Help!'" Fiasco heard a male voice scream inside the cab. He had assumed Talon had rescued the oil truck driver as he passed, but both had missed the man who must have been unconscious inside.

"Get back!" Fiasco shouted at a rain-soaked survivor who had straddled the guardrail to rescue the driver. "That railing could go at any moment!"

He appreciated that the citizen was at least trying, which said much about the people of New Haven, but the truck was already too far over the edge. Looking over his shoulder, the rescue workers were still trapped outside of the wreckage zone, having barely made any progress reaching the bridge. For his own worth, he was far less helpful, since his own power was engaged with both hands trying to keep the truck on the ledge, and his imagination went blank.

The truck jostled forward again, and Fiasco pulled hard against the momentum, fighting gravity that pulled on the tonnage, unsure if he was even making a difference.

"Maybe I should use my dick," Fiasco said through a strained jaw, a reflective reaction he had during crisis— but he couldn't bring himself to laugh.

"Pull it up," a voice said. Talon had saddled up next to him, silent as a cat. He stood there, arms crossed over his barrel chest and one hand holding his curved knife, staring at Fiasco behind that unyielding mask.

Rain slicked his shoulders and leather vest. "Stop thinking and pull it up," Talon continued, his voice a cool, even octave.

It took all the restraint Fiasco had not to lace his friend with a string of extreme expletives. "What are you talking about?" Fiasco asked, his throat sore from the strain the power was putting on his body. "I can't!"

Talon leaned his face in closer. "Yes, you can. Pull it up."

Fiasco ground his teeth as gravity forced his feet over the pavement. The power flickered and wavered as exhaustion drained his reserves. His hands curled to regain a tight grip on the tendrils.

"It doesn't work that way!" Fiasco said. "My power is not

proportional to what I make. Just because the hands are ten times as big doesn't make them ten times as strong. The truck is too heavy!"

That was the way Fiasco understood it and the way it had always been. He was able to take off car doors, but that was a combination of the tools he created and leverage, no different than a small jack's ability to lift a car. He could create a giant fist, or an unimaginative crowbar, but the manifestations he created were still attached to skinny arms.

His eyes stung from the perspiration on his brow. Strands on the webbing about the truck cracked and broke as fatigue set in and his power drained with it. He looked over at Talon, who stood like a statue and had not moved a muscle. Fiasco glanced between him and the truck. More webbing strands cracked and disappeared, and the truck budged.

"Help me! Please!"

The driver's petrified pleas echoed through the canyon, loud enough to be heard over the raging river below. Talon did not move. More New Haven survivors who made it to the east end of the bridge backed away as the tension between the two Megas grew.

"Stop standing there!" The left gauntlet on Fiasco's hand flickered like a light, then disappeared. Now bare, the tendrils from the net cut into the skin. He could smell the burning of his skin as he pulled along the rope. "Talon, he's going to die!"

The right gauntlet followed the left's fate, disappearing in a blink, and Fiasco had to hold the webbing with his bare hands. He dipped his head back, gritting his teeth with one last effort to hold the truck, but knew his efforts were in vain. Skin burned along the glowing rope and curled away. He could feel the power wane further like a candle wick running out of wax to burn. The hand from the cab clutched desperately at the top of the roof as the cab sunk further off the bridge. Fiasco held as long as he could until his aura flickered and died. The webbing around the truck evaporated like smoke and he fell onto the wet pavement with a splash. Landing on his hands, he watched, mouth agape in horror, as the remainder of the oil tanker careened over the side like a can kicked over a ledge.

Metal against asphalt wailed over the Modoc Bridge as the truck twisted onto its side, spilling black liquid gold. The driver's evaporating scream as he fell with the wreckage curdled the blood in Fiasco's veins.

You failed again, the voice reminded him, *and now that man will die.*

The ridicule heated the center of his chest and replenished a small portion of his power reserve. Fiasco told his arms and legs to pick himself up, but tired, exhausted muscles refused to comply, twitching before he fell back into the water with a splash. A mental command tried to reform the aura so he could fly and perhaps save the man inside, but the shield only sparked in starts, unable to stabilize from the dearth of energy. His internal fire had no fuel.

"Please God," he pleaded as he crawled. "Please don't let me let him die."

Fiasco's spine stiffened when he heard a deep splash below the bridge. The sound was followed by the crunching of heavy metal folding in on itself like a car in a compactor. An orange light bloomed from the darkness over the side of the bridge. The ground rumbled beneath his legs, spurring him to rise to his feet. Fiasco reached his hands out again, just as the first flash of orange light burst into the sky. Night turned to morning light and his ears rang from the explosion.

Scorching heat flowed over his restored aura, and a powerful wind pushed him back off his feet. The faces of survivors blurred as Fiasco rushed backward through the air. He reached out with his power, sending it outward, just before he plowed into a wrecked car. Metal scratched his aura like nails, wrapping the iron around his body and eyes, plunging the world into darkness.

In the blackness, Fiasco's heavy breathing pounded rhythmically along with the steady ringing in his ears. The aura had faded completely as he had pushed out the last of his reserves, and he was stuck within the twisted metal that cut into his skin everywhere he dared to twitch a muscle. Tired from the physical exertion, he relaxed in the wreckage, waiting for the remaining heat from the explosion to overtake him, letting his mind wander.

At the very least, they could say that he tried. Julianna would be proud. He chuckled until a beam of metal poked him in the back, piercing skin beneath the costume that sent warm blood trickling down his flesh. Fiasco stilled his body among the tangles. He had laughed because he knew being the town pariah, it was more likely that his efforts would be twisted worse than the wreckage he was trapped in. The scene of dead survivors that he failed to rescue would dominate the headline news, all his prior efforts ignored.

You are Fiasco, after all, the voice chastised, and Fiasco would have nodded in agreement if not for the shard of metal that uncomfortably poked the bottom of his neck.

As his breathing slowed, he heard the first scratches on the metal outside of his tomb. Muscles in his body tensed in preparation for an onslaught of fire and heat. Yet, morbid curiosity kept his eyes open. A hole punctured in the metal, letting in a stream of beige light. More holes followed. Water gathered and trickled when he saw what appeared to be fingers before his face. They gripped and peeled back the metal like a can opener, letting in more light. Sweet, refreshing air, thick with condensation, rushed into the gap. Something strong grabbed him beneath the armpits and pulled him to his feet in one swift motion.

Back on solid ground, Fiasco's legs quivered like jelly as he bent over and tried to hold back the bile that stung his throat. Talon crouched with him, saying words in his face that he could not discern because of the steady ringing in his ears.

"The people," Fiasco coughed and pushed through Talon's arms. "The driver! We have to help him!"

He could feel the heat on his exposed hands. Looking about, he thought that he must have been trapped within the rubble longer than he realized, since a fire truck had arrived on scene. Fiasco forced his legs towards the inferno, even though he knew there was little he could do to help or save the driver anymore.

As he passed, Talon grasped his arm. Fiasco tried to break free, but his fingers were strong. Talon moved between him and the inferno, shouting a string of sentences that Fiasco could not hear.

"What!?" Fiasco shouted and pointed to his head. "My ears, Talon. I can't hear you."

He felt a warm breeze when Talon breathed out in frustration, and grabbed him by the shoulders, forcing his body to turn right. He pointed towards a man who was splayed on the ground. The stranger was surrounded by two people dressed in rain-soaked medical gear who attended to a prominent wound on his forehead. The man clutched at a breathing mask around his nose and mouth, and Fiasco's eyes fixed on the gold watch the man wore that he recognized instantly.

"Is that...," he turned to Talon. "Is that the driver from the truck?"

Talon nodded and flashed a thumbs up at the man, who gave a weak one in return. The ground felt like water and Fiasco had to clutch his knees to stay upright. Somehow, after he lost the truck in his webbing, Talon must have turned on his incredible speed, sweeping over the truck in a blur, and rescued the man before the oil truck crashed into the riverbed. He never knew Talon could move that fast— not at Mega-level speed, at least— but as time went by in their friendship, he noticed that there were many things Talon kept hidden behind his mask.

Or he has proven, yet again, the significant gap between your abilities, the voice mocked.

"I get it," Fiasco thought. "He's better than me." The power burned in his chest and flowed upward. His ears tingled and crackled as the energy went about healing his damaged eardrum from the blast. Slowly, he was able to hear and comprehend the ambient sounds.

"...and I was able to get him out." Talon's voice sounded like he spoke through a plastic cup, but he could at least hear him again. "That barrier you made was quick thinking, Crooked F."

"Barrier?" Fiasco asked.

Talon turned back to him and crossed his arms over his chest. The rain had finally started to subside, but Talon was soaked to the bone. Somehow, he still looked like a statuesque God.

He looks far better than you. Julianna would love to trade up. Fiasco nodded begrudgingly.

Talon continued, his voice clearer with each passing second. "From what I could gather, you put up a barrier right when the blast reached the bridge," he nodded to where firefighters looked as if they had gained control of the blaze with the aid of the rain. "You must have funneled it away from the people and pushed it back over the river."

The evidence was there to support Talon's assessment. The scorch marks on the pavement pointed away from him like charred arrows. Leaves on the trees beyond the bridge were crisp and burned. A large portion of the asphalt where the truck had fallen over the bridge had been destroyed. Loose pieces of asphalt broke off the edges and fell into the conflagration below. Cracks from the edge widened as they webbed toward where he and Talon stood. The guardrails were ripped outward over the edge of the bridge, charred, and melted black, dripping with water. Around the bridge, the cars had been blown back from the gust that had knocked him off his feet, but there was clear delineation of damage where he manifested the barrier just before he burrowed into the car. Survivors glowered at him with wide-eyes and dirty faces that looked more scared of him than thankful. Yet, their hearts were still beating.

"So, I saved these people?" Fiasco asked as he wiped the rainwater from the portion of his face exposed beneath his mask.

Talon shrugged nonchalantly. "Apparently. But who is to say the blast would have even made it this far?"

Fiasco lowered his head. "Jerk."

"I heard that."

"I know. I wanted you to."

The power had healed him enough that Fiasco could finally stand upright. The urge to celebrate was almost overwhelming, but his triumph was marred by failure. The power inside swelled when he remembered that the driver of the truck had almost died because of his negligence and weakness. Rage almost quenched it when he remembered why the man was in such jeopardy to begin with. He looked up into Talon's blank white eyes. Talon smirked when he saw the recognition appear on Fiasco's face. Talon had left that poor driver hanging for a purpose he could not even begin to comprehend. But, before he could confront the Mega, Talon turned away and ran at high speed. Legs pumping, the leather vest flapped like a flag behind him as he hopped the tall firetruck in one powerful leap and disappeared behind it, leaving Fiasco alone on the bridge in a matter of seconds.

NHPD officers shouted and scrambled when they noticed Talon's exit. Unable to stop him, they pointed and walked towards Fiasco, angry. They shouted questions and instructions at Fiasco in one breath. Unable— but more likely unwilling to explain why he failed— Fiasco let the power flow outward like rolling fire from his chest, down into his legs, and over his arms until his aura returned. The power melted on his hands and the gauntlets returned, thick and shimmering a bright blue.

"Fiasco!" he shouted, his aura burning away the water beneath his feet as he took off straight up into the sky.

He cleared the Modoc Bridge like a bright blue train, speeding east towards New Haven. The sky was still dark with rolling gray clouds. The cool wind he let in through his aura felt refreshing, removing the stench of smoke and fire. He scanned the surrounding plains that were covered in darkness. It felt as if Talon had only just left the crash site before him but had already covered a significant distance. It took several minutes just to catch up to the Mega running below.

The night lights of a sleepless New Haven already loomed in the distance as Talon ran below him, his black boots splashing in the highland field thick with mud. He wasn't a Speedstra, a Mega whose main power was speed, but judging from the distance Talon had already covered, he definitely was in the enhanced category. Fiasco concluded he must have been at least a Delta or Charlie Mega speed.

"That answers the question of whether he could play in the Mega league," Fiasco thought. "Just how fast are you, Talon? And what else are you hiding?" The advantage of flight worked in his favor as he let the power feed his own velocity. "Only one way to find out," he thought as he sped forward, passing over his friend.

An unfamiliar sensation of apprehension seized his heart, as if he were afraid of the looming confrontation. It was something he found absurd, since Talon was his sometimes partner and long-time friend. He stamped the feeling deep down and arched like a rainbow toward the ground feet first. Letting the aura around his feet grow, he sliced trenches into the brown, muddy earth, turning on his heels to stop. Mud splashed about, hardening to chunks that slid off his aura shield in pieces. Fiasco looked up. Talon had stopped several feet from him, glaring, and with his strong arms held behind his back. He wasn't out of breath in the slightest.

"Nice Mega-hero pose there, Crooked F," he said. That bright, golden smile returned to Talon's face for the first time that night, but he still held the same intense gaze from the bridge. "Too bad you're not one."

The myriad of feelings Fiasco experienced at that moment ranged from happiness from saving lives, to sadness from failing the driver when the chips were down, and to anger at Talon for not helping him when he could. All the emotions played with his power level, causing it to fit and start. Sparks of blue power jumped from the crooked symbol on his chest and from the gloves on his hands. Muddy pools of water hissed and popped as he stomped towards Talon.

Unnerved, Talon flexed his arms held firmly behind his back as Fiasco approached. "I see you, Crooked F," he said in a cool tone.

Fiasco stopped just over a foot away from him and looked up into his eyes. Wet, black streams of hair fell on Talon's face, but the white screens on his eyes gave no hints of what he was truly thinking.

"I should hero pose you right in the face!" Fiasco said. It made no sense, but it felt good to say. Talon's lips pursed and his head tilted mockingly to the side as if offering his jaw.

He is not afraid of you at all.

"What the hell was that back there?" Fiasco continued. He ignored the voice. No matter what the circumstances were, he and Talon had shared the fire together. Respect was Fiasco's desire, not fear, and that began with the truth about why he almost let him get a man killed.

Talon's smile faded.

"You should have pulled him up," he said, repeating his line from the bridge.

"You told me to use both my hands. I did." Fiasco flexed his hands in Talon's face, letting the power dim enough to show him the scars on his palms that were still healing. "I was using both hands just to keep it from falling. How the hell was I supposed to pull up a two-ton vehicle!"

"With your arms."

He is mocking you.

Fiasco looked towards the sky and bit his lip so hard he thought he could break the skin. "I told you, it doesn't work like that! I don't physically become stronger the stronger my power gets."

Talon leaned in; his eyebrows cocked up. "Are you sure about that?"

The aura around Fiasco dimmed, since all he could feel was annoyance from the conversation. The 'I know your power better than you do' act was old at that point and grated on his nerves.

"Yes," Fiasco replied, his jaw clenched. "I am sure."

Talon leaned back. He pulled the hair away from his eyes, then rubbed his wet chin with his thumb and forefinger.

"Interesting," he said as he paced slowly around Fiasco. "So, tell me. When you are not powered up like you are now, can you rip car doors off the hinges like you did back there?" Fiasco swallowed hard about to answer, but Talon interrupted. "Better yet, can you pull that guardrail back with your bare hands, too?"

Fiasco looked at the ground. His shoulder still throbbed even though the power had sent a healing wave. Back at the bridge, he saved those people, and he pulled off those car doors to do so. But he couldn't take the credit. It would make more sense to credit the voice who fueled the energy.

"No, I can't," he finally said. "But that was the power and use of leverage, not me."

Talon sighed. It was the second time that night he seemed disappointed. "The power is you. An extension of you. You keep holding yourself back."

"Even if what you think is true, and it's not by the way, but even if it were. You compare doors to a truck?" Fiasco replied, his voice rising as he flustered. "No, not even just a truck. An actual tanker truck! With a tank full of oil. Get out of here, Talon!" Fiasco turned in a circle, then turned back again and pointed a finger. "I'm sorry to disappoint you, but I don't have that much power."

Deep down, he wished Talon was correct, that he could scale his power up by his manifestations, but the truth was the truth. There may have been an upper limit to his strength but pulling a tanker laden with thick heavy oil that was pulled by gravity as it leaned off the bridge was far more than what he could muster.

"Besides," Fiasco continued. "I'm street level, at best! The powers I have work with what I have to do."

Talon stopped before him. His mask crimped with his face, and the white screens on his eyes widened. "Street level?" he said.

"Yeah, like Wargone, or Redemption. Or even Salomon in Detroit. I go after the druggies, the drunk drivers, and occasionally robbers. We've done it together, in fact. You know what I'm about. It's not every day I'm asked to toss up a tanker."

"That was training," Talon rubbed the bridge of his nose, then looked back at him. "You really only see yourself that low? The street is your ceiling?"

It was a surprising question. Fiasco had never thought about going further as a Mega. They were in the Northwest. In New Haven, which was not even a major city, the rain was the greatest threat on most days. No Mals ever came to their neck of the woods, and he couldn't care to go to someone else's backyard to chase them down either— especially when he still failed at just being street level. The goal now was to impress Julianna, not the city, or the world for that matter. They never cared about him anyway.

"Do you know how much a fully packed medium tanker weighs?" Talon asked.

With his brain already tired and fatigued, Fiasco blurted out the first number he could think of.

"I don't know Talon," he said with exasperation. "I said two tons earlier."

"You need to read more," Talon said, mimicking the insult his parents would often say. "There are three types of trucks: heavy, light, and medium. That there was a medium truck, and fully loaded like you said. Well, nearly. Add the weight of the cab, and that's about twenty-five or twenty-six thousand pounds in total."

"So, two point six tons. Who cares?" Fiasco said.

Talon flinched back. "I can't even tell if you're pretending to be this dumb, but for the life of me I can't understand why you would want to." Then his face hardened, and he crossed his arms again— a gesture that Fiasco started to feel was condescending. "Twenty-six thousand pounds is around thirteen tons. If your power was not proportional, then your arms should have been pulled from your shoulders the minute you grabbed that net you made."

"That...that can't be right," Fiasco stuttered, but the analysis made sense. When he held the webbing on Modoc Bridge, it had felt as if his arm were being pulled from his body. He could almost hear the sinew being torn apart. He flexed his arms, which were sore at the elbows and biceps. Yet, there they were, whole and fully functional after holding up thirteen tons.

It was adrenaline. The heat of the moment.

"Was it though?" Fiasco thought. He questioned the voice, which never worked out in the past, and his faded aura was the result.

Yes, responded the voice, succinct and matter of fact. *You cannot replicate that success, nor should you try.*

Talon cocked an eyebrow and smirked. "What happened to all that power you had a few minutes ago? Did I shock you that much?" He laughed and walked towards him, each step sloshing in the mud. "If that got you, think about this. Your power... those things you make."

Fiasco looked up and cleaned the rain off his white goggles. "My manifestations."

Talon shrugged. "Okay, manifestations. They come from your imagination, right? What you conjure in your mind, they form?"

"Yes," Fiasco replied. He did not want to tell him how his power really worked. He did not want to tell him how the voice denigrated and berated, and how he fed off the emotion it churned. He had his own secrets to keep.

"So, if you can create what you think, and you didn't feel like you could pull up that tanker, then why did you just create a net?"

The question brought a grin to Fiasco's face. Talon had overreached in his judgmental assessment. The energized net he had manifested had covered the entire truck, and even he had already admitted earlier that it had saved it. Yes, a net was simple and crude, but it had worked. Besides, what exactly did his friend suspect he could do in such a short amount of time anyway?

"I had two seconds to think, and the net was the best I could do. Even you said it kept the truck up, so what's the big deal?" Fiasco countered, his voice confident that he had already won the argument.

"I also said you had two hands. You could have enhanced the net and held up that truck with one hand, while creating a crane or wench to pull it back up with the other. Or more arms and hands to push it back onto the bridge. You can fly, you know."

Fiasco's jaw tightened, not purely in anger, but more out of embarrassment and shame. Talon had got him again. He had pegged him correctly when he said that he never studied. In his off time being Fiasco, or even on the toilet, he could have looked at pictures of various useful objects, studied their form and structure, and practiced creating the manifestations. The embarrassment only grew in intensity when he wondered why it took a man to almost die before he thought to do so.

Because you are lazy, the voice said. *And you would have failed if you tried.*

Talon chortled and smiled. "Even behind those cheap goggles, I can see that I blew your mind again." He slapped a large hand on Fiasco's shoulder as he passed him by and walked towards New Haven. "It's okay. It took someone telling me something similar before I thought outside the box as well. You just think about that, Crooked F, because you need to get better."

Fiasco watched Talon's back as he walked away, the bird on the leather looking as if it would take off towards him. His friend had read him correctly, almost more apt than the voice. He had broken him down to the core. The bridge was not a triumph as it appeared and felt, but it was yet another loss. A defeat. A failure of his imagination and creativity. The voice was right; he was lazy. Nothing Julianna should be proud of.

Fiasco is what you are, the voice said, and Fiasco nodded.

The clouds swelled above, and the rain started up again. Feeling the first drops tap a drumbeat on his mask, Fiasco used the hurt, shame, and embarrassment to ignite his aura. The gauntlets returned to his hands, and he looked up at the dark gray sky that continued as far as he could see into the horizon.

"Hey, this rain is only going to get worse," he shouted at Talon. "Do you need a lift?"

New Haven was still miles away and the rain threatened to turn into a downpour. Talon crouched and his muscles tensed as he prepared to run again. He looked back over his shoulder, his mask emotionless and cold, and replied, "No. Do you?"

Interlude

Julianna's head felt light as a feather as she laid in Kevin's lap. His apartment was dark, except for the light coming from the television, its luminescence flickering off Julianna's face. As they watched the news, stock footage of the New Haven construction site filled the screen. With his left hand, he played with her soft, black hair, twisting long strands between his fingers down to her scalp like she insisted. With his free hand, Kevin massaged her shoulders, kneading out the knots of stress beneath her skin. Whenever her shoulders trembled again, he stopped the massaging and ran his hand up and down her arm. When the scene on the television faded into news anchors, their fingers interlocked on the curve of her hip. He pulled her hand to his lips and gave the top a kiss. Looking down, he delicately swept away the errant strands of hair that fell into the tears that trailed from her eyes.

"It'll be alright," he whispered in her ear. The power that roiled inside like a tumult said otherwise. He let the heat the power projected caress Julianna, hoping the warmth would provide some additional comfort.

Julianna sniffed. "I know," she said in a soft tone, but he didn't truly believe she meant it.

Most of the channels in New Haven told the same story that sent a pall over the city. Watching it again for what felt like the hundredth time, Kevin grew tired of the stale format on each channel. Two smartly dressed news anchors sat at a desk, their faces thick with makeup, both speaking with low, depressing voices, as if a national figure had passed away. That small square box that floated between their shoulders showed aerial footage of the Modoc Bridge that was taken from a helicopter as it circled the damage. He desperately wanted to pick up the remote and switch the channel or turn off the television completely. Then, he could take Julianna up into his arms and do something to lift her spirits. But the TV continued to play, grinding her down with its negativity.

The warmth in his lap escalated and Kevin lifted his hands as she squirmed to readjust. The hands hovered over her body, hesitant to re-establish the touch. In the end, he knew it was his alter ego's fault she was so distraught, and guilt consumed him as he realized the irony in providing her with comfort.

Noticing his distance, Julianna reached and pulled his hand back onto her hip. "Don't forget the hair," she said, voice cracking.

"Okay, Jay," Kevin replied, interlocking strand between his fingers.

"It's with a heavy heart that I say again," the leader anchor, Gwen Winston of WNHZ began, using the same phrase she had used the past three hours that made Kevin want to send a muscled blue fist through the TV screen. "The damage to the Modoc Bridge has been severe on highway one-twenty-six," she continued.

The small box over Gwen's shoulder expanded to cover the breadth of the screen. It was daylight when the footage was taken, long after Fiasco had left. The highway was damp from rain. The helicopter panned the charred wreckage in a slow semi-circle and lingered on the blackened hole where the oil truck had exploded upward like a volcano. In the light of day, Kevin noticed how extensive the blast truly was when the char on the pavement extended across nearly all four lanes.

The sear dominated the highway, except the area where he had created the barrier and saved several lives. Those lives mattered little to the media, not when the camera panned down to the web of support structures beneath the bridge that had taken the brunt of the blast. The pillars were blackened, twisted, and melted so severely that it was a miracle they all had not plummeted into the river that night. Since then, engineers had done their best to prop up the bridge in a short amount of time. They used concrete girders that leaned at an angle against the bottom of the bridge, down to the river that had calmed from the downpour, to keep the bridge upright. It was a stopgap until more permanent measures could be taken, but the damage was already done.

Gwen's annoying voice continued to speak over the footage.

"Not only has Modoc Bridge been closed indefinitely to incoming and outgoing traffic, but it is estimated that it will cost the city of New Haven millions in repair costs. This will affect the local economy, as imports will have to take highway ninety-seven, a route that will add additional tax and fuel costs for the foreseeable future."

"This is depressing," Julianna said through the frog that choked her throat. She dabbed a napkin at her pink eyes, swollen from tears.

"You want me to change it?" Kevin replied, hoping she would say yes, but she only shook her head in his lap.

"And the bad news does not end there," the insufferable Gwen continued, pouring salt into the wounds. Air blew out from Kevin's lips, and he couldn't help but think that there was a hidden glee behind her solemn expression. Negativity sold, and the local media was at the trough eating it up like starving hogs. "City officials are meeting at noon tomorrow to discuss the future of New Haven's Mega league team. Not only will the repair of the bridge cost millions, but the construction supplies also lost in the explosion have brought the stadium construction to a standstill."

Kevin wiped his face, sweeping the warmth over his nose.

Everyone involved in the stadium's construction, which appeared to be half the town given the uproar, were affected by the news. The travel industry that would have exploded with the new team was now just a fading memory. Mega league shirts became worthless overnight and acted as a stinging reminder of the loss. Citizens who had begun filing for new businesses, such as restaurants and gift stores in anticipation of the new fans and crowds, had their hopes dashed as well.

Worst of all, Josep, Julianna's father, was the lead foreman on the project, and was put on suspension until the city decided what they were going to do moving forward. The stress from that loss of income had descended on her parents' house, so much that Julianna had spent two nights at his apartment, testing the limits of her Christian values. All the while, he had to hide from the love of his life that it was his fault her home life was now in shambles. It was another lie forced into their relationship by his failure.

"Hero or hooligan?" said Brian, the co-anchor to Gwen. He wore a smug expression as he segued the news story to discuss his alter ego. "Many in New Haven blame Fiasco, the local Mega who botched yet another rescue." He pompously shuffled papers on the desk, and Kevin seethed inside as the footage switched again to a shaky camera that replaced Brian's smirking visage.

"As you can see from the footage, the Mega held up the oil tanker, trapping it in some net. Then, inexplicably, he let it plummet into the river below. This was followed by a spectacular explosion that damaged the legendary Modoc Bridge."

"No mention of Talon standing right next to me," Kevin thought.

It was the same footage they had played since the news of the construction suspension broke, taken by a survivor who was several yards away. The footage was exceptionally convenient for his partner, filmed at an angle that blocked Talon out of the shot by the shadow of another survivor looking on. The image was dominated by the blue light that gleamed off his leather mask, reflecting off his goggles like fire on glass. It also caught his embarrassingly thin frame that did not fill out his costume, and his skinny arms that struggled to hold his net manifestation. Then the image shook. The orange explosion blossomed outward and dropped the cameraman off his feet with a curse word just before his barrier would have gone up. The screen reverted to Brian with his mouth turned up and his head shaking slowly at the camera.

You looked pathetic in that footage. Kevin nodded in agreement.

"I hate him," Julianna said, as she wiped another tear from her eye. Her tone was full of poison that he did not know she possessed.

"Who? Brian?" Kevin replied. "Yeah, me too. He looks like a prick."

"No, not him," Julianna sniffed. He looked down and noticed that her face had hardened around her eyes and mouth. "Fiasco."

"Oh," Kevin replied softly. "Yeah. I hate him, too."

"Good," she replied.

Tell her about Fiasco now, the voice taunted.

"Ethan said he has access to that network the Megas use," she started.

"Who's Ethan?" Kevin interrupted.

"Ethan," Julianna replied in a tone as if he should have known who he was. "The guy always following Warren around."

"Oh yeah, him." Kevin replied. "And what did he say?"

She sniffed, using the napkin on her reddened nose. "Well, he said he has access to that Mega site, and he said the rumor is that Fiasco is such a loser because he's ugly and can't get laid. And that makes him go out into the field drunk and high. That's why he's such a screw up."

"Well, what does Ethan know about anything?" Kevin said.

Slowly, anger bled into the well of power Kevin kept inside. The tips of his fingers cooled from the loss, even though he knew what

Ethan said was a lie. The gorgeous woman lying over his legs proved that lie. Kevin breathed out to let the power drown the anger. The heat returned to his fingers, and he rubbed them along Julianna's arm. He was there for her, and nothing else.

Looking down, he noticed how the story Julianna told about Fiasco had made her feel better by the slight smile on her lips. "But I guess anything is possible right?" he continued.

"Well, I hope he burns in hell for what he's done to my father," Julianna said, mirthless. She turned over towards him, and he could see the tears accumulate in her light brown eyes. "I'm glad I'm here with you," she said. "I don't know how I would get through this without you."

"I'm your guy," Kevin replied. He tried to sound strong, to be there for his girl, but inside, his heart had sunk to his feet for being the cause of her discomfort. "I'll always be here for you when you need me, Jay. Always."

A smile sprinted on her face as she leaned up from his lap to share a warm kiss. When they parted, Julianna's hand caressed the side of his face. She looked at him directly in the eyes, her own shining with tears.

"I love you, Kevin Jones," she said.

Since she had met his parents, the words declaring her love seemed to come easier to Julianna. Every time she said them, they almost became easier to hear and believe. Kevin tried to smile back at her, but failed in his attempt, shackled by the truth: The pain she felt was his fault alone.

"I love you, too," he managed to say. "No matter what happens to us, I hope you always remember that Julianna."

The colors of the television projected on her face once more when she leaned back in his lap.

"What do you mean by what happens to us?" she questioned. Her eyes studied his face and her brow creased when she didn't find the answer she was searching for. Her hand went up between them. "You better not be breaking up with me, Kevin Jones, because seriously, I can't take that right now."

"Of course not," Kevin assured her. He rubbed her arms with his hands. "I'm just saying, sometimes I just think…"

His voice trailed off. He looked into her brown eyes with her black lashes stuck together by tears and couldn't bring himself to say aloud that sometimes he thought she deserved better. It wasn't often he thought about such things, but the frequency had increased, especially since he became aware of his mother's ultimatum. The doubt he felt continued to roll like a freight train after he took up the Fiasco name again. The consternation of her face told him that perhaps she sensed what he was going to say, and he knew that the way she nervously bit her lip was a sign that she did not want him to say it.

"Never mind," Kevin continued. There was an expectant pause as Julianna seemed to wait for him to change his mind.

"Well, I'm glad we're not breaking up," Julianna finally said with a laugh, giving him a sharp but playful poke into his side that made him squirm. Looking down, her fingers played with a piece of lint on his shirt. "You know you can tell me anything, right?"

His fingers ran down through her hair. "Yes," Kevin replied.

She did not return his gaze, still playing with his clothes, but said, "It's just, sometimes, every once in a while, I feel like there is more you want to say."

Kevin's eyebrows twitched from her words. Was it true what they said about women's intuition? That it might as well be classified as a Mega power when they could sense something wrong with their partner? He thought he had done a better job keeping that portion of his life hidden from her.

What is done in the dark will always come to light.

With his thumb and index finger, Kevin raised Julianna's chin to look into her eyes. "There's nothing, Julianna," Kevin assured her. *Another lie.*

"Either way, we've grown too close for me to ever lose you now. I'll always want you in my life, Kevin Jones." She waited for a reply again before letting out a heavy breath.

"You really mean that?" Kevin asked, surprised, but pleased by such a definitive statement.

As comforted as he felt at that moment, the Fiasco in him noticed her use of the words *either way*. They drilled through the good will of the words that preceded them. Kevin wondered if it was possible that she too, thought about ending their union?

"Yes, I mean it," her smile dropped a tear from the corner of her eye that trailed down her cheek. "It's strange to say this. I mean, we haven't even been together a year and I normally don't move this fast. But I feel like we've known each other all our lives, you know? Plus, I've told you more things than I've ever told anyone else. We share all this time together and I don't get tired of you. We share all this space, too, and you don't get tired of me."

She laughed and nodded toward the hallway. "You practically let me move in here to get away from my parents, even though I know you prefer your time alone. I'm just trying to say that you're the best friend I've ever had. I want you in my life any way that I can get you, Kevin."

"And I promise that I will be in your life for as long as you put up with me," Kevin chuckled, but the guilt of her pain quickly quenched the joy.

"I feel the same way, and I'm sorry, you're going through all of this now," he looked away, feeling a peculiar emotion build up. He did not know what to label the sensation, but he felt it burn behind his eyes. "I'm sure your father will get his job back."

"I hope so," she said softly and glanced at the television that had looped back to the beginning of the broadcast.

"He will," Kevin said, slouching down to look into her eyes. "What else are we going to do with that gigantic hole in the middle of nowhere?"

Her brown eyes fluttered upward before she said, "New Haven's first-ever waterpark?"

"In this climate?" Kevin's eyebrows checked up. "It's more likely to fill with rainwater and become the world's largest mudhole."

"At least we'd be known for something," Julianna replied, the widening grin brightening her eyes. "We can even take all that useless league memorabilia, slap an M on it, and call it the New Haven Mudhole. Then at least we could sell it as a collectible?" Her pink lips parted with a satisfied grin.

Kevin nodded as the two shared a laugh, amazed that she had indeed been paying attention to his infantile but satisfying hobby of collecting anything that could be considered a collectible.

"I really do love you, Julianna Jove." He said with the utmost sincerity. She was not the only one to whom the words came easier to as time went on, and whatever emotion it was that made his eyes burn compelled him to say it once more.

The power that surged inside sent heat to the hand lifting Julianna's chin before he kissed her again. Her lips felt soft against his, warm and welcoming, making his heart race, drowning out the noise from the television. His hand moved to the curve of her hips to pull her in. Her arms wrapped about his neck in kind, her soft body falling into him.

It was without question that Julianna had supplanted Warren in his friendship hierarchy. The baying and ridicule from the guys at work did little to change the fact that God had blessed him with the best possible friend that someone like him could hope to claim, a conviction he felt as their hearts seemed to beat with the same rhythm.

Yes, but she hates Fiasco, the voice said. *And you are the Fiasco in her life.*

They parted, and Kevin gently rubbed away a tear from her cheek with the knuckle of his index finger. Julianna leaned into his hand, still smiling. Given all the damage Fiasco had caused to not only Julianna's family, but to the city as well, he could not begrudge her hatred of the Mega.

Julianna's kind words should have been a salve to his own internal wounds, yet a swell of depression kept the power ebbing through his muscles and veins. It wasn't the hatred for him that permeated the city that hurt. All that acrimony from strangers he would never meet was something he could deal with since he had felt the negative chatter that surrounded Fiasco from the first day he put on the mask. It wasn't the vitriol spewing from the TV either that still had his power churning inside. Julianna's own words were the culprit. It was the smile on her face even though he knew how she truly felt inside that made the depression weigh heavy on his shoulders. It was those eyes that glistened in the television light, shedding tears that came from the pain he caused her with his failure.

Congratulations, the voice said. *You made your best friend cry.*

The Celebrity

It was nearly shoulder to shoulder in the food court of the Blanchet building where Kevin and Julianna worked. Tall, twin tripod stands were on either side of the glass door entrance advertising a sales conference in the gold ballroom, which explained the foot traffic. A cacophony of voices echoed off the high concrete walls, reminding Kevin of an airport wing. The air was thick from the multitude. It also captured the scents and aromas of the chicken shop, sandwich kiosk, salad bar, and other styles of food that populated the food court plaza and held them firm. The mingled scents had Kevin's stomach churning from hunger instead of nausea, but the massive lines that snaked from every counter and around tables crowded with people made them both shy away.

Julianna was next to him, dressed in simple jeans combined with a long-sleeved gray shirt whose frayed ends she twisted in her palms. Her ponytail brushed against her back as she stood on tiptoes, scanning the vendors for the shortest line. Warren and Jenni had already given up on the food court and braved downtown New Haven for an emptier venue, but she wanted to give the cafeteria one last shot. For a moment, it looked as if Ethan Johns was going to stay with them, until Warren pulled him along, knowing that he and Julianna needed their time alone together.

Kevin understood why Julianna wanted to stay in the food court.

She had put on a brave face at work, smiling and talking when she needed to, but he could tell from her sloped shoulders, the missing gleam in her eyes, and the way she played with her hair when she spoke, that her mood was still melancholic from the news of the construction site shutdown. He tried his best to cheer her up in the following days, but it seemed that she had to work it out on her time.

You cannot even be there for her when she needs it, the voice mocked. Kevin reluctantly agreed.

"Doesn't look too promising in here," Kevin said to her. He had to speak louder than usual to talk over the din of voices. Julianna didn't reply right away, still scanning until her calves gave up and she went back down.

"No," she replied. Her lips curled downward. "Maybe I won't eat anything. I'm kind of not even hungry."

If there was any doubt before about her disposition, that comment settled it as far as Kevin was concerned. Her murderous hourglass figure belied the fact, and as much as she tried to hide it when they first started dating, Julianna had a veracious appetite and loved to sample new food. Whenever he ordered something she had not tried before, Julianna would always sneak a piece off his plate when she thought he wasn't looking. When she got caught, she made that same shocked face from the balcony at his party when he caught her drinking that beer. Julianna declining to eat at that moment meant her mood had not improved much at all.

You will always fail her.

Kevin turned away from Julianna to concentrate. His fingers touched his chest, and the internal heat warmed not just the tips, but crept down his fingers into the palm. Counting to ten and breathing outward, he let the energy flow through his extremities to calm the power down. Since news of the suspension, the voice had been relentless in its mockery and degradation, and it took more effort to keep the well of energy at an acceptable level. As if ruled by the devil, it goaded him into prematurely revealing Fiasco to her by creating more energy than he could control, and Kevin knew that no matter what, he could not allow that to happen— not before he was ready.

"Are you okay?" Julianna asked and touched his shoulder. "Is it your stomach again?"

"Yeah, I think I'm just hungry." Kevin stood back up and forced a smile. Her hand almost went to his chest, but he caught it in his and played with her thin fingers. "And I just got a great idea. Let's go to Andy's."

A slick smirk tickled Julianna's lips and her nose wrinkled at the bridge. "Andy's? Your friend's pizza shop?" she said with that glimmer of interest in her voice that Kevin was hoping for. He was happy to see she wasn't so far gone that her favorite food couldn't cure the doldrums.

Given his affinity for the place, Kevin knew he should have taken Julianna to Andy's months ago, but a harsh fall and winter weather made the days they could venture there few and far between. Billed as an old school pizzeria, Andy's refused to deliver, sacrificing business to maintain the aesthetic of a family-friendly, walk-in-only restaurant of yesteryear.

Even with the temptation of a fresh pizza, Julianna pulled away from his hand, balancing on the back of her left heel. "I don't know. Isn't it kind of early for pizza? Plus, with your stomach messing up just now. Maybe we should just grab something premade and head back upstairs?" Her face scrunched as she glared at the cold bar of wrapped sandwiches that had to be stale, and the salad that she knew was already wilting.

She sees you as feeble and weak.

"I'm fine!" Kevin replied in a high pitch that made Julianna's eyes brighten. "Believe me, I can take it, so let's go. Besides, I can finally have you taste the perfect pie I have come up with, too."

Her smirk turned into a full-blown smile as she playfully swayed their hands like a swing.

"Oh yeah, the pizza di Jones," she laughed. "What's on it again?"

Kevin licked his lips. "Thin crust of course."

"Of course," she repeated.

Kevin continued. "Delicious thin cut pepperoni that crusts on the edges when cooked. The grease mixes with mozzarella made fresh daily, and spicy tomato sauce as the base. You know, the usual. But there's more." Julianna bit the side of her lip with anticipation, and Kevin reeled her in. He pulled her towards him slowly, staring into her eyes as he continued. "The following layer is slices of pineapple cut into tiny triangles for that bite of sweetness. Atop all of that, there's bacon fried crispy and crumbled all over. To finish it off, the entire pie is drizzled with a barbecue sauce of my choosing. All these flavors blend under an intense three-hundred-and-fifty degrees to crispy perfection."

By the end of his description, Kevin held both of Julianna's hands behind her back. People gave them side-eyed glances and queer stares at the public affection shown in a business setting, but he didn't care.

"I don't know. Do we have time?" Julianna still resisted.

Now part of the I.T. Department, working on the website's graphical design, Julianna was a salaried employee at Blanchet, so her hours varied to her whims. Kevin was still just a bill collector. He worked for eleven dollars an hour— plus commission on bills collected— and had a set timeframe for lunch. Any deviation from that time frame usually meant a reprimand from management. Three reprimands would push his name upstairs where Julianna worked, along with upper management who had little patience for uppity bill collectors breaking the rules.

Kevin chuckled at her concern but still marveled at the fact that she was always thinking of others.

"Well, Warren is the team lead now, and he just left with Jenni to get food, so I think I'm fine," Kevin said. "Plus, we'll get our food fast at Andy's. He's my guy. Trust me."

Julianna leaned back at the waist in his arms. "Is that so? Your guy? Well, now I'm intrigued, Kevin Jones," she said with a giggle. "Lead the way."

When he pushed through the glass doors, fresh, crisp air cooled his face. Outside, the skies were a deep, clear blue, and the afternoon sunlight hit his eyes like a flashlight as he held the door open with his back to let Julianna through.

"M'lady," Kevin said with a low, exaggerated bow. "Your feast awaits."

"Thank you, kind sir," Julianna replied with a coy expression. She held her hands out holding an imaginary dress to perform a curtsy.

Spring had come to New Haven, but the cool seasonal rains had dropped the temperature low enough to make his girlfriend shiver as she emerged onto the sidewalk, rubbing her arms against the cold. Kevin knew his boyfriend duty that Julianna had spent months training into him, and flexed his held-out hand, which she took eagerly into hers.

"Twice in one day you have me showing PDA," Kevin said as he pulled her in close to make her warm. "You're making me soft."

Before their relationship, he had detested personal displays of affection. The sight of a couple walking together as if they were attached at the hip was something he mocked. He always wondered how those men could smile while their space was so encroached by a woman hugging their body, directing where they moved. But when Julianna wrapped her arm around his torso that still ached from the Modoc Bridge incident and pressed her soft body close, Kevin caught a hint of the scent in her hair. With her head resting against his inside shoulder, he knew why the men he mocked in the past could smile so.

The brilliant sunshine had brought an end to a string of rainy days. New Haven citizens reclaimed the streets. Small, northern red oak trees were planted at intervals along the sidewalk, their blood red leaves contrasting with the serviceberry bushes planted in decorative square vases between them. Running his hand through the white petals, Kevin caressed Julianna as they walked with the flow of businessmen and women dressed in smart suits, and afternoon shoppers enjoying the break in weather.

They traveled south down 5th Street against the grain of cars and people traveling north. Citizens had begun to call the area where the Blanchet building resided Old Haven, since it clung to New Haven's small-town roots. Most surrounding buildings were two to four stories, built in a signature rectangular block, neoclassical Palladian style of architecture with red brick and cream-colored mortar keeping them upright like old English homes. Keeping with the architecture, the fronts of most buildings had large square windows, framed by porches that were held up by thick pillars and ivory white archways.

As they kept walking, the street darkened and fell into a shadow. Representing the new New Haven, the monstrous Savoy Tower was several blocks to the west. Nearly complete with fifty stories of modern glass and steel, it gleamed like the bright star it was meant to represent: The symbol of progress and the promise of prosperity. The sun was to its back, and its jagged shadow crept along every corner and side street, looming over Old Haven like a hand claiming its territory.

Heading west in the direction of the tower, the crowd thinned. Kevin nodded at most of those passing by but gave long glares to others. He noticed the side glances, and the jealous eyes leering at Julianna from the men that passed her. Tall or short; black or white;

old or young, it did not matter. Julianna's beauty was universal. They craved her with their looks and hated him with the same eyes.

Normal men may have felt threatened that they could lose their woman to a better man, but this was not the case for Kevin. He coveted the stares and the envy his presence begat. Outside of Julianna, he was just a loser in a low paying job, talking people into paying what they already owed, so there was a sense of pride knowing that they wanted to take her from him. His only regret was that there was no equivalent look from women for Julianna.

The sun grew brighter as they left the shadows of the taller buildings, and Julianna's mood seemed to brighten as well with each street they traveled. They shopped through the windows of the small local stores and thrift shops that lined the historic district as they walked. She always preferred their tight, cozy environments over the big box stores, and loved discovering strange items on their glass shelves.

Only two blocks away from Andy's, she had already identified several stores she planned to return to later, since they were pressed for time. When they reached the restaurant doors, a modicum of her true smile and brightness had returned to her countenance, quieting the cynicism from the voice.

A faded red sign hung over the entrance of the corner restaurant. 'Andy's Red Brick Oven' was painted in white letters, worn down by the harsh New Haven weather. A bell tingled as Kevin pulled out the small wooden door with its white chipping paint and let Julianna in first. Once he followed her inside, his nose was instantly flooded with the smell of freshly baked crusts, assorted meats, and delectable cheeses that made his mouth water.

The interior of Andy's embodied the sense of old New Haven. The floor was parquet pattern in a dull red and white from years of foot traffic. Clear glass spanned the entire left side of the restaurant from floor to ceiling, letting in sunlight. A small bar covered the wall across from them, where patrons sat on red stools that had seen better days, nearly shoulder to shoulder, enjoying single slices of pizza on white paper plates.

The old wooden tables around the restaurant still had fifties-style cloth with red and white squares covered by thin clear plastic over the top. Atop the counter were two enclosed glass cases that rotated already-baked pies on four levels of heated round wired racks. Behind the counter was a large red brick oven, where the restaurant borrowed its name, that glowed a dull orange.

The glower had returned to Julianna's face with the crowded interior threatening to derail any progress from their walk. "This place is almost as packed as the cafeteria," she said, and wasn't wrong.

At the counter, there was a separate register used specifically to order pizza by the slice from the display cases, which seemed to move fast as each slice was pulled and given to the customer within seconds. The main line, however, told a different story. Where Kevin would order his specialty pizza was a column of at least ten customers, their faces miserable as they were forced to wait for each pizza to cook slowly inside the oven.

The bridge of Julianna's nose wrinkled up again when she saw the long line.

"Do you want to just get a slice?" she asked, checking her phone for the time. Kevin could sense the disappointment in her tone but refused to give up the positive gains she had accomplished during their walk.

Kevin grinned. "No, there's no need. I promised you my pizza, didn't I?"

His hand waved above the line of customers to get the attention of the cashier behind the counter. He was a man who looked too old for that position, middle-aged and dressed in an off-white apron stained red in pizza sauce, wearing a red and white triangle hat atop thinning black hair. When the cashier noticed Kevin's waving hand, he tapped the shoulder of another employee behind him. Sweat misted the brow of the man who fed the brick oven with pizza from a long wooden pizza peel when he looked up.

Dressed in the same company attire, he looked like a younger version of the cashier, except with more hair on top. His face was twisted in annoyance from the interruption, until he saw the cashier pointing at Kevin. Recognition brightened his features and led to a smile on the cook's face as he waved in return. With pinched fingers, Kevin pantomimed scooping food to his mouth. The cook nodded then flashed an 'okay' hand sign back towards the couple before going to the ingredients table and rolling out dough.

Kevin returned the gesture, then turned to Julianna. "Done. You want to grab a seat?"

A left eyebrow cocked upward on Julianna's brow. "Well, now I'm impressed. Just a wave of your hand puts in your order," she said. That coy look returned to her face before she turned and led him by the hand towards the window. "You're like a Mega-hero in here."

"Told you. I have connections in high places," Kevin said as he was being pulled along. "I said that you hit the jackpot getting with me."

"Great." Julianna moved their held hand onto her shoulder as she weaved through the tables and said, "Jenni gets a boyfriend that gets made line lead, and my man can get me pizza with a wave of his hand."

He could only see her ponytail bouncing off her back as she walked and could not tell if she meant that comment from her tone. The thought of letting her down as Kevin Jones and not Fiasco nearly made the power rumble inside. It wasn't until she turned around fast in his arm that he saw the wily smirk playing on her lips before he allowed himself to relax.

"I think I got the best of the two," she finished with a chuckle.

Kevin laughed along with her, convincing himself that she meant the words.

At the table, a sweaty busboy finished clearing and cleaning off a table next to the window, his white t-shirt a cheetah print of dark red pizza sauce stains.

"Hey, Kevin," he said when he turned. His arms were laden with a gray plastic bucket that overflowed with red plastic cups, straws, dirty paper plates, and various garbage. Kevin bumped his forearm to his as a greeting.

"Hey, Tony," he said, and pulled a chair out for his girlfriend. "This is Julianna."

"Hi, Tony," she said in a sweet tone before taking her seat. The sun gleamed on her warm brown eyes and highlighted her full, pink lips that shined with a thin veneer.

The contents of the tray rattled as Tony lifted it to simulate a wave.

"Hello," Tony replied. His voice cracked, and he cleared his throat while a flush of red ran up his freckled neck. His green-specked eyes blinked rapidly behind thin glasses. Kevin knew that reaction well. It was the same look he saw on the faces of the men they passed by on the way to Andy's when Julianna's beauty hit like a sledgehammer.

"What are you even doing here, Tony?" Kevin asked as he took his seat opposite Julianna. "Shouldn't you be in school or something?"

Tony cleared his throat again and stopped looking at Julianna long enough to respond. "What? No, I have graduated already."

"Seriously?" Kevin said, truly surprised. It seemed like just yesterday when Tony was the little kid with the crusty nose that wouldn't leave him and Andy Jr. alone back in high school. Whenever they let down their guard, they nearly tripped over the little boy who buzzed around their feet. Now, Tony stood taller than his own meager height, and had graduated out into the world, joining the family business.

Tony's entire face had turned an apple red. "I'm seventeen, Kevin. God, you never remembered my birthday," he muttered then sat the tub down on the next table he was going to clean before walking off.

"They grow up so fast, don't they?" Julianna giggled before unwrapping the paper around her straw and waving the red plastic in his direction. "You're getting up there, old man."

Slipping off a thick, plastic, red ring, she unfolded a wine-colored napkin and spread it over her lap. Grabbing a separate one, she held it out for Kevin, who refused with a head shake. Behind her outstretched hand, she held an unwavering glare that told him what would happen if he allowed a drop of tomato sauce to get on his new work clothes. In return, Kevin's face hardened, crossing his arms over his chest to stand his ground. The brave stand lasted only until Julianna jutted out her bottom lip and tilted her head while slowly blinking those beautiful eyes. It was as if the woman had an innate Mega ability to weaken his resolve just by a simple look.

Kevin breathed out. Wilting under her adorable pout, he took the napkin and removed the plastic ring before stuffing the uncomfortable rag into the top of his shirt. "Dress shirt at work, and now napkins in it. What the heck are you doing to me, Julianna?"

"Making you civilized," she replied with a sly, but alluring gaze.

Tony returned with two red, pebbled, plastic tumblers filled with handmade lemonade. His face was still as red as the plastic straws in the cups. Kevin thought he had embarrassed the young man enough and let him get back to bussing tables without another word. After interlocking his fingers before him, he put his chin on top of his hands and looked over at Julianna who was studying the laminated food menu.

"I don't know why you're looking that over," he leaned in with both elbows on the table. "You are about to taste the best specialty pizza an average human being can concoct in his brain."

Julianna leaned in as well, her arms and breasts pressed against the table's edge. She licked her lips. "That's quite the hyperbolic statement from an average human being. You might be hyping this up too much, don't you think? Maybe it can no longer live up to the crazy standards you've set."

"I'll take my chances," he said below his breath. Julianna leaned in closer, as if inviting Kevin in, when an interruption came along.

"Now kids," Andy Jr. said with a toothy grin as he slid the twelve-inch pie between them. "This is a family restaurant. We'll have none of that funny stuff in here, or else I will have to ask you to leave."

White trails of heat rose from the pizza, mozzarella and red sauce still bubbling in some places. "Damn that was fast," Julianna muttered as she stared down at the pizza and bit the side of her lip.

"Well, we aim to please, ma'am," Andy said. Then, he turned to Kevin, put his hands out and said, "Kevin," in a long, slow drawl.

"Awe, shit," Kevin sighed, and his chair screeched as he stood up, removing his napkin to hug his old friend.

Normally in control of his emotions, joy dimmed his power re-serve inside from seeing the guy who shared the ridicule of growing up in nerd culture with him. The punches and jokes from the cool kids flowed equally between them. They had grown apart in the years since graduation. Andy Jr. was already married, while he was still finding himself with Julianna's help. But those times of trading comics, cards, and action figures, and being chased by crowing bullies while clutching the best of their collections to their chest, had formed a military-like bond that was hard to break.

He gave Andy Jr. a quick but strong embrace. "Hey, while you're here, let me introduce you to Julianna."

"Jules, this is, don't call him junior, Andy. The guy I told you about who took the same beatings I did growing up."

Caught by surprise, Julianna looked up with wide eyes. In the time it had taken Kevin to greet his friend, hug him, and walk to her side of the table, she had already separated the two white paper plates, putting one out for each of them. She had also pulled a steaming slice off the pie that she pinched gently by the crust and balanced on the tip of three other fingers. Seeing that both men were staring at the slice poised in front of her mouth, she put it back down. Embarrassed, Julianna quickly wiped the crumbs from her hands on her napkin, then stood up with a throat clear.

"Hi, Andy, not Junior," Julianna said with her hand held out. "This guy doesn't seem like he has many friends, so I've heard a lot about you two growing up."

Andy let out a hoarse laugh that he developed when they were still children from Julianna's comment. Observing the two shaking hands, Kevin appreciated the fact that his long-time friend had the courtesy to keep his eyes on his girlfriend's face. The jealousy and envy were fine from strangers but was always off-putting coming from a friend.

"Well, it's nice to meet you, too, Julianna," Andy replied. "We were not that popular growing up, were we, Kev? Which you probably already know if you heard the stories." He put his hands on his hips with a soiled rag curled up in his right fist. "Did he ever tell you about the Crutch?"

Julianna glanced at Kevin with a twisted grin, then said, "No, he hasn't. What's the Crutch?"

"Dude," Kevin tried to interject, but Andy's scratchy voice cut him off.

"Crutch is not a what, but a who," he said. "Mark Crutcher was a guy we grew up with. We didn't just call him the Crutch because of his last name, but for a kid, he was built like a tank."

With his hands out to his sides to emphasize the girth, Kevin nodded at Julianna. "Like a bowling ball with muscles," he contended.

"Yeah, and he would leave kids on crutches with that body, too," Andy snorted out a laugh, looking down as if he were picturing the scene before continuing. "One day, the Crutch was just picking on me while we walked. No idea why, but he was flipping the ends of my comics in my hands until they bent down over and over. I kept telling that beast to stop, but he wouldn't listen."

"And bending the edges is bad, right?" Julianna asked, looking between the two.

Kevin locked eyes with Andy and shrugged. "She's still learning."

Andy continued, never answering the question. "He kept flipping down the ends until they were practically ruined. And Kevin here," Andy held back laughter. "Kevin here, who was several inches shorter, mind you, just lost it. Next thing I know, he grabbed Crutch's shirt and pulled it over his head. Then, he unloaded on Crutch's gigantic head that was stuck inside. Once Crutch had tripped over his legs and stumbled into a pole, Kev here took off like a bullet around the corner."

Andy was at full throat by the time he finished the story— the short fight obviously a cherished memory.

"Fear makes you run faster," Kevin said to Julianna, thinking back to that morning and the terror he felt when he turned that corner and saw no teacher or kids to defend him. That open field behind the school might as well have been a graveyard, and he ran until his lungs breathed fire, thinking all the time that Crutcher was just behind him.

Amused by the story, Julianna clutched Kevin beneath the chin and said, "Awe, you saved him. My hero." Then, she gave him a swift peck on the lips. "Guess you're not the fearful little runt dad says you are."

"Your dad calls me a fearful little runt?" Kevin asked.

"Well, I embellished the *little* part," Julianna said as she rubbed his arm. "He was only joking. You know how he feels about you."

"Yeah, he thinks I'm a coward," Kevin thought, knowing what aspect of his life her father felt he was lacking. His thoughts were interrupted when Julianna asked a poignant question.

"So, what happened with Crutch?"

"Well, you know how they say that if you hit your bully in the mouth, you'll end up friends in the end?" Kevin answered. Julianna nodded. "Well, that wasn't the case with the Crutch. I said he was big, but he wasn't dumb. At least not when it came to inflicting psychological pain. He didn't catch me that day because I was meth-addict fast, but he let me wait days, sweating bullets during all my classes, until he caught up with me. He sniped me by the buses and just unloaded on my body, for some reason, ignoring my face."

"Like a true delinquent, he probably didn't want to leave any bruises on your face to get him into trouble," Andy Jr. said. As if noticing there was a woman in their midst for the first time, pride kicked in and he continued, "I wasn't there, Julianna, or else I would have helped him, of course."

"Of course," she said, letting Andy off the hook.

"Yeah, and you would have joined me in that ass kicking. Crutch was a possessed man," Kevin replied. He looked back at Julianna, mimicking the punches to his body. "It wasn't just the beating, either. The Crutch pulled me back up to my feet and gave me the deepest, most painful wedgie a young boy could endure." He lifted the chair, pulling it up and up and up, demonstrating just how deep the Crutch had pulled his underwear.

Andy keeled over, leaning down on the back of another chair while he burst into a lung emptying laughter. Julianna snorted. Her face reddened, but she had enough class to cover her mouth with the back of her hand to suppress the laughter.

"Yeah, keep laughing," Kevin said, hiding his own chuckle. "Just don't talk to me ever about children, Jules, because I'm sure Mark took care of that for me." The painful memory made his hand move and hover just above his crotch.

Julianna doubled over, putting her face in her hands, shoulders trembling. Andy's laugh turned to a high-pitched whine as he leaned on the back of the chair with his forearms.

"That wedgie went down in history in our school," Andy coughed out, almost choking on his own spittle. "When I found him, Julianna, it was almost stuck—"

"Hey, whoa, Andy," Kevin stepped in with his hand out in front of him. "No more details. I still have to walk her back to work, and you know, look her in the eyes."

Andy waved his hand before wiping the tears from his eyes and trying to catch his breath. "Okay, okay, I get it, pal. I'm just saying. That was brave of you, and I wanted her to know she has a stand-up guy."

"I'm glad you told me," Julianna said after recovering enough to keep the laughter down. "He knows all my embarrassing stories, so I'll just save this little Crutch story for a rainy day."

Andy noticed that she stole glances down at the pizza slice that still had steam rising from the cheese. Rubbing his chin, he spread white flour in his stubble and said, "So, you were just going to dive right in there, huh?" he asked. "Scalding tongue and all?"

"Oh, don't worry," Kevin said. "She's not that hungry."

Cheeks a cherry red, Julianna gave him a soft shove in the side with her elbow. "Shut up, Kevin," she replied.

Andy laughed. "Still have that mouth that used to get our asses kicked, I see." He looked at Julianna. "Do you think you can fix that little fault of his before he gets himself killed?"

Her eyelashes batted as she playfully rolled her eyes. "Please, I just got him to not wear t-shirts to work, so don't ask me for miracles." The two shared a laugh at his expense. It was typical Julianna. Just from the foolish grin on his friend's face, he knew she already had Andy in the palm of her hand like a pup nuzzling his mother. People were drawn to her.

"Well, that's because he knows he always has a job here. In the heat. Making some pies," Andy said as his heavy hands shook Kevin by the shoulders like a child. "Isn't that right, dad?" he shouted out behind him.

Customers at the table seemed used to the shouting and continued eating undisturbed. Hearing his son's voice echo through the restaurant, Andy Sr. looked up from the cashier, then waved his hand in a sharp upward motion.

"Get back to work, Junior!" he shouted, then muttered with a wave, "Hey there, Kevin...and woman."

"Hi, Mr. Amadeo," Kevin yelled in a lower tenor than Junior, saluting Senior with two fingers to his brow.

Andy Jr. let out a heavy sigh. "Well, let me get back to it," he said, then pointed to the pizza. "That should be cool enough to eat now by the way, Miss."

Julianna's eyes narrowed and her lips puckered. "Now, I see why you both got your asses kicked. Good day to you, Andy Junior."

Kevin and Junior laughed, shared a quick hug, and gave the obligatory promise to see more of each other in the future before parting. Kevin sat down and filled his plate with a large slice of his own when he noticed his friend had stopped by the bar against the far wall, just beyond Julianna's field of vision. He mouthed the word 'wow', nodding while he gave him a thumbs up, all with a silly grin that cracked the flour on his face. His appearance made Kevin laugh into his fist to not alert Julianna, and he gave Andy a curt nod up in reply. Concentrating on the food, Julianna didn't seem to notice the entire exchange as she held up and blew softly on her slice. Watching her, Kevin wondered if she had any clue what effect she had on the men around her.

"Hey," Kevin said and softly clapped three times. "Aren't you forgetting something, Jay?"

"Oh, shoot. Sorry," she said.

He put out his hands. For the second time, Julianna put down her slice of pizza, then put her hands within his. They both shut their eyes as Kevin led them through a quick prayer, thanking God for the happiness and the food they were about to receive. As their prayer concluded, Kevin knew the sideways looks they received from strangers around them were a source of pride for the couple. Their faith, and the backlash they faced by showing it openly, was at least something they could share together.

Julianna did not notice those glares since she was finally able to eat. She picked up the slice again with both hands. "Last chance," she said.

"Do it," Kevin replied, grinning in anticipation.

Julianna took a deep breath and then a large healthy bite that crunched from the thin crust. The sunlight streamed through the shop window like a spotlight on her face and body, both of which narrated her instant satisfaction. Her eyes were closed. Her chest heaved as she squirmed in her seat, chewing slowly, which Kevin knew meant she was enjoying the myriad of flavors. He took his own bite and was immediately hit with the same satisfying mixture. The pepperoni and bacon nearly tipped the balance into the sodium's flavor until the pineapple bit back, along with the barbecue drizzle that added a touch of sweetness to the salt again.

Julianna's ponytail bobbed as she nodded.

"You got me again," she said, though her mouth was nearly full of another bite. "I can't believe you put this together, Kevin Jones."

"Yeah, I'm great," he replied between chews. "I've been trying to get Andy to put it on the menu and name it after me, but Senior wouldn't have it. Guess he had enough of me leaning at that counter over there with Andy experimenting with different ingredients until we got it right."

There was another pie that made it to the menu instead of the pizza di Jones. Above the oven was a vintage pin-on menu board with black letters spelling out the specialty pizzas invented and available at Andy's. He failed to mention to Julianna the pizza di Fiasco, a pie Andy Jr. had said was the worst creation that his father could actualize. Angry at something he did at some point as the Mega, Senior piled on the onions, banana peppers, red peppers, and ghost pepper flakes, along with anchovies, small, deveined shrimps, canned tuna, and either egg or dill if the customer was so inclined.

It was filled with things teenagers would dare their friends to eat on a weekend. It was a badge of courage and bravery for those who attempted to stomach it. Next to the cashier station sat the ever-popular Fiasco wall, where pictures of the three brave souls who were able to keep their contents down.

With a tempered smile, Julianna chewed on the end of the garlic buttered crust while staring out the window. Where Andy's pizza shop occupied the corner of seventh street, the delineation between the old and new was clear. Just outside the window, they saw the dated parking meters that looked like metal baseball bats. Across the street there were modern parking meters that looked more plastic than metal, each with slots for credit cards, taking advantage of the bustling shopping in the new New Haven. Instead of the warm, red-colored bricks and arched porches, the buildings on the other side were cold, with dark gray and black features, and contemporary square glass storefronts. It looked emotionless compared to the New Haven they grew up with.

The sunlight caught the brown flecks in Julianna's eyes as she looked outside. "Everything is changing so fast," she said. Her tone was even, but several shades warmer than it was just an hour ago.

Kevin held his own crust in his hand. "Yeah," he replied. "Seems like I don't recognize this town with every passing day."

She took another slice in both hands and leaned on the table. "So, I know we hardly talk about this, but have you ever thought more about leaving New Haven?" she asked. The bite she took prevented her from answering any follow-up questions, but Kevin knew she was awaiting his answer, nonetheless.

He swallowed the mash in his mouth and took a sip of the lemonade that was bitter, so he knew Junior had made it. "Yeah, I've thought about it, but I don't know. I don't know what I would do if I left here. How would I make a living?" Kevin replied.

She pointed the bitten crust at him. "Well, lucky for you, people don't pay the bills all over the country. You could get a job anywhere in our field," she giggled. "I don't know. It just seems like there is so much more out there, and we're just getting a taste of it from here."

The bird is flexing her wings, ready to fly, the voice said. Kevin agreed.

The power smoldered inside, thrumming like a heartbeat as the warmth returned to his chest. The rising was partly from the voice's words, but mainly because it seemed bill collecting was the extent that Julianna viewed his abilities. The power ticked upward when he thought about the fact that he hadn't given her any reason to think otherwise. Any ambition was saved for the fledgling Fiasco, and even with all the recent failures, there remained hope that he could share that side of his life with her and raise his stock in her mind. He just had to figure a way out of the hole that he found himself in when it came to his status with the Mega.

"Yeah, I understand that. New Haven is just a drop in the bucket compared to the rest of the country. But do I really want to just be a collector forever?" he had to ask.

"Look at you, Kevin Jones. You've actually thought about this, haven't you?" Julianna's lips spread into a pleased smile. "Well, for now, at least, Kevin. It's a job you know but it doesn't have to be permanent. Oh, and besides, you're doing well at work. Don't think I haven't noticed, even though, for some reason, you try and hide it from me. Warren said you've been near the top of commissions for months now."

While breaking off pieces of his crust, Kevin muttered, "Well, Warren needs to keep his mouth shut."

Congratulations on succeeding at a dead-end job.

Kevin cleared his throat and asked, "Well, have you given it any more thought to where you would go if you did leave?"

"I haven't pinpointed any one place," her mouth turned up from the harsh lemonade, as she put the cup down. "But I have to narrow it down. Graduation seems right around the corner."

"Two months and nineteen days," Kevin lamented in silence. The countdown that was created at his family dinner was a ticking clock that fueled his sojourns as Fiasco since he felt the weight of losing her burgeoning every single day.

Julianna continued, "And I must start fielding these offers, too. I mean, if I don't, they'll go away. I'm great, but not that great that they will wait forever, you know?"

A swollen rain cloud must have crept over the sun outside because the ambient light in the restaurant seemed to slowly dim, turning the room a neutral shaded appearance that matched Kevin's mood. The subject of Julianna leaving was bound to happen sooner rather than later, as graduation loomed like a sword over their relationship. Yet, it was still agitating to take part in. Until he could spring Fiasco as his secret weapon, it was an ill-timed conversation to have.

"Do what you have to do, Julianna," he said in a harsher tone than he intended.

"What's wrong?" Julianna put down her slice. Her brow deepened like a ravine at the top of her nose as she glared at him. "What is that tone about?"

Kevin chewed faster and kept his eyes on the pizza in his hands. "It's not about anything. It's just, I'm saying, follow your heart."

"It doesn't sound like you're saying that at all," her voice had grown sterner. "I know you, Kevin. It sounds to me like you have something to say, but don't want to say it." Kevin shrugged in response, and Julianna flicked back in her seat. Her face was locked in an angry smile. "Now, what was that about!"

Kevin sighed, knowing that he had stepped into the mire. Julianna could be like a dog with a bone when she latched onto a subject she did not want to give up. He always thought if she ever failed at graphic design, she had a bright future as a lawyer or politician.

"I'm not going to L.A.," he said, smacking the elephant in the room on the head.

He heard what he thought were loud cracks of thunder in the distance. The sun fluttered on Julianna's face, as if a giant bird slowly flapped its wings in front of the window, and he thought about the clouds that must have been rolling in. It felt as if the dark weather had taken over Andy's and ruined the joy, as the tension increased with the passing silence.

"Who said anything about California?" Julianna said with a nervous laugh.

"You did," Kevin replied and took an exaggerated bite from his slice. His knee was jumping beneath the table as it sometimes did when he was anxious. "You, and my mom. When you two conspired against me at that dinner."

"Conspired against you? What am I, some Mal?" she smiled and reached across the table to grab and rub his hand with her thumb. "Oh, baby, you're being a bit dramatic. No one was conspiring against you. She asked me a question and I answered."

"Yeah, but you never told me about California being an option beforehand. It's like you didn't trust me with the knowledge or something."

"Is that why you have the attitude?" she sighed, leaning back, and clutching the ends of the table. "I never brought it up because I never truly considered it an option before."

Kevin stopped eating and finally looked up at her. "So, you're not going to go to L.A.?"

She chewed her bottom lip, and he noticed that she rubbed her hands on the napkin over her legs, a nervous tick of her own. "I didn't say that either, did I?"

Kevin smirked. "See, I knew it." Julianna moved faster than he expected and stopped him from taking another bite as she leaned in and seized his arms.

"There is nothing to see, Kevin. I must keep my options open, though." Her fingers played with the fabric of his shirt. "But I love you, and your opinion matters to me, so I want to talk about this."

Something Kevin could call a feeling of trepidation seized his chest like an iron fist and fed his power until his fingertips began to tingle. The thunder cracked outside again, and gray shadows darkened their faces.

"Can we not talk about it?" he asked. His arms retreated until he held both her hands. They were warm and clammy, and he knew she was just as nervous as he was discussing the subject.

"Why?" she said softly. A pall had fallen on the conversation, and he knew Julianna felt it, too.

"Because," he searched for the right words to lighten the conversation, to inject some levity and turn time back ten minutes prior when everything was going great, but the words escaped him.

You were never that bright, the voice said.

"Because," Kevin continued. It was his turn to bite his lip. "I just don't think I will like where this conversation would lead if we continued is all."

Julianna looked at him as a frown tightened on her lips. Her silence cut worse than any words. Kevin prepared himself because he could tell she was not about to let the subject go. The power continued to ascend as he lamented the fact that his mission to cheer her up from all the bad news going on in her life was now a failure.

"So, where does this go, Kevin?" she said softly.

While searching for an answer, white flashed like a camera bulb inside the restaurant. The thunder cracked outside, making Julianna's hands flinch in his. The restaurant was dark, and Kevin noticed an unnatural ash saturation as the thunderstorm rolled in on a bright, sunny day. A murmur rose in the establishment. Other patrons had stopped eating and noticed as well, looking around in fear and confusion. Some pointed out to the street.

Muffled shouts made it through the thick glass pane. On the street, cars screeched to a halt, leaving trails of rubber on the road as they barely missed the car in front of them. Citizens on the sidewalk hurriedly dropped their cellphones and shopping bags, shouting as they gathered small children in their arms and fled in all directions, their shouts pushed through the thick glass. A buzz reverberated off the pane next to them, causing it to rattle.

Kevin clutched Julianna's hand as the sunlight returned like a supernova. With a hard tug, he was barely able to pull her over the table, sending their plastic cups toppling over and sliding her gray shirt through the leftover slices, before a boom exploded on the street. Glass shattered in like a symphony of baritone harp music played off key. Pushing back on his heels, Kevin wrapped Julianna in his left arm and pressed her against his chest, which burned from the power. The concussion of whatever exploded outside swept them both off their feet, blowing out the overhead lights, bursting the bulbs that added to the conflagration of razor-sharp chaff. Julianna had shut her eyes and he could feel her scream vibrating through his shirt.

The power that was just under Kevin's skin from their conversation leaped outward like a fountain. It poured over his head and Julianna's, who was curled against his chest. It slithered like blue lava over the curves of her body, then down over his legs and feet, wrapping them both in a cocoon of thin blue light. The glass melted against his aura, turning into foggy white droplets that slid off his shield. Kevin held Julianna tight against his body with his arm wrapped about her waist, struggling against the shockwave to control their trajectory with his power. Then, instinctively, he reached out with the other hand.

Cups, tables, chairs, and debris floated like dandelions caught in the current as he concentrated. The errant glass glistened as it flew inward like shrapnel. The power focused in Kevin's outstretched hand, pulsing blue fire. His arm swept from left to right in an arching wave, as he and Julianna tousled in mid-air, covering Andy's in a large swath of burning, translucent blue light. He sent out streams of energy that attacked every splinter he could see, pulverizing the larger pieces of glass that could do the most damage. But as he should have expected, his efforts were in vain. The restaurant filled with sounds of pain and screams as the smaller pieces he missed cut the customers around him like tiny javelins.

You have failed them all.

The intertwined couple tumbled along the floor like a kicked barrel. Kevin's back cracked against the wall of the cashier station, and pain shot a bullet up his spine. Julianna whimpered as she jostled in his grip. He covered her tighter with his arm, but the aura had absorbed most of the impact. Dust covered stone wool tiles on the roof broke loose, and fell onto the upturned tables and chairs, breaking to pieces and scattering along the floor. Then, just as quickly as it started, the chaos ceased. Beeps, bells, and horns from car alarms played a concert in the street, filling Andy's with the discordant noise through the broken windowpanes.

Sunlight swayed through the air that was brown with smoke and debris. It took several moments before Kevin allowed his aura to disappear, not wanting anyone to see it through the haze. Instantly, his mouth and throat filled with grime that made him cough. He looked down at Julianna who still had her head buried into his chest and her eyes still shut tight, but he couldn't see any scratches or wounds on her face.

"Hey," he said to her. "Hey, it's okay now." She shook her head in his arms. "No. Julianna, look, we're okay." She looked up from his chest, still clutching his shirt in a tight fist.

"Oh my God, Kevin," she said with wide eyes.

The floating detritus made her run a trembling hand through her ponytail as she stood up on wary knees. Glass slid around on the floor as Kevin joined her, along with other patrons who looked around and gathered their bearings. An undertone of cries and whimpers carried through the still air, as those less injured helped the wounded. Meandering napkins floated down like doves from the ceiling. Bitter lemonade streaked the floor. The dust began to part, settling on broken tables and chairs, and the checkered tablecloths stained with Parmesan cheese and red sauce.

"Is everyone okay?" Andy Senior's voice echoed through the restaurant. He was behind the cashier counter that was pockmarked with holes. A dark red stream of blood ran down his head from a nasty gash on the side, but it didn't look life threatening. Glass crunched against the floor as Junior and a red-faced Tony slowly rose from behind the countertop, jaws slacked, and faces smudged with dirt. Julianna stumbled with a whoop as she inched forward in tiny steps and used an overturned table leg to keep her balance.

"Careful Juli," Kevin said as he reached out to steady her when a bright red light from the street mixed with the sun and dust and cast the restaurant in a pink smoke. The light acted as a siren call, pulling the customers forward, led by his girlfriend, who used other broken furniture to make her way over the glass and through the slippery dust.

"Julianna," Kevin called as he followed her. A napkin tickled his face as it fell that he crunched in his fist and tossed away. "Juli, where are you going?"

He wondered if New Haven was somehow under attack, and if the red light was some nefarious beam that controlled her mind as she wandered forward like a zombie.

"Kevin, it's him," Julianna turned back to him. The expression on her face was practically euphoric.

You are an idiot, the voice said, and Kevin agreed, slipping on another napkin that had settled in the dust with a curse word beneath his breath. *Did you think it would last forever?*

Kevin and Julianna neared the spot where their table used to be by the window. Long, thick scrapes were scratched along the linoleum from their chair legs that had slid against the ground. The pane glass windows had been blown inward, leaving shards on the top and bottom, resembling diamond-crusted teeth. Outside, a car had jumped a curb on the sidewalk. The hood wrapped around a parking meter that was wrenched from the concrete at the base, tossing quarters in the ground. Its roof was caved in down to the floorboard, as if someone had picked it up between their thumb and forefinger and had pinched it down the middle.

"Not safe to own a car in New Haven," Kevin thought as he wiped dust motes from his eyes. He blinked, not sure if what he saw was truly there. On top of the car, along the crumbled passenger side, he saw what looked like a hand that hung over the edge. The thick fingers were broken and twisted, with the bone of the index finger shattered in two, threatening to break through the skin. Blood streamed down the finger and dripped like red paint on the pavement. He clutched Julianna by the elbow to stop her from walking through the opening.

"Hold on. There's something off here," he told her.

A silhouette fell into the sunlight, dark, broad, and powerful. A small furnace burned above its head. Floating several feet above the sidewalk, the figure faced towards them, crouched on his haunches. A white cape snapped and billowed like a flag in the wind off to its left. A bare hand pushed up through the glass, crunching it beneath its palm.

"Is everyone okay in there?" the shadowed figure asked. His voice was strong and confident, and echoed off the walls. Julianna moved her arms from Kevin's grasp as she stepped forward, her mouth agape and wonder shining in her eyes. The figure looked at her and smiled, his white teeth standing out against his darkened features. "Here, take my hand. Be careful of the glass."

Her hand looked small within the palm of the man whose power could crush every bone with a twitch. Instead, it gently closed about Julianna's, and the silhouette floated backward to lead her safely out of the shattered pane. As if mesmerized, she followed the figure without a word and stepped over the lip of the windowpane onto the street. The rest of the customers followed, filing in line behind her. Even Junior did as commanded, ducking as he stepped through the shattered opening, a grin plastered on his face, even though he was wading through the rubble of his own restaurant.

"I can't believe he came back, Kev," he said, breathless, and without looking in his direction. "Remember when we used to talk about him as kids?"

Kevin was the last to join in the procession, exhaling as he reluctantly stepped into the sunlight. Dust particles still hung in the afternoon air and covered the street in a thin layer. Even with the choking mire, the New Haven crowd had rallied and returned in force to the scene to see their true hometown hero.

Unlike Kevin's own numerous crash sites as Fiasco, the scene in front of him was now almost festive in nature. Some citizens stood with a hand to their brow to block out the sun to see him. Cheers and laughter from the group could be heard over the bleating alarms. Those who still possessed their phones had taken them out, pointing the devices to the sky, filming and taking photos as they moved in closer just to catch a glimpse of the Mega.

Even the NHPD who had arrived on scene were enamored by his presence. With batons and arms spread out, they were barely able to hold the surging crowd back as they sneaked glances over their shoulders. None of the officers moved to question the Mega as they would if he was there as Fiasco. The handcuffs would have already been produced while a baying crowd, frothing at the mouth, would have cheered his incarceration. The Mega let go of Julianna's hand and floated upward. To Kevin's chagrin, she held the hand to her chest as if Christ himself had touched it, and he felt the power rumble inside.

As much as he did not want to, Kevin forced himself to look up at the person that could garner the kind of adulation in New Haven that alluded Fiasco no matter how hard he tried.

"Scarlet Valor," he sighed. His chest warmed as the power churned further.

That is true greatness, the voice said, almost in reverence. *Unlike Fiasco.* Kevin nodded, his thumb rubbing the center of his chest.

Smiling and waving, Scarlet Valor floated against a clear blue sky above the adoring crowd. His hair was a burning fire that trailed behind his head, strands moving with the wind. His eyes were a jade green on a tanned, chiseled face and square jaw. His double-breasted shirt hugged his chest and was a stark, bright red trimmed in black. Shiny onyx buttons were snapped in the shape of the letter L from left to right, two abreast, up to a round Nehru collar on his neck. The bottom of his jacket cut away like the bottom of the letter H to look like tails that sat on each leg. A gold belt held in place dark black pants. The pants were tucked in and belled over polished leather boots that gleamed nearly as brilliant as the buckle. He was the decorated warrior to Fiasco's savage.

"Excuse the mess, citizens," Scarlet Valor said, his voice loud and baritone enough to quiet the crowd. Even the cars seemed to listen as Kevin noticed that he couldn't hear the alarms anymore. "But as you can see, I got carried away while taking out the garbage." The crowed laughed in unison. Even Julianna.

"Please. That wasn't even funny," Kevin said, but no one was listening.

"It was worth the effort. The menace known as Bull Terror has been defeated," Valor pointed with his hand to the figure that had caved in the cartop.

Those who were close by moved in slowly, climbing on nearby hoods and trunks to take pictures of the Mal who was still out cold. He wore a simple brown armor that seemed to be fastened by large round studs running on either side of his body and down the side of his legs. Fist-shaped dents pockmarked various points on the armor. A champagne-colored chainmail helm covered his head. Sweat and blood soaked his brown hair, running down his face and around thick tusks, cracked from battle, that curved upward from the bottom of his jaw.

"Those thunder sounds must have been them fighting," Kevin thought as he leaned in and surveyed the unconscious Mal.

Even behind the chainmail, he could see that Bull Terror's face was a mask of purple and blue bruises. His eyes were nearly swollen shut with dark blood. The blood on Terror's hand was a shade darker and seemed to have come from Scarlet Valor, but from what Kevin could see, there was no damage to be found on his handsome face.

"He must be able to heal, too," Kevin surmised. The loss of that uniqueness to his skillset made his power flare up a notch.

Scarlet Valor held his billowing cape behind him with both hands as he continued. "And good, innocent people like you no longer need to fear him."

A cheer erupted from the crowd. So enamored by the scene, Kevin had not noticed the cars that had stopped at both ends, now honking their horns in solidarity. Looking up, he could see some people hanging out of office windows waving napkins or towels, and others leaning over crowded rooftops, lending their voices to the cheer of 'Val-or' that rang through the streets.

"Such admiration," Kevin thought as he scanned the merry faces in the crowd. "Fiasco is so far from this level of acceptance. This level of respect."

And he will never be on that level, the voice chimed in. What else could he do but agree when the proof was there before him?

Even his own Julianna was caught up in the ecstasy. She looked back at him, still grinning, oblivious of the red sauce stains on her shirt. Genuine tears welled in her eyes as she clapped and repeated his name along with the others. The power whipped about inside because of the pride that shined on her face for a man she didn't even know. Jealousy was a match to the fuel as Kevin realized that she adored the Mega, not knowing that she slept next to one each night. It was that love that Kevin wanted. It was that respect in her eyes that he craved. There was only one way to keep Julianna in town— something he realized when he looked back up at Scarlet Valor, who drank in the cheers with a thousand-dollar grin.

He is better than you.

"Remind me to thank you for the idea if we ever meet in

uniform," Kevin thought, stamping down the smile that made his mouth twitch.

Scarlet Valor laughed and clapped his hands so loud it took Kevin out of rumination. "I must go, but please keep your distance. A unit from the M.D.C. is on the way to take care of this mess," Valor said. He waved and smiled when a voice shouted their love for the original hometown Mega. "It's great to be back New Haven, and I love you, too! Remember to claim your Mal or Fiasco insurance so we can repair this damage. Take care!" Then, with a salute, Scarlet Valor shot up straight into the sky in a screaming trail of fire that dissipated seconds later when he curved and disappeared behind rolling clouds.

"The M.D.C. is coming here?" Kevin muttered and pulled Julianna by the arm. He had no doubt that such a high-level government organization had no idea who he was, but there was no need to risk being in the same vicinity given his current reputation after the Modoc Bridge disaster.

He tugged at Julianna's arm again. "C'mon Julianna, we have to go," he said.

Kevin took a step back when Julianna turned on her heels and whirled into his arms so fast that he stumbled after being caught off guard. She leaned back in his arms; her teeth parted in a grin as she smeared away a tear of joy from her cheek. Her two hands settled on his chest, and Kevin squirmed, but Julianna didn't seem to notice the warmth.

"Why are you in such a hurry?" she said. "I mean, he was here, Kevin. We just saw Scarlet Valor! How can you even think about getting back to work right now?"

Kevin marveled at his rare stroke of luck that, for once, seemed to favor him. Valor's appearance had all but erased the troubled tenor their conversation had taken before the Mega fight had spilled into their laps. He needed Julianna to bury the subject of that conversation deep down and far away so that the idea of L.A., leaving New Haven, or what that could mean for their future, would never return. Once it was gone, he would toss the dirt over the grave with his own actions.

"Lunch time is over, and we have to get back," Kevin said. "And I really have a lot of work to do."

As he led them away through the throng of gawkers and survivors who kept their eyes skyward, a wire-like smirk appeared on Kevin's lips as his thoughts coalesced into a grand plan that would tie up all their problems. Perhaps Talon was correct in his assessment that he, as Fiasco, thought too low of his own potential. Even if he captured a thousand drug dealers who sold their wares to handicapped babies, street level crime would never reach the level of respect necessary to receive that look Julianna had given to Scarlet Valor.

Women favored strength. They respected power and confidence. There was only one thing that could achieve this all at once, and he kicked himself for not having thought about it earlier. To demand that same esteem Scarlet Valor achieved throughout the city, he had to take on and defeat an actual real-life Mal.

Tamerlane

Kevin paced back and forth, elbow on his arm and hand beneath his chin, wearing thin his already threadbare rug even further. He stopped occasionally to glance at the computer monitor in his den. Small, plain green words formed together into sentences of various sizes that ticked up like stock prices, burying his message several mouse clicks down. It had been weeks since the run in with Scarlet Valor, and for Kevin, that time was spent formulating his plan, and trying to figure out what he was going to say to attract Talon's attention on the MegaStream.

Scarlet Valor's sudden reappearance in Oregon had flooded the regional stream. Megas of all levels who had access gushed about the celebrity who took time from feeding orphaned children to defeat the dastardly Mal, Bull Terror, and save all of Oregon. The praise was not quite that hyperbolic, but that was how it read to Kevin. As the stream ticked with the excitement— nearly too much to follow— he eventually decided to go with a simple message that would not be drowned by the noise.

His message read: **Talon. Ready to get better. Steel sharpens steel. Need to up comp.**

He had pressed enter on the keyboard over a day ago. The wait after the post went to the Stream had been an exercise in agony and frustration when Talon never responded. But the stream restricted access to news on Mals, at least as far as Fiasco's account was concerned. Kevin presumed that, given his proclivity for failure and property to get damaged, whoever controlled the MegaStream deemed him unworthy of knowing where the latest Mal activity was in his region. That choice essentially made him blind to the entire pacific northwest. Talon's access was needed if he was to confront a Malignant in the wild.

His eyes checked the stream again. Muscle memory read the streaming lines quickly, but there was still no response from Talon. The pace of his step quickened, along with the anxiety that raised his heartbeat and made him wipe his hands against his jeans. Time was slipping away. It was just over a month before Julianna was set to graduate, and the tightness in his back and chest made it feel as if it was imperative to succeed before that date.

After her graduation, once the celebration of her accomplishment began to fade, he would reveal to her that he was Fiasco. He wouldn't do it as the shamed Mega who always failed and cost her father his job, along with half the city, though. Rather, he would be on the heels of a win over a Mal, just like Scarlet Valor. Only then would she have that same admiration for dating a Mega. A hometown hero that she and New Haven deserved, and one that she could be proud to call their own.

End this buffoonery, the voice said. *Continue this line of reasoning, and you will fail, and someone will die if you face a malignant.*

"But Talon will have my back," Kevin said. "I've read about him on the Stream. He's taken down Charlies, and Beta Mals if rumors are true. We can take one together."

He has not responded because he knows you will fail.

Kevin was just about to return to his march when an off-yellow flashing light on the monitor caught his attention. Understanding the inner intricacies of the MegaStream, he knew it was a signal he had received a direct reply.

Seeing the blinking light sent his heart into his throat and made his mouth go dry. It could have been another joke reply, of which there were many before. Megas, even the supposed heroic ones, could be relentless with their mockery once a target was sighted. But there was still hope when he saw the blinking reply mingled among that day's activity. Quickly, Kevin made his way to the desk, sat in his green canvas folding chair, and clicked on the message.

The message he saw on the screen was as quick and concise as his own, using a code that proved it was from Talon. It read: **R5. Five meridiem. Be sharp as steel. T.** Kevin stood up from his chair, his grin broadening as he thought back to the night they created the cipher.

It was years ago while on a slow patrol of New Haven, that ended when Fiasco and Talon succumbed to boredom. They bought a case of beer that aided in concocting the secret code that was a shade more complicated than a simple Caesar cipher. That night was one of the rare occasions that his would-be mentor let down his shields and treated him as an equal, so Fiasco felt it was unnecessary to let Talon know about his tacit immunity to alcohol.

Taking their meeting to an empty field, Talon was able to carve a rather accurate facsimile of the town in the moist dirt with his index finger. Beer number six made Talon suggest breaking New Haven into fourteen regions. The region numbers would need to rotate counterclockwise monthly, where region one would turn to region fourteen and region two would turn to region one, and so forth. The 'R5' in the message corresponded to Township Middle that month, if Kevin had kept the regional movements correct.

He also remembered that beer number twelve had turned a normally stoic Talon into a paranoid conspiracy theorist.

"They are watching, Fiasco," Talon breathed, burping up ale. His dark hair was stringy and bedraggled, falling about his face as he steadied himself against the trunk of a tall honey locust tree with his hand. Fiasco could see how vulnerable Talon was, not knowing that it would be a rare occasion to witness him in such state. "They are always on that damn MegaStream," he burbled. "They see us, just as I see you."

"Who are they, Talon?" he remembers asking sheepishly.

Talon never answered his inquiry, but to placate his paranoia and throw off anyone who may have been paying attention on the Stream, they both decided that they would add fourteen hours to whatever time was given. How they came up with such a high number to add, Kevin could not recall, except a vague memory of Talon mocking his math abilities.

"Well, here we go," Kevin thought, closing the browser before rubbing his hands together, excited by the prospect of finally getting some action.

His mind raced with all the possibilities Talon could have designed. He hoped that he even understood the meaning of his short message. Breaking up a Chinzo-kai gun running ring would entail sharpening Fiasco's skillset instead of facing a Mal, as far as Talon was concerned. Speculation was useless, however, so he pushed the theorizing from his thoughts.

Five meridiem in the message meant 5 A.M. Looking at the Mega league clock on his wall, he saw that it was just past six-thirty, and the meeting with Talon was at seven sharp. Walking quickly towards the door, he grabbed the worn black backpack he kept so he could leave in a hurry. He didn't have to look inside to know that his Fiasco suit was stowed safely before he rushed out, letting the door slam shut behind him.

It was nearly 7 P.M. when Fiasco soared over the city, his head moving from side to side like a searchlight as he scanned the rooftops of new New Haven for a sign of Talon. Dusk had come, and the sky was a dark purple with a thin line of pink and orange clouds in the west.

"All that planning we did, and we never thought of coming up with a signal to find the other," Fiasco thought.

Spring was in full bloom and the warm air he let in through his aura caressed his suit. High in the atmosphere, Fiasco saw the tall four-bulb halogen light towers painted a bright orange, their heads angled down, illuminating the large chasm still leftover in the earth. Even with the loss of revenue, the city had decided to keep the lights on around the suspended Mega-league stadium. The narrative was they were left on to keep up the hope, but to Fiasco, it was as if the city decided to keep them on as a monument to his failure.

Township Middle citizens embraced their wealth, furnishing their roofs with complementing couches, sofas and chairs, firepits, and fake fabric along the top that was meant to resemble grass. Some rooftop restaurants had bars filled with posh-dressed customers who drank gin from mason jars and martinis of various colors. The Savoy Tower was in the distance that shined like a silver crystal spire in the night sky. Its fiftieth story was now complete and sat atop the edifice. Judging the distance between him and that building made Fiasco turn left towards the center of Township middle.

This plan is ludicrous, the voice said. *Losers always lose.*

The extra venom in its tone tipped off the well of energy Fiasco held in reserve inside. Often, before an anticipated run-in with the criminal element, the power would spark and churn inside from the wave of conflicting emotions that moved from anxiousness and stimulation, all the way to fright. Yet, as he neared the rendezvous with Talon, Fiasco was surprised by the sense of calm that permeated his being.

"Is this what real confidence feels likes?" he wondered, but the voice thought otherwise.

It is what embracing stupidity feels like. End this fallacy before you get yourself or others killed.

Fiasco breathed out.

It wasn't long before he spotted Talon. Having changed up his clothing once again, he wore a long-sleeved dark teal shirt that was loose against his body, allowing the gray eagle on his chest to flutter from the breeze. His sleeves were pulled up to his elbows as he waved Fiasco down like an airport marshaller taxiing in a plane on the runway. The blue aura around Fiasco flexed and thickened as he fed it internal energy and veered downward. Before he crashed head-first into the rooftop, he curled up in an arch and gently floated down to greet his friend.

"Thanks for finally reaching back to me," Fiasco said. He pulled the aura back inside, finding it best to conserve his power based off the austere expression on Talon's face behind his gray mask.

Three rings of necklaces hung from his neck with small, brown beads that were separated at intervals by bright red ones. He wore dark jeans that looked almost black in the light. He also had bracelets on both his wrists with amber gems that curled like teeth, long and thin. They were curious to Fiasco since he had never seen Talon wear those bands before.

He nodded at the bracelets. "What's with the jewelry?"

Talon's mouth curled upward. "Well, you said you were ready for battle, am I right?"

The gems looked carved out of wood but sounded like solid metal when Talon rubbed his left wrist, making the ornaments clang off each other. The knife belt hung at an angle on his waist, still armed with his bowie knife, silver throwing daggers pushed down into the usually empty loops.

Fiasco fidgeted with his goggles. "Guess that's why they call you Talon, right?"

Talon snorted. "Yeah. Something like that," he said, then turned to look out into New Haven.

The curved gems spread out like claws over his hands when he leaned onto the rooftop ledge. Fiasco watched him, ignoring the voice that mocked him for not having the muscles he saw rippling on Talon's broad shoulders through his shirt. Seeing Talon looking out onto the city, he wondered why the Mega seemed more subdued than normal. Leaning on his hands, Talon's gaze was fixed to the left; his gray mask squinted as if he was concentrating on something in the distance. The anxiousness to know why he was summoned made Fiasco's stomach tighten.

"So, are you going to tell me why we're out here? Or do I have to get us another case of beer before we get started?" Fiasco asked.

The night they came up with their New Haven code, Talon had revealed at least one weakness: his inability to handle any liquor. It took less than a six pack before he let slip some small morsels of information about his life. From clues dropped in his garbled words, Fiasco surmised that Talon was an Indian from the Modoc tribe, a lineage that was native to that area. The nicknames he used for the area signified that he was born and raised in New Haven, but most likely no longer lived within the city limits from the disdain he voiced for the Savoy corporation.

That night was the first time Fiasco had noticed the untanned ring around Talon's finger. There were even hints of a family. Realization that he had let down his shield, even for an instance, sobered Talon up quickly. Clarity returned his rigidity, and he ended the conversation and their team-up for that night with a swipe of his foot over the dirt map.

Talon huffed and looked down to the street. "So, you still remember that night, huh? Guess that beer didn't affect you as much as you made it appear, Crooked F," Talon said, but never turning around as he spoke. "Do me a favor and take a look at them down there."

With his arms crossed lazily over his chest, Fiasco walked to the edge of the roof where Talon stood and looked over.

"Do you see them?" Talon asked. His voice was calm and serene, like a teacher standing with his student before a grease board trying to teach a math problem.

"I see people," Fiasco replied with a nonchalant shrug. "Drunk douchebags that will probably cause trouble. Hot girls about to make them pay for their drinks. I see some cars, and things."

Talon's head turned to look at him. "Look closer."

The building they stood on was above Oak Avenue, deep in the heart of region five. Cars were nearly bumper to bumper as they cruised down New Haven's version of the Vegas strip. On the sidewalks on either side of the streets, diners waited by the entrances to elegant restaurants, holding clear plastic circles that would buzz when their table was available. The warm spring night had the street bustling with New Haven youth, in their best skirts, jeans, and t-shirts.

Their laughter wafted up to where the two Megas watched them. The sound made Fiasco remember himself at their age, and the joy he felt when winter finally broke, letting him venture outside again. Sadness made the power inside tingle when he thought about the fact that he was not that far removed from those kids by age, but the multiple failures since then made that period of his life feel so far away.

"I see them," Fiasco said. "I see New Haven."

Talon nodded. "Our tribe."

"Yeah. I guess." Unsure exactly where Talon was going, Fiasco leaned his backside against the lip of the roof and held himself up with both arms as he looked at the Mega by his side. "So, why are you asking me this now?"

Talon joined him in the stance with his arms crossed over his muscled chest.

"You're dumb, but I know you're not that dumb. I know you

know that I am Modoc, so for me, this is my home. The land is my true home. We were here first." Fiasco winced beneath his mask, hoping the conversation wouldn't go down a sensitive road that he was ill-prepared to deal with, but fortunately, Talon spared him the awkwardness.

Talon continued. "Now, I have adopted everyone in New Haven. When I see them all down there happy and oblivious, I fear they are unprepared for what is coming next."

That declaration made Fiasco squirm against the concrete. "What is coming next? Do you have some sort of inside information I should know about?"

"You should already know, because it's happening all around you," Talon said, waving his hand over Fiasco's head. Fiasco followed the arc and only saw the modern buildings behind him made of steel and glass.

"Are you talking about the buildings?" Fiasco asked, more than a bit confused. "I think I'm missing the point here, Talon."

Talon's countenance seemed to darken as the white screens on his eyes grew tight on his face.

"How can you not see it? New Haven is being bought and sold with promises of prosperity that always end up being chains to the seller," he replied. "This kind of wealth always brings greed, right? It's like that friend you invite to a party but are disappointed when they bring along their asshole spouse. Wealth and greed are joined at the hip. And certain bad elements circle that greed like sharks when chum is in the water. Ask yourself, why do you think you've been so busy lately?"

Fiasco bit his lip. He was so caught up in his own idea of earning Julianna's respect that he failed to notice the aches and pains that followed his town's growth. Talon was right. It was true that he had been able to patrol even further from his neighborhood, and still find crime. The dirty streets and darkened alleys went on for blocks instead of streets. It was as if the bad parts of town were spreading like a virus to the rest of New Haven.

The criminals had grown even more dangerous and brazen, as well. He had become so used to being able to stop bullets that he never thought about how he didn't have to do such a thing when he first started venturing out as Fiasco.

"Okay, I can admit, things have gotten worse," Fiasco admitted. "But I don't know. I never think that far out. I mean, I stay micro. It's easier to get by that way."

"Street level," Talon said dryly.

"Right," Fiasco agreed, but it felt as if the voice spoke through him, mocking in tone.

"Well, this is your tribe. Whether you admit it or not," Talon turned back toward the street. "That's why I don't like that poser, Scarlet Valor. Yes, he's from New Haven, but California is his home now. The pacific northwest is his kingdom. He doesn't care about the people down there anymore, even though they love him."

Unfurling his arms, Talon leaned on both hands on the roof's edge.

"New Haven needs more. To get the Mega they deserve as this growth continues," his head went down. "The Mega hero they deserve when I can't be there to keep them safe." He looked at Fiasco again. The darkness caught his face and cast a shadow on his cheeks, softening his features. Fiasco could almost feel the pleading in his visage. "You need to be better, Crooked F. I believe you can be, or I wouldn't be out here."

"Finally. We can be done with whatever this drama is and get to the battle already," Fiasco thought, confident their victory would pass whatever litmus test Talon had in mind. Alone, he would be more concerned about his prospects against a Mal of any level, but with Talon and his power level along with him, success was all but assured. All Fiasco needed to do was chip in when he could, have his back when needed, and stay out of Talon's way to claim the win. He could nearly picture it in his mind with such clarity.

Idiots never listen, the voice said.

"Do you have a line on a Mal?" Fiasco asked, crossing his arms over the crooked symbol on his chest. "Because that's why I'm out here. I want to get better, just like you keep saying."

"You sure about that, Crooked F?" Talon's mask didn't emote any emotions, but Fiasco could feel his eyes studying his face behind those white screens. "I see you."

He knows you are lying. He can see the lack of confidence, the voice said. *Flee before he calls you out for being a fraud.*

"Yes. I'm here, aren't I?" Fiasco said, almost entreating, as the longing to prove himself to Julianna poured out. "Believe me. I want this. I need this more than you know. You have no idea what it's like to try and fail time and time again. I thought I got that Modoc Bridge rescue right, but no. Just another failure."

The power flared and dipped, pulsating in indigo brightness and azure sparks that made Talon slowly rise and lean away. "I don't want to be known just for this for the rest of my life," Fiasco pointed to his chest. "This crooked symbol. A mistake that can't be corrected. Does that make sense?"

Talon's head tuned to the left again before he turned back to Fiasco. "Yes, it does," he said.

Talon stepped up on the ledge. "Follow me," he said as he crouched. Powerful legs pushed him off the roof in one, swift motion. The leap careened him over the double-laned street, arching like a rock tossed overhand. Then, he landed on the rooftop across the street, light as a feather. Talon's feet slid on the rooftop grit as he veered a hard left. Even with errant rubbish, loose stones, and furniture waiting to reach out and twist an ankle, Talon never broke stride as he raced across the roof, heading southeast.

The quickness of Talon's movements caught Fiasco off guard, and his aura returned all at once down to his gauntlets with a thrum. Stepping on the ledge, he leapt headfirst off the building with a shout of his name that echoed between the buildings. Nervousness and excitement played his power like a fiddle, and even four stories up, lack of concentration made him misjudge the distance. Screams and profanity from ducking citizens penetrated his shield as he buzzed over their heads, arching upward towards the roof where Talon landed, curving to the left like a blue shooting star to follow him. Talon had run over several buildings by the time he reached that level, but Fiasco was able to eventually pull even with the Mega in a burst of power that trailed blue behind.

Flying parallel with Talon, he asked, "Are you going to tell me where we're going?" Wind rushed against his aura shield, so he spoke louder to be heard.

Talon's arms pumped at his sides and Fiasco wondered if the Mega could hear him over the turbulence his sprint was creating.

"Do you know about the new exhibit at the Haven Museum?" Talon shouted, his voice deep enough to cut through the draft.

"We have a museum?" Fiasco replied with a grin that fell away from the glance Talon gave in his direction.

Another leap and another building behind him, Talon landed on the next roof and kept his stride. Fiasco poured on the power to keep up.

"Yes," Fiasco continued, flying even again. "I think I heard something about it."

Memories painted pictures of the dinner with his parents, and he wondered if that was the same exhibit his father had mentioned to Julianna. He could hardly remember though, since interest in what Howard Jones did after work was not something he often paid attention to.

Talon shook his head from side to side. "Do you read anything outside of your press clippings?" Not allowing Fiasco to answer, he continued, "The museum is hosting a new exhibit, The History of Civilization. They're displaying artifacts, scripts, and other antiquities from the middle east. Chief among them is the blood of Syriana."

"The blood of Syriana?" Fiasco asked. "What is it, and what's so special about it?"

"It's a stone, so dark that it looks red, like blood. Its value is immeasurable, and it's said to have certain properties." Talon leaped again to the next rooftop. Forced to dodge a couple who sat on swank, green chairs around a glass coffee table, he moved around them, graceful as a ballerina as he turned right and shot across until he jumped to a lower rooftop below. Touching his hand to the ground, Talon slid left again, arms pumping.

"Dammit," Fiasco grumbled.

His symbol flared like a rocket engine as he fed his aura with enough energy to keep up. The voice did its job to replenish the energy well when it reminded him, *Talon is so much better than you.* He veered up and over the rooftop edge, then down to the lower rooftop. An L-shaped pattern cut through the sky as he turned to his left. He appeared on Talon's right, level with his eyes.

"What kind of properties are you talking about?" he continued.

Talon's eyes remained forward. "That's irrelevant. What's important is that someone is trying to steal it."

Fiasco's head jerked back. "Steal it? When?"

"Right now."

"So that's what Talon was staring at back at the roof. He was watching the robbery happen in real time," Fiasco thought. Then he said, "You mean, we're headed to a robbery?" his voice higher pitched than normal.

"Not just any robbery. I told you. There is a powerful artifact involved."

"Can it hurt us?"

Talon shrugged his shoulders. "You, maybe. Depends on who has it at the time. But yes, in the right hands, it could be dangerous. By day, the exhibit is heavily guarded, NHPD and Phantom Watch mercs hired out of Anchorage, but at night, there's a skeleton crew, and they won't be enough. Not against that many criminals who are that heavily armed."

Artifacts, robbers, mercs, guns, and exhibits. It made Fiasco lightheaded from the sudden complexity.

"You can see how many there are?"

"Only when I jump." Talon crouched and sailed over to the next rooftop, arms and legs tensed as they prepared for the next move. He landed, crunching in the loose stones and gravel on the roof, then quickly jumped again. Arching over, he landed on a black steel fire escape. Talon grasped the railing and jumped over the edge with both legs sailing over. Falling onto the street, he was back to full sprint, now heading northeast. Fiasco kept pace, burning less energy than before as he rolled toward the street, flying in between a frightened couple holding hands who failed to notice his presence until he was over Talon's left shoulder.

"I count at least twelve of them, but there could be others lurking inside," Talon said without prompt. "The guards have already been taken out."

What!" Fiasco shouted. The aura flickered from the emotions of yet another failure. "They're dead? Why did you wait so long?"

Talon glanced up at him, "I don't think they're dead. I didn't hear any gunshots, did you? Besides, we needed the robbers to show up before we could intervene. We're not cops."

Satisfied with Talon's simple explanation, there was one question that burned in Fiasco's mind that his friend seemed to purposefully be dancing around. "Is there a Mega involved?" he asked.

Automobiles screeched to a halt, some blowing their horns in protest, as the Megas moved between the traffic with Talon on the ground and Fiasco flying faithfully overhead. Talon was silent as they left the lights of downtown New Haven, heading towards Yellow Tree Park. Fiasco and Talon were shoulder to shoulder in perfect unison as they passed over Deschutes Avenue.

"Yes," Talon finally answered. "There is a Mega involved. Technically."

The frustration he felt from the answer made Fiasco's aura shimmer and dim in luminescence. "Quit trying to purposefully be vague, Talon. It's not as cool as you think," he took a deep breath. "We're not on a date, so just tell me what you mean."

That made the corner of Talon's mouth curl upward. "I say technically because the blood of Syriana is being robbed by Tamerlane."

The name brought a jumble of clips, articles, TV specials, and pictures to Fiasco's memory. If he recalled correctly, Tamerlane was a Mega whose power was extreme intelligence. A Praetermind. Tamerlane had contributed to the M.D.C.'s futuristic armaments, designing their transport airships and body armor for their human police force. He also became independently wealthy for the encryption he added to the MegaStream. There was a falling out with the M.D.C. brass for his proclivity for malpractice and cruelty, and he went on to become a Mal, masterminding a high-end crime ring that had terrorized all regions of the United States.

Drugs, human trafficking, theft, kidnapping, and even assassination and murder. Nothing was out of bounds for the Tamerlane group— the world's very own Mal-Mega for hire. Talon had chosen properly. In the end, despite his vast intellect, Tamerlane was just a man with typical human speed, strength, and agility. If there was a Mal for Fiasco to cut his teeth on, it was with a bottom feeder delta like Vincent Tamerlane.

Fiasco smiled.

"Normally this would be a full M.D.C. operation. They would

love to put him in the oubliette," Talon said. "But this operation slipped through the cracks. It was just hanging on the Stream with no one attached. Guess a robbery in a mid-sized Oregon town was not important enough to attract their attention. Do you see why I emphasize our tribe? Now it's up to us to take care of him."

Mentioning the oubliette raised the hair on Fiasco's neck. The M.D.C. was bad all on their own, with their advanced training, and government backing, but, from what he could tell from the Stream chatter, the oubliette was the dungeon within the dungeon. There was a prison for most Mals with Charlie and Delta power levels that the world knew about where the inmates had their own separate rooms, exercise time, and rehabilitation efforts for good press. But it was a facade. Rumor had it that below that model of a prison was a special layer of hell for the more dangerous Charlie and all the Beta class Mals that needed additional security.

Mals who met the criteria of that higher level were captured then depowered by a device ringed about the neck that was created by the Praeterminds under government employment. They were then put into a containment box for an undetermined duration. In the box, they were drugged or hypnotized, reeducated so they would no longer be a danger to society. So the rumors said. It was not even supposed to exist, but the oubliette was often the boogeyman that Megas threatened Mals with to gain a psychological advantage during battle.

"So, what would someone like Tamerlane want with a rock in a small town in the pacific northwest?" Fiasco asked.

"I don't know." Talon allowed himself a smirk, and he turned his head towards Fiasco. "Why don't we go ask him?"

Fiasco gave a slick grin in return, then took off like a rocket into Yellow Tree Park. There was an audible muffled sound that played through his aura behind him, as if Talon had shouted something. He couldn't make out the words as the leaves and needles on the trees brushed and cracked against his shield. White bark from the aspen trees flipped by. Even with the warm spring weather, he could feel the cooler temperatures beneath the canopy of foliage.

The park opened before him into a clearing. Wooden picnic tables sat on gray slabs of concrete or were strategically placed beneath trees for the shade. Two white cobblestone paths crisscrossed through the park. Where the two paths met was a pavilion made of cedar. It was a large structure, dominated by a stage and a wooden roof whose freshly lacquered exterior glowed with the moonlight.

Fiasco stared at the stage area before veering off.

"This is where Julianna is going to graduate," he thought. He was surprised that that was the first time he had thought about her that night, since she was the sole reason for his adventure with Talon. Seeing the stage reminded him of the fact that she would soon be free of her scholastic anchor and would be making the final choice about their future.

That is when you will lose her. Fiasco agreed and fed off the negativity, the shock of power returning his concentration back to the business at hand.

The forest continued after the clearing, and he calculated that he still had several dozen yards before he reached the museum. It had been years since he had visited the institution from that direction, but a plan had been quickly formulated. The forest buffeted up next to the crescent road outside of the museum, ending in a line of tall, manicured trees. He could use the undergrowth as cover to get a lay of the criminal's location, and perhaps get an idea of where the guards were, as well.

The leaves of the trees scratched a hypnotic and calming tone against his aura shield as he passed through the forest.

"They had better still be alive, Talon," he thought. Fiasco as a brand name was already in the toilet when it came to the court of public opinion but would be flushed completely if it were linked to the loss of innocent life. If he wasn't chased out of town by a vicious mob, he would be forced to change his name— maybe even his costume— or retire as a Mega altogether.

"At least I would be able to fix this logo." The thought made him laugh, but as the universe usually decreed for the Mega, the laughter was short lived as he approached the forest edge.

The leaves and foliage thinned as they beat against his aura. Suddenly, in a burst of bright moonlight, his cover had fallen away, and Fiasco found himself out in a wide, open lawn with no tree in sight. Round patches of churned dirt marked where rows of trees had been cut and hauled away. It was the same on his left and right, with yards of cleared land in both directions. Fiasco curled up in a trail of blue, hovering in mid-air, bristling at his abrupt exposure.

"They've expanded the grassland leading up to the museum," he thought, suddenly feeling regretful that he did not have time to research.

You are not very bright.

In front of him were four white vans that lined the curved road of the museum. They were parked next to the curb by the tall, stone steps that led up to the doors. Once his eyes adjusted to the sudden light, Fiasco saw what had to be Tamerlane's men. They were hard to make out against the bright white coat of paint on the van. Since the men were dressed head to toe in stylish, white suits and matching masks that hid their faces, they almost blended in perfectly with the vans. The only way he saw them at all were the black automatic rifles they held in their hands that looked as if they floated in mid-air against their suits.

With his aura still burning bright, Fiasco realized he had advertised his presence like a shining blue star against the night sky. It wasn't long before they noticed, and the gang members bounded for cover behind the vans. Atop the steps of the museum, the large, white ornate pillars were perfect cover for the other Tamerlane members who dashed behind the thick stone.

Fiasco counted six smoke black barrels, two between each van.

"Ah, hell," Fiasco muttered, and pushed out his left hand just as shots rang out in a melody of rat-a-tat-tats. The power rushed out from his hand and poured into a thick, shimmering blue wall, growing until it covered the length of two parked vans. The bullets thumped against the manifestation like raindrops against a windshield, buzzing as they ricocheted off in all directions. Successive thumps penetrated the grass, sending blades and dirt adrift. Errant rounds tinged against the stone, brick, and windows atop the museum.

"It's not thick enough," Fiasco realized. The wall was larger than his usual manifestations that crushed bullets into harmless chunks of metal. Its large size spread out and diluted the energy to match the expanded proportion, thinning as it did so.

"Remember the bridge," he thought, and curved his hands.

The wall complied, curving away from him on his mental command. The hail of gunfire continued unabated, with the bass deepening as it played its woeful song against his creation. Scraps of black asphalt chipped off the road. The concave structure worked as planned, sending the ricochets back towards the shooters instead of randomly at the museum where the absent guards could be killed by an errant round. Chips of white dust still flaked off the stairs, pillars, and large white dome as the museum came under a barrage of caromed bullets.

Through the shimmering wall, Fiasco saw one of Tamerlane's gang members on the museum landing, stuck behind the decorative silver metal gates attached between two pillars. The separations between the bars on the gate were more than wide enough for bullets to filter through, and he panicked from the near misses that chipped the stone beside his head. Pushed into a frenzy, he tried to make a run for better cover behind the bulkier pillars, but was clipped in the shoulder, spinning him as his white suit was showered in a spray of crimson.

"I have to put an end to this before someone gets killed," Fiasco thought, but the staccato-like gunfire flashed from every direction he looked from behind his blue wall, freezing him in place.

The air was thick with an acrid odor, a mix of gun powder and lead dust from cheap bullets. A lull in the fusillade tempted Fiasco to risk pulling back his shield and move closer to the shooters, when he noticed that the back doors on the far right van were wide open. Unlike the street criminals who fired at him indiscriminately when he patrolled New Haven, Tamerlane's gang, it appeared, had a plan.

"I've been setup!" Fiasco shouted in his head.

Through the soft thumps against his shield, Fiasco never noticed the gang member kneeling a few feet away from the van, his suit still a pristine, frosty white. He didn't see the forest-green barrel of the rocket-propelled grenade launcher perched on a shoulder that they hoped would succeed where their rifles had failed, either.

A stream of curse words raced through Fiasco's mind but froze in his throat at the site of the metal warhead aimed at him. The escalation of the situation brought doubt, which led to the fear. The conflicting emotions drained his wealth of energy. In response, his wall manifestation blinked and wavered like a dying candle. A surge of blossoming heat made his head dizzy and sweat rolled beneath his costume as the power flooded back into his aura in a paralyzing rush while the wall disappeared.

The breech on the back of the RPG belched a bright orange that flamed in the night. A controlled *boom* shook Fiasco's lungs as the warhead fired in a burst of gray smoke. A snake-like hiss wafted through air, growing more strident the closer the projectile approached his elevated position. Instinctively, Fiasco glided back.

He flew backward to keep his eye on the missile as he tried to evade it, but the warhead kept pace, tracing his movements— no doubt an infernal creation of Tamerlane. Any clever thought on how to counteract the missile with a manifestation failed to materialize as fright stifled Fiasco's creativity. With his power frozen from shock and fear, the little he could do was cross his forearms before his face and brace for the impact.

His heart thumped like a snare drum beneath his costume. "Can I survive this?" Fiasco wondered frantically as the whining from the missile reverberated off his shield.

The missile was close, and the impact only a heartbeat away.

Losers always lose, the voice said in a churlish tone that cut to the heart. *And Julianna will not stay for a loser*. Fiasco agreed.

Instantly, the power burgeoned inside. It churned and bubbled upward like the main vent of a volcano. Pouring outward through his pores, it bled into his forearms like rolling, blue lava. The aura around his arms shined as the power pulsed, extending in azure streams from the influx of energy, before condensing down into iron bracelets that strengthened the arms crossed over his face.

A grunt escaped his lips when the grenade struck home with a loud *bang*. A brilliant white flash forced Fiasco to shut his eyes even behind the goggles. A splitting ring pained his eardrums. Heat filled his mouth when he breathed in. A concussive wave of power pounded through his shield, bruising his internal organs as they pushed against his spine. Wind whistled from below, swimming through his costume that was now exposed to the night air as the blast swatted Fiasco out of the sky. Grass and dirt filled his mouth as the earth gave way, and he plunged into the ground.

On his back, smoke curled off Fiasco's thin aura. Warm mud coughed up from his throat and splashed against his cheek. Still able to move, and seemingly in one piece, his fingers dug into the churned soil, and he slowly raised himself up. Fiasco rubbed his left wrist, massaging lightning strikes of pain down to his nerves and bones.

"Wrist is on fire. I must have broken something," Fiasco thought. Pain made the power roll over his sore body like soothing fingers along the wounds.

"He's still alive! Get another one!" shouted the Tamerlane gang member who had shot him down. Smoke still hung in the air around him. He was still kneeling, holding the RPG on his shoulder, waiting for his partner to arm another warhead for a second shot.

Fiasco's body seemed to ache from the thought. "I can't risk taking another one of those."

Reaching out with his right hand, a string of glimmering blue power stretched forth from his fingertips. Twisting and merging, the power transformed into a replica of his gauntlet, with the same intricate patterns along the back of the hand growing larger with each second he poured in more energy. Fiasco pushed out his shoulder. The gauntlet opened and reached out, clutching the RPG shooter within its glowing palm. Fiasco grinned when he felt the man's frightened screams reverberate through the manifestation.

The member who was rearming the RPG dropped the warhead. His white mask turned a soft blue from the glow of the oversized gauntlet as he followed it up into the air. The muzzle of his AK-47 sparked against the pavement, and he pulled the gun from behind his back, fleeing behind the van for cover. Fiasco kept his companion suspended in place.

With a mental command, the fingers moved, and Fiasco made the hand contract and squeeze. The RPG launcher that had sent him careening into the ground was pinned against the criminal's body. The hard metal pushed against the soft tissues of his diaphragm, making the criminal scream and shudder in agony as Fiasco lifted him further into the air. His wrist flicked and the gauntlet moved. The closest van rocked on its suspension as Fiasco pushed out, smashing the villain face-first into the side with a sickening wet crunch that surely fractured several bones in the criminal's face.

In a damp squeal, the well-dressed criminal slid down the side of the van, crumbling to the pavement. Left behind was a long stain that glistened a bright red on the white enamel on the van, proving that Fiasco had indeed broken something on the man's face.

"Okay, that might have been too hard," Fiasco thought as he looked down. "Well, that's for trying to kill me, loser."

From the count Talon had given him, there were still eleven members left— ten once he remembered the one who caught a slug in the shoulder. Peering through the gaps in the parked vans, he saw that many of them had secured their positions behind the strong, stone pillars and gates on the landing. It was almost too late when he noticed that those still on the ground had found new firing lanes behind their vehicles. His shield wall sprang up just as the gunfire resumed, playing an explosive song that echoed off the high walls of the museum.

Still stung from the RPG blast, Fiasco crouched behind his wall manifestation. On the ground, he presented a smaller target and was not able to create a manifestation large enough to disperse the bullets. Thumps vibrated against the walls with such force that the Mega took several steps back. Each impact made it feel as if the bullet had hit the broken bone in his wrist, making them grind together beneath his skin.

"Where is Talon?" he thought. The ache in his arm had spread to his shoulder. "He should be here by now." His eyes moved left, then right, then even searched the sky hoping to see Talon leaping into the fray, but the leading Mega was nowhere to be found.

Flee, the voice suggested. *They could have something more powerful than a rocket-propelled grenade, and you know that, deep down, you are a coward.*

Fiasco agreed and thought, "and Julianna won't stay for a coward."

Precisely.

The symbol on Fiasco's chest throbbed. He breathed and let the power pour down into his gauntlets. Pain screamed through his nerves as he spread out his hands in front of him, shoulder width apart. Shame of losing again gripped his will, and embarrassment of failing once more steeled his resolve against the barrage.

"Enough of this. I don't need him," Fiasco thought. His teeth clenched in determination. "I don't need Talon to lead me by the nose like some rookie. I can handle this myself!"

Yes, you do. And no, you cannot.

The doubt from the voice poured fuel on the pilot light that pushed Fiasco's power level into overdrive. The blue gauntlets sparked like wildfire as he pumped them with the surplus. The air crackled from the power build up as Fiasco stood. Sweat saturated his hands beneath the buzzing armaments that trembled from the influx, and he fed them even more power. The gunfire ceased from the gang members who had hunkered behind the vans. Seemingly frightened by the display that slowly turned night into a glorious blue daylight, they abandoned their positions and rushed up the museum steps for higher ground.

Azure light flashed over Fiasco's goggles. In his mind, he pictured the hug he would give Julianna at the airport when she left him behind in New Haven. The light on the gauntlets grew brighter. The image shifted. He then pictured Julianna, alone in his squalid one-bedroom apartment with her clothes worn and threadbare, sitting at a dilapidated table with chips in the wood. She was on the verge of tears, struggling over a stack of bills that neither of them could pay. In that vision, she had tied her future to his, and he had weighed her down. The ruminations and the images of their relationship ending with a broken heart, no matter which way it turned, made the power in the gauntlets explode.

Then, Fiasco lashed out, shouting the breath from his lungs.

Raw power, burning indigo flooded from his gauntlets. Two of the vans before him craned from the force that struck them like an ocean wave, lifting them off their wheels. The Tamerlane members still on the steps were swept up in the havoc, falling beneath the blue wave. Defying their weight, and the pull of gravity, the vans rolled up the steep sandstone museum steps, tumbling over in a torrent of broken steel and shattered glass. They were pushed by a firestorm of sky-blue flames that poured from Fiasco's outstretched arms. The right van broke loose from the cobalt storm. The wrought iron gate on the landing screamed as the vehicle ripped through the metal. Its molecular structure weakened by the rolling heat; the spine of the metal roof bent around the tall stone pillars that shook at the base from the impact.

The Tamerlane members who thought they were safe behind the dense stone backed away, seemingly mesmerized by the cracks that webbed on the thick pillars. Those who were not frozen from shock fled from the deluge of cobalt power. Some took the risk of broken ankles and legs by jumping over the gates at the end of the landing, plummeting down several feet below and out of sight into the dark declivity that was used for deliveries. Others ducked and covered their heads on the landing, while one brave soul crashed through the museum window, leaping headfirst through double pane glass to escape the rolling power and the debris it carried in its wake.

Caught in the tumult, the remaining van tumbled over the landing floor, plowing into the tall inlaid wooden entrance to the museum. The massive French doors shattered in a shower of splintered timbers. The stream of power from Fiasco's hands ceased. From his vantage point, he lost sight of the van, but heard the high-pitched screech as the van slid along the marble floors inside. His heart skipped when the sound of the van shattered into a wall, breaking glass in some back room he imagined was furnished wall to wall with priceless paintings and artifacts.

He looked at his hands that still glowered with cerulean energy.

"How the hell did I just do that?" he wondered, but the gauntlets only thrummed with energy.

Quit asking stupid questions that you already know the answer to.

At the museum landing, a piece of glass tinkled as it tumbled from the windowpane before shattering against the ground, startling Fiasco back to reality. He shook his head to return his focus to the task at hand. Drawing on the replenished well of energy, the aura returned about his body, and he took back to the sky. Slowly and cautiously, he floated over the bodies strewn on the stairway—four in total. He floated toward the museum entrance. Scattered along the stone floor landing amid the debris, he saw unconscious bodies and counted three more. Their white suits were stained with dark, scorched burn marks, as the heat from his powerful blast washed over their bodies and burned away the oxygen until they lost consciousness.

"Better to be lucky than good," he muttered after seeing the bodies.

The way of a fool is right in his own eyes, the voice taunted with the bible proverb.

The agonizing screams coming from the darkness on the delivery slope called to him. Fiasco floated to the end of the landing where he had seen the gang members jump for their lives. Peering over the edge of the metal rail that was bent downward, he saw how far the jump down to the concrete was. If he were to guess, it looked to be just over two stories. His eyes adjusted to the blackness. Below, two of the Tamerlane gang writhed on the ground, clutching at ankles and legs that bled from broken bones poking through tears in their white suits sullied red.

"Guess they aren't going anywhere," Fiasco thought. Compound fractures were painful, but not deadly, and there was little aid he could render for such an injury.

The darkness cleared like a fog as the light from his aura filled the chasm. There was a body beyond the gang members. It was on its back and far too still. Fiasco recognized the gray uniform, and the telltale green painted tactical ballistic goggles that covered the eyes. It was one of the Phantom Watch group Talon had mentioned before. Long, brown hair waved out behind the head, and he knew it was a woman. Blood trickled from her mouth, and her fingers were curled tight, gripping an invisible ball. The only way he could tell she was alive was from the tiny seizures that made her body slightly jerk.

Fiasco held onto the twisted metal railing, leaning over. "So much for magic users," he said.

The pale blue projected into the far corner. Three museum guards were in a circle back-to-back, their arms cuffed behind their backs, and dirty white strips of cloth placed about their eyes.

"At least some criminal tropes are still true," Fiasco thought after seeing the guards tied up like something out of a cartoon. Regardless, he thanked God that his energy wave was not able to reach the alcove. "There is nothing I can do here, especially for that watch member. There's no telling what's wrong with her, and I could only make it worse," he thought. "Might as well get back to finding that stone. And I still haven't seen Tamerlane at all."

In the front of the museum, the tall wooden door had been vaporized by the van. Powdered sandstone mingled with wood dust and hung around the entrance like a haze. Fiasco peeked his head through the haze and looked inside the museum. The soft overhead lights inside were still functioning. The van had spared the paintings inside the great hall but did a number to the clay statues that now littered the ground. His eyes followed the deep grooves in the dark marble left behind by the vehicle. Somehow the van had narrowly missed the crocodile-like Thalattosuchia bone fossil on the large wooden display at the center of the hall.

"Good. I've always liked that piece," Fiasco regarded as he eased his way through the dust and into the bowels of the grand hall.

The sound of falling glass thumping against soft carpet turned his attention. The gallery was nearly pitch black, but the ambient light from the great hall allowed him to make out the white suit of the Tamerlane gang member who had escaped his wave by jumping through the glass window, rising slow to his feet among the shard remains. Unwilling to waste more time with the rank and file, Fiasco turned back to move further into the museum.

"When they write about this victory, they are going to say I was merciful," he thought. He began to take a step but paused once again. "Or they are going to say I'm not as thorough as Scarlet Valor or Talon, and let one of the robbers escape?"

Making a choice, a thick beam of blue light shot from his right shoulder and into the sternum of the gang member, who was tossed off his feet. The beam curled upward, taking the robber with its momentum. Arms and legs spread out, the criminal grunted as his back struck the far wall with a crunching impact. Calling back his beam, the criminal slumped down into the rubble.

Groaning, Fiasco rubbed his sore wrist and walked through the gallery. As he walked, he kicked broken remains of glass and clay, alerting anyone of his looming presence. Recalling Talon's words of thinking ahead, the aura slipped over his body in a thin blue, and Fiasco raised himself up several inches off the floor, clear of any debris.

Trickling sweat tickled the hairs on his neck that he scratched away with his gauntlet. Floating forward, he passed the gift shop to the left with toppled shelves of trinkets and overpriced gifts that cluttered the ground. Floating to the fossil, the gauntlet on his right hand vanished, and he gave the pale bone a gentle pet with the tips of his fingers on its elongated skull as he passed. It was a move he would sneak behind his father's back as a child, standing on his tip toes— a memory that made him grin.

Leaving the display behind, the gauntlet returned with a buzz. The great hall opened into a grand gallery rotunda that was lit by medieval lanterns that glowered on the walls. Twin wide helical staircases parallel to each other curved upward to another level of the museum. On the first floor, glass displays that once held contemporary sculptures were broken and strewn in front of him in a tangle of a large brass chandelier, its decorative candelabra cracked and broken. He looked up at the high-domed ceiling that was painted in brilliant colors, mimicking some medieval tapestry he could not remember, and saw the wires from the metal mounting where the chandelier must have broken free.

"Some protector," he sighed, scratching his neck again as he glided over the chandelier towards the stairways.

On the far staircase to the left, the van had come to a halt on its side just outside of where the stairs curled up to the second floor. Further bucking the odds of physics, the van was wedged in the entrance of a hallway. The front end was shrouded in stripes of darkness, but he could see the back end from the gentle light shining from a lantern on the wall. Black marks scorched the top enamel of the van. The top door on the back looked jammed shut, its edges bent and mangled. But the bottom door was broken off the top hinge and tilted askew on the floor. From what he could tell, there was no sound coming from within the darkened interior.

Fiasco looked about. There were three other large galleries, two between the staircases that stretched far to the back, and one on the other side of the far-right flight of stairs, lost in shadow. All three had their lights turned down, and he realized that he was like a floating blue lightning bug in the wide-open rotunda. In addition to the fact that it was eerily silent, he had yet to see a glimpse of Tamerlane anywhere inside the museum or the supposed gallery that caught his attention. Any of the dark crevices or rooms that his aura light did not penetrate could be hiding the Mal or more of his gang members.

"Well, not if he's wearing one of those white suits," Fiasco muttered. A breath seeped through his lips, and he touched his chest, concentrating to pull back his power and dim his aura until it was thin around his body. "Now, to find this jerk before Talon suddenly shows up with him in hand to take all the credit."

Staring at the van, he decided that if he explored the vehicle, or the dark room beyond, he would be left vulnerable to an ambush on the other side, so instead, he floated to the right where the hallway was clear of any obstruction. Floating before the opening, his eyes could not cut through the gloom inside. The gauntlet on his right hand glowed as he thought about sending a tendril of power to light up a gallery inside. His arm pointed toward the room when a low, annoying buzz tickled his ear.

"You've got to be kidding me," he thought and waved his hand about his ears. "A fly. Now?"

His eyes searched the air through the goggles for the errant bug that chose the worst time for an interruption but failed to find it. The buzzing grew in intensity, transforming into a flutter that made his head tilt. Even with his ear pressed hard into his shoulder bone, the insufferable noise made it seem as if the bug had retreated directly inside his ear canal, the beating of its wings echoing off the walls. The noise rose to a crescendo, freezing all thought, when his head jerked back off his shoulder from the impact of a hard, solid object that struck just above his temple with a crunch.

Fiasco gasped from the intense and sudden pain. White flashed before his eyes as the agonizing sensation shot down his jaw and neck, jetting through his veins. About his body, his aura wavered as his mind was unable to maintain any thought outside of registering the agony that pounded against his head. Then, it disappeared in a blink, and he dropped to the floor.

Instinct made him land on his feet, which sent pain burning up his soles when he landed on the unforgiving marble. Feeling the pain, his legs buckled. Taking a weary step, he stumbled forward and slipped in shards of glass and clay that slid along the floor. He was barely able to stay upright from the never-ceasing pounding. Head throbbing from whatever had struck his temple, the impact made nausea grip his stomach, and he could feel the bile rising from the vertigo. Yet, his roiling stomach mattered little when something pierced his costume and bit him on the back of his neck.

"Ah!" Fiasco shouted, slapping his neck, but unsure if he hit anything at all.

The pain streamed with the pumping of his blood. It reminded him of the time he was bitten by a scorpion as a child, the searing agony that numbed his hand as he reached for a rock in his backyard. Now, the pain was in his veins as whatever bit him sent a bolt of searing electric current through his spine. Every heartbeat pushed that sensation swimming through his vertebrae. Sweat poured from him and sharp glass bit into his skin when he fell to his knees.

Just when it seemed that the pain would subside, a second current shot like a bullet through his body, contracting his spine and curving it backward in agony. His hands froze into strained claws. His mouth tried to scream, but his jaw was clenched shut, releasing only a suppressed mumble through taunt lips. Through the pain, he tried to call the power, hoping the aura would cancel the force ravaging his body, but he could not think beyond wanting the torment to end.

"I knew it!" a voice above him echoed off the walls.

The current forced tears in Fiasco's eyes, pooling in the wells. The smell of burning entered his nostrils when he breathed tight breaths. Behind his goggles that had grown so hot that the frame seared into his skin, he looked through the watery blur up to the second-floor balcony. Dressed all in white like his minions, Tamerlane floated down on round, white disks attached to the soles of his white leather shoes.

An overweight man, Tamerlane was round at the belly and stretched the blood red shirt he wore beneath his suit. His bald head glistened from perspiration and reflected the ambient light, and he wore safety goggles that covered both eyes with the black rubber strap digging into the fat around his head. They were tinted a shade of red to match his shirt, but Fiasco could still see his eyes dancing excitedly behind the glass. His chubby face wrinkled from his pubescent grin as he stopped his descent just above where Fiasco was forced to the ground.

He floated beside Fiasco's trembling head and crouched to speak, his eyes darting about, leering at him as if he were a lab subject. Identical silver spheres circled like sentries above his head.

"I always had a theory about you. That blue glow of yours," Tamerlane said. His breath was hot and smelled like earthy mold. "You can stop bullets with that emanation and survive heavy damage. But it's like a sponge, correct?" His eyes were wide, and his voice was giddy as he spoke.

You are pathetic to him, the voice said. Fiasco could hardly understand or comprehend the words through the intense pain.

"It's not a shield per se," Tamerlane continued, "but a malleable force field. You bounce around in that thing, and can feel pain if it's bent back towards you with enough pressure or force, correct?"

From the corner of his eyes, Fiasco saw Tamerlane lift his palm upward, a maze of circuitry lines. A haze of dust gathered just above his hand.

"That's where this thing comes in," Tamerlane said, and curled his fingers. The dust coalesced together to form into a small silver ball, a black ring in the middle that looked like an eye. "Nanorobots, my friend. Millions. You walked right through them at the door, and some adhered to your skin. They let me know when you arrived. I programmed them like those remarkable green ants, able to link together into what hit you in the head."

Fiasco's jaw ached and it felt like his teeth were going to break from the strain of being pressed together. Tears rolled down the side of his cheeks, and his eyes followed Tamerlane as he floated around to face him.

"Whizzball, I call it. You know, from the sound it makes." He laughed, his throat squeaking like a heavy smoker. "I know, not very clever, but that was never my specialty. But an interesting creation if I do say so myself. Combined, they are very solid, as you know, and can drill through solid objects. That takes some time, though, and I need to work on it. They can even create holograms." He grabbed the ball between two fingers and studied it in the light with a frown. "I am trying to make a projectile, but I am struggling with getting it to work at this size."

He snatched the ball into his hand and turned to Fiasco with a satisfied grin. "But I'm going to keep trying! That is the American way, correct?"

Tamerlane's countenance changed from joy to what resembled sorrow as he studied Fiasco's face, frozen in pain. "Oh dear, you probably haven't heard a word I've said, have you? I feel for you, truly. It was the dust that was on your skin. I tested the device attached to your neck on one man. It broke his jaw after three minutes. His neck followed when I turned it up a notch." He mimicked twisting close a bottle top with his hands to demonstrate. "He was a very useless man in life, but his death did allow me to test the proper voltage." His face was almost euphoric. "And also, the drilling function. Oh, such an experiment. It's like a knife through butter now."

The current made Fiasco's head jerk back, sending another tear following the other. The burning smell only grew in intensity.

Tamerlane's words struck home, and he thought he could hear his teeth grinding to dust in his skull. Then, there was that sound in his ears— the low crunching of strain as if the constant contraction of his spine was about to break his back at any moment.

Tamerlane stood to full height with a grunt and crack of his knees, and he looked down at Fiasco over his round belly. His face was in shadow, except for the red goggles that made him look like a sneering devil.

"I was told you were not very bright," Tamerlane said dryly. He released the whizzball in his hand, and it joined the others that orbited around his head like a halo. "And drawing in your force field like that? Tsk tsk, young man. You made it easy for me. You know, you don't have to live up to your namesake."

This false Mega human finds you beyond pathetic and he is going to crush you as he would an insect.

Fiasco agreed.

The smell of peony flowers wafted past Fiasco's nose. For a moment, he believed he could smell the flowery scent of Julianna's hair. Thin phantom fingers that felt like hers moved over his neck and down his back as if they tried to stem the tide of pain. Following the Christian faith, there were stories about angels who would come down and succor those in distress, calming the victim as they crossed the veiled into the afterlife. More phantom fingers, warm and soothing, slid under his rib cage, holding him in a tranquil embrace. He wondered if the angels were there, covered in the scent of his love, consoling his battered spirit, and preparing him for death.

"I am already behind schedule because of you, so it is time to move on." Tamerlane raised his left hand with the circuit side up. His right hand was poised over it, holding steady an inch above.

You will never see Julianna again, the voice whispered.

The voice, as always, spoke truth.

Tamerlane waved his right hand clockwise over the other. The embrace of his body grew warmer and tighter about his chest, pushing the breath from Fiasco's lungs. The pressure in his spine clenched again from the rise in electricity, making the crackling sound in his ears mushroom until he could hear little else. His clawed hand clenched tighter, trembling from the current.

As if sensing the pain, the phantom fingers rolled between the gaps in his fingers, holding his hand like Julianna would if she were there. Chest protruding out, the crooked symbol on his chest flared with his internal power. His aura flickered about his body, winking in a blue flash. As if grasping for air, the shield flickered on again, and for an instant, he was able to move a hand.

"Fascinating," Tamerlane said. "Given enough time, you might actually overtake my current. Are you that determined to stop me?" He rummaged around in the outside pocket of his jacket and produced a dark object that looked like a misshapen rock. It gleamed a dark red in the light when he held it out for Fiasco to see. "But I have what I came for."

The last bit of energy that burst from within healed Fiasco enough that he was at least able to think straight again. "The stone of Syriana," he thought. "I was too late. He has it already."

You already failed, the voice said with sharp mockery, and he felt the crooked *F* pulse with heat.

Hiding the gem behind his back, Tamerlane leaned down at the hip towards his face. "I really wish I could study you further. I wish I knew where this power you use originates."

"So would I," Fiasco managed to mutter through clenched teeth.

"Still more fight left in you." Tamerlane rubbed hairs on his chin that did not exist. His eyes behind the red goggles seemed to focus when Fiasco spoke. "Amazing. I would love to continue this banter, but time is of the essence and your friend could show up any minute." Tamerlane stood back up. "And since he's already blocked my escape route, it's time for plan B. It has been a pleasure meeting you, Fiasco, as short as it was, but I have preparations to make."

Tamerlane bowed then floated away on his white disks, out of Fiasco's field of vision.

"Is that what Talon yelled at me?" Fiasco thought. "That we were splitting up? But why didn't he tell me at the beginning?"

Think things through for once, the voice growled. *He did not split up with you. He knew you would fail.* The voice's words seemed as true as any other given his predicament.

"He knew I would fail and went to make sure Tamerlane could not escape afterwards."

The symbol on his chest pulsed hotter and brighter, surging against the current ravaging his body. Struggling, Fiasco was able to pull forward, striding against the current. He lowered his head far enough to find Tamerlane to his right. The round Mal was near the wedged-in van, his back turned to him as he worked. Two of the whizzballs bobbed near his head, their black eyes pointed back, keeping watch as their master configured an upright cylindrical device he had placed in the back of the broken vehicle.

"I need to stop him," Fiasco thought, and the gauntlets blinked at his hands. "If I don't, there is no coming back. The people. Julianna. Her father. Even my father. They would never forgive me for this failure."

But you will always fail.

Blue energy poured from the center of Fiasco's chest, spurred by the voice's words. It lurched over his torso, then to his back, and galloped up his neck in a wave. A high-pitched squeal screamed in his ears when the energy covered the top of his head, and the current ceased. With the device behind his neck that pumped electricity into his body destroyed, motor functions returned to his arms and legs. Falling forward on the marble, Fiasco reached and massaged the small of his back that throbbed burning aches up his spine and neck. Leaning over, particles slipped from his body like powder, coating the ground in a thin layer of dust that covered the glass and clay in debris.

Tethered by their shared programming, the whizzballs that floated near Tamerlane noticed the loss of their comrades. They had stopped bobbing around and floated ominously in mid-air, eyes fixed on him in a death stare. As if receiving a signal, Tamerlane noticed Fiasco's escape from the device, his fleshy mouth agape from the sudden turn of events and redoubled his efforts to work on the device. Sweat atop his bald head pooled then rolled down, staining his white collar as his hands worked feverishly below.

Fiasco rose on legs with circumspect strength that felt heavy from a muscle workout, and he wondered how much more they could handle. The well of power inside felt as if it were on fumes, barely chugging along, but he was still able to raise a hand towards Tamerlane. Pushing through the pain in his shoulder and elbow, a pale blue tendril shot forward from his palm. The glowing rope curled around the thick flesh of Tamerlane's neck. Turning, the overweight Mal cursed and wriggled within its grasp, clutching at his neck and the glowing line. Seeing their master's distress, the whizzballs zipped back and forth, blurry like gray comets, cutting away at the strand until Tamerlane was cut free.

Rubbing his throat, Tamerlane gasped and coughed. Snatching off his goggles, he glared at Fiasco with murderous brown eyes before activating the disk beneath his feet.

"You will pay for that," he growled, his voice hoarse as he floated up towards the second floor.

"Forget him. Get that device." Fiasco called what remained of the tendril back into his body, and let it strengthen his aura.

He glided toward the van with as much speed as he could muster with his meager power reserve, but it was still considerably slower than his usual pace. Passing the spiral staircase, he touched down just next to the van. Inside, he could see what looked like a cylinder of solid glass set on a silver base of buttons and wires. It appeared empty at first glance, but he realized that it was filled with a clear, thick liquid that he was almost afraid to touch. The little training he had done researching on the MegaStream, told him that what he was seeing was a liquid bomb— one of Tamerlane's more insidious creations. In it was a concentrated primer, far more powerful than the household chemicals used by terrorists. Given the size of the canister and the amount of liquid it held, he didn't want to guess how powerful it was, nor did he want to find out when the second chemical was introduced.

"I need to get this thing out of here." Fiasco wiped away the sweat above his eyes from beneath his goggles with hands quavering from shot nerves. Every movement was a demonstration in grinding pain, as all the energy he had was used to maintain his aura shield instead of healing. "I need to take it to the sky, away from the museum, before it explodes."

Gathering his last ebb of strength, Fiasco reached out with both hands, hoping to encase the capsule within his power. Internal energy rolled into his gauntlets, dark blue and thick. Then, he pushed outward with the power. The blue light resembled simplistic hands, but with only three fingers and a thumb. His thoughts were pressed by time, and he was too exhausted to add detail to the manifestation. Reaching the cylinder, he closed the gossamer fingers around the glass, but only felt the air as his manifestations passed clean through the device.

"What the hell?" Fiasco said.

He mentally commanded the hands to try again, but the results were the same, and they passed through the bomb as if he were trying to hug a phantom. His breaths shortened into quick gasps. Cold sweat ran from beneath his mask and down his face as he glanced about, hoping something he saw would help formulate another plan. Uninspired by his surroundings, he began creating a cocoon of energy between his outstretched arms, attempting to cover the entire van, praying he could gather enough power to blunt the explosion. The energy roiled like a blue storm before it streaked outward and swept over the scorched metal. Yet, this too passed harmlessly through the broken metal frame, stopping when it touched the solid back wall.

"Wait a minute," Fiasco thought. He glanced around again. The alcove he was in still had paintings on the wall, pristine and untouched. Above where the van was wedged in the gallery, he noticed that the wall had not taken any damage from the van's impact. Through the haze of pain, he tried to remember. He went back to when he first entered the gallery and walked past the statues.

"Left," he thought. He looked back at the grooves in the marble that veered away from him, passed the opposite staircase, and the realization hit him like a jackhammer. "I was turned around. The van is on the other side."

"Oops," a voice said above him. Fiasco looked up and saw Tamerlane standing on his anti-gravity disks, looking down on him with a sinister grin from ear to ear. "Come," he said.

The enamel of the van shimmered like a kaleidoscope of rainbow light, growing translucent when the brightness waned. In its stead was a whizzball, its black eye glaring as if taunting the Mega as it rose in a buzz to Tamerlane to join the two other units that orbited protectively about his body. Whole once again, the genius Mal rose and curved over the second-floor balcony out of sight. His cackling laughter bounced off the high dome, serving as a reminder to Fiasco of his impending failure.

"A hologram," Fiasco shuttered with a hint of defeat in his voice. With his power all but depleted, he thought about fleeing and using what energy he had left to get out of the museum before it exploded.

Flee. Everyone knows you are a coward. Be who you are, the voice said as Fiasco limped past the two staircases.

He reached the van on the other side that looked identical to what he had just witnessed. When he reached out with his bare hand, he felt the hard, cold steel beneath his fingers. Inside was the same cylindrical device, except the liquid appeared nearly spent.

Helplessly, he watched as the last of the liquid mixed, transforming into a beautifully green gas that swam to fill the canister to the top. It swirled inside like a captured storm cloud. Fiasco looked down at the canister, weariness sagging his shoulders, until the corners of his mouth turned upward as he let out a chuckle.

"Fiasco luck," he thought, just as the blast erupted before him in a light of pure green.

The stairs disintegrated in flames of the same color that washed over the gallery. The antechamber room went up in a glowing, grassy green burst that collapsed the second floor and added its priceless antiques to the conflagration. The mural on the dome curled from the heat before the entire structure succumbed to the concussion and imploded in a rain of stone and glass that careened through a cloud of choking dust.

Showering Fiasco in a wave of heat, the blast elevated the Mega off his feet, tossing him through the air. The aura strained to return, blinking on and off like a light switch, thin from his lack of strength. While some of the shrapnel bounced harmlessly against his shield, other pieces ripped through his shoulder and tore away chucks of flesh as he careened through the exhibitions in the gallery and back into the grand hall.

Pale Thalattosuchia bone scattered outward when Fiasco sailed face-first through his favorite exhibit. The fire leapt out from the tall entryway and spat Fiasco out, his body tumbling through sharp debris, ending when the top of his head struck the sandstone pillars outside. The pillars shook at the base from the impact and fine dust rained from the ceiling.

The green flame coughed from the doorway with a flamethrower sputter until it subsided and fell back inside the museum. Warm, copper-tasting blood trickled from the corner of his mouth when Fiasco turned over slowly and raised himself back to his knees. He coughed more blood onto the shining gauntlet on his hand that landed in a splat and began to sizzle.

Then, he heard it, a warbling sound that subsumed the flicking of burning fire. It was a scream, pitched like an eclectic mix of the A and E strings of a violin. Fiasco's fingers gripped the floor. He tried to move, but his body was transfixed by the pain that crowned from the top of his head. Green flames shot out from the window, scratching, and climbing upward. The shriek continued, bellowing outward in wavering tones that matched the roiling flames, as if someone was singing the last of their life away.

"I need help," he thought desperately, as convulsing pain made his hands tremble. He looked around for assistance, but all he saw were large stone pillars reaching up into the darkness of an awning being consumed by the unnatural green fire. He felt surrounded by the obelisks. He was alone and injured on a small patch of stone that had yet to catch fire.

"Say something," he pleaded, feeling the heat from the fire. "Tell me I'm a loser. Tell me how I failed and let someone die." He used his aura-covered knuckles to try and stand but fell back in a heap to the floor from broken ribs that scratched together inside his body.

"Tell me something. Anything." Silence greeted Fiasco, and he grit his teeth. The voice had never passed up a chance to berate him before, and he bristled in anger that it chose to do so when he needed it most. "Tell me how I've failed her. Tell me how she'll leave me! Tell me anything!"

Sirens echoed in what was left of the landing. Fire trucks emerged through the light gray smoke that swept over the curved driveway outside the museum. Angry at the voice's silence, Fiasco used his own strength and braced himself against the pillar. Ignoring the pain in his shoulder, he managed to slide up in a paint brushed streak of red as he clutched his sore ribs. There were cuts and gashes along his costume. His mask had fared better, coming out relatively whole, but he felt a throbbing beneath the leather from the whizzball that had pounded into his head. The goggles edges were nearly melted from when they had seared into Fiasco's face earlier.

Leaning away from the column, his left arm hung limp at the punctured hole in his shoulder, and blood trickled down from a jagged gash in his calf as he carefully limped down the stairway littered with remnants of the museum. The firefighters raced passed him, shouting, ready to douse the flames with their hoses.

After making it down to the street, he passed between the two remaining vans, pockmarked with holes, and the flaming ruins of the museum. Going against his best intuition, Fiasco glanced over his shoulder, and his mind went drunk from the sight. From the base to the apex, beautiful green flames gyrated in every broken window and opening of the museum. Just outside the landing, the firefighters fought valiantly against the fires, firing their cannon streams of water at the landing and at the floor of the grand hall. The pillars that held up the landing roof cracked from the heat, splintering from the weight of the stone roof. Rocks broke away and bounced down the steep stairway, bringing up chunks of stone in its path. Realizing the futility of their mission, the firefighters dropped the part of the hose they held, yelling at each other to retreat as gray smoke spewed from the landing. Then, the roof imploded.

The sight of the roof above the landing collapsing, the destruction rolling outward in both directions of the entryway like dominoes that broke as they struck against each other, made Fiasco laugh.

"Hey, Julianna," he said, his voice cracking as he watched. "Guess what I did today? You'll be so proud of me." Dust the color of sandstone swirled about his feet.

Walking slowly from the physical pain and depression caressing his heart, Fiasco's foot hit an object that made him stumble. Looking down, he saw a leg adorned in white attached to a body that laid face-first on the pavement. Glancing about, Fiasco realized that the Tamerlane gang members who were unconscious on the landing must have woken up while he was in the museum. They had made it as far as the vans, perhaps trying to escape when they noticed their boss had rabbited without them. But small, blood-red knives jutted out from their legs, tendons, and knees, rendering them inert. They could not walk, but he heard their screams as they grabbed at the unforgiving hilt of knives that seemed welded into their skin.

"Fiasco!" he heard a voice shout at his side. He turned to meet it, clutching his wounded ribs, blood dripping down the tips of his fingers.

Near a series of NHPD interceptors that had arrived at the museum, red and blue lights flashed rhythmically in turns. Talon stood there, holding an unconscious Tamerlane member with a badly misshapen arm in his hand by the scruff of his neck. Police officers took up positions in shouts behind the trunk and doors of the cars and pointed their service revolvers at Fiasco's direction. He nearly laughed at the .22s, .38s, and .9 millimeters that looked like popguns compared to the arms he faced earlier. Yet, something about the serious demeanor of the police made the sadness only increase inside.

"Where were you?" Fiasco said in a whisper.

Talon let the man in his grasp fall to the pavement and walked towards Fiasco. The white eyes on his mask were large and wide, and he had his hands splayed out wide.

"What happened!" Talon said. Fiasco's mind felt dizzy from the pain and loss of blood, and he had a hard time comprehending the words.

The world narrowed to the size of a pinhole, and the earth was liquid beneath Fiasco's feet. His arm clutched for his friend as he gathered his breath, and black dots floated like balloons over his vision. Wind swept through the tears in his uniform, and he hardly felt the impact when his back hit the pavement. The ground felt soothing against his spine, sending a tingling cold sensation out to his fingers and toes. The last image his exhausted mind processed was Talon leaning over him, face upside down at the top of his head, concern emoted clearly on his mask.

"I told you to wait for me," was the last thing he heard Talon say before the world went dark.

He knew you would fail, the voice said. *And so does she.*

Epilogue

Staring at the photo in his hands, Kevin thought about how Julianna's smile looked so bright that day. Her eyes were almost squinted shut from happiness and the sun that reflected off the snow around them. Her dark hair fell to her shoulders beneath a pink knitted snow cap. A grin sprinted about Kevin's lips at the pompom on the top that hung limp to one side.

The air was so frigid on the jagged northern ridge of Mount Washington that her flushed cheeks nearly matched the color of her hat against her brown skin. Even with the thick, pink parka, Julianna was able to hug him from the side, draping her arms around his. She pressed her face so hard against his cold cheek that he could barely give a smile when some stranger they had asked snapped the picture of them together. The trip felt like years ago when it had only been months.

Kevin didn't know whether this discrepancy in time meant that their relationship was in trouble, or if it simply alluded to the strength in their union— the fact that it felt as if they had known each other forever. He pondered the notion as he sat on the couch in his apartment, still in his Fiasco suit that was caked in dried blood. The suit still emanated the acrid smell of smoke, burnt flesh, fire, and blood. He sat mostly in darkness, rubbing his thumb across the picture in his hand.

Being an artist, Julianna always preferred to print out the pictures she thought were worth displaying. "To capture the spirit of the moment," she'd say. He always wondered why that hiking trip up the mountain had been so worthy of a store visit to resupply her expensive ink cartridges. He never understood, until he looked at the picture again and guessed that she had printed it out because it was one of the few times their genuine expression of joy was ever documented. A smile spread on Kevin's lips as he stared at the picture, before giving that happy Julianna a kiss.

A phone buzzed on the glass coffee table, breaking him from his reverie.

"Ssssss," Kevin hissed from the wound in his side as he reached over to grab the phone that sat next to his grime-covered Fiasco mask. Once he had the phone in hand, Kevin had to sit back against the couch and breathe out several times to gain control of the pain. He could feel the power beneath his skin, building with each breath, but he refused to use it to heal any further. After the museum, he never wanted to use his power again.

When he passed out at the museum, he had subconsciously encased himself in a cocoon of energy— something he was unaware he could do as he had never passed out from pain before. When he awoke, the world was a shimmering blue as if he were submerged underwater. He panicked for a moment until he reached out and touched the barrier that was smooth beneath his fingers. As if sensing his consciousness, the energy cocoon melted away. The cocoon had swirled with his energy and had healed his body enough to stand. Looking around for orientation, he was surrounded by a NHPD tactical squadron with their guns at the ready. Unable to penetrate his bubble, they must not have known what to do. Seeing the Mega rise, they kept their sights trained on him, raising their weapons in unison as he rose on steady, but sore, feet.

"Get on the ground with your hands out in front of you now!"

an officer shouted, emphasizing his command by pointing to the ground with his rifle tucked in his shoulder.

Candy cane colored lights flashed with the sirens in the distance. The NHPD TAC officers were screaming instructions at him, their voices hoarse with anger and hatred. Looking about, Talon was nowhere in sight, already having abandoned the sinking ship of their alliance. He couldn't tell how long he had been healing in the cocoon, but behind him, the fire that burned the museum to the ground looked nearly under control, with firefighters now able to penetrate the smoke to get inside. It was only a matter of that time before they found the remains of whoever was screaming inside. Screams that he could still hear in his mind.

Then, he turned to face the police again. He looked at those angry faces staring down their sights at him, and the power burned inside once again. The urge to get away was compelling, and in the end, overwhelming. Ignoring the officers' shouted instructions, the aura thrummed to life and Fiasco took off into the sky. To his surprise, no gunfire followed. His flight was silent, as he longed for the comfort of familiar walls and darkness.

In his apartment, the phone buzzed again in his hand, and he checked the name printed on the bright display. Staring at the photo in the other hand, he put the phone to his ear and answered, "Hello, Julianna."

"Kevin! Where have you been? I've been trying to call you all night!" she said. Her voice was high and brimming with excitement, and it was the first time since they began dating that he did not want to hear it.

"I've been sleeping," he said with a sigh. Another lie to add to the heap. "What's up?"

"What's up?" she asked. "You haven't been watching the news?" He wanted to tell her that he had been watching the news but had to turn it off since every channel just regurgitated his failure. They reported that one of Tamerlane's gang members had been caught in the explosion and died on the scene. Both Fiasco and Tamerlane were being blamed for the death, and the loss of the Haven Museum and its priceless possessions. 'Mega terrorist' and 'Mal' were the adjectives said before his name.

"No, I haven't, I said I was sleeping," he said dryly. He could hear the noise from the television playing the news in the background of Julianna's phone.

"Oh," she replied softly. Her voice was subdued, an indication that she had noticed his tone. It didn't last long before the enthusiasm returned. "Well, I'm over at Jenni's—"

"Who's all there?" he interrupted, wondering how many of his friends had witnessed his failure.

"Well, a few of the girls, Jenni, and Warren. And Ethan, of course." Julianna replied. "But that's not important. You missed how that asshole Fiasco finally got exposed for the fraud he is. He blew up our museum, and unfortunately, someone died. He was a bad guy, but still. Anyway, now he's being blamed for all the damage and murder, and that means that they'll finally get him off the streets!" Julianna giggled into the phone. "So maybe my dad can finally get back to work! Isn't that great?"

Something warm trailed down Kevin's cheek, tickling it like a feather. He wiped it away expecting to see blood from some head wound that he had missed but saw that his hand glisten like orange water in the pale streetlight that bled through his blinds. Surprised, he didn't realize he could still shed tears, yet there it was. And that one single tear was like a plug that had been pulled on a dam, and his throat burned as he fought back a deluge of more.

"Yeah, that's great," Kevin said. He tried to laugh but his voice cracked as he swallowed the lump that formed in his throat. "I guess it's hard to find good help around here, huh? New Haven's curse."

"Kevin, are you okay?" Julianna asked, concerned.

"Yeah," he cleared his throat. "I'm fine. I just woke up, so—"

"You don't sound okay," he heard a rustle of fabric through the phone as if she was getting off a bed or couch. "I'm coming over."

"No don't," Kevin replied and winched as he jumped forward. He couldn't imagine how he would peel that costume off without reopening the wounds and wasn't clever enough to come up with an explanation for it, either. At least that was the excuse he told himself for not wanting to see her.

You are a coward.

"You don't want me to come over?" she emphasized the word '*me*' when she spoke.

"No, Jay. I just," he tried to find the proper words, but all he could feel was the heat of pain from his tortured body, and another source of agony forming deep inside. "I want to be alone, that's all."

"Well, then I know something is wrong, Kevin Jones." He heard a door latch close behind her. The background noise on Julianna's end disappeared, and he guessed that she must have moved to an isolated location. "I know this because you've never said that to me before," she continued.

"I don't want to talk about it." He wondered why she always had to be so stubborn.

"It?" she had caught him in a word flub like she always did. Why did he allow her in? Why did she have to know him so well? "So, you admit something is wrong."

"Julianna..."

"No, Kevin. I can hear it in your voice. Why are you shutting me out again? Something is wrong, and we need to talk about it."

"No, we don't," Kevin sighed. The anger was building inside, and he desperately wanted to hang up.

"Why?" she asked, and it was her voice that strained from emotion this time. From the way it gave out in the end, he knew that he had made her cry again, and Kevin bit his lips to hold back his own.

Real men do not cry, the voice said. *Be a man and do the right thing.*

"I don't want to talk about it because," he said, fighting through the sadness, "I'm afraid of where our conversation would go if we did."

There was silence for a moment at Julianna's end, before she finally responded. "You've said that before. That time at Andy's...," her voice trailed off and was wet with tears. "And where will it go, Kevin?"

"You know, Julianna." He heard her sniff in reply.

"So, I don't have a say?" she sniffed again. "You're not going to give me a choice, or even tell me what's wrong? You are just going to make up my mind for me?"

"I'm giving you a say right now," Kevin replied, finding some strength to add to his resolve.

Julianna's tone quickly switched to anger as they descended into their first fight. "So, I leave it alone and pretend to forget about it, or we break up? Is that what you're saying?" The emotion in her voice was pointed and sharp, transformed as she too took a stand.

There was now silence through the receiver.

The question her father had asked him returned and rang in his ears, "Where will you be in five years?" The phrase played torturous strands in his thoughts, and he still did not have a remedy for it. He thought back to the beginning with her, when even Warren, his best friend, did not feel he deserved her love. The words were never spoken, but his actions said plenty when he refused to acknowledge Kevin as a rival for her love. Others believed it as well, with their sideways glances and accusing eyes as he and Julianna walked together. They were real-life beauty and the beast. Even his parents thought so highly of Julianna and her bright future that his own mother suggested she leave him.

How could he see a future with Julianna when so many others hardly believed that he even deserved to be her boyfriend?

You are doing the right thing for once in your life.

It had grown so silent on the phone that Kevin hoped that Julianna had enough of the fighting and hung up on him. He deserved nothing less.

"Hello?" he eked out into the phone.

"I'm still here," He could barely hear her voice.

"So, we're done? Can I go?" he waited for the line to go dead. With everything inside, the thoughts and emotions that conflicted and complimented each other at the same time, Kevin wanted to hang up as well. He wanted to be selfish, to keep her around longer, to smooth it over with dinner, movies, and flowers and a foot massage later. But the voice was right. It always was. He was a coward. It was right once again when it said she deserved something more.

There was an air of static that stabbed his heart with every passing second.

"No," Julianna finally replied. Her voice was thick with a sadness that equaled his own, her words stunted, barely able to speak through the pain. "We need to talk about this."

He could sense her tears through the phone and picture the anguish on her face, and Kevin could feel his cheek being tickled again by his own.

The voice was silent in that moment, but Kevin already knew what it would say.

The Truth

New Haven, Summer

A breeze swept softly over Fiasco's aura as he flew horizontally, cutting through the sky. The contents in the paper bag he had cradled like a small child in the nook of his left arm grew warm from his glowing blue gauntlets. The condensation from the bottles inside had soaked through the paper, turning the outside into a coffee-colored mush that made it nearly slip from his grasp when he turned south. Reaching beneath his goggles with his free de-powered hand, he wiped both eyes with his finger, attempting to clear the haze over his vision.

Attached to the Blanchet building, the setting sun made the gray parking garage glow a bright tan in the fading light. The garage appeared to move up and down as if Fiasco were in the front car of a roller coaster. He looked at the facade of the garage, shut his eyes, then opened them to the darkened interior of the second floor. He shut them once more and opened them to the fourth floor. If his timing was right, then he knew Warren would be on the fourth, lurking in the shadows to sneak a smoke break, letting the open-air cleanse the smell from his clothes to avoid Jenni's wrath.

Skeletal steel metal beams gave Fiasco something to concentrate on to keep his flight steady. In the corner, gray wisps of smoke rose from Warren's mouth. The last of the sunlight splashed orange against his face as he looked out. With a thought, the blue aura flickered and dimmed, and Fiasco slowed his flight to attempt a landing. A burbling hiccup rose through his throat that he hacked and coughed away. The darkness behind Warren grew as he approached, rising and falling, his view transitioning from the sand-colored concrete exterior to the dark interior and back again.

Up and down he soared until he became dizzy. "Look out!" Fiasco shouted to Warren, who quickly raised his hands and turned to the side to avoid him.

Fiasco entered the darkness headfirst but had misjudged his trajectory too low. As he entered the parking garage, the tip of his boot clipped the edge of the concrete wall. Caught for a moment on the sturdy structure, he tripped up with a curse word, hugging his package as he tumbled over. Fiasco let his power surge to correct his flight path as best he could and slid along his stomach across the floor. The aura dulled any harm he would feel from the sandpaper-like surface, freeing him up to scramble as he grasped at the bottles in the bag that tinkled while they rolled away along the pavement.

Coasting to a halt, a smile crept across Fiasco's face as he had managed to catch one of the bottles before it broke against a rigid parking block. Fiasco crawled through the dirt and mire, reaching after the other bottles to bring the errant siblings back together into a six pack.

Warren loomed over him, one hand on his hip between his suit jacket, shaking his head. Fiasco looked up huffing, giving him a weak smile.

"Ta-da!" Fiasco said. "Hey, Warren. I got one," he continued, holding up the bottle with pride. He chuckled as he rose on shaky feet, then adjusted his goggles that were tousled from his landing.

Warren took a long pull from his cigarette that turned the tip a bright red as he breathed in. "I see that you did," Warren replied.

Smoke curled around his head as he dropped the cigarette stump and crushed the butt with the bottom of his foot.

His best friend had adjusted well in the weeks since he caught a drunken Kevin changing into his Fiasco costume. Dressed only in his mask, goggles, and boxer shorts, Fiasco had to chase Warren down through the parking structure, capturing his best friend in a manifestation of a rope that curled him from head to toe, but kept him upright like a coiled spring. In the end, he had to cover Warren's mouth with another tendril to quiet his shouting once he took off his mask and goggles to reveal his face.

Since then, Warren revealed that, deep down, he had suspected that there was something Kevin held back, just like Julianna, but he couldn't quite put his finger on it. He listed a few things he thought it might've been, like a broken home, estranged sibling, or some weird past, but said he never would have guessed he was the maligned Mega. Once the thought settled in, Warren seemed almost proud to be best friends with the Mega that ravaged the city— the most notorious man in New Haven, and vowed to keep his secret, even from Jenni.

"You proud that you were able to catch that one bottle?" Warren asked with sarcasm, his voice echoing in the empty lot. "Is this what Megas are doing now? Skulk empty parking garages and drink beer?" He watched Fiasco stumble to pick up the rest of the beers— disheveled and costume filthy. "You know you don't have to wear that mask around me, Kevin," he continued. "It looks hot and dirty. In fact, your entire costume looks like trash. I bet you have serious swamp ass in that thing."

Fiasco stooped and peered back over his shoulder at him. "You sure you don't know Talon? He said something similar once." Turning, he reached down for another bottle. "Well, someone could see me, Warren, like you did, that's why I keep it on. And I'm a wanted fugitive, remember?" Fiasco responded with a bitter tinge in his voice. "That reminds me, where's your shadow?"

"Who? Jenni?" Warren replied, remembering to pant out his shirt to clear out the smoke stench. "Shit man, I have to show my ass just to get away from her and catch a smoke."

"Not her. The one that loves you more than Jenni. Your little peon, Ethan." Fiasco said. "Thought he would be out here lighting your cigarettes for you."

"Oh, him," Warren's expression darkened. "Well, he's grown beyond me, buddy. He's not even with the company anymore. Got some other job in IT, making decent money. We're not on speaking terms for..." he looked away as he thought of the right phrase to finish his sentence, "...other reasons."

"The butterfly has emerged from the cocoon, huh? Flew away." Fiasco fluttered his fingers. "Don't feel bad, though. We all have to grow eventually."

All but you.

Standing, Fiasco had gathered the remaining bottles; only one had broken, its contents saturating the concrete. He considered it a successful landing. The boots he wore were still covered in a layer of dark soot and scratched against the concrete as he walked towards Warren.

"Here, I saved you one. Should help take that sour expression off your face," Fiasco said as he shoved a bottle into Warren's chest. He twisted off the cap of his own bottle, and his mouth watered when he heard that hiss and watched the foam spill over the top.

"How many drinks in are you?" Warren asked.

Fiasco looked down at the remaining three pack. "This will finish off my second case."

"What's that, forty-two beers!?" Warren replied with that typical high pitch he gave when surprised. "And it's been this cheap rot gut? You can drink that much and not die?" He swished the bottle in the air.

"Well, it takes a lot to get me going and its cheaper with this swill," Fiasco said, and he waved at his friend. "Come on. Drink up and join me."

"I'm working, dude. I can't drink this," Warren said to Fiasco and turned to follow him. "You would be on shift, too, if you didn't get canned."

"Well, I don't want to drink alone," Fiasco said. "And I didn't get canned, I quit, remember?"

Since the breakup with Julianna, making phone calls to ensure strangers paid some billion-dollar company back became no more important than the gum on the sole of his shoe. The cafeteria glimpses, catching Julianna's lingering scent in the stairway, and seeing others enjoy her presence while he couldn't were too much for Kevin to bear. When Julianna finally set off for her graduation leave from the company, maintaining the silence between them, he knew he had to quit to save what was left of his life before she returned.

"Well, you sure made it seem like you wanted to get canned. Your fall off in collections was something that came up in the managers' meeting almost weekly." A dusk to dawn sensor light illuminated overhead, replacing the setting sun, and bathed the fourth floor in a soft, white light. Warren held his beer up and peered inside the bottle. "And this beer isn't even cold."

"Nag nag nag," Fiasco said as he rolled his eyes behind his goggles. He took a long pull from his bottle and slid his back down into the corner of the concrete wall to sit among the discarded cigarette butts. He placed his arms across his knees, lazily holding the skinny neck of the bottle.

Warren grimaced. "Dude, I saw Clint piss in that corner not two days ago."

"Well, you were just standing here in it," Fiasco retorted.

"Yeah, *standing*. Not ruining my clothes by sitting in someone's urine." Warren glanced down at his perfectly kept double-breasted navy jacket that he had paired with stainless steel cuff links that Jenni's dad had passed down to him.

"I'm sure I'll be fine," Fiasco sighed. He took another drink. "And you called me a Mega earlier. I'm no Mega. I just have to wear this when I fly. It's not like I can do that in normal clothes."

Warren looked to his right in the direction Fiasco flew in. "So, that smoke I see out there is not your doing?"

Fiasco laughed, then coughed when the beer choked his throat and burned his nose.

"That? No man. That over there is too funny," he coughed again, then let out a laugh that squeaked. "So, I was just at a gas station dressed like this, getting the beer, right. And when I walked out, bag in hand, a guy in a sedan who was pulling in saw me. I must have spooked him. You should have seen his face—eyes big as saucers. He must have panicked or something because he lost control and rammed right through a pump. Gas was everywhere." Fiasco's laugh rolled through the garage.

"Are you serious?" Warren said, walking toward him. "Was anyone hurt?"

Fiasco wiped the spittle from his mouth and took in a breath to control his laughter. "No. But when he bumped the curve, his undercarriage must have created a spark or something, because all the gas that had spilled before the emergency stop went up just like that." He snapped his fingers.

"You survived that fire?" Warren glanced again at the dark smoke in the distance. "Did the driver make it? Did you put the fire out?"

Playing with the label that was peeling from the bottle between his knees, Fiasco snorted. "Yeah, I did. And yeah, he did. Covered the guy in a shield the minute I saw him crash into that pump. Then suppressed the fire with my power so the whole station wouldn't explode. I'm good at putting out fires now since I'm around so many." He looked at the soot on his shoes. "I just stood there and laughed and laughed in the middle of that fire. We're old friends at this point."

"Well, that's something to be proud of, at least," Warren said. "Saving that guy."

"Yeah," Fiasco's head tipped back to finish the bottle and toss it aside. It was still bumping along the asphalt when he retrieved another from the pack. "I'm proud that someone was so scared of me that they risked blowing themselves up just to get away."

Warren leaned his hip against the wall and faced Fiasco. He crossed his arms over his chest, still holding onto the beer. "You've had a bad run, I admit. That museum thing...," his voice trailed off as he balanced his beer on the ledge. "People are going to be talking about that one for a while. Since. You know."

Fiasco finally looked up at his friend, the pain in his eyes hidden behind the goggles that reflected the overhead light. "I didn't kill anyone, Warren. I told you that was Tamerlane."

Fiasco believed the words he said, but the power still burned from guilt, knowing his failure allowed that man to die. A real Mega-hero would have remembered the man they had knocked unconscious the moment they entered the museum and found a way to save him before the fire from Tamerlane's bomb burned him alive, leaving just a charred husk for the authorities to find. Talon would have saved him if he were there. The criminals would have fled if Scarlet Valor had arrived instead of Fiasco. They were the real Megas.

"Yeah, public opinion is leaning that way— giving you some slack. But maybe it's time you moved on. Move past that incident," Warren replied. He studied the content in the bottle for a moment, the falling water droplets making his mouth water until he decided to break protocol. He twisted off the cap and it went rolling along the ground.

Fiasco lifted his bottle. The two toasted with a clink, and the silence lingered between them. Fiasco thought back to the last time they shared a drink together, realizing it had been few and far between since Warren and Jenni got engaged.

"I saw Julianna today," Warren said, as he stared down at his bottle. Fiasco kept his goggles forward, pretending not to hear. Every time they met, it seemed, he had to bring her up. He imagined Warren and Jenni going to sleep together, gossiping about them into the night. The couple had become insufferable to be around since the breakup, like that two-headed monster couple that always thought they knew what was best for their other couple friends. "I'm not the only one, either." Warren continued. "I noticed she's still getting attention from the fellas."

Fiasco glanced up and saw that bright grin on Warren's smooth brown skin. At least his best friend was kind enough to trigger enough anger to quell his power level, which would make getting drunk easier.

"She's very pretty. As always. And nice," Warren said. "She's not going to wait for you forever, Kev."

"Is there a point to this conversation?" Fiasco said, frustrated.

"Just what I said. Guys are driving hard to paint," Warren swallowed a pull, and his face contorted from the taste. "She'll never say it, but Jenni can tell. She told me she's waiting for you to come to your senses."

Fiasco looked down at his bottle and wondered how his six pack was going so fast. "I'm going to have to make another beer run. Maybe I can start a riot this time at the liquor store."

"Are you even listening to what I'm saying?" Warren's voice grew stern. "You're going to lose the best thing that has, or will ever, happen to your sorry life, and you're not even going to fight for it?"

The bottle between Fiasco's legs scratched against the concrete as he rolled it 'round and 'round with his palm over the top. "You don't understand, Warren. It's for the best that we're not together."

"Yeah, you keep saying that, but you never tell me why. Is it because of Fiasco? Because everyone hates him and you're not the greatest Mega in the world?"

"That's part of it," Fiasco said with a burble and laugh. "Who wants to date a loser Mega?"

"Then stop!" Warren leaned towards him. "Take off that costume, throw away that stupid mask and goggles, and just be Kevin Jones. She doesn't even know about Fiasco, and Kevin is who she loves, not him."

"You won't understand," Fiasco sighed.

"Sure I do," Warren said and slid down the wall to sit next to him.

"Hey, what the hell, Warren," Fiasco said, moving over to give them space. "I thought you said it was filthy down here. You're going to ruin that fancy suit, and Jenni is going to kick your ass."

"I said Clint pissed where you're sitting. It's fine over here," Warren chuckled. "And I do get it. You're no different than any man that has ever existed. Don't you think that the first man who realized he could run faster than the rest of the tribe wasn't running everywhere he went to show off? Fiasco makes you special. He is your niche that separates you from most people. You think being him will somehow make you deserving of Juli."

Fiasco lifted the beer bottle to his lips and could smell the sweet amber contents, but decided against taking another sip, staring at the ground instead. He had no response because Warren was right, and it stabbed like a knife. He thought about the power, and the voice that had taken over his life. Even in the months he had not been Fiasco, at the beginning of the relationship with Julianna, both were still there, clawing at his consciousness, begging to be utilized.

"It's not that easy to just stop," Fiasco said. "If I could just quit, don't you think I would have already? But I am Fiasco. This is who I am."

You are the Fiasco, the voice said.

Warren continued, his words twisting the blade. "Sure, it is that easy. You're just scared is all. You're scared that plain old Kevin the bill collector is not good enough for her. I'm your best friend, I think. So just admit it."

"Of course he's not!" Fiasco shouted, making Warren's eyes twitch. "She was going to leave Kevin Jones the minute she graduated. Or grow beyond him later. Can you blame me for trying to give her something meaningful to hold on to?"

"But she wouldn't leave Fiasco the Mega-hero, right?" Warren replied, maintaining his normal, calm persona.

"Probably not," Fiasco replied softer. Warren pushed him on the shoulder into the wall with a laugh. "Damn that hurt," Fiasco sat down the beer and rubbed his sore shoulder. "I can feel pain when my aura is down, you know."

"Yeah, I know," Warren sniggered. "Oh man, Julianna really is your first real girlfriend, huh? Like ever." He chuckled again. "Listen, Kevin or Fiasco," saying the Mega name with sarcasm, "if she wanted to leave, she was going to leave regardless. You being Fiasco won't pay her bills, and she has her own life and dreams to chase."

The logic made sense, but it was far too late for reason.

"Well, now she can leave, and not have to worry about me or Kevin." The thought of no longer having her brought back the urge to drink, and Fiasco took a swallow. "We were just holding her back anyway. Everyone holding onto us are threatened with being dragged down themselves."

"Don't be such a drama queen," Warren sighed. "Fiasco is not that significant, to be perfectly honest with you. And I don't think you really believe what you just said." Warren's legs slid up so he could also rest his arms along his knees. "But now I can see that this is a confidence thing."

Silence descended between the two, as his friend kept his head bowed between his legs for several moments so that Fiasco could see the perfect waves glistening in his hair.

Then, Warren finally lifted his head back up and said, "Do you know how much it actually hurt when you told me how you two kissed at that party?" Fiasco looked and saw that grin, but also noticed the sincerity in Warren's eyes. "I really liked Juli and felt like I gave her my best game. And yet, she still straight up chose you over me."

"That was a good party," Fiasco said, and his mouth twitched up to a smirk. The memory of her body shivering in his arms as he dared a kiss spread his lips wide. "I didn't think you were that hung up about it."

"Well, I was. It took a good week before my injured pride healed. And I get everything you've done since then. I mean, you out kicked your coverage with her. I don't even know how you got her because...no offense or anything...but she is so far out of your league," he said, with a laugh. "My point is, it's only natural when a man is with a woman like Juli to feel like he has to overcompensate," Warren continued and took a drink.

Although Fiasco felt as though anger was the appropriate emotion in response to Warren's sentiment, he realized that anyone would be upset at losing Julianna. For that reason, he found it in himself to empathize with his friend. He knew just how he felt— only worse, and far more miserable because he once had her.

"But look at me," Warren stood. He cleaned the dirt off the back of his pants then waved his hand over his chiseled face with its five o'clock shadow, and down his jacket that Fiasco knew hid a fit body. "She turned down *this* to be with you."

"Thanks jerk," Fiasco guffawed and flexed his skinny arm. "I'm not that bad, you know." His costume hung even more off his body with the weight he had lost since the breakup.

"No, Kevin, you're actually not," Warren said with a snicker. "I wouldn't be friends with you if you were as bad as you seem to think. And given all the choices of guys who Juli could have dated instead, she must think highly of you, as well."

Fiasco snorted a succinct laugh. "The competition for her was pretty fierce, right? Seemed like our entire sales floor had a crush on her back then."

"Man, you could have thrown a rock on our floor and Julianna could have been with any man it hit. Probably most women, too," Warren huffed, then finished off the bottle with a smack of his lips. "Buddy, you won the greatest battle in your life that night and didn't even know it when you got her."

That's because losers will always lose, the voice said.

Warren tongued the last of the beer from the bottle and sat it on the ledge. "But then you had to go and get selfish."

"Now you're talking crazy," the sudden movement of standing rushed the booze to Fiasco's brain to the point where he stumbled enough to clutch the wall to steady himself.

"How am I being selfish? I'm the one that let her go so she didn't have to worry about us when she left," Fiasco said. "I did it to free her."

"No. All you did was tell her that she wasn't worth moving away from your bland, boring life," Warren said. "She believed in you and you, being scared that you're not good enough, chose the coward's way out. You were being selfish by not even giving her a chance."

The soft light in the parking garage morphed into a pale blue glow as the power inside Fiasco burned to the surface. His aura covered his body, nearly double its normal size, burning like the tail of a shooting star. Sparks burst off his body and the gauntlets on his hand, fizzling in the air before landing on the concrete in wisps of dark smoke. Warren put his hand up and took a step back, mistaking the display as a sign of anger, instead of the spectacle of unadulterated depression that it truly was.

"I'm sorry, man, I didn't mean to upset you," Warren said, his mouth open as he studied the spectacle. The air around him grew so warm that he had to slowly remove his suit jacket and drape it over his arm.

"It's okay. I'm not angry," Fiasco said meekly. His gauntlet covered hands curled into fists. "Did I ever tell you how my power works?"

"No, you haven't." Looking an ashen blue against the light of his aura, Warren laid his jacket over the concrete wall, then waved his hand. "Go on, tell me."

Fiasco hesitated, almost embarrassed to tell him the truth. Every time he said it out loud to himself, he wanted to laugh from the insanity of it. "Long story short," Fiasco swallowed. "The worse I feel, the stronger I get."

Warren's eyebrows arched upward. "The worse you feel, as in physically? Is this why your stomach is always upset?"

He is going to laugh at you. Fiasco agreed but felt compelled to continue.

"No. Emotionally," Fiasco continued. "Depression, misery, malaise, despondency." He touched the light blue luminescence that surrounded the crooked *F* symbol on his chest. "Anything negative. When I feel those emotions and hold onto them, they turn into...this inside."

Mentioning the voice, Fiasco decided, was a step too far that would only make his story sound even more absurd. That was one secret he had to keep close, since he really didn't know whether it was real or a sign of lunacy.

The lashes on Warren's eyes fluttered as if his brain was processing the information like a computer. "Let me get this right," he leaned against the wall and spoke with his hands. "Whenever we see you, like this, you're feeling as depressed and miserable as possible?"

"On that day, at that time, yes."

Warren's head jerked back in surprise. "Wow. Just like that movie," he muttered, shaking his head as he put his hands on his hips and turned to walk away.

The warm night breeze brushed against Fiasco's chin and played through his mask ties as he rested the back of his elbows on the concrete wall, watching his friend walk a circle inside the garage. The aura dimmed and boosted in luminosity as he waited for that laugh— the mockery Warren was about to heap on him once he contemplated everything he was told. There was a reason he never shared his secret with anyone, not even Julianna. Sure, there were Megas and Mals alike whose powers caused abnormalities and sometimes physical deformities, but even with those examples, no one would truly believe a person could be cursed with such a terribly ridiculous gift.

Apparently, the concept of his power was done baking. Warren saddled up next to him, eyes closed and hands in prayer pressed to his lips. The two stood silent together for several moments.

"Well, I never expected you to say that," Warren said, opening his eyes. "But I have to tell you, you've never been more of a real Mega in my eyes than now."

Fiasco lifted his head and looked at his friend. "Don't patronize me. That's not funny."

"I'm not joking," Warren's face was grim and his voice mellow. "To think. Just to put on that costume and try and help people means that it has to make you miserable, yet you continued to do it? I don't care what your reasons were regarding Julianna because you were Fiasco way before her. That's amazing to me, man. I don't know if I could be that—"

"Stupid," Fiasco laughed.

Warren's face remained stoic. "I was going to say courageous."

"Thanks." Fiasco exhaled and allowed an awkward smile. "That really means a lot coming from you." Whether Warren truly meant it or not, he had to give his friend credit for trying.

"You ever think about telling her all of this?" his friend asked.

"Yes. I was going to tell her until the museum thing happened. I thought after that win I would have something solid to stand on when I did. Not just the lame 'woe is me, look at my bad power' thing."

"Damn," Warren scratched his head then smoothed the hair that stood up down with his palm. "I can't say that wasn't a bad idea, to be honest. That's if you believe that Fiasco was something that would be important to her. But give her more credit than that. Juli is not that shallow."

"Okay, I get it, Warren. I messed up. But it made sense at the time," Fiasco said, then turned and looked back to New Haven. The sun had gone down upon the city, and streetlights made it twinkle like stars. The smoke had turned gray in the distance, and he could see the red and white lights flashing at the gas station. "She hates me, though. This me. She blames Fiasco for her dad losing his job. She thinks I'm a murderer, for God's sake. Do you know how that feels? To have the woman you love hate an aspect of yourself that much?"

"That's what I'm saying, though. She doesn't know about Fiasco," Warren countered, his voice sounding exasperated like a parent having to explain something to a child for the tenth time.

"I couldn't lie to her again, Ren," Fiasco shook his head. "I couldn't take keeping it from her."

"Well, then again, give Julianna more credit. I bet if she knew you were Fiasco, she wouldn't hate you. Hell, she might even help you get over that terrible part of your gift. The thing is, though, you won't know until you try and give her that chance you denied her by breaking up in the first place."

Fiasco leaned over and laid his chin on the back of his hands on the balcony, contemplating Warren's words as he stared into the distance.

"You could be right," he said, then snorted. "The funny part is, I couldn't even be Fiasco when me and her began. There just wasn't enough sadness there to plug into. The happiness she brought killed it. When you really think about it, I guess she's another person who could defeat Fiasco." Their shared laughter echoed against the concrete walls of the empty lot.

"That's why it hurt when you said that I was being selfish. How I didn't give our love a chance. I had never felt anything like it before, so to me, that love was everything...," His voice weakened as he choked on the sadness. "Look at you, though," Fiasco finally said, twisting his head to look at Warren, his face brightening with a grin beneath his mask.

Warren's eyebrow kicked up. "What did I do?"

"Being engaged. Giving me advice about my relationships. Hell, not even railing me over how my power works, which would have been a softball tossed underhand to the Warren I knew. When did you get so wise and mature?"

Warren's laugh echoed, "Don't give me too much credit. I'm not that deep." He took a breath and said, "Blame Jenni. She domesticated me."

"She's really been good for you, huh?"

"Yeah," Warren smiled, using his right thumb to flick at the palm of his left hand. "I'm not going to lie. At first, she was just a rebound from my failure with Juli. But Jenni knew something I didn't when I was going after her friend. That she and I were the ones really meant to be together. She said she knew me, and Juli would never get together. Apparently, she liked you even before the party. It took me awhile to realize that she was right."

"When?" Fiasco asked. "When did you know Jenni was the right one for you?"

"I don't know," Warren grinned, showing his white teeth. "When she left, I would smell the pillow and smile. Hell, I didn't even mind finding that damn red hair in everything like I normally would in the past. When I discovered or thought of something new, I couldn't wait to tell her. I guess that's when I realized that she wasn't just someone I could live with, but someone I couldn't live without."

"She became your best friend."

"Yeah, I suppose so. Sorry."

"It's okay," Fiasco smiled, thinking of Julianna. "I get it."

Warren continued, "Once I realized that, it's all been a blessing. But that's your answer right there."

"What is?" Fiasco said.

"Julianna is the answer," Warren replied. "Like I said, she was the best thing that ever happened to you. Fiasco makes you miserable and obviously unhappy. God gifted her to you so you wouldn't have to do it anymore. She is your blessing. I guess she's a gift for having to put up with the depressing shit for so long. But forget the power. Forget trying to be special, and just be Kevin Jones."

"Well, thanks friend," Fiasco sniffed out a chuckle.

Realizing the failure of his own phrasing, Warren returned the mirthful facial expression. "You know what I meant. All I'm saying is that you still have time to fix this, if you leave Fiasco behind."

It wasn't what Fiasco expected to hear but knowing that Warren and Jenni both thought he still had a chance, splashed cool water on the power that burned inside. There had been so many clues of her presence in his apartment, it was almost as if she had planted the items there purposefully to be discovered. There was no doubt his heart ached whenever he smelled Julianna's lingering scent on his pillow or found a hair clip between the couch cushions. Drives felt empty without her voice, and he couldn't deny how his heart leapt any time his phone rang, nor could he deny the depths his heart sunk to when it wasn't her name flashing on the screen. Without even knowing it, Julianna had stabbed deep into almost every aspect of his life with harpoons, and he felt the pain of trying to remove her barbs whenever he moved.

"You know, this reminds me of something," Warren said, shuffling towards him. "You know that bar down the street, the one you don't like, and only went with me like, once?"

Fiasco nodded, "Too many people."

"Right," Warren replied. "There was this one regular there, Dale, a firefighter. But he wasn't the typical fire fighter you would see. He was fat. Out of shape. Not stoic or humble at all, but more lecherous than honorable. The kind of guy who would say he was off duty if you told him there was a fire in the kitchen."

"Okay," Fiasco said as he kept his gaze towards the horizon.

"We always ragged on him that he just wasn't the normal, proud, honorable firefighter," Warren stopped when he stood close. "And I remember one time I said that line again, and a drunken Dale looked at me and replied, well Warren, we can't all be heroes."

Fiasco looked up and over to his laughing friend. A huff went through his nose, along with a grin that spread with each nod of his head. "Point taken Warren."

Powered by the remaining embers inside, the glowing blue aura dimmed until it framed Fiasco. Standing in that drafty garage, he wondered if it was even possible to go back in time. The wise maxim went that one could never truly go home again, and he probably had already crossed that time threshold with Julianna in the months they had been apart. So much had changed in that time between losing his job and Julianna graduating and departing for only God knows where.

It was all too much to think about in just one night, especially with the booze pumping through his veins. Without a word, Fiasco leaned over to the corner and gathered the one beer he had left, then floated up to the ledge with the package tucked deep in his arm, trailing sparkling blue dust behind him.

"I have to go. I think I have some liquor at home, and I'm going to need much more than this bottle to process everything," he said, the power already burning through his buzz.

You are headed towards catastrophe, the voice warned, and Fiasco wondered why it had been nearly silent until that point. It let Warren speak unabated, as if it were uninterested in the conversation until there was hope that Julianna could return. Perhaps it feared being defeated by her once again. It was either the insidious jiminy cricket or her, and it knew which would win.

"Thanks, Warren, I needed to hear all this," Fiasco said. He looked down at his friend who stared up at him, leaning against the wall with an assuring smile. "And I have to admit, it felt good to finally tell someone about everything."

"Well, that's what friends are for. To tell you the truth, right? Glad you finally felt you could confide in me," Warren replied. Grabbing his jacket, he turned to walk away before pausing, then turned to wag an accusing finger at the Mega. "Oh, before you go. You look like hell. For real. Shave. Take a shower. Clean yourself up before you meet her. Have some self-respect and get your shit together, man."

"Thanks, dad. If I ever see Talon again, I'll introduce the two of you since you have the same advice," Fiasco laughed, then took a step off the ledge, his aura rippling like the top of a lake as he floated in the soft breeze.

"Do you really think there's still a chance of fixing this?" he asked, still feeling that pang of doubt that he reckoned must have been the remnants of the voice's rebuke.

"Of course. There is always a chance. For some damned reason, that amazing woman loves you. And if you can get through managing that awful power of yours for this long, then it shouldn't be a problem to get her back," Warren replied, then his smile faded, and his intense eyes bore into Fiasco's. His voice darkened when he said, "But don't take too long, Kevin. Like I said, she's not going to wait on you forever."

The Callout

It was mid-day in New Haven, and translucent gold sunlight beamed through the drawn vertical blinds on Kevin's sliding glass balcony door. He was pacing again. He stared at the dark screen in his hand, still wondering if he was doing the right thing by reaching out to Julianna. Despite the reassurance from Warren, and an angry phone call from his fiancée that was more expletives than words day later, he was still paralyzed by fear.

No, you are not doing the right thing. End this now and save yourself the pain.

"Shut up," Kevin muttered. His stomach turned like a wheel of pain and his pace increased. Sweat misted on his forehead from the exercise and frayed nerves. With captured breath, he quickly found Julianna's contact entry in his phone.

Kevin laughed. "A for angel. First entry. Dear Lord, I am such a wuss," he thought, and hit her name. His heart pumped in his chest with each successive ring. The palm of his hands felt damp as a swamp, and he thought about ending the call before she could pick up.

"Hello, Kevin," Julianna said. The sweat on his body turned cold as if he had been caught stealing candy by his mother. There were no inflections he could hold onto in her voice that said she was happy to speak to him, and his courage began to melt all over again.

"Hello, Jay," his mouth felt dry as sandpaper. "Long time no talk."

That was pathetic. Kevin agreed and felt the perspiration from his pits tickle his skin as sweat dripped down his sides, and he wondered why he hadn't rehearsed the call beforehand.

"Well, not since you broke up with me, right?" her sarcastic tone made his heart sink further in his chest.

"Right," Kevin breathed out, then cleared his throat. "Well, I've been thinking and honestly, I miss you. I miss us. Together."

There was an expectation of some reply, but all he heard was heartbreaking silence. That stillness deepened the well of power reserve inside—power that he chose to ignore.

"I miss us, too," Julianna said sheepishly, and paused. "Sometimes."

"Well, I'll take sometimes. That's something, at least," Kevin sighed, and his chest warmed from the swell inside. "I know you probably hate me, but there are some things I want to talk to you about. Do you think we can meet and, you know, talk?"

"Oh, so the phone isn't good enough anymore?" Julianna replied in that same angry tone she had when they last spoke.

The anger-filled argument that ensued on the phone that night, was the major impetus that kept Kevin from reaching out to her sooner. Even the power that fed off misery could not take hearing that heartache in her voice ever again. To hear that similar tone in her voice once more meant they were closer to having their second argument than reconciling, but it was something Kevin could at least hold onto. Anger meant she still cared.

"It was good enough to end us," Julianna continued, her voice rising, "but now that you have *something important* to discuss, you want to talk face-to-face?" Her words felt more like a statement than an actual question.

"She's still spitting mad," he thought. "This is going to be harder than I thought."

You are going to fail, the voice said, and Kevin agreed.

A half cup of room temperature water sat on the coffee table that Kevin quickly picked up to slake his parched throat.

"I didn't say that, Julianna, but I get it," he felt like he was losing the conversation, and a deep breath calmed the power that continued to spike. "I'm sorry. There were things going on that night, but you're right. I should have let you come over. You always deserved more than I gave you. But I was scared."

"What were you scared of?" her tone had softened. It was a sign that she was willing to listen, plus she had not hung up yet— two circumstances that gave him a modicum of hope. There was an urge to tell her everything, about the museum, about his power, about the forays as Fiasco while she slept. But he had made the mistake of doing something important over the phone before, as Julianna just reminded him, and he couldn't let it happen twice.

The pacing resumed and brought him to his bedroom. He looked at his Fiasco costume laid out on the bed, wrinkled like a deflated doll. Since talking to Warren, he had used his advice and taken the time to wash out the blood that stained the garment and sewn up the rips and tears as best he could. The repairs resembled bundled scar stitches, but it was better than seeing bare skin beneath. The acrid stench of smoke still lingered in the threads, but the new black stitching on the side and legs gave the uniform an air of toughness that it lacked before.

"Well, there was a lot going on back then, and even now, that scares me, Jay. But things will make more sense if I tell and show you in person. But I understand if you don't want to. I don't blame you for hating me right now. I'm not a fan of myself, either."

Well, you are the Fiasco, the voice said.

"It's not that I don't want to see you. Not really. I guess I'm just scared, too." Julianna paused again. "But I agree. We do need to talk. I have some things I need to discuss with you, as well."

She is leaving you, the voice mocked.

Months ago, that would have pierced Kevin's heart like the voice intended— sent his power soaring and pouring forth in blue light— but Julianna leaving was something Kevin had already anticipated. Time continued to march, even after the breakup, and she had already graduated with honors. He could only imagine the offers that must have been pouring in vying for her services. Warren had already hinted that things were changing in Julianna's life, and he emphasized that the time to repair the breach between them was fleeting.

"So, you're agreeing to meet up?" he asked and bit his bottom lip as he waited for a response.

"I guess," she said, not with the confidence Kevin was hoping for, but beggars could not be choosers.

"Well, you know my rules, Jules. Since I'm asking you to come out, you pick the place and I'll pay."

Julianna chuckled. "Yeah, you're an old soul." She went quiet for a moment then said, "How about Black Deer?"

"I knew it! You love that place!" Kevin laughed, solo at first, until she joined in.

"Best chicken fried steak in New Haven." she said, and Kevin thought he could feel her smile.

Black Deer was her version of Andy's Red Brick Oven. It was the first place they went after their first kiss. It was their go-to place whenever they celebrated a milestone. But since the breakup, Kevin couldn't even bare to walk past the restaurant's doors, fearful she might be inside.

"Well, I can't argue with that," he said, jumping at her olive branch. "So, when do you want to meet up? I'm free anytime."

"Still not working?" she asked.

Kevin's mouth twisted up and he wished she had kept that question to herself. He was saving the fact that he was scheduled to start at ACS the following week for their dinner. It was another collecting job at the rival firm of Blanchet— not in the mire of credit delinquency of his old job, but one that worked with customers to reasonably pay expensive medical bills. It was not as lucrative as the massive credit debt, but it felt less sleazy to work that mission instead. It was a needed change to combat all the negativity that controlled his narrative for far too long.

"No, not yet, but I have something lined up." Kevin quickly changed the subject. "So, what day are you thinking?"

"How about this Friday? Does six work for you?"

It was Wednesday, so that gave him more time to make his final preparations. "That's great, and I can do six," he replied as he tried to hide his eagerness. It would be in the heart of happy hour in Black Deer at that time, but Julianna practically had a seat reserved for her there at any hour.

"Okay," there was a pause again that continued to make him nervous. "Well, I guess I'll see you there."

"Okay. Bye Julianna. I lo—" he knew he made a mistake while he said it, but the habit of talking to her again made him say the word.

"Don't you dare," Julianna hissed before he heard the beep that ended the conversation.

That was not a wise move, the voice said. *You were never very smart.*

"Couldn't agree more," Kevin thought as he tossed his phone on the bed next to his costume.

The leather mask, colored a tone like one of his bruises, was near the edge of the bed, wrapped with his goggles. He pulled it free and thumbed the stitches on the repairs he made to the side.

"That wound could have killed me," he thought. "Warren's right. Why even be Fiasco when I'm bad at it?" he tossed the mask back down on the bed. "If your dumbass can actually get her back, you need to put all of this behind you, and hope Kevin Jones is good enough for her," he said to himself.

He picked up the dark cyan costume top, held it out before him, and stared at the crooked *F* with its maroon rorschach-like stains of dried blood in the white circle. The failure to even create his suit correctly should have been his first sign that he was not meant to be a Mega. Now, the new stitches were a metaphor for each blunder that he had patched over, hoping each time out would be different. He realized his thought process was the definition of lunacy.

"I'm going to need a bigger suit." He held the garment up to his chest, then looked at the skinny suits of various earth tones he had hanging in his closet. "It's time she knew every single damn thing. Warts and all."

******

On Friday, Kevin stood across the street from the Black Deer. The previous days seemed to blow by in a flurry of store visits to find the perfect suit, large enough to fit over his Fiasco suit but still look presentable. Standing in the shadows of a thin alley, he squinted his eyes to get a clearer look at the windows that lined the side of Black Deer, scanning the restaurant for Julianna. He had arrived early to do some reconnaissance and had not seen her among the stream of customers. As anticipation grew, he felt a tinge inside. It was as if he could feel that she was waiting. Rubbing a hand to smooth out his tan suit, he wondered if she could feel him, too.

From his pocket, he retrieved the Fiasco mask and raised it to his lips, giving it a kiss for good luck. He paused and added a prayer, since luck was non-existent for the Mega. Then, he hastily shoved it back into his pocket before crossing the street that was just beginning to stall from weekend traffic.

The smell from the rose he held close to this chest wafted to his nose as he hopped up the curb and squeezed through the loiterers in front of Black Deer. The cast iron handles made to resemble prancing black deer's parted as he shouldered through the wooden doors that creaked at the hinges. Instantly, he was struck with a clamor of loud conversation and revelry. The inside of Black Deer was shaped like the capital letter 'L', dominated by a bar that stretched from the far corner to halfway down the middle of the building. The décor was hunter-themed with deep, dark wood used for the tabletop of the bar, and the tables and chairs that clustered the main floor.

Intricately framed pictures of majestic deer taken or painted by enthusiasts around the world adorned the wall, along with stuffed mounts of ten-point whitetails looking out at the customers with pride captured in their thick necks. Their dark brown eyes seemed to follow Kevin as he walked past families waiting for free tables in the foyer. The pretty female hostess flashed him a knowing smile as she pointed to the back.

With a nod, Kevin turned to the right and walked towards an elevated portion of the restaurant. The aroma of grilled steaks and venison mixed with roasted potatoes and vegetables filled his nostrils as he walked through the crowds. The area in the back was partially walled off from the rest of the bar by dark wood railings inlaid with falling forest leaves. The dais held rows of wooden booths with one row on each side, where Kevin knew Julianna would be. She preferred more intimate settings when they talked, away from the drunken crowds and noise. As predicted, he found her in the third booth down that she always chose.

Julianna sat on the far side of the booth and greeted Kevin with a wave and a brief smile.

"You found me," she said, rehashing the memory of their first meeting at the restaurant.

Kevin watched as Julianna stood and noticed that her hair and choice of clothing seemed to mock his stupidity for breaking up with her. Her dark blue jeans wrinkled at the curved hourglass hips that his hands were once allowed to caress. Contrary to her usual conservative way of dressing that only hinted at her fantastic body, she wore a tight-fitted black tank top that fanned out at the top of her waist, hugged her flat stomach, and cupped her breasts that seemed to spill ever so slightly over the top, revealing an eyebrow-raising amount of cleavage.

Her face was as angelic as ever, with her smooth brown skin and red, full, lips glistening under the light. She hid her eyes behind a pair of black-framed glasses she sometimes wore. They were non-prescription, but she liked the look with certain outfits, and it was a perfect complement to her attire. As if adding to his regret, she had her dark shiny hair pulled tight into a ponytail, parted on the left side like he loved, cascading down her back in waves. Walking towards her, Kevin drank in Julianna in all her glory, involuntarily licking his lips as he let her beauty sear into his mind.

Flee, the voice said breathlessly. *You cannot win this battle.*

"It's not a battle, idiot," Kevin thought. "It's Julianna. My Julianna. We love each other. I can do this." Yet, he bit his lip and mumbled another prayer.

Behind her, he saw a man sitting in a booth tap his friend across from him. Both turned their heads to look at her with those jealous eyes that he used to love. Now those eyes only brought swift anger inside that tempted the power. To let them know he noticed their leering gazes, he responded with an angry stare of his own, eyes intense beneath a wrinkled brow that made them both men quickly turn around like chastised puppies caught stealing a treat.

"Hi, Kevin," Julianna said in an even tone.

The countenance on Kevin's face softened when his gaze turned back to her. The two stood and looked at each other, neither moving, both unsure of how they were to act post-breakup. Even Julianna— who always seemed to know how to carry herself in public with their affections— stared at him with the top of her fingers glued inside her jean pockets. He wondered if he was even allowed to touch her at all anymore, because her standoffish posture suggested otherwise.

Then, Julianna broke the tension. Rolling her eyes and sighing with a sarcastic smirk, she finally took her hands out of her pockets to give him a hug. Her arms wrapped around his neck. The flowery fragrance of her hair sent pleasant memories cascading through Kevin's mind that made his skin tingle with bliss. He noticed that she hugged him with her hips pulled back, rather than with her entire body pressing into his as she used to do. He rationalized receiving the unemotional hug, convincing himself that it at least kept her from feeling the bumps of his costume beneath his clothes. Still, he felt his power swirl inside from disappointment.

The two parted far sooner than Kevin wanted.

"And you're wearing cologne," Julianna said with puckered lips and an approving nod. She thumbed the hem of his jacket. "And you got a new suit without me, I see. "

"I did good?" Kevin replied with his best country accent that usually made Julianna laugh. Instead, she eyed the suit, still nodding.

"It's a bit big, but I like the color," she said with an adorable giggle that he missed more than he cared to admit. "It brings out the color in your...oh my God."

She had finally noticed the thin, black-framed glasses on his face. When they were together, he sometimes complained about painful headaches. He chalked up the episodes to stress from work, being in a relationship, and being Fiasco— which was a strain on everything. But Julianna always suggested that his eyes might have been overworked from staring at the computer screens at work, and that glasses could possibly cure his headaches.

Julianna squealed when she saw the glasses on his face, further splintering any remaining tension. The high-pitched noises she made brought unwanted eyes from other diners around them, but Kevin could hardly care given her obvious joy at seeing him wear them.

"I cannot believe you actually listened to me and got them!" she said with a bright grin.

Kevin had to lean back as she jumped up and down in front of him, before pulling the glasses off his face. She removed her own and tossed them on their table to don his.

"Wow," she said, stretching out the word. Her head moved around Black Deer, and he could see the white around her light brown eyes. "Everything looks so much sharper now."

"It does! It's not the biggest prescription, just twenty thirty, but you can tell the difference. But wait a minute," Kevin said, and his mouth curled upward. "Are you telling me you need glasses, too? All that time getting on my case about it, and you needed to go yourself?"

Julianna wrinkled up her nose as she kept looking around. "I guess so. Who knew?"

"Classic Julianna," Kevin laughed, pointing out that she hardly followed her own advice. It was a quirk that complimented his proclivity for procrastination. "Now give them back."

No," she replied, pulling away. She smiled and her hand instinctively went up to guard the frames.

"Stop playing, Julianna. I need them."

"No, you don't," her cheeks flushed. "You just said they were low prescription, and I want to see how I look in them. You chose cute frames."

Kevin grinned and feigned for the glasses that made Julianna flinch, then cover her mouth in laughter. The sound soothed the rising power within, and it felt as if they had never skipped a beat together.

"Fine, keep them on. They look good on you," Kevin sighed. "And here, I got you this."

Julianna pushed the glasses up her nose, and her face turned to surprise. She let out an audible gasp as if she had just noticed the lavender rose in his hand. It had taken trips to five different flower stores on the busy day before to find the correct flower, but he remembered she mentioned how she preferred the fragrant deep purple plume over the traditional red.

Julianna held the stem with both hands under her nose, closed her eyes, and breathed in deep. "I love this scent," she said. Her eyes opened and her mouth settled into a frown. "I know what you're trying to do, Kevin."

"What?" he said like his father, but she only narrowed her eyes in response.

Kevin gestured with his hand at their table. Julianna's mouth twisted up, and she cocked an eyebrow at him before she gave a slight curtsy that made Kevin chuckle. She slid into the booth.

"She's relaxed. This is good so far," he thought as he followed suit and sat on the stiff bench on the opposite side. "So far. she is the same. That wonderful girl that I know. My beautiful dork."

People only saw the surface of Julianna, but behind her elegance and class, there was a lighter, goofy side that laughed at dirty jokes, rubbed his leg during steamy movie scenes, and enjoyed the spectacle of any geek convention he took her to.

After the tall, handsome server— whose gaze lingered too long at Julianna's chest for Kevin's liking— took their order and left, she said, "So, we're here. Which one of us goes first?"

Kevin's mouth went tight and thinned to a line as he thought about where to even begin. Did he start by admitting his stupidity, pleading on his hands and knees, and begging her for forgiveness? Or did he remain stoic, admitting very little, and discussing how it was important to put the past behind them and move forward? He imagined Julianna would respond more to the latter response, since she typically loathed male weakness, but neither reaction felt ideal to fully pass along what he wanted to say.

As his silence lingered, Julianna began, "Listen Kevin, I probably should just tell you—"

"I took you for granted," Kevin interrupted before she could tell him about her eventual move to Eugene, California, or some other state that needed her graphic design talent. Her mouth fell open from his words, and her eyes fluttered as she changed her train of thought.

Her hands busily rearranged the silverware on the table before her. "Wow, okay," she said flustered. "I have to say, you're full of surprises tonight. But I'm curious, what made you come to that conclusion?"

"Because it's true. I did. I took you for granted. They always say absence makes the heart grow fonder, right? Well, our time away has shown me a lot. Everything, in fact," he said. "We were great together. And I just got used to you being there. I should have appreciated you more when we were together. Been more honest."

"Kevin, I never felt underappreciated," she replied, setting her rose down on the table to cross her arms over her chest. "Give me more credit than that. I never would have stayed with you if I felt that way."

You are losing her, the voice said.

"Wait, you're mad at me now?" Kevin said, more than confused. "I'm telling you how I feel here, I thought that's what you wanted?"

"I am. And it is," Julianna said sharply. "But it's not the truth. Not completely. It doesn't explain how you could take what we have," she paused and caught her words, "or had, and just poof, throw it all away. Over the phone."

"I know. I have a lot of explaining to do, and I will. It's just. Before I do, I wanted you to know that that was how I felt before I told you something that might," he searched for the right words, "change how you see or feel about me."

"Did you cheat on me, Kevin?" Julianna leaned in fast enough that he caught a hint of the scent of her hair.

"What?" Kevin leaned back against the back of the booth and waved his hand away. "Whoa now! That's insane, Julianna. I don't even know how you jumped to that!"

She sighed and played with the butter knife, tapping the curved tip against the table. "Well, listen to the way you're talking. Saying I would see you differently or change how I feel about you. It was just my first thought. That you cheated," she smoothed out her hair, rubbing her hands over the top, and breathed out. "This is just frustrating, Kevin. I thought we trusted each other, but I always had a feeling that you were holding back. I tried and tried to break through your walls."

"You did, Julianna. I promise." It was Kevin's turn to lean towards her. He felt the sweat begin to bead beneath his suit from the turn of conversation.

"Then why are we here!" she asked, raising her voice loud enough that made her sheepishly look around to see who noticed.

"We're here because I wanted to tell you how I feel, and to talk about us."

She leaned back again, and he saw the swivel of her hips as her legs crossed beneath the table. "In person this time," she said.

Kevin flushed, coupled with a pinch of anger. It felt as if she was purposefully talking him in circles. "I've apologized for that already, Jay."

"No, Kevin," she replied, matching his attitude. "You really haven't yet. Not in my book."

"I apologize for what I did over the phone," he said, probably with more consternation in his tone than he originally intended.

She crossed her arms over her stomach. "For breaking up with me. Over the phone."

"Yes," Kevin sighed. "For breaking up with you over the phone."

Silence returned when the server brought their drinks, hers a sparkling blue curacao margarita, and his a tall glass of beer. The waiter lingered again, smiling like a loon, and asking too many follow-up questions.

He is far superior to you physically.

Fed up with the waiter's interference, Kevin fixed him a look and said in an icy tone "Thanks. We're fine."

The waiter's smile washed out from the withering gaze. "Are you ready to order then, sir?" he asked.

"I'll have the usual, Jerry," Julianna said. "And he'll have the fish and chips. Right?"

Kevin nodded, shooting glances up at the flustered waiter who took down their order, then walked away with haste.

Kevin nodded after him. "Is that new?"

"New-ish. He's been here a few weeks," she replied.

"You two seem friendly," Kevin replied, reminding himself to sit up straight instead of the pout he felt coming.

"Kind of late to be jealous now, isn't it Kevin? Don't take whatever this is out on him," Julianna admonished. Yet, even in the soft shadow of the faux torchlight, he noticed that there was a small grin on her lips. "It's not Jerry's fault we're here," she finished.

Julianna shook her head, grinning as she mixed the ice by moving her straw up and down. Satisfied that she had properly merged the tequila with the curacao, she took a long sip. Kevin followed suit, swallowing the fermented liquid that chilled the anxiety. The power would attack the liquor, but it did relax him enough to make him think that Julianna was justified in her acrimony towards him. It was wrong and disrespectful to break up with her over the phone. She earned far more respect than that.

The decibel level in the restaurant turned up as the time moved later in the hour. Over the banister, shot glasses clanged against wood at the bar, followed by uproarious celebratory laughter. At the table, Kevin unfurled his own silverware out of the napkin, then began tearing off strips of white from the towelette, stalling for time while he gathered his thoughts.

"I get it, Julianna. And you were right in asking me to apologize in person. You deserved nothing less." He finally said. "I had a reason for not wanting you to come over that night, but what I did was weak."

"It was bullshit," she glared at him over her drink.

"Yes, it was. But I didn't want us to meet like this—just to talk about this one thing." Ceasing from destroying his napkin, Kevin unbuttoned the top button of his shirt and loosened his tie, pulling down the knot to let in the conditioned air. "Will you accept my apology now so we can move forward?"

Julianna's mouth puckered, eyes glued to her drink as if it were a scrying pool that would give her the answer. "I guess."

Kevin couldn't tell whether she actually accepted his apology, or if she just wanted to move on to the next subject. He waved his shirt to cool his warm neck.

"This is getting me nowhere," he thought, removing the tie and twisting open another button on his shirt, getting tantalizingly close to the top of his Fiasco costume beneath.

"I can't believe she was right," Julianna said after another sip, ice clinking against the glass.

The top of Kevin's brow creased. "Who was right?" he asked.

"Mrs. Caitlyn. Your mom," she replied. "She told me you had a problem with commitment, but like a fool I thought, 'Oh I can change him. Everything will work out because never had I gotten along with someone so well. We're soulmates,' I thought. 'We'll get marr—'" She stopped and covered her mouth with her hand. Even behind his glasses he could see the red in her eyes, the romantic lighting shining off her budding tears.

You have made her cry for the third time, the voice said with anger. *Leave now and let her move on without you.*

"You really wanted to get married?" To me?" Kevin said, almost whispering so no one else could hear.

In all the time since that dinner, they still had not spoken about his mom throwing him under the bus in any detail. Variables like her graduation, work, and her future made it seem like a futile endeavor. In retrospect, he saw how foolish he had been to allow that ultimatum to go unchallenged.

A loser never imagines greatness.

"Yes, I did, Kevin," Julianna replied. She removed his glasses off the bridge of her nose and swiped tears away beneath both eyes with her hand. "You obviously didn't, though."

"But my mom was wrong, Jay," he said in an elevated voice. The anger returned in a flash from the sight of her tears, and he made a point to remember to confront his mom about that subject later. "I was committed to you, Julianna. I am now."

"Were you really, though?" Her wet eyes reflected the soft torchlight.

"Yes," Kevin replied in a stern tone. "Seriously, Julianna? You ask me if I cheated, and now you ask me if I was really committed. How could you ask me these things? Were you always questioning my commitment?"

Julianna didn't reply. Instead, she held up her left hand, turned it around with her palm facing towards her, and wiggled her empty ring finger.

"And you never thought to bring it up? Or discuss it with me? Was I supposed to read your mind? I guess I wasn't the only one holding back then, huh?" Kevin sat back, proud that he got in at least one point that she could not counter. Perhaps the fault of their breakup wasn't heaped entirely on his shoulder alone.

"I never brought it up," Julianna said, her voice a hoarse whisper as she spoke. She could not bring herself to look him in the eye. "Because I didn't want to chase you away."

The anger Kevin felt inside gave way to a surge of burning power that swelled like a turbulent river from her words. Warren, his mother, and everyone who had any interest in their relationship, were all right. He had put Julianna on an astronomical pedestal in his mind, but Kevin realized that he had failed to let Julianna know— or even feel— that elevated status. It was a wonder that she even stuck around for as long as she did. A blessing. He imagined how she must have felt, believing that her hold on their love was so tenuous that she could not even broach a subject that was important to her.

He watched the water well up in her eyes and the red flood Julianna's cheeks. It took everything in him to not hug the pain away for her. The pain he seemingly kept inflicting on the one he supposedly loved.

You are the Fiasco in her life.

"It doesn't even matter now," Julianna sniffed. "Kevin, I really have to tell you—"

"Excuse me, Julianna, but I have to go to the bathroom," was all Kevin could say through the knotted fist that burned his throat. Napkin strips fluttered across the table as he scooted off the bench and stood up. He was gone before Julianna could gather her breath to respond.

Happy hour at Black Deer had just begun, which meant there was no line to the men's bathroom. Inside, the air smelled of fresh bleach. Modern cream tiles covered the floors and went halfway up the wall, separated by a line of white tile at his waist, before being replaced by brown and cream wood. The bathroom light was so bright it made him see speckles of black as his eyes adjusted.

"How can she not know how I feel about her?" he thought. "How did I even screw that part up?"

The power clawed at Kevin's chest as if it wanted to force itself over his body. He paced before the four decorative sinks against the wall and palmed his chest, hoping to massage the energy away. He caught his reflection as he passed by the silver-gilded mirrors above the sinks and paused his brisk pace. Kevin looked at the red eyes staring back at him, the sweat on the brow that made his forehead glisten, and the baggy ill-fitted suit that Julianna gave too much credit. Time was a wound his power could not heal. Even with a full shave, his skin looked weathered and blotchy from stress and years fighting as Fiasco, and his hair already looked bedraggled from the sweat and anxiety that made it stick up in random places.

"You really are a loser," he said to his reflection, taking over the voice's role.

The image of his face in the mirror turned in a mask of pale blue as he curled his hand into a fist and brought it down on the ceramic bathroom sink with a growling shout. The bathroom echoed from the sound of the edge that cracked in spirals, then shattered before his blow. Broken pieces of white stone tingled as they fell, breaking further as the pieces spread and rolled across the floor, echoing a rattling tune. With his anger and frustration sated, Kevin ran the faucet and splashed cold water over his face that spilled onto his collar, trickling beneath his suit.

A bathroom stall door creaked open behind him. Kevin looked in the mirror and followed the well-dressed man who eased his way towards the exit as if he were evading a dangerous animal. The man's blonde hair was matted with sweat, and his eyes were wide as he surveyed the floor and broken sink pieces scattered about.

"You okay, bro?" the man's voice wavered as he spoke.

Turning off the faucet, Kevin wiped the water onto his face, then turned and leaned against what remained of the sink.

"I'm fine. Are you doing okay? You're sweating a lot there," he said while wagging a finger in a circular motion.

The man's face struck a chord as if Kevin had seen him somewhere in Blanchet before, but before he could pinpoint the memory, the stranger's eyes widened. Slipping on a film of water that had trickled from the pool forming beneath the sink, he fled the bathroom quickly, pushing the door open with his forearms, letting out a curse word. Loud voices from the bar briefly filled the bathroom before the door slammed shut behind him, bringing back the welcomed silence.

"That was weird," Kevin thought. He wondered what had spooked the man so, until he looked down to see what the man was staring at. The outline of the white circle and the dark thread of the crooked *F* was partially visible from the water that saturated his shirt. The sight made him chuckle, and he waved the shirt back and forth to dry it out.

"Well, guess the cat's out of the bag," he joked over the sound of his whipping shirt. "Now, I just have to tell Julianna before that guy steals my thunder."

He turned to the mirror. The shirt had not dried enough to leave the bathroom without anyone else seeing the symbol, so he released a wave of power from inside that grew steadily warmer until the shirt lost its gossamer appearance. Tides of stained sweat weaved between dirty wrinkles, making the shirt appear as if he had just retrieved it from a dirty hamper. Kevin shook his head and snorted. "Classic Fiasco." He buttoned up his suit jacket to cover his shirt.

Water from the sink did little to pat down the stimulated hair. A forlorn face stared back at him in the mirror, sad and pitiful, and he took in a deep breath. His neck muscles cracked as he rolled his head around his shoulders while exhaling the breath he held. Then hopped between feet to steel his nerves.

"Okay. Time to rip off the band-aid. If anything happens tonight, at the very least, she has to know how you truly feel," Kevin said to his reflection, then closed his eyes. "Please God, don't let me lose her. Even more, don't let me hurt her again."

Opening his eyes, Kevin nodded at his reflection. Walking to the door, and with a deep inhale, he pushed it open, turning down the hallway back towards the bar. Almost instantly, he ran into a standing crowd. As he walked towards his booth through the bodies, he noticed that Julianna's side of the booth was empty. The din in the bar had reached a fevered pitch, and he looked about. Other booths were abandoned, with plates of unfinished food resting on top, their various delicious aromas mixing together. Happy hour or not, it was an abnormal number of bodies, and the air of excitement and energy in the bar raised the hackles on the back of Kevin's neck.

"Kevin!" he heard a voice shout over the clamor.

Most of the standing people faced to the right towards the bar. The average height of the men seemed to be inches above his own. Even the women seemed to dwarf him, wearing their Friday night heels, as he waded through the crowd trying to follow the sound of his name being called.

"Kevin!" the voice said again. He noticed Warren's head among the throng.

"Warren? What is he doing here?" Kevin thought. Heat from the packed bodies created a musty stench. As he shouldered by, their loud voices rang in his ear. As he neared Warren, he saw Julianna standing next to him, talking very animatedly with Jenni, her shiny, red hair cascading down over a tight, white shirt, and simple gray skirt that hugged her hips and belled outward at mid-thigh. Neither looked in his direction.

"What the hell is going on?" Kevin said to his friend.

"Hey, turn that up!' Warren yelled as he reached him.

Dressed in a crisp gray suit, Warren waved his hand up at the male bartender who was being shouted at by partygoers as they leaned over the bar like fans at a concert. The poor, overwhelmed barkeeper wore an agitated expression on his face that was a dark shade of red. He held a remote above his head, moving it about to dodge grabbing hands. Shouting down the customers, he pointed the remote at the satellite box perched on a ledge high above the bar and was unsuccessfully fidgeting and pressing buttons at random.

Julianna's eyes finally caught Kevin's and lingered before she retreated closer to Jenni. Warren leaned towards him.

"What's going on?" Kevin said again, loud enough to pierce the noise.

His best friend's face was solemn, and his eyes belayed the worry he felt. "You have to see, dude," Warren replied. "It's about--" And he made the letter F with his fingers.

Kevin glanced down at his shirt to make sure his costume was still hidden before he turned towards the bar. The large televisions that hung over bottles of liquor were normally reserved for sporting events but were now telecasting programs from three different news stations. He noticed the fancy symbols in the corners of the screens, indicating that the broadcasts were national instead of local. Whatever was going on was being seen by the nation.

"Is that live?" Kevin said to Warren, who shook his head to affirm.

Julianna had moved next to him, and he felt her warmth against his arm as the two faced the televisions together. The screens on either side of the main television were muted but showed images of police activity cordoning off streets. A cheer went up in the restaurant as the volume increased. Then, the patrons of Black Deer fell silent. For a moment, the screen was dark, but Kevin could hear helicopters blades chopping through the wind. The camera was shaky as it followed an unsteady spotlight aimed at the top of a building. The helicopter turned and the camera panned around the large rooftop.

"Wait a second," Kevin said to Julianna, who had her mouth covered with both hands. "Is that our building? Is that Blanchet?"

From the spotlight's luminescence, he could see black-clad NHPD S.W.A.T. officers standing around three of four edges of the rooftop at Blanchet. They resembled medieval statues, stiff and unmoving, pointing their guns towards the square, red brick entrance that jutted out from the rooftop. He had been up there several times since the alarm on the door was disabled. Many collectors used the area to get away from the stress of being yelled at by delinquent debtors before the carport was built. The thin metal door of the entrance was propped open by what looked like the piece of a broken cinder block.

The entryway was filled with a tan light that was broken when Blanchet's evening collectors streamed out, holding canvas bags in their arms that bulged with what he guessed were expensive, stolen items. The account information found in BCR blade servers alone could be worth millions on the black market to the right buyer. Hardware being more valuable since it was virtually untraceable compared to a hack.

The camera view zoomed out. Inexplicably, there was a red and white car on the roof that shone under the shaky spotlight. Gleaned from his obsession with monster cars as a kid, Kevin thought it looked like a Cadillac convertible Deville, with its long white stripe down the side, and red fins that jutted out the back for headlights. Walking in a steady line, the workers, still dressed in their fashionable work clothes, were depositing the sacks in an unusually large backseat, stacking them in a pile before turning on their heels back into the building.

"Now that is something I thought I would never see," Kevin said aloud.

"Wait," Warren replied with a shout. "It gets worse."

"To repeat our previous coverage," the faceless female anchor said through the television speakers. "Mal-Megahumans have seized the Blanchet building in the town of New Haven. They have taken several hostages, and called out the infamous Mega, Fiasco—"

"What?" Kevin said. The blood in his veins could have frozen an ocean. Beneath his suit, his knees buckled from the shock, but he managed to take a step forward, unsure if he heard the anchor correctly over the din. Her tone was far too jubilant for such a shocking statement.

The voice continued in her singsong television tone, "The Mals known as Mimicker and Enrapture have called out the Mega in his own town, claiming they would kill the hostages if he did not appear within the hour. According to multiple reports from those with access to the secret MegaStream, the two up-and-comers want to cut their teeth against a Mega, whose current notoriety spiked from recent footage of his debacle at the Haven museum. The museum was destroyed in the fight."

"Thanks for that last part, lady," Kevin thought. His racing heart galloped in his chest, and his power stirred inside when the voice said, *none of them respect you.*

"Hey, let's go check it out!" a voice shouted near the bar. Others agreed. The cacophony grew as people filtered out from Black Deer, bumping into him and his friends as they moved out into the street. As the crowd thinned, Kevin turned and looked at Warren who was biting his lips, his brow creased with concern.

"I need to go with them," Kevin told him.

"Are you crazy?" Julianna shouted and grabbed the fabric on his forearm. "Don't you dare go out there, Kevin Jones. Those lunatics are dangerous, and who knows who will get hurt or killed once that criminal Fiasco shows up."

She tugged at his arm, and he replied, "I'll be fine. Trust me."

Then, he turned and whispered to Warren. "Keep them safe and keep them here."

Warren nodded. "Okay, I will." He leaned in and whispered back, "Are you sure about this? She's right, those are real Mals out there this time dude."

"What choice do I have?" Kevin said in a loud whisper. "You saw that footage. We know some of those people, and they'll die if I don't go."

"Those two are low beam and are just trying to raise their credit. Do you think they would really do that?"

The two locked eyes. "Do you think I can risk it?" Kevin asked.

Warren held his gaze, then looked away. "No, I guess not."

"Just keep them safe. That's all I ask," Kevin urged. "If it gets out of hand—if somehow, things get close to here, get them out."

Black Deer was a Blanchet hangout. Just on the edge of new New Haven, it was only several blocks away. The fallout of a real Mega on Mal fight could reach that far based on other battles Kevin had seen, and Warren understood from the look in his eyes. His friend gave him one final nod and a hard slap on the shoulder. Then, Kevin turned and looked at Julianna. Her eyes were glazed over with tears, as if she could sense there was more to his story than just taking a look. His power swelled at the sight.

"You better not go out there, Kevin," she said. Her hands flinched as if she was about to force him into staying with a hug, but instead, she crossed her arms below her chest. "I won't forgive you if you did."

"I'm just going to look, that's all. This is a once in a lifetime chance."

"Men," Jenni said as she saddled up to Julianna in an act of solidarity. "They are always chasing after that next testosterone fix." She shooed Kevin away with her head. "Go on. Go get some building dropped on you then, Kevin. Be an idiot like the rest of these losers."

"Nice to see you too, Jen, and shut up," Kevin said. Although her words were harsh and biting, he could still feel the concern behind them. They matched the worry on Warren's face, and he flashed both of his friends an assuring smile. "Julianna, I'll be right back. I promise."

That is a lie, the voice scoffed.

He fought the urge to wrap Julianna up in his arms. To hold her close again in a cocoon of his energy and tell her why he had to leave. He imagined using the power for himself, for once. To transport her to the pacific through the sky, and dive far below. He imagined fighting the crushing depths of the ocean, feeling her heartbeat against his chest while his blue light illuminated the wonders found deep in the ocean that most people could never witness.

But it was all a dream since, in the end, the voice was right. It was always right. A fight with Mals would be dangerous, and possibly deadly. Mals were not the comic book villains he grew up reading about that were incapable, dimwitted, or selfish to the point of self-defeat. In real life, they were smart, deadly, capable of performing high-level crimes, and often, frighteningly vicious. The MegaStream was rife with stories of fallen Megas who bit off more than they could handle. Often, their bodies were found garishly harmed or mutilated, usually for everyone to see as a warning, or stripes of credit in the Mal community. They had also established a community much like the Megas, often seen working together on jobs, or just out to murder Megas for fun. There was no certainty that he would return to her. It was true that the promise was another lie, but it was one well worth telling if he could give Julianna even an ounce of comfort. He owed her that in the end.

"You can hang onto those glasses," he said to her. "I'll be back for them."

Instead of the embrace he imagined, Kevin leaned in, smelling the peony scent of her hair, but careful not to get close enough for

Julianna to feel his costume. He cradled her chin with his hand, letting the power flow to his fingertips to make them tingle with warmth, and lifted her head. Her eyes sparkled, the light brown irises seeming to beg him for a kiss. Fighting the urge to fulfill that desire, Kevin gave her a soft, but warm peck on her forehead instead, letting his lips linger for just a moment. He had yet to tell her the absolute truth about Fiasco and his power, and thus, had not earned the right to feel her lips once more.

"Be careful," Julianna mouthed. The noise in the bar had grown too loud to speak over.

Kevin mouthed back, "I will. I promise."

Fearing that looking at Julianna any longer would shatter his nerves, Kevin turned and joined the flow of the crowd, leaving through the Black Deer doors among a group of people who seemed to froth for the coming violence. The cooler air outdoors was a relief to his face, which was warm from his racing pulse. A shiver made him realize just how damp his skin was, and he wiped his sweaty palms against his pants. Cars shined under the glow of the street-lights, stopped by the flowing patrons from Black Deer and other bars that clogged the lanes. Horns blew like trumpets, even though most of the drivers had left their cars parked in the street as the news of the oncoming battle swept through the crowd.

The surge of the crowd flowed south towards old New Haven and the Blanchet building, while Kevin edged his way north, sliding between people as he searched for an empty place to change. Words of derision played through the multitude— most of which were at his expense. Hopes of a Fiasco throttling seemed the prevalent choice, along with the sentiment that he deserved what was coming to him. Not everyone agreed. Moving through the throng, he would occasionally hear someone say that Fiasco was local, and wanted him to win, but they were few and far between, and he could never find the face who spoke the words when he looked. Overall, most sentiments were negative outbursts that wished him bodily harm or worse in the coming battle.

They all despise you, the voice said, and Kevin's chest tingled with a blooming heat.

The crowd thinned once he reached the edge of the street. Still, pockets of people could be seen on the sidewalks, under the restaurant awnings, and occupying the front of store entrances, lingering as they stared at their phones. Scanning the crowds, there were some recesses he thought were dark enough to slip out of his suit, but there were too many eyes and street cameras perched high above for him to risk being seen. If things went as badly as the crowd wished, he could not allow anything to connect Fiasco to his family or Julianna.

In his pocket, the seams and metal rings that held his mask ties pressed against his leg as Kevin rolled it over nervously in his hand. No one seemed to notice him as he walked further north at a brisk pace, anxiously searching for an empty street or alley. As he walked further, the brightly lit downtown gave way to domestic row houses. There were far fewer people on Elm Avenue, but still enough loitered on porches and stoops, gossiping about the news. His heart raced when he thought about the limited time frame he had to get to Blanchet before the Mals kept their promise.

"They said an hour. How much time has it been?" He said aloud as he looked down at the silver watch on his wrist, realizing it was pointless since he had no idea when the countdown had started. It could have begun at the moment of the broadcast, or before he even saw Warren in the bar. Either way, he had no way of knowing. He retrieved the mask and goggles from his pocket.

"To hell with it."

Then, Kevin ran. He ran towards the dark patches between streetlights where there were less people and donned the mask. He pressed the metal, so it pinched the dorsum of his nose, and quickly tied the straps behind his head. He ran through a spotlight of orange on the sidewalk. When he reached the next strip of darkness, he slipped the goggles over the eyeholes, pulling the straps on either side to make them snug against his face. Quickly he moved, arms pumping, and his suit jacket snapping behind him. Running below the next streetlight, the power bled from his chest, pouring over his head and body like molten blue gold, burning bright and hot.

The baggy tan suit darkened, cracking like dry skin before burning away like a newspaper tossed into a fire. The fabric spread to the wind in gray bits of ash, shaking loose with every footfall, until only his costume was left behind. The glowing gauntlets on his hands were the last to form, twinkling like azure stars, before he took flight.

"Fiasco!" he shouted, stretching the syllables until his throat burned. He realized it was most likely the last time he would get to say it. As his name echoed off the row houses, he streaked into the sky like a gleaming arrow.

Fiasco arched back like a rainbow, turning south towards Blanchet. The cool wind felt soothing as he let it through his aura to chill the skin beneath his suit. It had only been a few weeks since he rode the skies, yet the mask and goggles felt unfamiliar, tight and stifling on his head. His stomach tightened from the vertigo. Yet, when he saw the line of white headlights going north and south on the ninety-seven, and the square patterns of orange lights that marked the New Haven suburbs from the shimmering downtown buildings, there emerged a sense of belonging that he was Fiasco again.

Enough. Only failure will come of this, the voice asserted, wrenching Fiasco back into reality as he looked down. The NHPD had blocked off all four corners around the ten-story Blanchet building with wooden barricades that bristled with New Havenites. The scene appeared more like a block party than it did a Mal hostage situation. The citizens' laughter and clamor rose as Fiasco approached Blanchet, flying over the crowd before increasing his altitude to get a bird's eye view of the rooftop.

The sky was thick with helicopters who had moved farther away from the Blanchet building— perhaps predicting the chaos that was inevitably near. The pale moonlight brightened the rooftop, giving Fiasco an overview of the situation. He could make out the NHPD S.W.A.T. officers that lined the edges of the roof. Their arms were still aimed toward the hostages, as if their muscles were made of stone. The improbably placed Deville was still parked on the center of the roof, its backseat now piled high with stolen contraband from the river of hostages that continued to find room for more.

"Why does everyone choose roofs with me?" Fiasco thought as he surveyed the scene. "Do Megas who have water-based powers always get called out to oceans or rivers? Tired of roofs." Hovering high above so as not be spotted by the guards, he made a slow circle through the sky. "Looks like at least fifteen hostages," he muttered, counting the bodies moving about. "Sixteen officers, too. So, one for each hostage with an extra for me. Good planning."

A figure in a large, brimmed hat leaned on his shoulder against the square brick, his arms crossed as he watched the workers. Judging from his shadow, he looked well over six feet tall. The moonlight clashed with the garish, light green suit that was three times baggier than the suit he wore to Black Deer. The man wore a white shirt beneath the green jacket, opened wide at the top like a butterfly collar. His pants cascaded down in waves about his legs and tapered near his feet, which were adorned with shiny black shoes with bright white insets. Two long chains made of gold looped down one side of his leg and glamoured in the moonlight. A broad grin was on his olive-toned face framed by a square elongated jaw, but his eyes were hidden in the shadow of his fedora that was striped around the middle with a black band.

"That must be Mimicker. The skin changer," Fiasco thought.

Even though Talon continuously mocked his lack of studying, the Mals always interested him more than the Mega-humans. From what he could remember, Mimicker's power was his ability to change his form and imitate other people. Somehow, it extended to even their voices and mannerisms, which were said to be nearly perfect imitations. Mind-Megas speculated that he could even mimic brain patterns of those he targets, but it has never been scientifically proven. There was also a ghastly rumor that the suit he wore was the extra flesh he needed to impersonate others, but he never gave that hearsay any credit.

"That suit is hideous. Green is such an ugly color," Fiasco thought, flexing his blue aura about his body. "Now where's the other one? Enrapture."

Mimicker's profile was linked with Enrapture on the MegaStream and vice versa, as one could not be found without the other. As if summoned by his query, Enrapture emerged from the rooftop entrance dressed equally in the height of fashion of some bygone era. A purple bandana with paisley black and white icing held her blonde hair up in a bun in the back, while curly locks on either side fell down her temples and passed her thin jaw. She wore framed glasses of the same color that tapered off her face in triangled edges, and dark purple lipstick that appeared close to black. A tight-fitted plaid shirt patterned with mauve and light blue hues was curled up to her elbows and tied in a knot just above her navel and jean shorts cut at her upper thigh that frayed at the ends. Her long, toned legs ended in dark leather cowboy boots embroidered with purple flowers.

There was something in her smooth gait—and the way her hips swayed, and her chest bounced—that made Fiasco have to shake his head in attempt to peel his eyes off her. "You want Julianna," he reminded himself. "You love Julianna."

Even with her innocent yet seductive appearance, Fiasco knew Enrapture was most likely the more dangerous of the two Mals. With a unique Mega power, her voice was able to overpower someone's inhibitions and control their mind. There was no video evidence of her performing the act, but even at Fiasco's safe distance, he could still feel her pull. It also explained why the officers were threatening the hostages, and why they were stealing from their own office, pliant and docile.

The blue power streamed behind him as he flew towards the roof. Once he was far enough away that he could handle gunfire, Fiasco let his power flow freely, burning a bright cobalt, his aura grew large enough to get the two Mals' attention.

"So, why are you two bothering me?" Fiasco shouted, hovering above the rooftop.

With that same silly grin, Mimicker unfolded his arms and moved away from the entrance, walking slowly towards the Deville. "You finally decided you had the balls to show. Guess I owe you more of the cut, dear. Now we can get out of this hellhole town." His ashen skin seemed to glow beneath the moonlight, yet his eyes stood shadowed by his large brim.

"Why dont'cha come down here. Fiasco, and we'll tell ya why we are in this armpit of a town," he shouted back, his voice harsh and throaty.

"You want me to grab you a cup of water first?" Fiasco replied.

"Don't make fun of my man," Enrapture said in a sultry tone that made her sound older than she looked. She slid into Mimicker's long arm and wrapped her arms around his thin torso. "And we're not askin' you, either."

She pointed a skinny arm at Fiasco, hand limp and lazy. A grin changed her young countenance into something wicked as she licked her dark lips and flicked her index finger. As if their marionette strings had been pulled, in unison, the officers took a step forward, shouldering their weapons at the hostages who stopped dead in their tracks.

Fiasco surveyed the situation and realized that there was no way to stop them all from gunning the hostages down, given their distance apart from each other— even with his speed. Reluctantly, Fiasco floated down to the rooftop. Mimicker and Enrapture moved behind the human shields, making their way towards their waiting car.

"So, are you going to tell me why you dragged me out here?" Fiasco asked, trying to sound calm, even though his stomach felt like he had swallowed a brick. His eyes followed the Mals as they moved behind the hostages. "Is this to gain some credit or something? Because I have to tell you," he laughed. "I'm not too high on the Mega paradigm these days."

The Deville was facing away from him, the fin of the taillights pointing to the left of his shoulder. Mimicker and Enrapture stood together a few feet away, just outside the passenger side door.

"Well, someone has been talking about you. You've been in the news a lot lately, and your profile has never been higher," Mimicker replied. "And so we thought, what the hell."

"Yeah," Enrapture chimed in drawing out the word. Her blue eyes gleamed behind her glasses. "We thought, 'Might as well mess with the worst Mega on the planet, gain a little cred and loot at the same time.'" They laughed together, hers a high-pitched squeak, and Mimicker's a cement mixer turned on high.

They do not respect you, the voice said, and Fiasco agreed. His aura flickered and grew brighter, making Mimicker grip Enrapture tighter.

"They may not respect me, but they are afraid of me, at least," Fiasco thought as he took a step forward.

Enrapture's arm shot back in the air. "Stop right there, Mega, or you'll get brains on that pretty little force field of yours."

Fiasco cocked his head to the side. "Who told you it was a force field?" he asked.

Mimicker's lips flicked up to a smirk. In the light, Fiasco noted how his teeth looked elongated and far too big for his mouth.

"Your old friend told us. You know, Tamerlane," he said before giving a guttural laugh. "Once he found out we were going to mess with you, he provided that sweet ride to get the job done. He's highly upset with you. Said something about being choked?"

"So that's how the car got up on the roof. Those flying disks Tamerlane used," Fiasco thought. "Who would have thought Mals would actually work together just to humiliate me, of all Megas?"

The strong prey on the weak, the voice said. Fiasco nodded.

"So, what are you doing up here? Are we just going to wait around and talk?" Fiasco said. "You all pulled me away from a date and I would like to get back to it."

"Awe," Enrapture purred and rubbed her man's chest, fingers moving through a mass of shirt that Fiasco could only imagine felt like greasy skin. "He has a date. Poor girl, you're not really filling out that suit." The power inside rose from her laughter. Even though Fiasco had never met the woman before, something in her melodic voice made the words sting. She looked up at Mimicker's shadowed face. "Maybe we should keep him. I could show him a few things that he could take back to please the poor girl."

Mimicker guffawed; an unnatural sound that made the hair on Fiasco's neck stand on end. "If he even has a girl. Probably some overweight whore. The talk of the town that one." His accent shifted from southern to northern Irish as if the Mal could not decide on just one form.

"She's not a whore," Fiasco said, his teeth gritted with true anger. "Not like the one on your arm."

Enrapture jumped away from Mimicker, who stood up taller now that his arm was free. With her hands curled into fists, her blue eyes burned into him, full of fury.

"Uh oh," Mimicker grinned. He eased towards the car to open the side door, sliding over the gravel with his gaze on Fiasco. "Looks like you made her mad. Give us our head start, dear, and let's split from this mudhole."

The menacing grin returned to Enrapture's face. "Hurt him! All of you! Make him bleed for me!" she said. Her voice was angelic as she sang the words.

The hostages wasted little time rushing in, their faces contorted with the unbridled rage from their puppet master. Arms swam in his direction. Soft thuds rang inside, and Fiasco curled down as they pounded at his aura with pipes, rocks, and debris that littered the rooftop. Some even used their bare fists, striking against his shield with foaming mouths spewing obscenities. Not wanting to hurt anyone, Fiasco stepped back from the throng, trying to create distance as he anticipated bullets flying through any moment since he lost sight of the officers.

Suddenly, his head jacked forward from a blow from behind that gonged like a bell within his shield. He turned around to see that, instead of firing, the S.W.A.T. members were physically attacking him, beating him down with ferocious strikes with the curved heels of their rifles. Between the hostages and the police, Fiasco wilted, falling to his knees from the onslaught.

Through the mass of arms and legs, and over the drumming against his aura, he heard Mimicker's voice along the air, "Get in the car and leave him, babe!"

"No" he heard her snap back. "I want to see this!"

"We have our orders. He's here and it's time to go. Get in. Now!"

Enrapture's voice trailed off as she playfully sang, "Have fun playing with my toys, scumbag."

The weapons pounding against his shield continued unabated. Still crouching, Fiasco heard the engine quicken and accelerate in the Deville and felt the pelts of small rocks spitting out from beneath the wheels as it drove away.

"Can't let them get away," he thought as he covered his head. The crowd pressed against him, stifling his light with their mass. Fiasco had difficulty breathing within the cocoon of energy and blows that rained against him. The power rushed inside as the heat and saturation of bodies pushed Fiasco to the verge of panic.

Now you will even lose to civilians, the voice mocked. *Pathetic.* Fiasco agreed, and finally lashed out.

"Get off of me!" he shouted, his arm sweeping out in a blue tidal wave of energy.

The wave of power collected the bodies pressed around him in the curve of its thick arc. Hostages and police alike were pushed off their feet, uncontrollably grinding along the gravel by the strength of the energy, before striking the raised rooftop edges in bodies that piled up at the base. Shouts brought Fiasco to his feet in time to see that a few of the flailing bodies had broken away from the pack. It was as if an invisible storm front had moved them along with their arms and legs twisted over the edge, falling over the roof in a cacophony of terrified screams. He counted five in total, with a sixth barely able to hold on, arms swimming in the air against the current that threatened to push her over.

Her panicked screams rang in his ears, and Fiasco rushed forward. Reaching out with a tendril of blue power, he lassoed a former colleague named Vanessa, and was able to grasp her arm as she teetered over the edge. The string snaked up her wrist and to her forearm, and he pulled hard, lurching her forward over the gravel. Her high heels caught in the grit, and she whooped before falling to her hands and knees. But that victory was short-lived when the wails of the civilians lost over the ledge resounded off the buildings, singing their horror in the wind.

"Oh, give me a break," Fiasco muttered.

The Deville had already taken flight, utilizing the same white anti-gravity disks beneath the tires that allowed Tamerlane to float back at the museum.

The power kicked up in a blue flash, and Fiasco dived over the edge. A woman had her face covered by brunette hair that fluttered upward as she fell backward, but he could still hear her terrified screams. Blanchet was ten stories high, but even in the brief time it took him to fly, the five who fell before Vanessa were nearly halfway down, descending faster with every breath.

A tendril wormed from his hand and caught the shrieking woman about the wrist. He curled the end into a barb in his palm. With a grunt and a prayer, he tossed the barb at the Blanchet building. For once, luck was on his side and his aim was truth. The harpoon sparked against the brick, bouncing as it was dragged along, before it dug into the concrete, breaking off portions of rock as the barb took hold. The line went taunt, halting the woman's descent with a jerk.

"One," he muttered.

Fiasco ignored her shriek of pain and released more power to accelerate downward. It felt as if it had only taken seconds to rescue the woman, yet the other four had already passed the halfway point, gravity pulling them to the fourth floor. The cold, hard street loomed below them.

Adjusting, he lassoed the leg of a large man who was falling headfirst, and around another that tumbled around like floating paper, but gave enough slack so he wouldn't stop them cold like the woman. He created five blue mini barbs on his fingertips and shot them in the glass building opposite Blanchet. The barbs shrieked as they cut long, jagged lines into the thick pane of glass, then suddenly tightened as it hooked into the other side.

"No, no, no," he heard the larger man yell as he covered his face with his arms. His momentum whipped them both to the right, flinging them into the windows below. The glass cracked from the impact with a resonant thud. The distance was not that far by Fiasco's standards, but the two hung limp like prize fishes on the line, dangling unconscious from the lasso around their legs, blood dripping down various wounds.

"Sorry," Fiasco shouted as he blazed past them. "That's three." He muttered.

Wind screamed around his mask. There were still two left who had fallen from the roof. His breath quickened. There were only three stories left in the building. Given the amount of time it had taken to rescue the first three, he calculated there was enough time to save one if he used the same methods, but not the other.

You will have to choose one, the voice said. *And fail the other.*

"But I have to try," Fiasco said.

But the voice's words rang true, and the negative emotion refilled his well of energy that he pushed out behind him like a jet engine in a fiery blue flame. He gritted his teeth against the turbulence as he streaked down headfirst. The woman's screams sang through his aura as he passed. Falling backwards, the obese man appeared shocked silent, his face calm and serene when Fiasco passed him.

Approaching the first story, Fiasco slowed to curve upward and turned about. Floating parallel between the hostages and the street, he drew in all his power, his aura dimming as he closed his eyes. He concentrated on the image of Julianna, and the tears in her beautiful eyes back in the booth when she admitted she was afraid to talk about marriage because she thought he would leave. He imagined letting her finish her sentence before he went to the bathroom, telling him that she was moving to L.A., leaving everything in New

Haven— including him— behind. The anguish from the thought of losing her moved the power like crashing particles inside, causing more and more energy to build.

The aura doubled around him. Fiasco opened his eyes and unleashed the accumulation from within. Beams coiled in all directions from his aura, thick and strong bands that carried weight. They crisscrossed left and right, weaving over and under with each other. Thrust outward like bullets, the barbed ends stuck into the glass and concrete on first strike until they formed a shimmering azure net between the two buildings.

"I hope this works," Fiasco thought. His question was quickly answered.

The large man hit first like an anvil, pushing the net down and making Fiasco exert additional energy outward to reinforce the net. The woman followed soon after, straining the manifestation further from the combined weight, and Fiasco worried they would still hit the concrete below from the drastic curvature. More energy flowed from his hands, pushing the two bodies back into the air like a trampoline until they landed again, with the woman bouncing atop the big man's girth. Their rebounding decreased until she settled atop his bare stomach that had finally burst through the buttons.

Fiasco floated closer to check on their well-being, hoping they did not accrue additional injuries from the landing. He anticipated screams or strings of curse words from the survivors if they were not too injured, but instead, to his surprise, he heard laughter.

The woman pulled her hair back from her face, still laughing. "Well, that was fun," she said with a grin and tapped the man's stomach. "Thanks for the soft landing, Frank."

Frank looked up, thick black hair blown out as if he had been in a wind tunnel, and his eyes still wide from the experience. "No problem, Marie," he looked over at Fiasco. "Th...than...thank you."

"Yes, thank you," Marie echoed, her eyes reddening from the realization that she had survived a near-death incident.

Fiasco nodded at the two, unable to take in any joy from their words as it would threaten his dwindling power reserve and took off straight up. He passed the dangling hostages who made up for the two below with curses hurled at him as he headed towards the Blanchet roof. When he approached, he called in the line and harpoon around the first woman he saved and scooped her up in his arms, reasoning that her injuries were too severe and her position too high to make a speedy rescue.

Arching over the raised edge and landing on the rooftop, she groaned as Fiasco laid her softly on the stone.

"Thanks for breaking my arm, you dick," she lashed out, a statement which Fiasco took to heart to replenish his strength.

He turned in the gravel, facing northwest towards the Cascade district where he last saw the Deville and took off again, not minding the injured woman who yelped from the gale he created, swirling the loose rock. Flying just below a row of clouds turned cotton white by the moon, the ninety-seven looked like a curving, white snake of headlights going north. He followed Antler Street out of the city. The roads had been cleared from the police barricades for hours, so he picked up the strong acrid stench of exhaust fumes through his aura that still lingered in the air and followed it. He fed his aura more energy and surged forward like a hound picking up a scent.

Passing the highway, the view turned into square parking garages, manicured lawns and trees, and skinny driveways of asphalt laid before single family homes. Fiasco flew low, buzzing over family-sized cars parked along the street, his copious speed fluttering the leaves of chestnut trees as he passed.

"Why would they go to the suburbs?" Fiasco thought, turning

right on Cascade Street. "Maybe the traffic jam forced them this way?"

The unmistakable stench grew stronger through his aura, stinging his eyes, when he saw round silver taillights and gleaming red fins in the distance.

"They must think they've already beaten me," he thought.

They know you are weak and feeble, the voice said.

Fiasco grinned and the houses on either side blurred. The Deville came into view, and he noticed that Tamerlane's strange disks had moved from beneath the tires and coalesced together into one object, a stark white that was draped over the backseat to keep their stolen goods from jostling as the Mal's tore down the street at a breakneck a speed.

The Deville jumped over a speed bump, which elicited a scream of joy and laughter from Enrapture. Fiasco took that time to cut the distance between them in half with a burst of speed. He saw Mimicker adjust the rear-view mirror as the glow from his aura crept onto the car, creeping like a translucent blue shadow. Not glancing back, the Mal leaned over and whispered something to Enrapture that made her finally notice his presence behind them.

She turned around, her knees digging into the light brown leather bucket seat, with both hands steadying her on the white headrest. Seeing him made her smile return, sharp and just as sinister. She removed her glasses and tossed them aside. She then untied the purple bandana that held up her hair and shook loose her blonde tresses, letting them flow about her face while they were pushed by the wind. She then opened her mouth and began to sing as she pointed a finger at Fiasco.

The melody was instantly striking. The lyrics were audibly indecipherable, but they impaled Fiasco's mind. To the Mega, it sounded like multiple voices singing in unison, but at different tones and octaves that harmonized a strange, beautiful tune he could feel within his soul. The Deville disappeared, and he saw only Enrapture in his mind. Her fingers and hands moved at angles with the melody, massaging the words into his heart as they poured over his body in melodic waves.

"Yes, I'll do what you say," Fiasco stammered. "I love you."

The gossamer image of Enrapture smiled, floating closer to caress his chin and turn his head. She warbled the music directly into his ear. Her dark purple lips moved slower than the words, yet he heard the music at normal speed. It felt like love personified, heating Fiasco's skin as he struggled to catch his breath. Her smile broadened and her fingers felt like heaven against his skin, the soft yellow rays of light tickling his face. An urge welled up, strong and overpowering like a tsunami rushing ashore. Whatever she wanted Fiasco to do, he would comply without hesitation or doubt. He would do anything if it meant he could take her in his arms.

You said you loved her, the voice chastised. *You have failed her again.*

"No, I didn't," Fiasco said. His thoughts ached as he remembered the gleam of Julianna's ponytail, the wrinkle in her nose, and the way her eyes closed when she smiled and laughed. "I do love her."

The floating Enrapture's words were shaken and began to sound off key, the notes spoiled by a voice not in tune with the others, breaking the harmony.

"You resist," he heard the apparition sing. Drifting, it pulled back from his side and glared with striking ocean blue eyes. She licked her lips that gleamed like jewels and whispered, "Don't resist me. You love me."

The aperture smiled, but Fiasco still heard the song as he drifted forward, ready to take her face in her hands when the image of Enrapture fell before him with a scream. The soothing light darkened blue like ink poured into water. A growl interrupted the beautiful song. He looked down. Straddling Enrapture's chest, and with both hands around the Mal's neck, was an image of Julianna, burning a cobalt iridescent. Her face was the mirror of rage, a dark and twisted visage that he had never seen on the real version of her. The Julianna impression pulled at the shocked and wide-eyed Enrapture, pulling her close to eyes that smoldered with a blue radiance.

"*He's mine!*" the Julianna image spat out, but it was not in Julianna's usual, soft inflection.

To Fiasco's ears, she sounded like that voice, but darker, pregnant with vitriol and wrath. Enrapture's terrified screams sounded like cold death, separate voices whaling in different octaves that chilled his spine. In an instant, both images disappeared in a flash of rainbow light, and he returned to the real world, evident by the stench of burned rubber as the Deville swerved left then right in a haze of gray. In the passenger seat, Enrapture screamed. Eyes wet with tears, her hands clutched at her throat, and she fell back onto the floorboard, bumping Mimicker on the way as he struggled to keep the muscle car on the road.

Leaving the Enrapture world was jarring and disorienting for the Mega. The houses still blurred from his speed, and the wind played through his cheeks. Fiasco glanced about to regain his bearing when he looked down and noticed those cursed yellow lines that separated the street. Instantly, his stomach lurched, and bile stung his throat from the lemon-colored strips that pulsed into his eyes. His aura waned, losing power as his altitude fell, veering into the pavement.

Careening down, his shoulder nicked the asphalt until he skipped along like a painted blue rock atop lake water. With his flying momentum, the aura shield pulled up chunks of pavements as he bowled head over heels down Cascade Street. Metal screamed and glass shattered as his back scraped against the side of a car that he caromed off. Air rushed from his lungs as his ribs struck a high-rise concrete curb that he tumbled over with a thump, before finally coming to a stop when he cut a thick groove of dirt and grass—ruining a pristine lawn.

Dirt turned to mud in his mouth, mixed with the bile that still piqued his throat.

"Always throwing up. You're so weak," Fiasco croaked as he wiped his mouth. "No wonder she wants to leave you."

The aura had taken the brunt of the impact, and Fiasco lifted his head, still reeling from the experience. The taillights of the Deville flashed red as Mimicker regained control and continued down the street, tires squealing. He was in someone's front yard and stopped mere meters from plunging through their garage door. He quickly got back to his feet, clutching his queasy stomach, when someone whose yard he had just ruined stirred.

A light clicked on in the foyer. Before he could fly away to escape the homeowner's wrath, the front door opened with a creak, and he saw a young, black girl peak her head out through the opening to look around. Her brown eyes were wide when she saw him standing in her front yard. Fiasco did not dare to move unless he wanted to frighten the small child.

"Sorry," Fiasco said through a weak grin. "Stay inside, honey, and stay off the grass. There might be sharp things in your yard that could hurt your feet. Just tell your mom to call the police, okay?"

"Okay," she replied. Before she closed the door she said, "Mr. Fiasco?"

He turned back to her. "Yeah?"

"You can beat them," her smile was even more adorable than he had expected because of the two front teeth that were missing. Obviously embarrassed, she giggled and quickly ran back inside and closed the door.

"Thanks, little girl," Fiasco mumbled, then took to the skies to continue the pursuit.

You are going to fail her, as well, the voice said when he crested over the trees.

"Welcome back, prick," Fiasco responded, still tasting of bile. "And what the hell was that back there with Enrapture? Was that just me fighting back with the power, or did you actually help for once?"

There was no response and Fiasco bristled at the disrespect. But the voice wasn't going anywhere, so he pushed the desire for answers from his mind, deciding it was more important to concentrate on capturing the Mals who were endangering citizens like the little girl he had just met.

The smell from the Deville's exhaust fume still lingered in the air. He used it to follow them down turns, putting him onto McCastle road that led out of town. He followed the road for several blocks and ended at a T-section hedged by a tall chain-link fence. Turning left and flying parallel, he followed barbed wire that circled over the top of the fence. On his right, rows of tall lights at the municipal airport lit up runways that were stained with black streaks of rubber. On the opposite side, sagebrush was incandescent under the moonlight that looked like skeletal trees as they rolled along the dark, desert floor. He veered upward towards the firmament to gain a better vantage point.

The entire view of the Cimmerian desert came into focus. In the distance, the airport looked like a string of Christmas lights. Looking about the landscape, it wasn't long until Fiasco had a hunch where Mimicker and Enrapture fled when he saw a ring of towering lights a few miles down the road that stood out in the darkness.

"They went to the abandoned Mega League stadium just to taunt me," Fiasco thought with a grimace. He imagined a plane parked in the massive crater, or a futuristic jetpack supplied by a bitter Tamerlane to ferry them away with a haul of stolen goods, and his pride in their pocket. "I need to get there before they escape. If they do, I'll never be able to look at Julianna again. If she doesn't leave me first, that is."

The thought still brought with it a pang of sadness that roiled his emotions and replenished his power reserve, which he then used to rush towards the excavation. He careened over the desert like a blue missile. Arriving at the site, tall thin cranes rose into the sky like frozen yellow crosses. The tower lights ringed the large aperture in the ground like a halo, turning the night into synthetic daylight. Around the edges were staggered levels of dirt-like stairs carved out of earth, which led down to the nearly flat ground. The surface of the hole was cluttered with dirt-coated metal containers and orange construction equipment that had clearly not been used in some time.

Fiasco turned to the west end of the opening, where he saw another stack of metal containers and the large foreman trailer Julianna's father must have used to oversee construction. Beyond the trailer, he saw the Deville parked among pickup trucks and a few small loaders he always wanted to drive as a child. The Deville was empty except for the Tamerlane shield that covered the back. A quick inspection of the area did not turn up Mimicker or Enrapture.

He supposed that they parked at the site to hide from his pursuit, but, in their genius, did not account for his ability to fly. But that was wishful thinking. Mals were cunning, evident by the high body count of murdered Megas. He would be foolish to underestimate Mimicker and Enrapture, especially since they have already proven their worth by trapping him and evading his pursuit thus far.

"Talon always said to never follow a Mal without getting their location first," Fiasco ruminated. That did not seem to be an option, since the blazing halogen lights created large dark shadows around the site where the two Mals could easily hide. He'd have to give his position away just to search them all.

Fiasco curled downward and his aura dimmed as he landed between a stack of red and blue storage containers stacked double high just a few feet away from the foreman's trailer. The gravel crunched beneath his feet— which couldn't be helped— as he crept in the shadows to the edge of the shipping container and peered out far enough to see the trailer door. It resembled a long ranch-style mobile home. Three halogen lights were attached to the red roof and pointed down to illuminate the porch. There were two windows on either side of the front, and two black staircases that led up to separate doors. Caked in dirt, a bulky, white air conditioner jutted out of a small window. It chugged to life, which told him someone was there—or had been there recently.

"Can't believe this cloak and dagger stuff works," Fiasco thought as he slid forward, his back against the side of the container to stay in the shadows.

The window closest to him on the right was dark on the inside. Being that close, he could see the flashing lights of a television reflecting in the other. While he contemplated how to get to the other end of the trailer without being seen, the door crashed open and banged against the side with an aluminum clatter.

The round wooden end of a baseball bat was the first thing to emerge from the door.

"Who the hell is out 'ere!" an old man yelled, spittle flying from his mouth as he spoke. He stood at the top of the staircase platform; his back hunched over as he held the bat with two withered hands. Dingy overalls hung limp on his body over a stained white t-shirt that was just as loose over his skinny, haggard frame. His mouth was tight and puckered as if he got up too fast to put in his dentures. Deep wrinkles lined his face, and his eyes were half covered with thick, gray, bushy eyebrows. Ironically, his head was nearly bald, except for wisps of silver hair that dangled in the front.

Not wanting to give the old man a heart attack, Fiasco emerged from the shadow with his hands up and with his light barely surrounding his body.

"It's just me, sir. Fiasco," he said.

"Fie-ass-co?" he replied with a strong, southern twang and a croaking tone. The old man tapped his palm with the barrel of the bat. "What tha hell is Fie-ass-co?"

"Me, sir. New Haven's favorite son?" Fiasco said, almost laughing as he said the words. "You got a name, old man?"

His caterpillar-like eyebrows flicked upward. "It sure as hell ain't old man," he licked his lips then leaned on the bat like a cane. "It's Bill. Bill Kramer. I'm watching over this site until they get it back up again. Now you gonna tell me what the hell you're doing here, Fie-ass-co, before I call the po'lice?"

Fiasco lowered his arms and slowly approached Bill.

"I'm here looking for some Mals sir that robbed a building in New Haven and put some innocent people in danger. Have you seen anyone around here?"

"Can't say that I have," Bill's shoulders straightened up. "And I heard your ass comin', so I'm guessin' they ain't around here."

"Well, I saw their car parked a few yards away. These people are dangerous, sir. Mind if I look around?"

"Well, I'm coming with ya. We've had a problem with kids coming here screwin', stealin', or smokin' pot, and I can't have some stranger walking around here even if he does wear some gay, blue costume." Bill's defiant demeanor told Fiasco that he wasn't going to take no for an answer.

"Well, just stay behind me," Fiasco sighed. "I don't want you getting hurt during this. And if something happens, I'm going to need you to get out of here." He began to walk but stopped in his tracks, paused, pointing a finger at the old man. "And just so you know, this suit is dark cyan. Studies show it's a top masculine color."

"Shut up. I don't need no protectin'. Got ol' merciless here for any brats we find," Bill replied and banged his bat against the porch twice. "And only an ass sniff'r would know the damn name of a color like that."

Fiasco chuckled and decided that he liked the old man's obstinate temperament as he moved passed the foreman's trailer. Bill did well to stay quiet behind him as they moved between containers and storage units packed with stadium parts. Fiasco called in his aura and gauntlets, until both disappeared as they approached where he thought the Deville would be. Beyond a pickup truck laden with bags of cement, he finally saw the empty Deville.

"They have to be around here somewhere," Fiasco whispered.

"Who is? Dammit boy, you better tell me what's goin' on around 'ere," Bill said.

Fiasco waved his hand back to quiet him down. "You forgot already, old timer? The two Mals I mentioned earlier," he turned to face Bill. "I'm going to look inside the hole. Stay here and remember, if something happens, get back to the trailer. Call the cops if you need to."

Beads of sweat streamed down Bill's forehead as he nodded, holding the bat as if it would do any good against the Mals. Quietly, Fiasco skulked away. As he passed a pickup truck, he stood on his tiptoes to look inside the cab but saw nothing except fast food refuse and empty cans of beer, most likely from an out-of-work construction worker lamenting the loss of steady pay on a lonely night. The reminder that all of this was his fault made his power rise inside. Then, a pleasant giggle echoed up from the chasm and caught his attention, spurring him forward. A red compact loader was near the edge, and he couldn't help but touch the hard exterior before he knelt in the long shadow at its side.

Looking over the edge of the chasm, he saw Enrapture sitting between the treads of a bulldozer, one leg crossed over the other. Her hair was still down, but she had donned her purple glasses again. The tower lights highlighted her toned body and smooth legs. Even though the Julianna apparition in the Enrapture had fiercely choked her slender throat, there was no sign of bruising that he could see. She leaned back on her palms, chewing gum and looking up into the sky without a care.

"Well, isn't that the most enticingly beautiful trap I've ever seen." The remnants of her song played like a soft, lonely voice, enticing him to float down and join her, and Fiasco shook his head to try and release it. "Damn, her power really lingers."

"Ain't she gorgeous," Bill said in his ear, making Fiasco flinch in surprise. Lost in Enrapture's magnetism, he didn't hear the old man approach from behind.

Fiasco flicked his shoulder from the man's hot breath against his neck. "I told you to stay back," he asserted.

Bill stood up holding his bat as his furrowed brow created more wrinkles on his face. "I ain't scared."

"Well, you should be," Fiasco whispered and turned back to the hole. "That lady down there could probably kill us both with just a song."

"Don't I know it," Bill replied.

Gone was his accent, or even the old inflection in his tone, replaced by a deep gravelly voice. Fiasco began to turn when he felt a sting in the back of his head in a flash of white light that jerked it forward. The bat moaned as it cracked and splintered, breaking into shards from the blow to the back of his head. Fiasco spun in the dirt on his heels and stood in one motion. He could finally see the brown of Bill's wide eyes as he looked at Fiasco, then to his bat, as if it somehow failed him by shattering into pieces.

"Nice try," Fiasco said with a sly grin. He clutched the old man by his skinny arm that felt like bone covered in flesh. "Contrary to some, I do learn from my mistakes, and you can thank your friend,

Tamerlane, for that. It took me weeks to learn how to make my aura low enough not to be seen, but still effective. You moved too soon."

No longer stricken with old age, Bill stood at full height and stared at Fiasco with his cold, brown eyes. The overall pants on his right leg quivered, rippling upward, squirming like liquid. Then, the leg transformed into a hulking veined mass. Pink skin pulsated on the limb, and muscled tentacles protruded out from the foot. Faster than Fiasco could react, old man Bill thrust forward and kicked the massive, clubbed foot forward, covering Fiasco's body from stomach to throat.

Breath rushed from Fiasco's lungs. Pain rippled through his bones, and it felt as though he had been hit in the chest by a Mack truck at full speed. So swift was the blow that Fiasco had little time to strengthen his thin aura, and he was pushed backward in a burst of dust beneath his feet. He saw Bill's clothes and skin ripple upward several times in rapid succession until he was replaced by the Mimicker in his green, baggy suit, eyes still shadowed in darkness from the oversized fedora that leaned on his head, and a leering grin as he approached the ledge. Then, Fiasco slipped backward off the edge.

Coarse, brown dirt saturated his suit as he rebounded off the wall, which wreaked havoc with his orientation when he thought to fly. Sharp dirt and rock outcroppings ripped open his poorly threaded repairs and created fresh holes in his costume on his shoulder and thighs. The dirt pushed him along, increasing the speed of his plummet. He broke through another ledge, his side plowing through in a shower of grime. Then, he fell further and caromed off the lowest jut of a dirt overhang that forced his headfirst slide along the gravelly stadium floor that pushed soil and stones into his open wounds. He slid to a stop a few feet from the bulldozer where Enrapture sat, her shrill laughter floating through the canyon.

Fingers of fire squeezed Fiasco's lungs as he writhed, trying to force in air. Jumping off the tracks in one hop, the heels of Enrapture's cowboy boots padded the rough gravel as she approached, giggling all the while. The same gravel cut like glass when Fiasco pushed himself to his hands and knees. Deep, panicked breaths made his side and back ache.

"How many damn times am I going to fall today?" he thought as his breath began to return to normal, his lungs taking in phosphorous-tasting air.

With hands on her hips, Enrapture leaned over and blew a bubble from her gum that smelled faintly like strawberry before it popped. "That's what you get for messing with my man," she said quietly through a smirk. Then, she stood upright to deliver a swift, sharp knee to Fiasco's side that tumbled him over and drove the newly arrived air from his lungs once more. "And that's for choking me, and calling me a whore, asshole."

"We're running out of time, babe!" Mimicker shouted with his gravelly voice that must have been his normal inflection.

Still on his side and clutching his aching ribs, Fiasco watched as Enrapture practically skipped to the lowest jut on the dirt wall. A long, green arm, muscled and throbbing with red veins, slithered down behind her, and curled itself around her waist and body. Instead of being repulsed, Enrapture caressed the writhing appendages with her arms. She waved at Fiasco with her skinny fingers as the grotesque arm lifted her up the long, dirt wall to where Mimicker was leaning over with his other hand braced on his knee.

Reaching the top, the arm wormed its way back into his Mimicker's body, and the two Mals embraced, then exchanged a long kiss as if they had been away for hours instead of the minutes it truly was. With Enrapture's arm wrapped around Mimicker's waist and her other hand rubbing his chest, the couple gave Fiasco one last look, admiring their ingenuity and victory, before moving away from the edge. Then, Fiasco heard a clicking sound. Out of his sight, the Mals tripped a switch that canceled the light towers and cast the area in a sea of darkness, with only the pallid glow from the moon as a source of illumination.

You have failed once again, the voice said. *Give up now.*

The roaring engine from the Deville, mixed with Mimicker's eerie laughter, reverberated down to where Fiasco laid on his side, then trailed off in a buzz of engine roar.

"Get up, dammit," Fiasco grunted, wincing from the pain as he crushed dirt and gravel in his fist. The disheartening words from the voice— who was always right— stirred an emotion of humiliation and replenished the depleted energy inside. Warmth ran through his skin and bones and rolled over the stinging wounds like stitches of light. Quickly, it moved over his body to staunch the wounds that tickled from the blood he felt welling up in the new cuts and gashes. The gauntlets on his hands returned and glowed blue, shedding light on his surroundings. The power healed Fiasco enough to get him back on his knees.

"You took their best shot," Fiasco spat out the blood that pooled in his mouth, lungs breathing in wheezing air. "Don't let them win again. What would Julianna think?"

You cannot win, the voice mocked with relentless glee. *End this farce of being a Mega. End your dream of being with her.*

"No!" Fiasco gritted his teeth, his fist slamming against the ground in frustration.

The scream of an airplane engine zoomed overhead, trailing as it passed him by. Looking up, he could not see it in the firmament and stars, but he could feel the vibrations through the ground given his proximity to the airport. He imagined Julianna sitting alone on the plane, her face close to the oval window that dripped condensation, looking down on New Haven as she moved on to a better life. The voice wanted him to let her go. And the voice was always right.

Fiasco's shoulder slumped as despair descended on his being. The pungent taste of copper on his tongue reminded him of his failures thus far. But, before he could make a move towards either choice, a coruscating light blinked on in the distance. It flashed his shadow against the dirt wall— a thin silhouette down on his hands and knees.

"What is this?" Fiasco said, his voice shallow from the lack of air. He put up a hand to block the brilliance. "Another attack from Mimicker and Enrapture? Seriously?"

"Mega-fugitive Fiasco," a voice boomed through the chasm in a commanding tone. "This is the Mega-human Defense Command authorized by the United States Government."

The blood in Fiasco's veins cooled, even though his heart raced as he whispered, "the M.D.C.? Here?"

The floating voice continued, "You are hereby remanded to our custody for murder, and in violation of the misuse of Mega powers to harm citizens and personal property. Power down and await M.D.C. officials to bring you into custody. Any actions on your part outside of these parameters will be viewed as force and be responded to in kind. You will comply."

The light narrowed into a white spotlight. Sweat chilled Fiasco's skin as he sat back on his heels. His shoulders dipped further, shivering from the sudden cold, and he stared at his shimmering gauntlet-covered hands that he had cupped on his knees, almost in sublimation.

"I am so screwed," Fiasco wheezed out.

Above, he heard the mechanical sound of a door opening behind the light. It whirled like a chain being released, then clanged open to a stop. A shadow played in the light, moving like a dark creature. It slowly descended to the ground, landing just in front of him, nearly hidden by the brightness.

Yes, the voice agreed. *Yes, you are.*

The M.D.C.

"You never even questioned why those two Mals ran in the first place," Fiasco thought. "You're so stupid."

Still sitting on his heels, Fiasco held his bare hand up to the light to see him better. The Mega was told to power down his gauntlets, and he complied, seeing no other option. John Hammond, a high-ranking member of the M.D.C. stood within the light. He was dressed in a full-body suit that was patterned a suppressed gray and black camouflage. In the light, his head looked rather square to Fiasco. Although his face was lined with wrinkles, he still looked rather young, with a head full of ginger curls, and a matching five o'clock shadow. Fiasco knew though that despite Hammond's youthful appearance, his high rank in the M.D.C. indicated that he was at least his father's age.

"Hello Fiasco," Hammond said, his voice eerily calm given the situation. His hands were open and accepting as he slowly approached, black combat boots crunching gravel. "There is no reason this has to go any other way but peacefully."

On the MegaStream, Fiasco had watched Hammond conduct press briefings and action reports. He was the public face of the M.D.C. and was responsible for ensuring the organization was viewed positively by citizens who sometimes saw their actions as overreaching. Despite civil liberty organizations' constant derision,

Hammond's appeal to the public seemed to work, as the people accepted their actions with little push back. Although he did not appear to be a Mega himself, to any Mal or Mega who broke the rules, Hammond's presence always meant a one-way trip to the Oubliette. Fiasco nearly saw it as an honor to have someone of his stature being there.

You will never see Julianna after this day, the voice said.

"Why are you here?" Fiasco asked, his voice still strained from pain.

"You know why, Fiasco," Hammond replied calmly.

You are a failure.

Fiasco laughed and slowly shook his head from side to side. "So, you lured me out here using those two Mals? I should be flattered."

"We agreed to reduce their sentences. It's complicated, political, and not really your concern right now," Hammond said as he continued walking towards him, slow and with caution. "We needed to draw you out because you're dangerous, Fiasco. We couldn't risk civilian casualties if you decided to resist. You won't resist though, will you?" Hammond waited for a reply, but Fiasco just stared directly at him, processing all that had happened so far. Hammond continued, "This hole here seemed like the perfect location. Not much more damage you could do around here, is there?"

The wounds on Fiasco's legs, back, and arms from the fall stung and bled with the aura no longer healing them. One arm moved to the ribs Enrapture had kneed that ached whenever he took a breath. His tongue moved loose molars in the back as his mouth that again filled with the taste of blood. But he swallowed the taste of copper instead of spitting it out, not wanting to lose even more face in front of Hammond. Taking inventory of all his injuries, he was in little shape to resist even if he wanted to, yet he did not answer Hammond's questions.

Hammond stopped, head tilted when he noticed the silence.

"Come now, Fiasco. Don't be as ignorant as I heard you can be. Assess the situation." He waved his arm, and the spotlight changed to a dull orange, almost as if the stadium had been illuminated by candlelight. "Perhaps this will remove any rebellious thoughts you might be entertaining."

Fiasco heard a hiss of machinery in the air. He looked up and saw only the stars, yet in the firmament, a cargo lift door was open like a tear in the sky, vomiting light out and pouring it downward. Four darkened figures emerged, standing at the edge of the light before jumping to the ground. Fiasco felt them land through the dirt but could not see their faces in the spotlight.

"You brought a skychaser?" Fiasco asked, remembering how the M.D.C. capture squad were known to travel in airships developed by Praeterminds. Although he could not see it in the sky, it was not invisible, either. Instead, the metal exterior was shined to such a sheen that it reflected the environment and mimicked invisibility, even in daylight.

"We come prepared," Hammond said, his head tilted back to the people who had joined him on the ground. "As you can see."

Three of the four figures emerged from the shadows, and Fiasco recognized them instantly from browsing the MegaStream under the M.D.C. tab.

"Megas," Fiasco thought as he looked at each of their faces. "Trained M.D.C. Megas."

You are going to fail.

One of the Megas stepped forward, speaking first.

"No es tan valiente, verdad?" Flash Freeze said on the left. White clouds puffed from his mouth as he spoke. Jet black hair sat messily atop his head, like frozen black spikes frosted white. He wore dark tactical pants, but was barefoot on the tough gravel, and shirtless in the night air. His skin seemed translucent with icy blue lines that zigzagged though his face, arms, and feet. A grin played across his youthful face, his eyes two frigid pools of blue.

A giant of a man stood in the middle of the trio, and said in a thick, brooding voice, "What the hell did he say, Sonance?"

Fiasco recognized him as the Mega called Rush and noticed how his shadow seemed to swallow the two Megas on either side of him. He was armored from his neck down to his feet with titanium-colored plates. Dark skin hid his facial definitions in the poor light, but Fiasco could see the outline of his round, black manicured afro.

"He said he doesn't look so tough or brave," Sonance said beside him on the right. The thin girl was practically clutching Rush's massive arm, her voice shivering. She was dressed in the same M.D.C. tactical gear as Hammond, but all-black, with an additional mask that covered everything but her pink lips, and large hazel eyes that trembled as they peered at Fiasco.

"Sonance. She must be the rookie," Fiasco thought as he sized up the Megas. The M.D.C. were known to send a rookie on easy capture campaigns to give the new recruits fieldwork experience.

They do not respect you.

"Well, why the hell didn't you say that in English, then?" Rush asked Flash Freeze who was standing at his side. His voice was deep, but light, like a teenage boy just entering manhood. Sonance giggled, making it clear that she was accustomed to the two squabbling Megas.

"Puta, I gave you books," Flash Freeze replied, speaking English in a thick, latin accent. "Plus, that is a simple sentence. You should know that one by now if you had studied it."

Rush's lips pursed. "Not the time for conversational lessons in Spanish here, Freeze."

"Quit the side chatter," a voice said behind them to which they all seemed to defer, ending the conversation instantly. "Stay frosty. Fiasco is down, but he's still very dangerous."

On his knees, Fiasco reared his head back and began to laugh, the sound bouncing along the dirt walls. He laughed with such vigor that his bruised side ached like fire, yet he paid it little mind. Tears trailed down his cheeks, stinging the cuts on his exposed cheeks and jaws. As his laughter subsided, he lifted his fist, grains of dirt falling from his hand as he held it up to the light.

"I was wondering if you would show," Fiasco said, crestfallen, watching the dirt pour from his palm. "It's funny. For a moment, I was actually hoping that you'd show up to help me."

"Well, that was foolish, wasn't it, Crooked F?" the voice said behind the Megas.

The trio of Megas parted, and Talon emerged, his presence swallowing the light. His head was adorned with a wonderful, beaded headdress with short, stiff turquoise feathers with black tips, pointing downward as they flowed back and over his shoulders. The mask he wore was bone white. The white screens hid his eyes, but the mask impressed the intensity of his brow that arrowed down over his nose. Red bracelets of knives gleamed over his muscled wrists that veined from the clenched fists at his sides.

Talon stopped just behind Hammond, flanking his back. An unbuttoned, sleeveless, leather vest, the same turquoise color as his headdress, fell past his leather belt armed with knives, over dark slacks. Stitched on the right of his vest was the image of the Modoc Chief Yellow Hammer riding a steed of white and dressed in the height of Indian fashion of his time, his fellow warriors trailing behind him on an Oregon plain.

You do not have any friends besides her. the voice taunted. *That is assuming you even have her.*

Talon crossed his arms over his chest, tapping a blood red knife that gleamed in the light. "You seem disappointed" he observed.

"No," replied Fiasco as he rose from the ground, groaning as he clutched his side, hardly able to breath from the pain. "Disappointed is when you find holes in the middle of your loaf of bread. What I feel now is...something else entirely." He stood as tall as he could but was still hunched over. "You were supposed to be my friend."

"I was your friend," Talon replied tensely. "Didn't I warn you that others were watching?"

"You never said you were one of them."

"Sure, I did," Talon said, jaw clenching tight. "I tried with you. I tried making you better. I patrolled with you. Gave you access to the Stream. But you disregarded my instructions at every turn, going off half-cocked with little training, and no idea how to control your power. And then the museum—" He cut himself off as his voice teemed with anger. He rolled his fist in circles around to calm his emotions, then continued, "So here we are."

"Yes, here we are," Fiasco parroted. "With you betraying me in the end."

And you will lose her, too.

Talon took a step forward but was stopped by Hammond, who waved him back.

"Whether you think it's a betrayal or not, Fiasco, doesn't matter now," Hammond said, his voice still serene. There is no need for violence here," he paused, and looked back at the Megas in his charge. "Or insults."

Hammond turned back to Fiasco, his green eyes steady. "There won't be any violence here, right Fiasco?"

"You keep asking me that," Fiasco replied. "Like you're scared I'd say no."

"Scared my ass," Rush mumbled from behind Hammond. "Skinny little wimp or not, just give me the word, sir, and I'll rip—"

"Enough!" Hammond said in an octave that approached a shout.

Fiasco glared past Hammond to Rush, whose right hand twitched at his side.

You are weak and he wants to punish you, the voice said.

"That one is itching for a fight," Fiasco thought. He turned his gaze back to Hammond, whose face had darkened from the sudden outburst of anger.

"We're not scared, Fiasco, because you must understand the situation. You're surrounded, and outnumbered," he said as he walked forward. "You are facing four highly trained M.D.C. agents chosen specifically for your skill set." Hammond peered around. "And you're alone out here, in the middle of nowhere. With no aid coming."

He is right. You are alone.

Hammond's left eye shined a bright green, battling the overhead light with its own as he approached. "Again, we can end this with no bloodshed. No one wants to hurt you."

They all do and will if you resist. Yield.

"Please, I implore you. Analyze the situation, Fiasco." The gleam in Hammond's eye grew brighter, the light itching into Fiasco's brain. "You really have little choice here." Hammond stopped and gently put a hand on Fiasco's shoulder. His hand felt light and his touch comforting as he leaned in and smiled like a father would consoling his son. A wave of calm enveloped Fiasco the closer Hammond stood, and a feeling of destiny fell upon Fiasco's beleaguered mind. "Are we in agreement, Fiasco?" Hammond added.

Fiasco's head dropped as he accepted his fate, and the weight of his situation was lifted. A lifetime of failure had brought him to that moment. A culmination of years making the wrong choices. Turning left when he should have gone right. Bereft of the drive, ambition, or intelligence to propel him forward. Not until her. Not until Julianna entered his life and turned it around.

She was the strength that pushed him when he did not move.

And all he did in response was bring ruin to her life. None of the happiness that sprouted up sporadically overshadowed the negativity his presence imposed upon her. The current predicament of their relationship was a testament to that failure. Given how much he had disappointed Julianna during their time together, the best thing he could do for her in the end would be to spend time in the Oubliette.

The air smelled mountain fresh with the gained clarity. Hammond's question hung in the silence, so he asked it again. "Do we agree, Fiasco?"

"Yes," Fiasco replied beneath his breath.

Hammond smiled, then breathed out as if relieved. "Good. You made the right choice." The green flecks in his left eye glimmered like an emerald as his face relaxed.

You are a coward who does not deserve her, the voice said, and Fiasco agreed, and he thought he could still hear the whine of the plane engines in the distance.

Fiasco looked up at Hammond. In the shadow of the light, the glint emanating from Hammond's eye changed from green to blue, stifled by a source of light between them. Hammond looked down. His eyes widened, and the azure glow made his skin and red hair look pale blue in the reflection.

Knocking off Hammond's hands from his shoulder, Fiasco reached out his right fist that shined with a gauntlet covered in intricate blue lines and pushed the glove into the M.D.C. commander's chest. The power rippled outward from the crooked *F* in the middle of his chest in a blue ocean of waves that coalesced into a surge of energy at the tip of his fist. Fiasco stepped forward into the gravel with his left foot, pushing in his heel to gain traction. Behind his goggles, he met Hammond's eyes. The blue energy swirled between them, resembling the top of a tornado. Fiasco grunted through a clenched jaw, twisting his hips, and punching upward with all the strength he could muster from his battered body.

A thrum reverberated off the dirt walls, cascading and pushing outward from where the two Megas stood. Fiasco watched, his jaw slackened, as Hammond lifted off his feet, his chest sparking shards of his blue light. "Oh shit," he muttered as the M.D.C. commander's body arched like a doll tossed overhand, a reaction to a punch that he poured far more power into than intended.

Reactively, Talon glided to his right. Rush ducked beneath the oncoming body, pulling Sonance by the back of her head down with him. Their commander's body soared overhead, trailing blue smoke from his chest. His arms reached out for something to hold, but only finding air. Then, weighed down by his tactical gear, he lost momentum and arched towards the ground. With a thud, Hammond landed behind the group of Megas, tumbling through the dirt and grime that extinguished Fiasco's energy on his chest. After a slow glide that turned him around three hundred and sixty degrees— face eating dirt— his body finally stopped in a mound of rocks and gravel. Tan dust hung in the air. Hammond lay prone on the ground, arms akimbo over his head as the dirt and smoke settled around his still body.

A loser will always lose. The voice warned. *This will cause you pain.*

"No kidding," Fiasco thought. He grimaced, his bruised side burning from the sudden movement. "But he tried to get into my mind, just like Enrapture did."

The four M.D.C. Megas stood between him and their fallen commander, almost afraid to move.

Flash Freeze glared at him with sky blue eyes before looking back at his commander. "Estàs bien, señor?" he murmured. His ice-covered eyes blinked rapidly as he touched a cross over his body.

Kneeling with one knee on the ground, Rush flashed a furious look at Fiasco. His forehead creased as he turned back to Hammond. "Boss?" he stammered.

"Oh my God," Sonance gasped at his side. She also looked back at the M.D.C. leader, her hand covering the mouth beneath her mask. "Is he dead?" she squeaked between her fingers.

Talon did not say a word, mouth tight and jaw clamped with concentration. He kept the white screens of his eyes on Fiasco, and the two met gazes. Still stung by the feeling of loss and betrayal, Fiasco raised up straight, biting back against the pain in defiance, then twisted on his back heel. His right foot glided back through the gravel in an arch kicking up dirt, and his gauntlet-covered hand shot skyward. Without a second thought, he released barbed tendrils of light into the sky from his fingers and palm. On his mental command, the barbs curled and twisted together, melding into a beam of light that lifted northeast like an azure missile.

A boom bounced off the walls that made even Talon flinch and shake loose chunks of dirt and rocks from the edge of the chasm that tumbled into the hole. Metal screeched and cried as Fiasco's beam ripped through the bottom of the skychaser, before shooting out the top of the craft. Debris pushed up through the gap, shining like jewels in the moonlight before falling back to earth. The Megas who were sent to capture him were caught beneath the fallout.

Fiasco watched as Flash Freeze raised his arms to create an umbrella of thick, glistening ice that rainbowed between both hands, and spared him from the dangerous debris that stuck into the ice block. Rush leaned on his hands and covered Sonance from the falling shrapnel with his own body, letting the chunks of metal careen off his armor with clangs as it fell harmlessly into the dirt while the smaller Mega cowered beneath his large frame. Fiasco could not find Talon in the rain of metal that pummeled the dirt, so his eyes returned to the sky.

Black smoke followed by orange fire billowed from the skycraft, concealing the stars as the skychaser listed to the left. The awkward trajectory allowed Fiasco to see part of the frame. To him, it looked like a cargo plane, with short thick wings that kept it hovering in the sky, but far more robust and armored. Red lights flashed a warning on the wings. Its body was oblong and lengthy, and it tapered at the back to a tail that still reflected the stars. Fiasco noticed the top was dominated by a round structure that resembled an eye, yellow and almond shaped. He assumed that sirens were blaring from the inside. Shadowy figures ran through the backlight of the eye as the skychaser pulled away, still coughing smoke.

The air was thick with the smell of oil, fire, and smoke when Hammond's groan brought Fiasco's eyes back to the ground. The M.D.C. commander struggled up to his elbow and spat dark red blood into the dirt. With each heavy breath, caramel dust fell from his red hair. He rose further, gray smoke simmering from the armor on his chest, until he propped himself on his hands. A long breath whistled from Hammond's lips as he moved to sit on his haunches, hands on his knees. Touching the melted iron on his chest from his now-ruined tactical vest, he rubbed his fingers together. His green eyes, that had previously appeared calm and pleasant, were now bloodshot, piercing Fiasco.

"Take him down," Hammond bellowed. Blood from a cut at the top of his head streaked his face that was twisted in rage. "Now!"

"Uh oh," Fiasco thought as he watched the Megas turn toward him.

Silent, and like a switch had been flipped on, the trio of Megas attacked him as if they were one unit. In the rear of the quartet, Flash Freeze's ice blue veins flowed in his translucent body down to his hands, and he rose into the sky on a thick column of ice that formed from his palms. This maneuver nearly distracted Fiasco from the silver brute that lumbered towards him. Bending at the waist, he barely ducked under Rush's massive forearm that sailed inches over his head, strong enough that he could feel the breeze beat against his leather mask. He heard the gravel spitting outward as the big man's momentum pushed him forward. Fiasco took the moment to return his aura shield back to full power with an audible thrum.

"What am I doing, what am I doing?" Fiasco panicked.

Looking back at the remaining Megas, Fiasco noticed Sonance shivering next to the tall column of glistening ice, legs bent, and hands parted out in front of her at shoulder length. Her wide, hazel eyes darted back and forth behind her black mask, alone and confused. Fiasco decided to attack her first.

Flying upright, leaning forward, and with his gauntlet curled into a fist near his head, he sped towards the Mega, leaving a trail of blue dust in his wake.

"I never hit a girl before," Fiasco thought as he approached, skimming over the gravelly floor. "Maybe I can just give her a strong tap or something to knock her out?" Teeth bit into his bottom lip when he couldn't decide what to do. "Talon's right," he admitted. "I should have studied my power more. Nearly caved in Hammond's chest back there."

Sonance finally reacted to his assault, and he saw the whites of her eyes expand further, contrasting with her black mask. Fiasco's flight pushed the wind into Sonance's face, making her eyes flutter. Only inches away, she unexpectedly turned her back to him. Fiasco skidded to a halt along the gravel when she raised both her hands and dropped down to the dirt. "Stop! Stop! Stop! Please!" she pleaded. Fiasco couldn't see her face behind her arms but felt a pang of guilt from her voice that was full of terror. "Don't hit me! I give up!"

Walking through the kicked up haze, Fiasco put up his gloved hands to try and console the young Mega that now reminded him of his little sister, Angie.

"Whoa, calm down. Calm down! I'm not going to hurt you," he said.

Fiasco reached out to Sonance, focused on consoling her sobs, missing the whistling sound that came from his left. His hand went numb. Looking down, Fiasco blinked behind his goggles, stunned as he stared at the hilt of a blood red iron knife that curved out from the back of his left gauntlet that had shattered at the center.

"Shit!" Fiasco cried.

He turned on his heels in the grit, clutching the wound to his body to staunch the flow of warm blood he felt building inside the glove. A scream caught in his throat when he wrenched the flechette from the back of his hand in a spray of red. The blade felt light and balanced, with both edges sharpened to fine points.

"I didn't even feel that go in. It went right through my shield. How the hell did he do that?" Fiasco thought as he tossed the knife aside. The blue gauntlet flowed and stretched over his wound, and he released more power to try and hasten the speed of healing.

Fiasco searched the darkness, but his visibility was poor. The spotlight from the skychaser was still aimed at the hole, but having floated farther away, its white light created long angled shadows among the construction vehicles and palettes piled high with equipment. Fiasco knew Talon could be in any one of them with another throwing knife ready.

As he peered through the shadows, his breath turned to clouds of white frost that swirled into the sky. Even with his aura, the cold seeped into his skin and bones, and he began to shiver. His injured hand froze to his body in a block of ice tinted red. Fiasco tried to turn again, but his lower body was frozen in place, and the cold crept up his chest, leaving stalactite spikes of ice hanging off his outstretched hand. The cold moved over his face and the world turned an icy blue as crystals slithered over his goggles and mask, crackling upward.

"Got him!" Flash Freeze shouted atop a tower of ice. His

outstretched hands looked blurry, and to Fiasco, his voice sounded as if it were underwater. "Get out of there, Mija. Rush, you're up!"

Fiasco felt his muscles tense, but he could not move. His head felt heavy, as if it were encased in fast-drying cement. Locked in his cold tomb, he felt the ground rumble up through the ice. He saw the murky image of Sonance on the ground, who gave him an upward glance, feet slipping in the dirt before fleeing beyond his field of vision.

"No. Got to get out of this. Help me get out," Fiasco thought, trying to call on his power or aid from the voice, but the chill that froze him made it difficult to concentrate.

His heart that was pumping strong from adrenaline, began to slow. The intensity of the freeze drained the heat from his aura and body, while the vigorous shivers racking his bones siphoned what remained. Being entirely encased in ice made Fiasco breathe in the limited air supply with panicked ingests, adding weight to his eyelids that made the world dim.

A muffled voice penetrated the ice. "Rush! Stand down!" Fiasco thought he heard Hammond say, but it was hard to tell with frozen ears.

The rumble in the ground grew in ferociousness, which forced Fiasco's eyes to open again. A bright white light gained in intensity in the ice, like the headlights of a locomotive barreling straight towards him. The ground swam like an earthquake beneath his feet, rocking his ice tomb and making it teeter. The shine of the light expanded brighter, until he heard the ice splinter and crack like a spider's web. Then, it shattered into crystalline shards from an explosion of pain that launched him skyward.

Fiasco's throat felt like it had fallen into his stomach. Cool wind whistled over his ears, and the stars rushed up to greet him, twinkling their song. He tried to jumpstart his aura with thoughts of Julianna, but the swooping air only made the water against his skin feel frigid. The lights of downtown New Haven blurred through the pieces of broken ice that had followed him into the sky. He thought about how beautiful its radiance looked against the night before the cold moisture in the clouds embraced him, and the world turned a misty gray.

Downtown

Muted trumpets stirred Fiasco from a dreamless sleep. His eyes fluttered open, and he was greeted by a wall of blue. At first he thought he was still frozen in a block of ice, losing breathable air, but then he felt the warm rush of blood in his body as it moved freely once again. He reached out to the edge of the barrier with his bare hand. A triangle-shaped scar an inch long had healed into a smooth mound of flesh on the back, and dried blood dyed his fingernails. The healing cocoon disappeared at his touch in a blink. Dirt thumped against his mask and goggles, smaller pieces falling into his mouth. The sound of a blaring alarm stampeded in to fill the silence.

"Am I dead?" Fiasco thought. The realization that he was touching dirt made him shoot up at the waist in a start. The filth fell away from his goggles, leaving dark smudges on the lenses that he had to wipe away. "Not again," he sighed.

Looking up, he saw the sky, but the stars were partially hidden behind a tan ambiance. All around him was an inclining wall of earth that led up to a lip of broken asphalt. Fiasco rose to his feet, joints in his knees cracking from ache, and surveyed how deep he had fallen. Unable to guess beyond the fact that the depth would make a decent underground bunker, he let out a lung clearing cough and began his ascent. Dirt covered hands and feet dug into the cold mud and earth as he lifted himself up, each movement sending waves of sharp pain through his body.

"Tired of holes today," he thought, keeping his eyes up towards the light. "And getting my butt kicked by everyone on this side of the pacific."

You are a loser who will fail, as always, the voice said. Fiasco agreed, letting the severe words recharge his near depleted well of power that forced him to climb instead of fly.

The beeping alarm bounced off the walls, growing louder the further as he marched upward. After some time, he finally reached the lip of the hole. His left hand nearly gave way from needles of pain where Talon's knife had pierced, and he strained to push himself over the edge. After clearing his body from the hole, Fiasco stood.

Wiping off the dirt and grime from his costume with downward swipes, he looked around. He saw that his descent had carved through a parked car. Its alarm trumpeted like a mocking siren. Its headlight had been sheared off by his energy cocoon, along with a portion of the hood.

Beyond the car was a square park with closely cropped grass. Osculating sprinklers stood at various points, ticking as they sprayed arches of water. Newly paved streets ran along the four sides of the square, dark and clean. Elm and Northern oak trees rose high into the sky around the park edges, creating a canopy of limbs and leaves. The canopy hung over gray brick running trails that were lit with interspersed lamps that radiated a soft, beige light.

Fiasco turned slowly and looked at the luxurious line of two-story townhomes behind the street, their fronts dominated by large, formatted windows. They weren't made of brick but appeared more like Fiasco proofed metal laid smoothly in panels and colored a modern hard gray. "I know where this is," Fiasco thought as he looked up. "I'm in Enterprise Square."

Above the trees sat the new crown jewel of New Haven piercing into the sky. The Savoy Tower looked every bit as beautiful up close as it was when he saw it in the sky. All fifty stories gleamed and reflected the stars and moon. The spires peaked at the top to give the building its shining crown. He was indeed in the new square, but there was something strange about his surroundings.

On a normal night, the streets and parks are bustling with teenagers and couples kissing beneath the trees. Runners would be on the trails, taking advantage of the clean air, yet the area was eerily quiet. There was not a soul in the park, and the scene looked like a mocked-up Hollywood set version of a small town. Even the car alarm that blared in the background didn't stir up any angry homeowners. A thin blue tendril sprouted from his hand that curled inside the broken automobile's window and ripped out random wires beneath the steering wheel to silence the noise.

"They evacuated the area that fast?" he thought as he called in the line. "How long was I out?"

Then, he remembered that it was the M.D.C. he was facing. The powerful government entity that employed equally powerful Megas. It would take little effort to empty the streets of a park— a fact that reminded Fiasco that he was in over his head. The whirling of a helicopter caught his attention, and he looked up to see one of the news copters he saw flying near Blanchet earlier. A small light aimed towards him, with a cameraman leaning through the opening to film.

"Here to broadcast my humiliation to the rest of the world, huh?" Fiasco muttered, wondering if their cameras were good enough to capture the movement of his lips.

He had no time to contemplate the answer as a whine from an engine forced his gaze to the left. There, the skychaser floated just outside the park. He saw it among the gray smoke that smoldered from the hole his blast had caused, yet it had stabilized its flight, and the spotlight from its hull found him with ease. Fiasco let his aura thicken, releasing more energy from inside. The side of the craft opened again. A thin column of ice fell from the hole, skinny and tall. It grew wide as clear water flowed over the exterior and froze, twisting down into the asphalt to gain hold.

Fiasco looked the column up and down. "Ice that can dig through asphalt? How powerful are these guys?"

They are stronger than you.

The three Megas, Rush, Sonance, and Flash Freeze, flanked by Hammond in the rear, stepped onto the pillar. Rush stood near the edge of the column with Sonance still at his side. Flash Freeze knelt in the middle of the pillar, his arms out wide, as his hands melded with the ice. His blue veins pulsed, and the pylon melted and descended, bringing the Megas down to ground level. Clear water darkened the asphalt as it spread outward from the base of the column. Fiasco stepped back while the water crept close to his toes, wary of what might happen if he were to step in the liquid created from the Mega's own body. Standing at the edge of the skychaser bay, Talon rejected that method of transport, and instead leapt straight from the hull, landing beside the others in his group in a small splash of water.

"Always showing off, huh Talon?" he thought as he followed the Megas movements. They were less than a block away, and muscles tensed from their proximity.

Hammond stood behind the quartet, the twisted melted armor breastplate still hugging his chest. "Let's try and get it right this time," he demanded in a shout. His red hair was still caked with dirt, but he no longer seemed concerned with his appearance.

"Get off my case, Hammond!" Rush snapped back, peering over his shoulder. "I said I was sorry already." Unnerved, Sonance twitched and stepped away from the Mega's raised voice.

"You will refer to him as sir," Talon interjected sharply. Rush bandied an angry look in Talon's direction but lowered his head when he saw his leader's stern expression.

"We specifically chose that designated area, Rush, to lower property damage, and not endanger lives," Hammond continued.

"Yes, sir," Rush grumbled.

Hammond nodded at Talon, then also to the Megas, "Now, follow your orders, and end this quickly."

The instructions made Rush smile broadly. "Yes, sir," he responded.

Without further orders, Rush turned in Fiasco's direction and ran. His feet sloshed through puddles of melted ice, arms pumping at his sides like an Olympic sprinter.

This will hurt your feeble frame, the voice said.

"You're kidding me, right?" Fiasco thought, expecting something entirely more vicious from his acrimonious partner. Still, he used the insult to enforce his aura even further.

Rumbling forward, Rush lowered his head. His gallop trembled the ground beneath Fiasco's feet, just as it felt back at the stadium. White streams of light darted in front of Rush's black hair, growing in intensity with every quaking stride. Fiasco thrust out his right hand, and the thin gauntlet melted back into place, shimmering a dark blue. The power darted between his curled fingers, then blended into a ball of swirling energy an inch before his palm.

The ground shook with such ferocity that it forced Fiasco to hover above just to keep his stomach from lurching. Fiasco clenched his jaw. The two competing energies met and instantly clashed, biting at each other like fighting canines. The air smelled like welded metal as the two fought against each other in sparks of turquoise flames. Fiasco's shoulder was nearly pushed from its socket as he struggled against whatever energy Rush had conjured.

"Where did they find this guy?" Fiasco thought as his arm began to tire. "Where is this energy coming from?"

Still bowed, Fiasco's energy slowed Rush slightly, but he still pressed forward, forcing him back in the air. The white light from Rush threatened to envelope his own meager ball, so Fiasco brought up both hands against it. The bones in his hands ached from the rattling. Still, he crouched at the knees and poured more energy into the sphere that whistled from his power, draining his reserve well that nearly made Rush's feet stop moving. The air screamed like an injured plane engine, and Fiasco felt as though the air was being pulled from his lungs.

Rush peered over the light blue energy. His countenance was made sinister by the pale glow on his dark skin. Still, there was little strain to be found on his face, while Fiasco felt he was barely hanging on. "Are you trying to embarrass me in front of the boss?" Rush asked with his eyebrows arched, his voice sounding almost sarcastic.

With a sudden twitch, Rush's body jerked forward, and his massive fist swung upward, punching the white current that fought with Fiasco's power. An explosion ended the stalemate with a boom that shattered the windows on the cars on either side of the Megas in a shower of glass. Fiasco's jaw clacked shut as the concussion forced him backward through the air in streams of white light. Losing concentration and altitude, his foot clipped the asphalt and he tumbled backward, a victim to the push of energy, sliding along the road until he used his aura to stop and regain control of his flight just above the ground.

The twin energies coalesced and coursed through his frame, pricking nerve-endings like fine needles, before traveling down to his feet and dying off. Shaken, Fiasco floated to the ground and noticed that Rush was several yards away. The air smelled like a firework show that had spent all its munitions. Having been bounced against his aura shield, blood trickled down from a cut on Fiasco's lip that warmed with his healing power.

"So that's how he knocked me into the troposphere at the excavation site," Fiasco pondered, remembering how he found himself in Enterprise Square, launched from the stadium by some force he couldn't identify at the time.

Rolling his right arm helped Fiasco alleviate the lingering pain in his shoulder. Down the street, Rush held a wide grin. He crouched down at the waist and put his fingers to the ground like a lineman preparing to crush a quarterback. A growl from the large Mega chilled Fiasco's spine before Rush charged at him again. The ground thumped, as each step methodically counted down to more agony, reviving the streaks of white light before him.

"His running is creating that energy," Fiasco observed, watching the white coalesce. "He's aptly named."

Fiasco's eyes flitted left and right as he tried to think of another memory to replenish his strength and energy. Then, he remembered. "This is when Flash Freeze suckered me last time," he thought, as the heat in his aura increased to combat such a threat but left his well of power woefully short to deal with the oncoming onslaught.

Rush powered forward, pounding the pavement, huffing like a bull while the white energy gathered before him with each step. Fiasco breathed in to brace for the impact and pushed out his hands to counter it once more. Then, a sonic noise screamed about his head, intense and high-pitched, nearly bursting his eardrums. A stinging siren of white noise drowned out all ambient noise from Rush. Unable to hold back the offensive decibels, Fiasco clutched his ears, using his palms to plug the openings, which did little to end the shrill horn. A scream escaped his lips but was submerged by the auditory misery that forced him down to one knee. Tears blurred his eyes, and his lungs burned from having shouted out all the air that did not alleviate the sensation paralyzing his arms and legs.

When Fiasco opened his eyes, the world looped sideways from his loss of equilibrium. A lump of bile rose in his throat. He dared to put his hand down on the street to stop him from falling over completely, groping about until his fingers spread on the welcoming hard asphalt. Through the airy edges of Rush's light, he caught a glimpse of Sonance standing near the drop zone. Her arms were outstretched before her, a similar pose she struck at the stadium, except her small, gloved hands were closed together like a clap.

Her image only lasted an instance before Rush punched the white energy with a right cross and it exploded against his side. The wind hissed at Fiasco's back as the power of the punch rocketed him into Enterprise Park. A thick oak tree splintered in two as Fiasco plowed diagonally through the trunk like a cobalt cannonball. Flying uncontrollably, he careened through a concrete barrier near the running trails that disintegrated into gray rubble, before landing in a soft patch of wet, damp grass.

You are failing again, the voice mocked as water from a nearby sprinkler thumped the stream against his mask. From the muddy earth, Fiasco raised his head then rose on his palms, replenishing his lungs with heavy breaths.

"Tell me something I don't know."

Water dripped down Fiasco's chin. He coughed and spat out grime that was mixed with red. "More blood," he thought. On his hands and knees, he called back his aura and gauntlets with a rush of energy that pushed out the blades of grass beneath him. A piercing whine rang in his ears, his left earlobe tickling from what he thought had to be blood. He knew he couldn't take another hit from Rush.

"Hammond wasn't lying. Everything these Megas throw at me targets all my weaknesses. The shield is barely keeping me together, and everything they use is circumventing its protection." Speaking aloud to focus his thoughts as he returned to his feet, hunched over to stave off pain.

Fiasco looked about and saw that he was deep in the park. The punch had moved him past the picnic tables under the black light posts and running trails, and he was just beyond the shadow of the tall trees that swayed overhead. His eyes adjusted to the gloom. The mayhem he left in his wake was like a trail that led back to the road. Looking to the other side of the park, he found Sonance beyond the illuminated running trail. Dressed in black, she was nearly invisible in the shadow of the trees, but he could see the white of her bare hands. Knocking Fiasco to his knees must have replenished her courage because she seemed to be searching for him through the foliage, without backup from Rush.

Releasing a thimble of power from inside, Fiasco took to the air and sped, fists-first, like a bullet aimed at his target. "Don't hold back this time," he thought, psyching himself out. The world darkened to a pinhole as he focused on the young Mega who was responsible for that terrible sound that had blood trickling from his ears. "Get passed the fact that she's a young, skinny girl. She's too dangerous."

The lights glared against his goggles as he sped past their lined bricks. He had nearly cleared the running trails when the air whistled again. He heard glass cracking once more. A gasp escaped his lips when a stinging pain bit into the back of his calf. The aura wavered from the agony clawing up his leg, and Fiasco slid along the cold brick, his left leg dragging limp behind, painting a smear of his blood on his trail.

"Can't believe that prick got me again!" he thought.

Exhaling, he looked down at the red knife buried deep enough inside the meat of his calf that he was almost afraid to touch it. Blood seeped around the edges of the wound, running down both sides, making the flechette slippery when he tried to take hold. Gritting his teeth, he reached over with both hands to quicken the process. Fire rose like liquid up the veins on his legs as he pushed and pulled the knife back and forth to work it loose, widening the wound with its sharp edges. The red knife rose slowly through the flesh before he finally pulled it free with a sudden jerk that nearly made him fall backward. Blood fountained from the opening but was instantly staunched by his aura that flowed down his leg like blue water, stinging the wound.

He held up the knife in the moonlight. "Sucker punching asshole," Fiasco said, then tossed the knife to the side. He searched the shadows in vain hope but did not see his friend. Using his good leg, he tried to stand. Having hardly been injured since he became a Mega, Fiasco put pressure on the left with one mistaken step.

"Mother fuc—" he shouted, bending down from the shotgun blast he felt burning in his calf, the curse word freezing in his throat.

He began to fall until he felt the burning fingers of cold caress the bottom of his jaw. The cold crept over his body, numbing his muscles and nerves, making drowsiness descend like a curtain from the falling temperature. In response, the reservoir of energy he kept inside flared wildly in a flash of blue behind the ice, nearly melting the casing in one outburst. Fiasco almost felt a strange sensation of delight as he watched the ice weep from his power, but that emotion quickly disappeared when he saw a blurry glow of white light out of the corner of his eye that had grown too familiar.

"Just one break, that's all I ask," Fiasco pleaded before the ice shattered with a bone fracturing explosion.

A wave of chalky colored energy pushed by a large brown fist lifted Fiasco off his feet. Splinters of wood rained against his shield as more of New Haven's trees fell victim to Rush's power as he careened out of the park. The wood turned into an avalanche of glass before jagged curls of metal covered his goggles in a whining groan. His back dug into the side of a sedan, pushing the driver's seat into the passenger side with a rending tear. The car skidded against the ground, burning rubber against the asphalt, until it struck the sidewalk curb, kicking up on two wheels before crashing back down.

"Deja vu," Fiasco thought, moving his eyes about. "Dirty holes.

Falling on the ground. Explosions and car tombs. The story of my career."

Failing is the story of your life, the voice chimed in. Fiasco agreed.

The power roiled inside from the voice's reminder of his failures, which allowed him to shoot tendrils out from his hands. The coils snaked forward, the ends transforming into imitations of his gauntlets that grasped the edges of the car. Taking a firm grip with his manifestations, he called the power back in like a fishing line, using the leverage to wrench himself free from the wreck. Fiasco spilled out onto the pavement. He coughed up a substance that made his stomach wretch and spat a patch of blood that spread like an inkblot on the ground.

His tongue searched around his mouth for additional cuts or wounds but felt nothing. "I must be bleeding on the inside," he concluded.

The sweat turned cold beneath his filthy and torn suit, when a dark shadow draped over the road. Fiasco looked up and saw Talon standing over him, headdress looking like knives, and fists at his side. White eyes glared down at him. His silhouette loomed over him like a muscled Adonis. He gazed up into Talon's shadowed face and gave his friend a smile— red blood coating his teeth.

"Ta-da," Fiasco said, trying to ignore the pain that wracked his body as he struggled to stand at full height.

"I can hear your bones grinding together as you breathe," Talon said. His white mask held an eerie glow under the moonlight, emoting concern as he looked Fiasco over. "I can hear the gurgle as liquid fills your punctured lung."

"Is that so?" Fiasco asked, smearing the blood away against his chin with the back of his gauntlet.

"I can smell the blood coming from all your injuries. You can't heal from all this damage." Talon finished.

Yes, the voice asserted. *Admit your failure and yield to your betters.*

Fiasco wavered on his feet, leaning to the right to alleviate the pain still pulsing from his left calf. "I'll manage it," he breathed out. "So, you ready to team up and take these guys out?" he asked with sarcasm to mask the disappointment he felt at Talon's betrayal.

He would never admit it aloud, but the treachery hurt his soul—nearly as painful as the breakup with Julianna. He thought back to all the patrols he and Talon had shared together. They had talked about his relationship with Julianna, and Fiasco had taken Talon's sage-like advice when he presented it. The trip to Mount Washington was his idea, telling him that little adversity defeated together could make two people grow stronger. The climb they accomplished did exactly that, keeping them strong for several months until his failures wrecked it all.

Fiasco wondered if Talon's advice was also true about their friendship.

He never liked you, the voice whispered, adding gas to the fire that fueled Fiasco's anger and disappointment. Fiasco agreed and drank in the anguish.

Talon snorted. "Always joking, huh, Crooked F?"

Fiasco looked up. "Don't call me that," he said in a stern tone that took Talon back. He stood as tall as he could, and pain burned down to his tendon below his bleeding calf. "You lost the privilege of calling me that."

"Well, Fiasco," Talon corrected himself, sneering his name. "That joking is why we're here with you bleeding like a stuck pig on our own streets."

"No, we're here because you betrayed me," Fiasco shot back. "To the same government you used to rail against. What happened to you? How long have you been an agent of the state?"

Talon shook his head, and his mask furrowed at the brow and nose. "It's not that simple, and you're too short -sighted for me to explain it any further."

"You haven't explained it at all—"

"I didn't come here to argue Croo—Fiasco," Talon interrupted in a shout, his muscles tensing in his toned arms. "I'm here to end this now before you cause any more damage."

"Your damage is already done Talon, and you don't even know it," Fiasco grimaced, crouching at the hip.

"Don't even think about it," Talon's jaw stiffened. "I see you...Crooked F."

Fiasco bristled at that epithet. "You sellout," he countered.

His gauntlet curled into a fist, and he launched a punch with his right hand that Talon swiped away with ease. The muscled Mega returned the punch with three of his own that ignored Fiasco's aura, slapping the flesh on his stomach, chest, and swiftly across his face. Blood splashed from Fiasco's mouth as his back bounced against the wreckage behind him. Taking advantage of the rebound, Talon grabbed him, twisted up his costume at the neck in his fist, and tossed him down the street.

"It's like my aura shield isn't even there," Fiasco thought and rubbed his jaw. "I need to keep him away."

He sent out tendrils of blue light from both hands that curled together attempting to snag his foe. With a quick push from his calves, Talon jumped, and the tendrils folded together, hugging nothing but air. Two gleaming, red knives cracked through the trunk of the beams, pinning the manifestations to the blacktop. Shuffling to his feet, Fiasco lost track of the Mega in the glare of the streetlights, until the treads of a size twelve boot nearly caved in his chest, pushing him back and separating him from the strands. Fiasco reeled back from an additional blow to his sternum that doubled him over. Sharp bones on knuckles pushed passed his ribs, and air rushed from his lungs in a spray of red. He stumbled over his feet from a left hook that struck his temple with a sickening crunch, pushing him off balance.

Talon ceased his assault and glared down at Fiasco, who could barely stand on legs that seemed to be made of wicker. Reaching out, Fiasco clutched his friend's shoulder to stop from tipping over, smearing blood on Talon's leather vest.

"I can see you, Fiasco," Talon said, repeating a phrase he had used many times before. "I can see your energy signature. I've been reading you since day one. You're a kitten fighting a bear. This is a fight you can't win."

Yield, the voice urged mournfully.

Fiasco grinned, salmon-colored slaver dripping like a tear from the corner of his mouth.

"Screw you, Talon," he breathed, and let the voice's sorrowful tone energize his gauntlets.

His gloves sparked and glowed from the influx of energy. Fiasco only had a moment to catch his breath before Talon flicked the gauntlet off his shoulder and held the luminous glove up in his hand. The air was still between the two, and their eyes met behind their masks, sharing the silence. Then, Talon flexed his arm. Veins ballooned from his wrist and crawled up his arm like mesh when his strong fingers shattered the gauntlets like thin, blue glass down to the flesh beneath. Talon twisted his hand outward at the wrist.

A scream terminated in Fiasco's throat when he felt popping sensations on each side of his wrist, tendons snapping, separating muscle from bone. What followed was a conflagration of pain that blazed through his being and shocked his brain silent.

Holding the wrist tight, with his head bowed, Talon mumbled, "You never learned, even when I tried."

He released Fiasco's injured arm that hung limp at the wrist. Twisting on the ground, Talon's left leg curved backward, skidding along the asphalt, sweeping Fiasco off his feet, and launching him into the air. The M.D.C. Mega used his centrifugal force and spun into the air like a top. Utilizing the same grace Fiasco had admired from a distance for years, Talon twisted and delivered a back kick that cracked through the aura, leaving a muddy footprint on the crooked *F* on his chest.

Fiasco did not feel the impact of the door he ripped through, nor the two separate drywalls inside the townhome that imploded from his broken body. But he tasted the course chalk on his tongue when their dust exploded like a gas grenade. Wood furniture and fixtures fragmented from his body tumbling through the air, cutting deep through flesh. He broke through a third wall, crashing head-long into a square sunroom in the far back of some poor citizen's home.

Hearing the glass crack like ice above, weakly, Fiasco curled up, knees to his stomach to protect his vulnerable chest. The panes fragmented into pieces, falling like hail, bouncing off his shield, and creating droplets that skittered along the ground. The discordant sounds made the Mega-hero flinch behind his arms, clutching his shattered wrist close to his protected chest. Once the sounds had ceased, Fiasco unfurled and lay on his back on the tile floor, glass surrounding him like a chalk outline.

"Wow," Fiasco said in a raspy voice. "Talon was fast."

His aura shield flickered like a lightning bug near the hole over his chest, until it faded and blinked away. Without the low thrum, there was only silence.

Rejuvenation

Scarlet liquid made the glass shards resemble a pink and red puzzle as it spread down the floor. The warm night air frisked the cuts and tears in Fiasco's suit, blowing stinging heat into the various wounds that leaked blood into a pool beneath him. Shallow breaths blew over his cracked lips as his meager and tortured body tried to heal.

Why would a true born loser persist? the voice asked.

The beige porcelain flooring was cold against Fiasco's back. Blood crawled from his mouth and nose, itching like a line of crawling ants— but his body hurt too much to scratch it away. The skyline of the sunroom was a broken canopy of leftover bits of glass. Beyond the lattice of wood beams that remained, the stars twinkled peacefully above, oblivious to the chaos Fiasco had just endured.

"I want to make Julianna proud," Fiasco replied. His lungs ached when he breathed in.

That is a lie, the voice responded.

"What?" His head moved, scraping glass against the tile as he lifted up so his chin touched his chest. "Why would you say that?"

That is only a partial truth. Losers tend to lie. Why did you fight?

"I guess I don't understand the question, or why you're even asking."

Why did you fight when you knew you would lose?

Fiasco let his head rest against the ground again, looking up at the heavens that resembled a broken mirror of stars through his hopelessly cracked goggles.

"I didn't know that," he replied.

There was a pause, and then the voice said, *after all your failures, you did not know you would lose against four government trained Mega-humans, one of whom you believed was your best friend and is your superior in every way?*

"No, I guess I didn't." He tried to shrug, but only managed a twitch of his left shoulder that hurt the least of the two. "Sometimes I feel like you don't know me at all."

Interesting, the voice said in a low tone.

Fiasco waited for a follow up, but only heard an animal rustling in the bush outside the sunroom wall. "Why did you ask me that?" he asked again. "I know you don't care. You never say anything that isn't mockery or condemnation."

You will never see her again, the voice said, almost in spite to prove Fiasco's words true. *Yet, like a halfwit, you fought, nonetheless.*

A smile tortured every muscle in Fiasco's face, curling into the purple bruises that swelled on either cheek. "Now whose lying?"

Explain.

"Of course, I will see Julianna again. I have to. We have so much left to do together."

Delusions of grandeur is a sign of psychosis.

Fiasco snorted a laugh that made his heart skip from a stab of agony.

"Yeah, that might be true," he whispered, exhaling to control the sensation. "It doesn't change the fact that I believe it. I'll see her again because I love her. Somehow, she didn't know how much. I have to let her know that or die trying to get back to her."

If you persist, then you shall surely perish, the voice mocked. *You have angered the Modoc, and he will not let you pass.*

"I meant figuratively. I think," Fiasco replied.

Either way, you will lose.

"Again, why do you even care? Are you even real? Is it just me talking to me, or are you a part of my gift? Just another asshole aspect of this awful power?"

As fiasco predicted, the voice did not respond. The question of its existence was something he bandied about before, back when the power first began manifesting. He kept asking its true origin— even back in high school— and received nothing but silence in return. It took years until he had grown used to the slander and ridicule, letting it act as fuel, until he eventually stopped posing the question.

Perhaps that was his main issue in life. Perhaps that was why there was always a thorn in his relationships, even Julianna. She was his salvation, pulling him up from the mire the voice made him wallow in. Even when he responded by giving her only portion of himself, she persisted, bringing light to the darkness that was his existence. She earned the right to see him truly for what he was. The voice and all.

Perhaps that was the answer to the voices questions as well, he thought. The reason why he chose to fight. It was clear that the Oubliette was his future, but he still had to reach her. To reveal all of himself to the one person who deserved to know why she was kept at such a distance. Yes, she hated Fiasco, but it was worth that hate for her to know the truth. That final act would be the warmth when he was depowered, and shackled in that government dungeon, where he couldn't ruin her life further.

All it would take for resolution was to get past government Megas with powers that negated his own, who also seemed to hate his guts.

"Should be simple enough," Fiasco joked aloud.

Embrace who you are. Embrace the cowardice within you. Yield to your betters, the voice said.

Small chips of glass fell from tears in Fiasco's mask as he gingerly rose with one hand, the other still throbbing fire from the injury Talon inflicted.

"No," Fiasco responded, groaning as he pushed through the pain to stand tall.

Fresh blood leaked from the wound Talon put into his left calf, yet he was able to apply some pressure on it when he stood, but left it bent at the knee. Moonlight reflected and sparkled in large shards of glass scattered by his feet. Fiasco removed his goggles that were now cracked and broken and tossed them among the sea of glass. He pulled the string behind his mask to loosen the leather against his skin. Biting against great pain as he bent over, he lifted the broken pane in his left hand and held it up until the moonlight shined on the glass and he studied the face staring back at him.

The makeshift mirror trembled from exhaustion until Fiasco breathed out to steady his hand. Where his skin was visible beneath his mask, his visage was a misshapen mass of lumps and bruises. Cuts lined his jaw and chin, with a thick gash on his bottom lip. A large contusion on his cheek gleamed a dark purple and burned when he touched it. A tuft of hair jutted from a rip atop his mask. The pane slipped from his hand as it gave out, shattering by his bloodstained boots. Fiasco sighed as his head dipped to his chest.

Yield.

"I've given up on everything in my life. I gave up on school when it got too hard. I lost my job. I stopped being Fiasco," he said. "I even gave up on Julianna at the peak of our relationship, when she was the best thing in my life. I always quit. I always yield. Where has that gotten me?"

Here. On the verge of yet another defeat, the voice responded earnestly.

"Yeah. But listening to you has got me here too." Fiasco nudged off a shard of glass that had landed on another with the tip of his boot.

You are flirting with the biggest failure of your lifetime.

Fiasco lifted his head. "You're lying."

You will fail.

Fiasco turned his head slowly from side to side. "I don't believe you. Not this time. I refuse to. What I believe is that I will see her again. I won't surrender to cowardice. Not this time." The power roiled inside, and the aura returned with a sudden hum, buzzing like a lamp to break the silence of the sunroom. "If not, then at least I can create my own shield to go out on."

How did you ever get someone like her with such tripe?

Fiasco thought he heard what sounded like a laugh from the voice, but he chalked it up to the wind blowing over the empty rafters. The rumination over the voice's criticism sent the power pouring over his body in cascading waves that discharged therapeutic heat.

Fiasco huffed. "To answer your question, I really don't know why she chose me either," he said, shaking his head.

His breathing inched close to capacity as the warmth spread. Feeling the tingling along his extremities, he dared to bend from side to side to stretch out the soreness in his mending ribs. The pain was still prevalent, like little stabs from a prison shiv in his side, but he couldn't complain— at least he was able to breathe again. The gauntlets returned to his hands, but without the edges that normally curled up to a point halfway up his forearms; there wasn't enough power. With a mental command, he concentrated energy into the right glove, sending rivers of light to heal whatever he felt pop inside his wrist. After some time, his fingers inside twitched and moved, and he was able to curl his hand into a fist. It was weak, but it was all he had, and he would make do with it.

"But since you're so full of questions all of a sudden, about me and Julianna," he said. "Why don't we get out of this stupid room and ask her why she chose me?"

Do not include me in this fallacy.

"Sure," Fiasco replied, turning slowly in the glass as if he were searching for the voice. "We are a packaged deal. It took me some time, but I realize that now. She must see and accept us in our totality, something I should not have kept from her to begin with. You and I, we're one."

Once again, the voice did not respond.

Glass crunched beneath Fiasco's feet as he limped to the opening in the structure where he had plowed through the drywall. From the outside, the townhomes looked small, but they extended farther back by several rooms— much larger than they appeared from the street.

His lower back protested as he bent over, peering through the twin holes in the walls where Talon had kicked him through. Fiasco looked about, and he was thankful that everyone was evacuated by the M.D.C. before he was launched inside. The ground was strewn with items from the broken home. Looking past it all, Fiasco saw the streetlight streaming through the chasm where the door once was. Four shadows moved back and forth on the street near the entrance, growing bigger as they approached the craggy hole.

Losers always lose, the voice said— almost as if it sensed the Megas moving forward to finish their mission.

The buzz of the aura grew louder, and the antechamber was cast in his blue light. Grinning from a sudden idea as he tied his mask snugly on his face, liquid blue power twinkled about his temples. The power twisted like a figure eight over his eyes, morphing to create new goggles, that shimmered with his blue light, replacing the broken pair. He wasn't going to yield.

"Yes. You're right. Losers do always lose," Fiasco agreed in a whisper. "But at least they keep trying."

There was silence from the voice, as if it searched for the greatest comeback that would cut him to the core. *One should die proudly when it is no longer possible to live proudly*, it finally replied.

"Nietzsche," Fiasco snorted, grinning from the quotation that was one of his father's favorites.

Looking through the power-infused goggles, the world appeared before him in high definition, dyed crystal blue. The gauntlets on his hands shined, and he saw white flakes of power floating away from the lines on the back like smoke from a furnace as he formed them into fists.

"Amen," he replied.

Fracas

The Megas' whispers grew louder as Fiasco approached the entrance. While keeping his aura low to the point of invisibility, hands jutting out behind him, he glided forward through the home, swirling the debris that littered the floor below his feet. Light tinted ocean blue from his goggles filtered ahead, gleaming through the holes in the drywalls. As Fiasco approached, the M.D.C. Megas' shadows grew larger against the wall inside the home, their voices turning into audible conversation.

"Why should I go in, when it was Talon who put him in there?" Rush said. His massive body moved, and his shadow dominated the left side of the hole his body made through the townhome door.

Flash Freeze answered, "Because he's the field commander. We have to follow orders. You know what will happen if we don't."

From their tone of voice and demeanor, Fiasco recognized that the Megas were nearly cavalier about the danger. They continued to bicker with one another, even during a battle, casual and flippant.

They do not fear you.

At the opening, Rush's massive arms crossed, casting a shadow against the rubble on the ground that resembled a strong pile of rocks. "Then why don't you go in there if you're so gung-ho about following orders?" he countered.

"Because you're sturdier, and because he told you to go, not me,"

Flash Freeze replied, unwilling to give in and completely ignoring Sonance's advice. "You know what Talon—wait a minute. Hold on," his words ended suddenly. Fiasco saw Flash Freeze's icy blue eyes glowing like pools as he looked around inside. "I think I see something in there."

"Be careful, you guys," he heard Sonance say in her mousy voice. She was somewhere outside the opening, her silhouette swallowed by the other two Megas.

Rush put a large hand up at the edge of the broken entrance and leaned forward. The metal about his body gleamed in the streetlights. Not a hair was out of place on his round afro, as his head looked left and right inside the home. "I don't see anything," he said, turning towards Flash Freeze.

"I'm telling you; I saw something back there," Flash Freeze replied and pointed a pale arm inside. With the light behind them, the interior looked pitched.

Looking down, Rush noticed that the chaff along the floor trembled. A low hum sang in his ears, making his head tilt to listen closer before he looked up at his hand that was cupped under the top of the entryway, feeling the rhythm vibrating through the fingers. When his eyes moved to the back of the room, it appeared as though his eyes had finally adjusted to the darkness, and he saw what Flash Freeze had warned. Rush's head flicked backward.

"Get back!" Rush shouted with a shove to Flash Freeze's shoulder, pushing him away from the opening. The surprise that spread on his sharp features emoted that he knew his warning came far too late.

"Dammit!" Fiasco exclaimed beneath his breath.

With his approach discovered, the aura returned to full bore, rousing about his body. A burst of speed cast the room in navy blue. The current from his acceleration tossed debris clattering against what was left of the townhouse walls. Cobalt light from his aura shined like a rising sun on Rush's face as he scrambled back from the chasm. Fiasco barreled toward the opening, finally raising his arms.

The remnants of the door exploded from blue horns that curled outward into sharp, manicured points. They were attached to stampeding bulls that glimmered a dark blue ambiance about their powerful, brawny frames. Their broad chests were rippled with muscles, and their mouths frothed with light blue spittle as they charged through the rubble. Their horns thrashed about, taking out a large portion of the window frame and wall in a burst of concrete and glass that careened out onto the sidewalk.

Fiasco followed the herd out of the breach, floating behind the manifestations with his arms outstretched before him. The fingers on his gauntlets moved the pale blue tendrils that curved down, controlling the bulls. There were three on his left and two on his right, and he played each creation like marionettes on strings. As he strained to control the raging beasts, he licked the sweat above his lip, the salty liquid stinging the gash that still had not healed.

"You wanted me to think outside the box, Talon," he thought.

Muscles flexed and strained on the bovines as Fiasco steered them around Sonance, who was crouched on the ground frozen in fear, covering her head from the charge. Two bulls on his right hand broke free from their lines and encircled the frightened Mega. Their hooves clacked against the ground, each hot on the heels of the other, running in a circle to keep her pinned down.

The remaining three attached to his gauntlet veered to the left, their hooves resonating like thunder as they clattered against the asphalt. They moved toward their target in unison. Having recovered from the initial surge, Rush crouched in the middle of the street, lowering his center of gravity into his sturdy legs. His metal reflected the cerulean glow as the bulls centered on his form, charging towards him.

Rush's forehead wrinkled, setting his face in stone. Two fingers on his right hand bent at the tips when he touched them to the ground. Dark brown eyes, twitchy and manic for a fight, studied the savage opposition. With the target fixed, and teeth clenched hard in his jaw, Rush exploded forward to meet the manifestations head on. Heavy footfalls shook the ground. His rumbling and Fiasco's manifestations threatened to fissure the ground as they neared a clash.

"At least you got balls, Rush; I'll give you that," Fiasco murmured, flicking his gloved left hand forward.

The horns on Fiasco's creations bobbed at different intervals as they ran, rearing their heads to bellow deep from their diaphragms. Rush responded with a growl of his own. White streaks dashed before the Mega during his sprint. They formed together, resembling lines of thunder that grew larger with every step Rush took. Yet, the short distance between him and the bulls did not allow the Mega enough time or space to generate the same amount of energy he had used to punish Fiasco earlier in the night. To Fiasco, the white looked hardly a quarter of the size it looked before, and his creations bounded forward to their destiny.

Solid blue horns smacked against tempered metal with clangs, and the two opposing forces met in a thunderclap. White streaks flew outward at the impact point. Dull moans from the bulls rolled down the street from splintering cracks that formed along their horns. Rush grimaced, reeling from the impact. The bull's gait never wavered. Muscled arms flailing and grasping at the sky, Rush disappeared beneath a mass of cobalt radiance that plowed over the M.D.C. agent with thick hooves spitting blue sparks against metal.

"Hope that hurts, you prick" Fiasco shouted, trying not to let the joy of revenge affect his energy levels.

Across the street, the park remained free of civilians. Red and white lights flashed rhythmically off the row houses. With his vision enhanced by his manifested goggles, he saw clearly in either direction and noticed that the New Haven civilians had filtered away from the fight at Blanchet. The people had gathered behind police barricades at the far end of the four street arteries that made a square of the area. Heavily armed NHPD officers and S.W.A.T. team members carrying rifles marched up and down lines, keeping the raucous crowd at bay behind thick wooden barricades painted police blue.

They came to witness your failure, the voice said. *You are the criminal fed to the lion for all in the Colosseum to see.*

Fiasco agreed when he found what he was searching for. Looking further right, he finally saw the Mega who was pushed back from the door just before his bulls pressed through. The ice blue blood in Flash Freeze's veins churned like a river inside. He sloshed white snow that flowed from his hands down to the street and pooled about his bare feet. Even with his translucent skin, panic shone on his thin face. His ice-blue eyes flitted back and forth as if the choice between fight or flight were still running through his head.

"Can't let him get the higher ground and do that trick again," Fiasco realized, his body involuntarily shivering from the thought of being encased in ice.

Seeing the sliver of an opening, Fiasco flicked a finger at the Mega. The command sent one of his bovine manifestations rushing forward. The charging bull roared when it struck the Mega with the thick mast of its head, a sickening thump resonating as it sent Flash Freeze bowling down the street, skimming over slosh.

"Think ahead, press the advantage," Fiasco uttered like a mantra.

He followed the M.D.C. agent's path with a burst of blue speed that parted the shallow water over the street. His quarry had stopped yards down First Street. Seemingly as tough as the very ice he could conjure, Flash Freeze had already regained his footing, standing on his bare feet in the middle of the street, straightening when he saw Fiasco flying towards him.

Fiasco saw the Mega's mouth move. Veins in his translucent face and neck pulsated. His lips twisted up as if he were about to whistle. Thick, white breath rolled out from bellowing cheeks, twinkling with flakes of ice that blew across the air like storm clouds. The white cloud dissipated before it reached Fiasco, but an itch began beneath his costume, sweeping across the small hairs on his skin.

"What the hell was that?" Fiasco said as his own breath blew white out of his mouth.

A cold whisked over his body, and the sweat froze a crystalline sheen over his exposed skin. Fiasco tried to scream, but ice froze his trachea. Through the rips in his costume, the cuts from the night of violence distended from the freeze, opening the scars, and exposing the meat beneath from water freezing and expanding in his veins. Blood tried to pour out of his wounds but froze into crystals of red ice upon meeting the cold air, forcing his cuts to split open even wider. His shimmering gloves clutched at his throat from a lack of oxygen, with lungs that refused to open and close from the accumulated ice that formed within.

What followed was a blinding agony that made Fiasco's aura waver like a light with a shorted circuit. He slowly veered toward the ground. The bulls raged behind him wailed their master's pain, blasting indigo light from their broad nostrils, before disappearing as the suffering continued inside Fiasco unabated.

"He's solidifying the water in my body," Fiasco thought, through the panic from the sense of drowning. "He's freezing me to death."

He is better than you, the voice reminded him. *It ends here, and you will never see her again.*

A lack of oxygen made dark spots crash over Fiasco's vision. In the spots of light that fit together like puzzle pieces, he thought he saw Julianna. She was at Black Deer, sitting at their booth in front of plates of food that were already cold. She tapped her credit card against the table as she checked her phone obsessively, glancing at the door every time she looked up from her screen.

"She's waiting for me," Fiasco thought. The power rose within, churning out from the center of his chest, combating the cold with its own heat. "And I have to see her."

The fire dashed through his veins like molten liquid. As the fire spread, his muscles relaxed, allowing Fiasco to move once more. As Fiasco gained movement in his limbs, he shook off the frozen crystals that fell from his body, flexing out his arms and legs with a guttural scream. The sudden movement sent kinetic energy through his aching bones. His lungs gasped for air as the chill that gripped them melted. Water gurgled in his raw throat with each heavy cough. He spat out pink phlegm that was still cold in his mouth.

With the water cleared, Fiasco gasped, letting in New Haven air. The threat of a migraine drilled against his temples when his brain finally reacted to the spreading heat. Fresh red streaked his costume from the blood that melted in the cuts and tears along his skin, simmering as they dripped into his shield. A weakened aura spread over him, adding to the warmth, working overtime to stitch his wrecked body back together.

"That bastard really tried to kill me," Fiasco thought. His teeth clattered in his mouth.

Angry and slighted, the goggles on his eyes fixed on their target. Fiasco waited for the voice to negate his persistence, but his ears were met with silence instead. Two glimmering blue fingers lightly tapped the ground, and Fiasco pushed himself upward. He swallowed down cold saliva that tasted like spoiled copper to moisten his thawed esophagus. Blue goggles glared forward, looking at Flash Freeze, whose iced-over eyes expanded, shocked that his quarry had survived his attack.

"Maldito bastardo!" he heard the Mega shout. Spanish was one of the courses Fiasco nearly failed, so his translation was less than stellar; however, the curse words stuck, and he got the gist of what was said.

"That all you got!?" Fiasco shouted, voice straining but once again aiming towards the M.D.C. agent.

"Damn, this guy," he read on his frostbit lips as Flash Freeze's icy jaw clenched.

Reaching back with his left hand, water spread along the asphalt behind Flash Freeze, who then kicked back on his heels and glided along the top, increasing the distance between them. He pushed his right-hand forward. A small brume of ice was suspended before his palm like a gathering snowball. The tips of Flash Freeze's fingers tapped the air, and the slosh froze solid, expanding and forming into a large round circle of ice as he retreated. He tapped the air again, and again. Sliding backward, he left a series of traps spread almost evenly apart, as they enveloped Fiasco in ice when he rocketed forward, bursting through each barrier, aware of the setup, but aching for revenge.

Using the anguish from random memories the voice was able to conjure, Fiasco fed the power into his gauntlets, strengthening and doubling them in size. Then, he used them to punch through each successive ice wall, grunting out the pain and frustration with each blow. Ice shattered from each swing. Each slash sent splashes of water and slush that hissed against his goggles and sprayed his mask until he was nearly in front of the M.D.C. agent.

"Why can't I stop you!" he heard Flash Freeze shout, accent deepening.

With the proximity between the two shrunken to inches, Fiasco recognized terror in Flash Freeze's icy pool of eyes. For the first time since the battle began, he was the cause of fear instead of the victim of it, and Fiasco grinned.

"Surprised, jerk?" he asked as he floated towards his enemy. His lips curled upward, splitting the skin once again.

Twisting from his hips, the gauntlet whistled as it flew and cracked upward, striking against Flash Freeze's jaw in a splash. Water and ice spread outward from the blow that glowered an indigo blue from a cloud of Fiasco's own power. He released the energy from the gauntlet into the Megas chin as he followed through with the punch. Flash Freeze stumbled backward, trailing the azure stream that floated about his head. Fiasco's own momentum forced him forward. Lowering his altitude that curved downward like a frown, he pushed his feet outward until he stumbled to a landing onto the street, involuntarily clutching at the calf Talon's knife had cut open.

"Damn, he must have cut me deep. This wound still hasn't healed," Fiasco said. Pulling his fingers back, he saw the red blood that bubbled and darkened on his gauntlet. Still, he knew the fight was not over. He gingerly turned, favoring his injured leg.

Several yards away, a roiling blue cloud of energy surrounded Flash Freeze's head. It multiplied, spreading along his body, glowing like a blue nebula, crackling with ice-blue lightning that coursed back and forth. The kinetic power from the storm acted like a cauldron that churned the heat, and Flash Freeze breathed in the storm. His screams gurgled within his throat before filling his mouth.

Cold water sprang like a geyser from Flash Freeze's mouth. His translucent skin cried teardrops as water seeped from his pores. His frosted hair melted, turning black as it stuck to his forehead that wrinkled with anguish. The light blue liquid in the Mega's veins faded when the brown pigmentation returned, and his skin solidified. His iced-over pupils were the last things to revert to normal, changing to a dark brown that lazily scanned the night sky before he slumped unconscious on the soaked pavement with a splash.

Curly strands of white vapor rose from Flash Freeze's still frame, twisting into the sky before disappearing against the gray color of the townhouse. But beneath the steam, the Mega's chest continued to rise and fall. Fiasco breathed out. "Well, that's another down," Fiasco thought.

The momentum of their battle had moved him closer to the

crowd behind the barrier that crossed First and Tomas Avenue. Behind the police barricades, the clamor among the multitude of New Havenites grew, and they laced him with negativity and pent-up condemnation for his past failures. The noise grew even more vociferous when they saw the M.D.C. agent lying in a pool of his own fluid several yards away.

Hunched from exhaustion, Fiasco lazily glanced at the crowd behind the wall of law enforcement. Ribbons that were torn from his costume caught in the breeze, scratching his still mending wounds that leaked blood over his costume. He muttered, "Thanks for the unnecessary commentary, citizens." He allowed their spiteful words to replenish a nearly exhausted reserve of power.

Then an audible burst exploded about his head in a cacophony of horns and high-pitched screams that made even the crowd behind the barrier flinch. NHPD officers let their rifles hang loose on their slings about their shoulders as they covered their ears with both hands. Fiasco clutched at his ears and forced himself to the ground onto one knee. The blue glow from the gauntlet molded over the openings, scrambling in vain to block out the noise that punched and kicked his eardrums.

His mind swam with a confusion of voices and noises, but he was able to peer through the clouding fluster in his mind. With his enhanced vision, down the street, he saw the car he had caved in. Sonance stood beside Talon. Her thin body shivered even in the mild night air, and her skinny arms were held out in a clap as she looked up at her field commander for his approval. Two feathers were gone from each side of Talon's headdress. He held the knives in both hands, gleaming as he rolled clenched fists. He did not return Sonance's gaze but kept the white screen of his eyes on Fiasco.

Gravity faltered from the noise assaulting his hearing, and Fiasco swam on the asphalt from the equilibrium turned upside down. Barbed chain links, the color of cobalt, exploded out from his aura.

Several shot up harmlessly into the sky, while others sailed wildly in other directions, striking nothing. Finally, several barbs pierced the blacktop of the street, and instantly, Fiasco pumped energy into the chains that caught hold. The chains stiffened, solidifying into rods that steadied the Mega. Using the rods as a guide, his hand touched the ground to steady him further.

"Talon must have defeated my bulls that kept Sonance pinned down," he thought as he massaged his temple with his thumb. The ringing in his ear made tears mist his eyes, but the screams were dissipating inside. "I won't be able to get to her with him around."

He shut his eyes tight, pushing the welled tears down his cheek. In that darkness, he saw Julianna on the crest of mount Washington. He saw her bright smile that kept him warm, even at such a high elevation. He heard her laughter that infected the rest of the tour group. He was sure he could smell the flowery scent of her hair. Sadness landed hard on Fiasco's shoulders when he remembered that he was on the verge of never seeing or feeling Julianna's warmth again.

Fiasco's eyes flashed open when Sonance's scream reverberated back to him in a high pitch that rivaled her own power. Through his goggles, the street looked like a long map of the Mississippi river, with all its connecting tributaries burning a low indigo. Blue strands leaked from his gloved fingers that touched the ground, hiding through the cracks and seams in the asphalt. When they found their target, the beams reached up like fingers, coiling around the Mega's skinny calf. Her leg kicked out, but the strands persisted upward, morphing into various species of snakeheads that hissed and flicked their tongues.

Tiny hands covered in black leather gloves tried to push the heads away, beating against the thick, writhing bodies wrapping around her. "Help me!" Sonance begged.

Talon heard her pleas. His movements were almost a blur of turquoise mixed with streaks of red. Thick, muscled arms swung down, then up, cutting away at the snake strands with crescent swipes of his blades. But for every one he hacked away, two more grew from the stumps, flicking their blue tongues as they moved upward. Soon, the young Mega was wrapped up to her neck in slithering snakes glowing in an indigo fire.

"Sonance!" Talon shouted, forgoing the knives that clattered against the ground to pull at the manifestation with his bare hands.

Fiasco pushed more power into his gauntlet. The tributaries in the street brightened, and Sonance was launched up into the night on a pillar of blue. The thick, rubbery column arched down, leaning lazily to the right before Fiasco tossed Sonance and the snake manifestations into the brush of the park inside Enterprise Square. Her shrieks played through the trees until the sound was swallowed by the thick canopy. Talon glanced back at him, his white mask a mix of anger and horror, before darting off into the park after his charge.

The New Haven citizens roared behind the barriers, but the ringing in Fiasco's ears made their derision sound like someone was screaming at him while he was underwater. But with Sonance gone, the ringing began to subside further. Fiasco chewed the side of his lip as relief washed over his ear, and the ambient sounds of the world rushed in. "That was rougher than I wanted," he thought. "And that look on Talon's face...I hope she's not hurt."

You most likely killed her.

"I'm sure she's fine," he said, but wondered if he was trying to convince himself of that truth. "I just have to keep going. Julianna is waiting for me."

The gleaming poles that steadied him to the ground pulled back into his aura, sounding like metal chains being reeled in. His aura hummed from the additional power, and his ear healed enough for him to stand on both feet again. With Talon occupied, he looked around, half expecting to be sucker-punched again. Far across the other side of the park, back at the drop zone where the fight began, he spied Hammond under the skychaser spotlight. He paced back and forth, adamantly speaking into a mic that curved near his mouth.

"Him," Fiasco said to himself. "If I can get to Hammond, I can end this. I can convince him they're wrong about me or force the M.D.C. to leave me be."

With his mind made up, Fiasco raised his aura and floated off the ground, preparing to fly as fast as he could towards Hammond, hoping to reach him before Talon— or anyone else— could interfere. He floated several feet forward before asphalt flew up in a shower and pelted off his shield. Fiasco curved away from a brown fist that missed his chin by inches but could not dodge a follow-up punch that dug into his sternum and pushed him into the park. Fiasco's aura thrummed, and he corrected his flight. Rush followed him into the park at a gallop.

"You are trying to embarrass me, aren't you, twerp? It's going to take a lot more than some lame ass cartoon bulls to take me down," Rush said. His brown eyes were broad and dancing with rage, and he glanced to the right. "Don't even think about going after the boss. This ends between you and me."

The massive Mega punched again with his left fist, and Fiasco flew back away from the blow. This maneuver seemed to please Rush, who flashed a smirk and ran several steps to conjure a fragment of the white energy before him. With a snarl that curved his lip, he pushed that energy towards Fiasco with a right cross that broke the wind with a boom. Fiasco quickly reached out his hands to counter with a ball of swirling blue energy. The two energies met with a squeal, then burst into a miniature explosion of light blue that flipped Fiasco back even further into the park. A smell of burning lingered in the air. Fiasco concentrated, and his aura burst about him like a star, cracking the brick as he slid to a halt on the running trail.

Fiasco wiped a trickle of warm blood from the corner of his mouth. "This guy is relentless. How am I supposed to stop him?" he thought.

You are going to fail against his strength, the voice asserted.

With a hop, Rush stomped towards him at a trot that quickly turned into a sprint. His head disappeared behind the strips of white energy, when Fiasco heard a spine stiffening whistle in the air. Instinctively, he turned and pushed his hand out through his aura. A stream of power followed like a wave and flicked the flying red blade away that tinkled against the stone pavement.

Anger threatened to deplete his repository within. His eyes scanned the shadows that swayed from the tree canopy but could not see his foe in the darkness. "Why hide if you're so much better than me?" Fiasco shouted to try and coerce Talon out from whatever shadow he hid.

The pounding ground reminded him that he was not alone in the park. Frustration mounting, and with no more power to spare searching for his friend, he turned his attention back to Rush. The massive Mega could hardly be seen as he charged forward, head down like a raging rhino behind his white, darting energy. The way he used his power to stop Talon's blade, and the voices mockery sparked an idea.

With his hands out at his sides, Fiasco allowed the power to flow freely. Streams of energy roiled and coursed through his crooked *F*, then poured over his shoulders. It crawled down his back and spread outward, flowing like a cloth that he clutched with both hands and pulled out to his sides.

"I can have a cape too, Valor," he thought, his shimmering goggles keeping vigil as Rush sped forward.

The cape billowed behind him from the turbulence Rush's power created. Fiasco held his position as the bench beside him rattled and bounced against the stone. The sparkling white energy was close enough to reflect off his goggles, and he could feel the heat from Rush's power. Covered in a white glow, Fiasco finally side-stepped, twisting on his heel to the right. His left hand rose, and the cape of energy belled outward. Rolls unfurled, spreading outward, sweeping over the white. Rush shouted as the cape folded over his head, until he was trapped within its many folds. The white energy exploded with a muffled pop within the piece of cloth that Fiasco had manifested.

"Your power is proportional. Your power is proportional," Fiasco repeated like an intonation as he held the cape with both hands and turned, remembering Talon's advice from the Modoc Bridge that his manifestations were as strong as they appear.

With clenched teeth, he pulled as he twisted on the concrete, using Rush's centrifugal force to complete circles over the stone running trail. His injured leg screamed in agony. Leaves and dust swirled outward beneath Fiasco's feet as the M.D.C. agent slowly lifted off the ground. Inside the shimmering folds of the cape, he could hear Rush's angry curses stifled by the glowing fabric. His growl was just as menacing as punches bit into the folds, each blow sending streams of blue lights sailing. Still, Fiasco kept turning, raising Rush higher.

Talon emerged from the edge of the shadows running towards Fiasco with a raised hand. "Fiasco don't!" he shouted, the screens on his white mask wide with alarm.

"You always said I didn't listen to you, Talon," Fiasco thought.

His arms strained from the lumbering brute's weight, but he kept turning until his shoulders burned and elbows felt as if they would break. Grunting to release the pain, his hands parted. The folds of the cape parted like shimmering water, and Rush careened upward through the night sky. His baritone scream trailed as he rose into the ether. A spell of dizziness sent bile to Fiasco's throat, as he watched Rush become a small speck in the night sky.

"Got you!" Fiasco shouted at the Mega with glee that made his aura waver, wiping wretch from the corner of his lips.

Then, gravity took hold and the heavy Mega began to descend, and Fiasco realized why Talon had instructed him to stop. His shoulders dropped. "Ah shit, not again," Fiasco shuddered, watching in horror as the Mega plummeted downward like a rock.

The wind screamed around Rush's form. With a thundering crash, he plummeted through the top of the Savoy Tower, sending bricks and steel tumbling over the edge. Fiasco's aura blinked and his shoulders cringed from the sound as the destruction magnified. Floors designed to hold the weight of an office whined as they imploded inward and crashed down to the next, sending ceiling panels, concrete, furniture, and glass to the next floor—a continued chain reaction of devastation.

As each floor was demolished, stylish windows that reached from the base of the floor to the top of the ceiling exploded outward. The rainstorm of glass was followed by clouds of gray that sailed through the empty panes like smoke. Wreckage careened out of the openings, tumbling down to the street in an avalanche, caving in the roofs of the expensive, high-end cars parked below.

Fiasco thought about using the distraction to flee and take off his costume, burn it, and never think to put it on again. He wanted to hide, but the M.D.C. would only hunt him down. Especially after his count reached twenty-two floors. His jaw slackened as the pride of New Haven caved inward on steel-framed beams that bent along stress lines, ruined by his own folly.

The remaining floors were spared, and Fiasco guessed that Rush had stopped just above the middle of the building. It was not a total collapse, but what remained resembled a crown tossed to the ground, with spindles of jagged metal on either side twisting upward. Clouds of misty smoke hung over First Street near the base of the tower and floated out to the shouting onlookers who covered their mouths, cringing to protect their eyes from the haze.

"They are going to want to kill me," Fiasco thought of the crowd, and they were not the only ones.

Talon

He looked for Talon and found him standing just outside the edge of the shadows inside the park. The dust wafted over his back, giving his turquoise vest a veneer of dirt. He was staring at Fiasco, as well, his white mask twisted in anger, and hands curled up into tight fists at his side.

"Enough of this," he read on Talon's lips. Then, he watched as his friend ran with such speed that he shook loose the dirt clinging to his clothing.

In an instant, he was in front of Fiasco— so close that he could feel the angry blast from Talon's nostrils as he exhaled. Talon landed two hammering blows to his face before the Mega-hero could dare to blink, slapping hard against skin and bone. Fiasco stumbled back on his heels. He responded with blue lines of energy that he shot out from both hands. Talon deftly dodged the attack, ducking low below one, then sliding to his left in a blur to avoid the other. Talon wound his way in between the tendrils and pushed a straight jab into Fiasco's stomach that forced the wind from his lungs, sending him sliding back along the stone walkway.

Pain scratched along his back from the lack of air. Wheezing in air, he sent barbed-tipped strands of light from his fingertips to try and stop his former friend from punching him again—at least until he could catch his breath. They curled in random directions from his mental command to create a sense of confusion, but Talon pirouetted away, slashing, and breaking the strands with a feather knife plucked from his headdress.

Fiasco felt pressure below, close to where Talon's punch had taken his breath. Two stings bit into Fiasco's stomach after Talon had hurled the smaller, thinner knives from his bracelet in quick succession. Talon materialized before him and grabbed both gauntlets by the wrists. He twisted both wrists outward. Fiasco gasped and his knees wavered when he felt twin pops on either side.

Talon pushed his face close to his that Fiasco could feel his warm breath against his exposed skin. "Guess I'm going to have to do more damage to these before you end this," he said in a growl. Talon twisted outward further, and Fiasco heard his gauntlets begin to splinter and crack.

Sweat dripped off Fiasco's nose, and he gritted his teeth against the pain. "Good thing I have more than just hands, right?" Fiasco replied, his mouth twisting into a grin, revealing pink teeth stained with blood.

The rim of his incandescent goggles on his face twinkled in a figure eight before the lenses spat out solid sparks of blue light. Talon's head jerked backward from the blast, and he shouted out an intelligible curse. His hands loosened from Fiasco's gauntlets, then clutched at his eyes that smoked an indigo from Fiasco's beams. Seeing an opening, Fiasco pumped energy reserves into his gauntlets to reinforce his injured wrists, and rushed forward, landing a thudding punch to the side of Talon's face that moved him backward several steps. The blow was weak from his injury, but Talon didn't see it coming. The punch pushed his hands away from his eyes, revealing the scorched, black skin around his mask that was burning in blue fire.

"Don't be stupid, Crooked F," Fiasco thought, flying forward as he rung out his right hand. "There is no need to even use your fist."

A large replica of his gauntlet pushed from his right hand, streaking like a bolt in an arch that struck Talon again with a cross. It drew blood from a gash that was left behind on his cheek. Fiasco ducked, and a slow left hook from Talon sailed over his head. Fiasco shot a thick beam of light from his goggles at the ground in an azure flash. Pressure and heat broke the stone. The debris rose and tangled in Talon's feet, tripping up the usually graceful Mega. With a twist of his hip, Fiasco lifted his right fist that was buffered by a broad, blue gauntlet manifestation, catching Talon under the chin. Iron feathers were knocked loose from his headdress, and his jaw clacked shut from the uppercut that sent him reeling backward.

Fiasco fell to one knee. Rivulets of red streaked down his uniform from the wounds where Talon's blades protruded from his abdomen. Moving to sit back on his calves, Fiasco's painful grunts echoed through the clearing as he worked the knives loose with manifested pincers. The pain shocked his skin cold, and he gasped when the blades finally slid out. Giving the knives a quick glance, he tossed them aside. Blood followed the red razors extraction, almost tickling his skin as the liquid pushed outward. He coughed as a reminder to breathe in, and stretched his fingers out over the twin wounds, letting the heat of the energy from his gauntlets pour over the cuts.

Like an apparition, Talon appeared just outside his arms' reach, and pulled him up by the scruff of his costume before he could topple over from momentum. Fiasco's friend lifted him up with one hand and drew him in until they were eye to eye. The white mask Talon wore had burned away, leaving dark, melted particles embedded in his skin. It was replaced by scarred flesh, black and charred, set by amazing green eyes that shone with wrath.

"Cute trick with the mask," Talon said with a grin that held no mirth.

With a shove, Fiasco felt himself tumble back several steps. A blow that felt like a plank of wood dug into the side of his neck, but instead of a fist, it was the broad side of Talon's hand. His legs weakened, and Talon blurred. The debilitating blow was followed by a series of punches that seemed to come from every direction all at once. Talon's body was a musical, playing a gruesome tune on his battered body, piercing his shield. The aura around Fiasco's body withered and splintered from the onslaught, breaking away in pieces like crushed porcelain. He watched as Talon twisted on his heel, turned, then pushed his left foot deep into his gut. Acrid bile filled his mouth as he rolled backward along the running trail.

Talon was stalking forward. Reaching back, he pulled two feathers from his headdress, striped with the colors of the American flag. "This doesn't end well for you, Fiasco," Talon said. He held the blades out beside him. His green eyes glowered. "You can't beat me. You never could. Not the way you are. If you had listened to me, you would have been better by now, but that time has passed. I'm ending this."

You tried and failed, as we both knew you would, the voice said with melancholy. *There is little shame in yielding now. He is better than you.*

"No," Fiasco said. The stench from his retch stung his nose as he lifted himself up on his hands. The manifested cape covered his back like a glowing shroud. "That's not going to happen. I'm not going with you, Talon. There's someone who needs me."

"That girlfriend of yours?" Talon replied. "If you listened to me, you would be with her right now. But I would get that thought out of your head now. You're never going to see her again."

Fiasco gritted his teeth and brought his gloved fist down against the ground in frustration. "You're not listening to me. I can't go with you. I'm not letting her go again."

Talon stopped, studying the fallen Mega. "Your aura just changed. Is that anger I see? Interesting. Finally, another emotion from you. Took long enough, but it's too late now."

"Now you're the one who's failed." Blood trickled from Fiasco's mouth when he grinned. "You think you know me, Talon, but you only know a part of me. What I allow you to see. There is only one person in the world who deserves to know me, and I'm going to be with her again tonight."

Do not be delusional, Fiasco heard the voice say. *You will never see her again.*

The crooked *F* on his chest flashed with a burst of power that poured over his body as he stood on weary legs. He imagined hearing the long creak as the heavy cell door slammed shut at the Oubliette. He would never feel the warmth of Julianna's skin, cherish her flowery scent, or twist her hair between his fingers again. He would just be another prisoner. A statistic on the M.D.C. ledger. The *F* that pulsated on his chest would just be a symbol of his failure. He would waste away in that dungeon, only remembered by Julianna, who hated him for being who he was.

The mix of emotions made Fiasco's aura shift before erupting outward in flashes of blue sparks. Swiftly, he lifted off the ground, hovering over his old friend. Talon looked up and stepped back from the spangles that shot out from Fiasco's aura. He watched as they twisted to the ground about him, burning like pyrotechnic from a blue flare. Glowing gauntlets held the edge of the cape that sailed behind Fiasco, and the aura shined so brilliantly that Talon had to shield his eyes from the radiance with the back of his hand.

"You say you see me, Talon," Fiasco said. His goggles shined, the luminescence shadowing his face in blue. "But I have so much left to show you, friend."

Fiasco concentrated, and his crooked symbol exploded with power that sprang forth like water from a broken dam— as if it were angry for being contained for so long. The power hurled stars across the sky that arched to the ground, spreading outward in glowing pools. As one pool landed near Talon's feet, its light morphed and changed. A glowing knob formed at the top, rising upward from the loch. The light shifted as it grew upward, splitting into what appeared to be arms and legs. The light rolled back in angles and curves until it became a gossamer blue version of Fiasco. It looked nearly solid, three dimensional, but sheer in appearance. An outline of the Mega-hero traced in cerulean neon.

It turned and looked at Talon. Pale tears misted the manifestation's goggles and spilled out, glowing down its chin as it rushed towards the Mega. "You betrayed me," it sobbed, punching outward with a right jab that Talon dodged.

Still gliding to the left, his arm rose and fell, and Talon slipped the blade he had pulled from his headdress through the top of the Fiasco manifestation's skull that cracked from the impact. The creation stopped its attack and sobbed one last time before winking out of existence. Twisting on a heel, Talon caught the knife before it hit the ground, crouching as he held it behind his back.

Energy sprang forth from Fiasco and continued to land on the grass and brick trail. Floating above, he watched as Talon's head moved from left to right as copies of Fiasco sprang up around the M.D.C. agent. It began with two, then turned to four. Six more sprung up about him, surrounding Talon, each manifesting an emotion that Fiasco had learned to hold and manage inside.

A round, cherub-faced Fiasco looked about like a curious child, its head looking over the top of the trees and night sky before it looked down and saw Talon. It let out an immature giggle and glided vertically until it slid over the stone to tightly hug the Mega with both arms around the bottom of his legs.

The clone looked up with sad, drooping goggles on his eyes and said, "Brother," in a soft voice.

The Mega struggled to pull from the creations grip, but the innocent Fiasco copy held tight, wrapping Talon's pants legs in blue fists strengthened by gauntlets similar to its master's.

Another clone lumbered up to Talon, a garish smile spread wide across its face as it dragged a heavy blue mallet behind it that clanged against the stone with every bump. Cobalt blue spittle dripped from its mouth as it reached up and swung the mallet against the side of Talon's face with maniacal laughter. The thick face of the weapon slapped against brown skin, whipping Talon's head to the side.

Strong legs kicked the child-Fiasco away as it cried and thrashed about on the trail. Talon hopped backwards to keep away from its flailing hands. Wasting little motion, the Mega's arm arched backward, releasing a blade at the club-wielding manifestation that struck in-between its eyes with an audible thunk. Its goggles split where the knife was deeply embedded. The specter screamed an obscenity before it cracked and tumbled to the ground.

Talon retrieved a knife from his headdress to replace the one he had just used, backing up into a manifestation that wrapped its glowing arms around his body. The arms of the duplicate were as thin as the original but were reinforced with its own gauntlets that formed together in front of Talon, locking him in place. The clone floated behind him, leaning close to Talon's head so it could scream obscenities into his ears.

"I thought you fucking liked me!" the Fiasco imitation shouted, its voice dripping from the devastating emotion Talon's betrayal had created. It squeezed hard enough to force Talon to release a grunt through gritted teeth. "I thought we were friends!"

Then, another Fiasco approached, bounding in small hops until it reached close enough to land several crosses to Talon's face with whoops of excitement. Talon tried to wiggle within the cartoonish arms, but two more copies had reached out and held his legs in place. One lamented how it would never be as good as him, while the other was far more confident that it had already surpassed him in every way. The two manifestations bickered with each other over their positions as they wrapped glowing arms and legs about Talon's trunk, anchoring him to the ground.

The avalanche of attacks continued. Fear, disgust, confusion, rejection, despair, and apathy followed, moving among the others like a colony. Each one was a clone of the original, and each one was a manifestation of its own emotion.

"I'm sorry," Fiasco murmured, his voice cracking as the attack continued.

Talon finally freed himself as his veins rippled on his arms, pushing outward with the broadsides of his hands to crack the forearms of the Fiasco that held him. A backward head flick from Talon caved a blue nose inward on the clone's face. The clone's arms loosened, allowing Talon to retrieve a knife from his headdress that he stabbed down twice in swift succession. The glowing clones about his legs screamed before cracking like brittle, dying as they fluttered away into the night.

Freed, Talon twisted at the hip to plunge the blade deep into the neck of the manifestation that held him in the tight lock. Blue light spilled out from its wound, and the duplicate clutched at its neck, mouth open as it melted away. Talon's arm arched backward, sending the red, white, and blue blade deep into the maniacal Fiasco who had started the attack. The blade stuck deep into the center of its chest, cutting the crooked F in half before it flashed from existence.

Talon stood under the tan light of the lamppost. Blood trailed down his turquoise vest that was torn and tattered as it hung off his broad shoulders like a bloodied rag. The headdress on Talon's head was missing several feathers, which left gaping holes throughout. The bracelets on both his wrists were more beads than blades. Talon's fingers played with the knives that tingled when they clanged together, realizing he was running out of knives to launch.

Seeing Talon bloodied, hair disheveled, and forlorn, made a tinge of guilt well within, to the point where Fiasco pondered ending his assault but abandoned the idea when he noticed his creations being tossed into the air to his right.

"What the hell is going on over there?" he thought, wondering what new horror the M.D.C. had unleashed to stop him.

The creations that manifested aspects of his fear scampered away, flying, or running as they cried blue tears. Rush barreled through the blue sea of Fiasco's, using his white energy as a ram to batter them away. The silver metal along his body lost its luster, smeared with grime and dirt from plummeting through Savoy Tower. One frightened Fiasco clone was not as swift as the others. Its scream gurgled in the dirt as Rush stampeded over its back, crushing it beneath his feet.

Still, some of the creations remained as they manifested his judgmental nature, aversion, revulsion, disapproval, and loathing, emotions. They looked upon the M.D.C. Mega and found his presence among their lofty ranks repugnant. They sent makeshift weapons that extended from their own light, swinging bats, wrenches, and blue crowbars that smashed against Rush's armor.

"Get away from him, you freaks!" Rush grumbled, ignoring the manifested clones that clung to his massive neck, feet sailing behind them. Others were pulled along the brick, clinging to his legs. The shimmering white energy in front of Rush dwindled further when he punched through the clones toward Talon.

Twin clones of Fiasco held onto Talon's body like leaches, lazily clawing at his face, one yawning as it gouged at his eyes. Rush's field commander pushed the two back, stretching out his arm and pressing against their jaws with his palms. Rush moved forward to assist, but Talon's eyes caught him, and he groaned the word, "No."

Talon twisted left and then right, lashing out with quick slashes against the clones' blue throats with the last knife in his headdress, sending light streaming from gaping wounds as two more clones dissipated.

With full-body breaths, Talon stumbled forward, forcing Rush to scramble to catch the Mega who fell into his arms. The minutes of fighting felt like hours to muscles weary from use beneath bruised and swollen flesh, and Talon finally succumbed to exhaustion once he felt a sense of safety. Face stoic, Rush held up his leader with a hand on his chest, draping his bloodied arm over his shoulders to keep him on his feet, unwilling to give the real Fiasco the satisfaction of seeing his commander fall.

"What's our status?" Talon asked Rush as he leaned inside the arm of his fellow agent.

"Bad news. We got the word," Rush touched a finger to his ear and flashed an angry look up at Fiasco who hovered above, staring down at the two M.D.C. agents and reading the words on their lips. "We're getting out of here."

"What?" Talon perked up, his scorched eyes blinking. He leaned in close to Rush's ear and shouted, "Hammond, stop. We're not done here."

Rush cringed from Talon's breath against his ear. But before his field commander could resist further, he lifted Talon, curling his arm under his legs and neck. Then, Rush bent at his waist, crouched low to the ground, and jumped away from the manifestations that had begun to counterattack in a mass.

Fiasco followed his arching trajectory. Near the landing zone, he saw Hammond standing with Sonance. Her black outfit was covered in dirt and leaves, and she had her face buried into his chest. Hammond waved a hand in a circle in the air as Rush finally made it into the spotlight, landing with a deep thump against the asphalt just outside the edge of the park. There were various Fiasco imitations running or flying through the brush, hot on his heels.

Flash Freeze limped into frame; his icy blue veins etched onto his skin once more. When all five of the M.D.C. Megas were close enough to each other, Flash Freeze sent a blast of cold to the ground from his hands and raised a pillar of ice that lifted them all into the sky. Fiasco's creations tried to claw and climb the glistening column but fell back to the ground from the slickness of the ice. Blue trails curled upward, heading toward an orange breach in the sky. Fiasco could not see the Megas boarding the skychaser obscured by the trees; he could only hear the mechanical door slam shut and the engine sputter. The spotlight widened on the ground as the ship floated south.

Fiasco hung in the air. Dozens of his doppelgangers crowded below. All were silent, mimicking his movements and looking skyward. Fiasco's weary muscles tensed when the skychaser floated overhead, coughing smoke. If anything, the M.D.C. were persistent in their pursuit, and as far as he knew, they never lost a Mega they hunted.

The glowing cape fluttered behind Fiasco as the ship let out a powerful gust. Fiasco grabbed it toward him with one hand and shielded his eyes from the light of the ship with the other. The clones did the same, nearly in unison, appearing like a Mega league team saluting the flag. The skychaser floated further south and its spotlight below was extinguished. Fiasco lost sight of the craft when it leaned away, reflecting the atmosphere, becoming invisible.

With the skychaser gone, the hum from the Fiasco clones below sounded like an electric cable stripped bare. Leaves rustled through the swaying trees, disturbed by the multitude of news helicopters that flew low over the park. Fiasco floated down with hands out to his sides, letting his cape spread out behind him. The clones parted to make room, and he landed on the wet grass.

Being back on solid ground seemed to remind his brain of all his injuries, and he bent over in pain. Looking around, the manifestations stared at him, their faces blank and devoid of the emotions that gave them life just moments prior. With the danger subsided, they walked into him, melting back into Fiasco's aura, one after the other, until all were gone. Only the park light remained. With his power fully restored, the skin on Fiasco's stomach itched as the energy worked to heal his wounds.

For an instant, Fiasco felt his emotions shift, vacillating between confusion and sadness as he thought of Talon's betrayal. Pride, surprise, and even excitement made their appearances, each getting a chance to reign. After so many series of failures that occurred over the years, his mind could not fathom what it meant to win.

Losers cannot handle nor comprehend success, the voice said, making Fiasco chuckle.

The voice sounded warbled, like an old record rolling over a curve in its plastic from a long absence. Still, Fiasco welcomed its presence since it made him feel less alone.

"Thank you, I needed that reality check," he said. "Prick."

He limped toward the north end of the park holding his wounds, moving towards the Savoy Tower to survey the damage Rush's body had caused. Firefighters and EMTs rushed up the staircase to search for any injuries that may have occurred from Rush's fall. "This was all so big." Fiasco muttered.

On the left periphery, he noticed a police officer, one hand out and the other on his sidearms, attempting to hold back the New Havenites who had broken through the abandoned blockade at the end of the street. Catching his breath, Fiasco stood upright as far as he could on an injured leg and mending wounds. The citizens ran into the park from all four corners like a flood, jumping, whooping, and yelling. Fiasco tensed and his aura thickened and pushed outward with a thrum. He turned in a circle, alarmed, and checked the citizens' hands for pipes or weapons, suspecting that Enrapture had returned to finish him off. That was before the crowd broke out in a chant.

"Fi-as-co! Fi-as-co!"

It began low at first, with those closest to him, before being picked up by others in the back, until it morphed into a chorus of his name. Fiasco shrank.

They do not love you, the voice said.

"Too late to kiss up now, New Haven," Fiasco thought, yet his mouth twitched as he suppressed a smile that pained the cuts on his lips and cheeks still mending under his aura.

Instead of holding weapons, their hands held phones that flashed around him, with flashing red lights recording the moment of his victory. For the first time, instead of curse words and avarice, there were smiles; their faces were grinning, drunk off his victory. The Mega team loss was forgotten. The failure at the bridge was forgiven. No longer was he the murderer who let Tamerlane escape. Nor was he the black sheep Mega forever tucked away in the shadows of Talon and Scarlet Valor. For that moment, he knew that they had seen him. That night, Fiasco was New Haven's favorite hero.

The citizens pushed against the reporters who did their best to stay upright. Bright circles of light shined in his face as they spoke over each other, peppering him with an endless stream of questions.

"How many people have you killed?"

"Do you believe this attempt of apprehension has something to do with the museum disaster?"

"Fiasco! How do you feel being wanted by the M.D.C.?"

"How will you pay for the destruction of yet another New Haven treasure?"

"What will you do now as the most wanted man in the pacific northwest?"

The attention was overwhelming. The fact that he had gone toe to toe with the M.D.C. and was still alive made his head swim. There was no reason why he had inexplicably won. Judging by their questions, Fiasco knew that the public was still apprehensive about him, but also realized that he did not owe them anything. Even if he could explain his victory, the media were the last who deserved the details. There was only one person who deserved to know about the conflict, and he didn't see her in the crowd.

"I don't have time for this. I have to talk to Julianna," Fiasco thought. His aura expanded, frightening the reporters and citizens alike who flinched back from the light. "She has to know about everything, and there won't ever be a better time."

He crouched and let the power flow out from his crooked *F* down to his cape that rippled from the current. The ground trembled from the gathering strength before he launched into the air in a swirl of grass, leaves, and dust that wafted over his newfound fans.

"Fiasco!" he shouted.

His name sang over the soiled crowd who let out a cheer even though they were covered in his spinning grit. The sky greeted Fiasco, embracing him with the warm air that coursed through the pores he allowed in his aura. He veered left towards Black Deer, painting a glowing blue arch in the night. Even through the blood, sweat, and pain, Fiasco was no longer able to hold back a smile as he lifted into the starry night sky that seemed to twinkle with brightness, celebrating his inexplicable and life-defining victory. Now that he had finally won as Fiasco, he knew that nothing could stand between him and Julianna, and he planned to love her for the rest of their lives.

You Are the Fiasco

The congestion on the roads outside Black Deer had nearly cleared by the time Fiasco circled above. Paranoia reigned, but one loop of the area was enough to convince him that there were no more Mal or M.D.C. traps awaiting him in the darkened alcoves or alleyways. Sailing above, he studied the faces still in the area. It appeared that Warren had done what Fiasco asked, since he did not see him, Jenni, or Julianna among the people milling about on the sidewalk.

Fiasco chose a rooftop three buildings down. His aura dimmed as he landed so he would not be seen by anyone, wincing as he knelt on one knee onto the gravel rooftop. From his vantage point, he peered over a red brick riser that ran along the edge and saw the dancing deer handle on the bar door through his goggles.

"I can't go back to being Fiasco," he realized on the flight back to Black Deer from Enterprise Square. His aura felt different, as if his victory had changed its composition. Yet, even as the wind cooled his burning wounds, he knew the M.D.C. wouldn't be happy after the battle. He couldn't risk putting his family, or Julianna, in harm's way. It was time for a fresh start anyway, and he was going to ensure he and Julianna got that chance.

This is wise for someone who is not that bright. While he looked over the rooftop ledge, the voice continued, *but perhaps the point is moot. Perhaps the M.D.C. already know who you are outside the mask.*

Kneeling in the grit on the rooftop, the questions made Fiasco tighten his grip of the brick on the riser. The query turned over in his mind, then he shook his head.

"No. I never told Talon my real name, and he's never seen my face."

You spoke about her.

Fiasco swallowed hard. "Yeah, we talked about Julianna, but I never said her name, either."

He gave you access to the Stream.

"The MegaStream is independent for that reason. It's encrypted and piped through so many servers to make it all anonymous," he reasoned. "Once Talon got me in, that was it. I don't think even the M.D.C. could crack that code created by guys like Tamerlane. I think I'm okay." Fiasco's grin widened, and he went back to look at the bar door, waiting for Julianna to appear. "I think we're going to be okay without Fiasco."

Horns blared on the boulevard, and exuberant voices resounded up to his perch. The crowd seemed to thin even further as news of his victory trickled outward. During the battle, Fiasco had not noticed anyone broadcasting the struggle— too focused on dodging punches, thawing himself from ice encasements, and pulling knives from his flesh. But when he counted the number of reports present after the battle had finally ended, he knew that there had to be at least a dozen present—local and national. He was sure that the entire town had either seen the battle unfold. Feeling the euphoria of the hometown kid done good, the whooping revelers were compelled to join the festivities that were mere blocks away.

Apprehension tightened Fiasco's chest as more people filtered out of Black Deer, but he did not see Julianna. The crowd petered out with the rest on the street, and he wondered if perhaps he had missed her and the others in the crowd. It was nearly impossible from his altitude to account for every face within the hundreds that were gathered near the park. It was very possible she had grown tired of waiting for him. What was even more possible was that she saw the destruction on the news, the bodies tumbling over their buildings, and could no longer fight against her concern, and had joined the crowd to check on his well-being.

You are not together anymore. She would not search for you.

Fiasco shook his head. "You never did understand her, did you? She absolutely would look for me, just as I would for her. And she has to be down there since we weren't done talking yet," he replied. The power fluttered inside, reacting to the truth and sentiment behind his words. "Julianna needs this just as much as me. She'll want to hear the truth because she knows, just like me, that we're meant to be together."

Perhaps she believes you left her. Yet again, the voice said, relentless in its interrogation. *Kept at the same distance that drove you apart.*

"What, are you a psychologist now? What do you know about real feelings?" Fiasco's gauntlets flashed on in blue lights. "What do you know about love for that matter?" He stood, winching from sharp pain that pricked his nerves, and looked around. "All you do is bring me down. But I defeated you as much as the M.D.C. tonight. For once I overcame your venom to finally become the Mega that I was always meant to be." Fiasco turned back to the ledge, kneeling again and the glow fading from his hands. "And now I don't need to be a Mega at all. She is all I need."

New voices rose to his perch, and Fiasco lifted his head off the brick. The door to Black Deer jostled open, and more customers spilled outward into the streetlight, talking and laughing in their inebriation. The streetlight buzzed as the people quickly dispersed from its lights. Then, as if summoned by his argument, Julianna emerged, catching the tall wooden door just before it closed. The sight of her made Fiasco's heart leap, and he wiped sweaty palms gently against his legs. Pushing open the door, she stepped outside into the glow of the streetlamp that cast a triangle light on the sidewalk.

It was if the battle had made her even more radiant. The wind played through her long, dark hair that was free from the ponytail, cascading like a waterfall down her back. Even at his elevated height, Fiasco's mind conjured her familiar flower scent, bold and striking, as if she were standing beside him and not several streets away. She still had on his glasses that she pushed up her nose. Julianna's face held no smile, nor the anger he expected. Her head looked east then west down the street, searching for something— or someone— as she walked closer to the edge of the sidewalk.

"She must be waiting for Kevin," Fiasco concluded.

Fiasco made a mental note of all the things he had to apologize to her for, including how long he had kept her waiting while he battled the M.D.C. and, of course, keeping his secret from her all this time. Fiasco wondered what it would feel like once he let his walls down. Would she throw herself into his arms after seeing his multiple wounds, overjoyed that he was even alive? Or would she recoil in horror from his mere presence, knowing the harm Fiasco had caused to her family and the town? The blood in Fiasco's veins hastened his heart from the range of possibilities, and he licked away the salty sweat above his scabbed over lip. He stood up and took several deep breaths to calm his nerves.

"Amazing. I can't believe I'm more nervous now than I was at any point during the battle," he said as he limped back and forth, gingerly wringing his aching hands out at his sides. Several short hops made his bones throb throughout his body, so he ended that practice quickly.

For some reason, he looked down and examined his uniform to see if he was presentable but realized any attempt to tidy up was an effort in futility. Dirt from multiple falls had changed the color from blue green to a mud brown. There were rips and tears scattered along the fabric wherever his eyes landed, filled with strands of grass and bits of dirt. Some were crusted with long streaks of dry blood from the knives Talon had thrown into his body that he knew Julianna would find worrisome. Futile as it was, he still put his hair back into the top of his mask and adjusted it over so it would not poke out again.

End this cowardly delay, the voice chided.

Fiasco breathed out. "You're right this time. I can do this."

The temperature had fallen, but Fiasco still felt the sweat begin to form beneath his mask. Anxiousness, anxiety, and fear sapped the power's presence as he stepped up onto the ledge. Julianna was still standing under the lamp, waiting, and he knew it was time to come clean. Yet, before he could leap and float down to the street, the door of Black Deer creaked open again, and he watched as Julianna turned away. Warren was behind her, holding onto the door as he leaned out of the restaurant. His jacket was off, sleeves rolled up on his untucked shirt.

There was something off-putting about Warren in that state, disheveled and unkempt. As he approached Julianna, it looked as if they had picked up a conversation that they were in the middle of back inside the restaurant. Even with his goggles enhancing the image, he could not read their lips, but he could read their body language. Each moved their hands sharply through the air for emphasis as they spoke. Their voices bounced off the street in muted shouts.

"Are they arguing?" he thought as he witnessed the exchange. "Could something have happened between them when he tried to get her to stay? Could it be about me?"

Their barking resounded off the buildings, but he could not make out a word through the echo. Moments later, Jenni appeared at Warren's side, pulling him by the elbow with both hands, as if imploring him to return to the bar. Jenni looked between the man she was to marry and her best friend. Her normally indignant expression was now soft, pleading for him end the fighting. Finally, her appeals seemed to be effective, and Warren's head dipped down, hands on his sides. Relenting, his best friend said one last statement to Julianna, and waited for her reply. Fiasco couldn't see Julianna's face with her back turned to him, but she simply wrapped her arms around herself, protecting her skin from the breeze. Warren shook his head, throwing his hands up in frustration before walking back into the restaurant with Jenni rubbing his back.

Julianna turned back around, her phone bathing her face in soft light.

"She looks so angry," Fiasco thought, watching her face flush red as she walked up and down the sidewalk. "I really hope that wasn't about me." Fiasco knew he needed to swallow his nervousness and confront the situation.

The aura rippled about him, and he pushed one foot out, ready to take the first step to a new life. Fiasco breathed out again, harnessing his courage, until he was interrupted again by the squealing of brakes from a silver sports car that pulled up to the curve. Julianna stopped her pacing. She turned back to face the car, and Fiasco took a step back off the ledge, kneeling on the rocks and gripping the edge. Julianna's face shift from anger to joy. A genuine smile spread across her cheeks, triggering that adorable wrinkle above her nose. The car windows were tinted too dark for Fiasco to see within, and he wondered who could elicit such a reaction from his girl.

The fancy car pulled to a stop next to the curb. A door clicked, and the suspension groaned when a man emerged from the driver's side. His hair was brown and trimmed, fading into his thin beard. He was tall, fit, and well-dressed. His smile was bright enough that Fiasco could see his perfect teeth—probably even without the aid of the goggles—as he walked to where Julianna stood on the sidewalk.

"Ethan?" Fiasco muttered. He moved closer to the edge, grinding his sore knee into the gravel. "Is that Ethan Johns? Didn't Warren say he left Blanchet for a better tech job? What the hell is he doing here?"

But he was not the Ethan Johns Fiasco remembered. He was not the Ethan who had received his first kiss ever from a woman at his party so long ago. In the time since he had last seen him, Warren's mentorship had transformed him into someone completely different. Strong arms stretched within the sleeves of his tan suit jacket. The spare tire he carried just months ago had vanished, replaced by what looked like a flat stomach based on the fitted button-down shirt he wore beneath his jacket. His chubby cheeks had transformed into a square jaw made of steel, and his hair was parted at the top, shining a healthy brown glow.

Julianna quickly took the glasses off her eyes, and slyly stowed them in a purse that hung on her arm. She pulled back a lock of hair that had blown over her eyes and smiled at Ethan. Then, she stood on her toes, hugging Ethan by the neck. Fiasco flexed his left hand, still sore from Talon's knife, while Ethan's hands went to her curved hips, just as his once did. Julianna's body pressed into Ethan, and Fiasco could almost feel her warmth. She caressed the back of Ethan's head, her thin fingers stroking the small hairs at the nape of his neck. Then, Fiasco's heart froze when the two shared a long, passionate kiss, Ethan leaning her over in his arms.

Fiasco's jaw slackened, sending pain through fractured bones on the mend. His throat seemed to close as it dried up from the cold that gripped his heart, as if he were caught within Flash Freeze's murderous attack again. "This can't be right," he muttered, feeling dizzy. "Why is that prick kissing my girl?"

The aura came back, buzzing and wavering from the myriad of emotions within. Leaning in against the rising that pressed on his torso, he watched as Ethan led Julianna by the hand toward the passenger door, opening it for her and leaning in to meet her at eye-level. Red bricks melted beneath Fiasco's gauntlet as the two kissed again. Julianna's eyes twinkled with ecstasy as Ethan closed the door on a car Kevin could never afford.

The voice's whisper seemed to hang in the breeze. *That liar.*

Pain gripped Fiasco's chest and spread outward, hurting more than any knife that had pierced his skin earlier that evening. The aura rolled about his body as Ethan walked briskly to the driver's side, still beaming from Julianna's kiss that used to fill him with the same warmth and vigor. The car's suspension bounced as Ethan sat inside, clicking the door shut. The brake lights flashed white, then red as the glistening Lexus moved down the street.

The air felt thick, choking Fiasco's neck, and the voice groaned, *Yet another betrayal.*

"No. Maybe it's a trick," Fiasco reckoned. His head was drowning in feelings as he searched for meaning. "Maybe Warren knew I was close, and he and Julianna are playing a prank on me." His heart fluttered with irregularity as heat swept over his neck to quench the cold within. "Or maybe I'm still Enraptured? Maybe she's pulling out my worst nightmare to torture me? Maybe none of this is real?"

His rough gauntlet, glowing along the ornate lines on the back, brushed the bare skin beneath his mask and tested the flesh with its heat. The sensations were tangible, and within his depths, Fiasco knew what he saw was true, and his mind raced, trying to make sense of it all.

The treachery, the voice said— its tone poisonous.

The goggles about Fiasco's eyes glimmered, thickening with a new surge of energy. "Warren." He thought back to his best friend, and their last meaningful conversation. "He tried to warn me. In the garage at Blanchet. He said I was running out of time, didn't he? He said that she wouldn't wait forever."

The depth of Fiasco's humiliation became apparent the more

the memories churned in his mind, pulling on strings to unfurl the events. "Julianna told Jenni about Ethan, and she told Warren," the realization was a splash of scalding water. "So, he knew all along. He knew that little asshole protege of his actually stole her from me."

It was a double-cross, the voice hissed.

The thought of the turn of events took Fiasco's breath away. Questions cascaded like daggers through his heart, carving his soul. He wondered how long it had been going on. Was it days? Weeks? Months? It could have been the day after they broke up. It could have been something that was already in the works before their last conversation when he foolishly broke up with her over the phone.

The tips of his fingers were numb as they held onto the concrete ledge that dripped red brick. Were all of them talking behind his back? Warren, Jenni, and Julianna? Were they mocking his misery while she moved on with their handpicked replacement, created from the ground up by his best friend just for her?

The depth of this deception is boundless, the voice said, growing louder in volume.

"She would never do that," Fiasco choked out, his voice wavering.

The Lexus stopped several streets down from the bar, and Fiasco leaned in further, pressing his stomach against the rising until the knife cuts in his stomach bled again. He hoped that Julianna would get out of the car, realizing that she hadn't even given him a chance to explain his side of the story yet. He imagined her exiting the vehicle, eyes misting with tears. Then, she would lean into the passenger window, pulling her hair behind her ear as she told Ethan that she had unfinished business. Then, Ethan would share Fiasco's pain, feeling his heart being wrenched out from beneath his skin.

It was then that he would sail down the road on a trail of blue light. He would land next to that insufferable silver car. His goggles would be ablaze with his power as he tore the car door from its hinges from a manifest head of a dragon. Shimmering in indigo, it would roar into the night as he dragged the usurper of his dreams out by the collar with the gauntlet on his other hand. He would pull Ethan away, letting his legs drag behind him as he lifted into the sky. It was only then that he would warn Ethan against seeing Julianna again. He would smell the fear on his breath, and see it play in his blue eyes before dropping him back to a heap against the concrete. Then, Ethan would know. Julianna would know. They would all know who was better.

Your dreams never come true.

Then, the car moved again, Julianna still inside. A yellow light blinked on the right taillight before it turned down Antler Street, disappearing behind the edge of a darkened coffee shop that seemed to have closed early to celebrate Fiasco's victory. The blue aura fluctuated and sputtered about him as Fiasco floated upward, trying to a catch a glimpse of her again. But the Lexus was lost in a sea of red lights leaving the downtown of old New Haven, taking his heart with it.

"It all makes sense," Fiasco stammered, swallowing hard to wet his dry throat. He thought back to the conversation between him and Julianna moments before being called out by Mimicker and Enrapture. He put himself back in Black Deer, sitting in their booth before all the madness had exploded that night. "She had something to tell me, didn't she? She was insistent, but I interrupted her. She was going to tell me about this." The thought sank in, and his chest felt as if it were about to implode. "She was going to tell me to my face. She doesn't need me anymore."

Did she ever need you? the voice asked.

Fiasco floated higher, gaining altitude until the cold in the atmosphere whipped through the tears in his uniform that were still caked with blood. "She lied to me, didn't she?" Fiasco said. "They all did. Warren and Jenni. They did this, too. But it was her. It was Julianna who lied the most."

A memory rushed forward of their time together after his failure on the Modoc Bridge. They were together the night after, in his apartment. He remembered the warmth of Julianna as she leaned over his lap, tears glistening on her cheek, with the newscast about the stadium closure playing behind her. That night, she told him that no matter what happened, she always wanted him in his life.

Behind his goggles, Fiasco's eyes reddened, and he swallowed the frog that bloated in his throat, covering his mouth with the back of his glowing hand to stop his lips from trembling. He had believed her when she said those words. He had even asked her twice to ensure that she meant them, and she said yes each time.

His aura flashed outward, and his gauntlets curled into tight fists. "But that was all a lie, wasn't it? You never meant a word, did you?"

Every word she said was a lie, the voice said with a low growl that sounded like captured thunder.

The indigo aura spit and burst, curling outward like spouts of lava of his skin. "You only met up with me at Black Deer to throw this new guy in my face, didn't you?" His goggles thickened, glowing a bright azure to match his shield.

Using the energy, Fiasco shot up through the clouds, leaving round holes in each layer of the stratus behind him. Air whistled over his aura, matching his racing heart. The sadness inside fueled his power, pushing him further upward. The power flexed from his hands, and he soared upward through a field of gray and white. The moonlight shined down on his face, and the clouds below were a puffy meadow of white that rolled into the horizon.

He floated between the moon and the earth, arms out, leaning back against the wind. Fiasco contemplated the time he had spent with Julianna. Although he did not share everything with her, it was more than he had shared with anyone else. Yet, in the end, that mattered little. He kept things from her for a reason. He had a plan, but she didn't trust him enough to see it to fruition. She had moved on so quickly.

The growl in the voice rose in intensity, mixing with the power that raged into a turmoil. *How much did she ever really love you?* it sneered.

Fiasco's throat burned. "I wasted all this time." His jaw clenched. "I gave her what I could, but it wasn't enough," he whispered. His teeth bit down hard enough to make his jaw ache. "Why does this keep happening to me?"

You are the Fiasco, the voice grumbled.

"Yes. Even when I win, I lose!" Fiasco snarled. His breath clouded about his face, chilled from the altitude, and his own voice grew louder.

Losers will always lose, the voice replied, almost maniacal in its mockery.

The cloud over the moon shifted, and the dinner his parents hosted played like a movie reel in his mind.

You asked if she ever needed you, the voice continued, *but did you ever need her?*

The reel played on. As if watching from a distance, Fiasco recalled how much his entire family had loved her. His father had even opened up to her, more than he did his own son. The dagger twisted in Fiasco's chest as memories that once brought him joy now only brought pain.

It was all a sham, the voice said as it leaned in, erecting the hair on the back of Fiasco's neck with its malice.

The emotional wheel turned inside Fiasco, glancing over the less extreme emotions until it landed on one more severe. It was the most insidious emotion that he always tried to keep at bay, since it was poison to his well of energy. Anger burned like an inferno from the well inside, shooting out through the crooked *F* on his chest.

She lied to us! the voice shouted, mimicking the anger Fiasco felt as he nodded in agreement.

The voice was always right.

"I wasted all this time!" Fiasco shouted, emptying his lungs.

The power filled Fiasco's mouth, gurgling within his throat as he shouted upward. The gauntlets glowed a bright blue that expanded, adding thick streams of light that joined the conflagration. The tears in his eyes burned away, replaced by the power that could no longer be contained as rage and anger filled his reserve, pushing it out in lariats of energy that whipped like lightening all about him. Fiasco's entire being glowed white as the power left his body in a steady stream that careened into the sky.

His power raged as he saw Julianna kissing Ethan in his mind. It vomited anger, hate, and aggression into the atmosphere. His shout was thunder that gave voice to the storm until his lungs strained from the thin air. Fiasco could not sustain the fury that consumed the power like a ravenous cancer. Then, with the power spent and his rage failing, the aura faded away.

Physically and emotionally spent, Fiasco's limbs went limp. Frosty wind whistled through his uniform as he plummeted downward. The stars turned a gossamer fog of white. Crystalline dew stung like pins against his half-healed wounds as he passed through the moist clouds. A strong current kicked up and spun Fiasco on his back as his descent to the earth quickened with every heartbeat.

The straps behind his head drummed a beat against the side of his leather mask. A strong updraft blew kisses of wind against his bare eyes, but he kept them open to experience the pain.

"I can't believe she did this to us," Fiasco thought, giving little care to his plunge. "I gave her as much as I could, and she still rejected me."

Has your tantrum concluded? the voice asked, its tone now serene.

Fiasco thought for once they would be on the same page. That for once, he and the voice would agree for one time in his miserable life.

"Shut up you insufferable—" Fiasco's brow furrowed beneath his mask. The costume grew cold against his skin.

You took her for granted.

"No," Fiasco blinked. "No, I didn't. She said so herself. I tried with her."

Only losers lie. You held back. You did not tell her about us. The late nights. The distance. You only shared a part of you, and she felt it. The voice paused, and then said, *you lied first.*

Fiasco shook his head. "You know I couldn't do that. Tell her about this. About us. She would have been ashamed of me. I had a plan to make her proud."

You were ashamed of us. You lacked belief in us. In the end, you lacked belief in her, as well.

Fiasco searched for words to counter the logic, but his mind only went to a new question. "Does that explain why Warren and Jenni set her up with Ethan?" Fiasco growled. "Why Talon betrayed me? Why my own friends betrayed me? Did my lack of faith in us do that, too?"

No, the voice said softly, conceding that small victory. *Not for the Modoc. But Warren did not betray you.*

"He knew."

He tried to warn you.

"But he set them up!" Fiasco shouted. "He created this man who stole my future from me!"

Or he stopped being Ethan's friend when he found out about their relationship.

"But...he and Jenni kept it from me."

Perhaps they would not have felt the need to do so if you had listened and been honest with her.

"You told me to leave her."

I also said to tell her the truth. I told you this would only lead to heartache in the end. Look at us now.

Fiasco agreed. As always, the voice told the truth, whether he liked it or not. The truth always hurt, and the dagger cleaved what was left of his heart.

"So, it was my fault," he finally said. "I deserved this. I deserved to lose her to some other guy like our time together never mattered?"

Yes.

Falling through the sky, extremities to the point of freezing from the cold cascading winds that swept through his ruined costume, Fiasco finally realized why Julianna's father disagreed with his answer when he posed the question, 'Where do you see yourself in five years'. The answer should have been simple in retrospect. At that moment he knew that any answer that did not start with, "I want to be with Julianna" was the wrong answer.

Thin drops of liquid floated upward from Fiasco's eyes. "So, what do I do?" Fiasco whispered, his voice trailing in the howling current. "I can't even think about being without her."

Let her go, the voice said. *Be a true Mega once more.*

"Let her go, huh?" Fiasco's breath caught in his throat. "Just like that?"

Yes. The voice said, matter of fact. *Giving up should come naturally to you.*

Fiasco snorted and wiped a cold hand over his eyes. He looked over his shoulder, down at the ground that raced forward, dirt and steel waiting at the bottom. "Well, why don't you give me something if you don't want us to die."

What is your answer?

"To your suggestion? That I just let her go?"

Yes.

Fiasco paused, mulling over the question before replying, "I'll consider it."

He glanced over his shoulder again, "Now are you going to say something to refill the well?"

You already contain it. You always have.

Before him was a gossamer image of Julianna, similar to how he saw her in the Enrapture, shimmering a brilliant indigo. Her brown eyes stared back at him, shining like elegant stars. Her painted lips grinned, and her cheeks flushed as she laughed. Her eyes closed and the image leaned into the warmth of his fingers, then it disappeared. The pain of loss acted as salt to his open wounds. With a sudden thrum, the aura spread over his body, cutting off the howling wind. His descent slowed, then ceased. With his arms spread outward, Fiasco released energy, and he turned up to a vertical position. His descent slowed before touching down lightly on the street.

Yellow streetlights blinked against the dark asphalt. It was well past midnight, and the streets were bare on either side. Beneath the blinking streetlights and limp cameras that were affected by his power release, Fiasco peeled away his mask and wiped the caked dirt and grime from his face that had gathered during the battle. He looked towards Black Deer a block away, wondering if Warren and Jenni were still inside.

Further down, his eyes moved to Antler Street, where he had watched Julianna and Ethan turn down in his Lexus. It was lost. Just like that one muscle car he had chased long ago. He snorted a laugh, not understanding why that specific memory returned. Of all things to remember. The streetlights swayed slightly, creaking from a stiff wind, and with a faint nod, Kevin turned and walked in the opposite direction.